"Edited by the venerable queen of horror anthologies, Ellen Datlow. . . . The stories in this collection feel both classic and innovative, while never losing the primary ingredient of great horror writing: fear."

—*The New York Times*

"A decade of celebrating the darkest gems of the genre as selected by Hugo-winning editor Ellen Datlow, whose name, by this point, is almost synonymous with quality frights . . . [and] contributed by a murderer's row of horror authors. . . . Essential."

—*B&N Sci-Fi and Fantasy Blog*, "Our Favorite Science Fiction & Fantasy Books of 2018"

"With the quality ranging from very good, to fantastic, to sublime, there just isn't the space to discuss them all. . . . If I need to make a pronouncement—based on Datlow's fantastic distillation of the genre—it's that horror is alive, well, and still getting under people's skin. If you have even a vague interest in dark fiction, then pick up this book."

—Ian Mond, *Locus*

"A survey of some of the best horror writing of the last decade . . . highly recommended for anyone interested in contemporary horror and dark fantasy, as well as anyone looking for a collection of some of the best and most horrifying short fiction currently available."

—*Booklist* (starred review), for *The Best of the Best Horror of the Year*

"A stunning and flawless collection that showcases the most terrifyingly beautiful writing of the genre. Datlow's palate for the fearful and the chilling knows no genre constraint, encompassing the undead, the supernatural, and the cruelty perpetrated by ordinary humans. Exciting, literary, and utterly scary, this anthology is nothing short of exceptional."

—*Publishers Weekly* (starred review), for *The Best of the Best Horror of the Year*

"Datlow's survey of the first decade of her Best Horror of the Year series is also an argument about the field's major talents and trends. Its contents make a compelling case for the robustness of the field, a condition Datlow herself has done much to nourish."

—*Locus*, "Horror in 2018" by John Langan

"Award-winning editor Ellen Datlow has assembled a tasty collection of twenty-one terrifying and unsettling treats. In addition to providing excellent fiction to read, this is the perfect book for discovering new authors and enriching your life through short fiction."

—*Kirkus Reviews*

"For more than three decades, Ellen Datlow has been at the center of horror. Bringing you the most frightening and terrifying stories, Datlow always has her finger on the pulse of what horror fans crave . . . and the anthologies just keep getting better and better. She's an icon in the industry."

—*Signal Horizon*

"Datlow's The Best Horror of the Year series is one of the best investments you can make in short fiction. The current volume is no exception."

—*Adventures Fantastic*

"As usual, Datlow delivers what she promises, 'the best horror of the year,' whether it's written by the famous (Neil Gaiman) or the should-be famous (Laird Barron and many others)."

—*Washington Post*

"You just can't have a list of recommended speculative anthologies without including an Ellen Datlow anthology. It's. Not. Possible. The line-up in *The Best Horror of the Year Volume Eight* is absolutely stupendous, featuring the most frighteningly talented authors in horror fiction."

—*Tor.com*

"Once again, [Ellen Datlow supplies] an invaluable book, featuring excellent short fiction and, in addition, providing as always precious information about what happened in the horror field last year."

—Mario Guslandi, British Fantasy Society

"Datlow unfailingly presents notable scary tales and—since her choices come from an immense variety of sources—even avid readers are unlikely to have encountered them all . . . . This is a perennial must-read for anyone who enjoys dark fiction."

—Paula Guran, *Locus*

"Ellen Datlow has been called the 'venerable queen of horror anthologies' by the paper of record itself [*New York Times*], and the 22 stories within the twelfth volume of her annual Best Horror of the Year anthology cement her status as royalty in the genre."

—Tonia Ransom, *Nightfire*

"Even with the overall high quality of the latest of Datlow's anthology series, there are some remarkable highlights . . . this excellent anthology demonstrates that Datlow's reputation as one of the best editors in the field is more than well-deserved."

—*Booklist* (starred review)

"Datlow has drawn her selections from a wide variety of sources that even the most dedicated fans may have overlooked, and her comprehensive introductory overview of the year in horror will uncover still more venues for great scares. This is an indispensable volume for horror readers."

—*Publishers Weekly* (starred review)

Also Edited by Ellen Datlow

A Wolf at the Door and Other Retold Fairy Tales (with Terri Windling)

After (with Terri Windling)

Alien Sex

Black Feathers: Dark Avian Tales

Black Heart, Ivory Bones (with Terri Windling)

Black Swan, White Raven (with Terri Windling)

Black Thorn, White Rose (with Terri Windling)

Blood Is Not Enough: 17 Stories of Vampirism

Blood and Other Cravings

Body Shocks: Extreme Tales of Body Horror

Children of Lovecraft

Darkness: Two Decades of Modern Horror

Digital Domains: A Decade of Science Fiction & Fantasy

Echoes: The Saga Anthology of Ghost Stories Edited By

Fearful Symmetries

Final Cuts: New Tales of Hollywood Horror and Other Spectacles

Haunted Legends (with Nick Mamatas)

Haunted Nights (with Lisa Morton)

Hauntings

Inferno: New Tales of Terror and the Supernatural

Lethal Kisses

Little Deaths

Lovecraft Unbound

Lovecraft's Monsters

Mad Hatters and March Hares

Naked City: Tales of Urban Fantasy

Nebula Awards Showcase 2009

Nightmare Carnival

Nightmares: A New Decade of Modern Horror

Off Limits: Tales of Alien Sex

Omni Best Science Fiction: Volumes One through Three

The Omni Books of Science Fiction: Volumes One through Seven

Omni Visions One and *Two*

Poe: 19 New Tales Inspired by Edgar Allan Poe

Queen Victoria's Book of Spells (with Terri Windling)

Ruby Slippers, Golden Tears (with Terri Windling)

Salon Fantastique: Fifteen Original Tales of Fantasy (with Terri Windling)

Screams From the Dark: 29 Tales of Monsters and the Monstrous

Silver Birch, Blood Moon (with Terri Windling)

Sirens and Other Daemon Lovers (with Terri Windling)

Snow White, Blood Red (with Terri Windling)

Supernatural Noir

Swan Sister (with Terri Windling)

Tails of Wonder and Imagination: Cat Stories

Teeth: Vampire Tales (with Terri Windling)

Telling Tales: The Clarion West 30th Anniversary Anthology

The Beastly Bride: And Other Tales of the Animal People (with Terri Windling)

The Best Horror of the Year: Volumes One through Thirteen

The Coyote Road: Trickster Tales (with Terri Windling)

The Cutting Room: Dark Reflections of the Silver Screen

The Dark: New Ghost Stories

The Del Rey Book of Science Fiction and Fantasy

The Devil and the Deep: Horror Stories of the Sea

The Doll Collection

The Faery Reel: Tales from the Twilight Realm

The Green Man: Tales from the Mythic Forest (with Terri Windling)

The Monstrous

Troll's-Eye View: A Book of Villainous Tales (with Terri Windling)

Twists of the Tale

Vanishing Acts

When Things Get Dark: Stories Inspired by Shirley Jackson

The Year's Best Fantasy and Horror (with Terri Windling, and with Gavin J. Grant and Kelly Link) Volumes One through Twenty-One

THE BEST HORROR
OF THE YEAR

VOLUME
FOURTEEN

EDITED BY ELLEN DATLOW

NIGHT SHADE BOOKS

NEW YORK

Night Shade books may be purchased in bulk at special discounts for sales promotion,
corporate gifts, fund-raising, or educational purposes. Special editions can also
be created to specifications. For details, contact the Special Sales Department,
Night Shade Books, 307 West 36th Street, 11th Floor, New York, NY 10018
or info@skyhorsepublishing.com.

Night Shade Books™ is a trademark of Skyhorse Publishing, Inc.®, a Delaware corporation.

Visit our website at www.nightshadebooks.com.

10 9 8 7 6 5 4 3 2 1

Library of Congress Cataloging-in-Publication Data is available on file.

Cover illustration by Samuel Araya
Cover design by Claudia Noble

Print ISBN: 978-1-949102-67-3

Printed in the United States of America

ACKNOWLEDGMENTS

The Nightfire blog for keeping me informed as to the horror novels published in 2021.

Dave Axler, Kam-Yung Soh, Mike Winter, and David Erik Nelson for recommendations.

A big thanks to Tegan Moore, Theresa DeLucci, and Troix Jackson for helping me in my reading

And a special thank you to my always patient and supportive in-house editor, Jason Katzman.

TABLE OF CONTENTS

Summation of the Year 2021—Ellen Datlow i

Redwater – Simon Bestwick 1

Caker's Man – Matthew Holness 19

Black Leg – Glen Hirshberg 42

The Offering – Michael Marshall Smith 56

Fox Girl – Lee Murray 77

Shuck – G. V. Anderson 79

The Hunt at Rotherdam – A. C. Wise 85

Dancing Sober in the Dust – Steve Toase 107

The God Bag – Christopher Golden 122

The Strathantine Imps – Steve Duffy 140

The Quizmasters – Gerard McKeown 162

All Those Lost Days – Brian Evenson 169

Anne Gare's Rare and Import Video Catalogue October 2022
– Jonathan Raab 183
   "Elephant Subjected to the Predations of a Mentalist"
   – Dir. B.S. Stockton, 1921 183
   "Ol' Will's Birthday Bash and Dither Family Reunion"
   – Dir. Various, 1952 184

Three Sisters Bog – Eóin Murphy 186

The Steering Wheel Club – Kaaron Warren 200

The King of Stones – Simon Strantzas 210

Stolen Property – Sarah Lamparelli 226

Shards – Ian Rogers 241

Chit Chit – Steve Toase 267

Poor Butcher-Bird – Gemma Files 279

Trap – Carly Holmes 286

I'll Be Gone By Then – Eric LaRocca 311

Jack-in-the-Box – Robin Furth 322

Tiptoe – Laird Barron 350

Honorable Mentions 374

About the Authors 376

Acknowledgment of Copyright 381

About the Editor 384

SUMMATION 2021

Here are 2021's numbers: There are twenty-three stories and novelettes, and one poem in this volume. The story lengths range from 550 words (actually shorter, as two pieces are combined) to 10,200 words. There are seven stories and one poem by women and sixteen stories by men. One contributor has two stories in the book. Nine stories are by contributors living in the United States, three in Canada, one in New Zealand, six in the United Kingdom, one in Estonia, one in Germany, one in Australia, and one in Northern Ireland. Nine of the contributors have never before been published in any volume of my Best of the Year series.

AWARDS

The Horror Writers Association announced the 2020 Bram Stoker Awards® winners on a YouTube Live presentation May 22, 2021—after Stokercon's in-person convention, scheduled to take place in Denver, Colorado, May 20–23, was changed to virtual as a result of the ongoing Covid-19 pandemic.

Superior Achievement in a Novel: Stephen Graham Jones: *The Only Good Indians* (Gallery/Saga Press); **Superior Achievement in a First Novel**: EV Knight: *The Fourth Whore* (Raw Dog Screaming Press); **Superior Achievement in a Graphic Novel:** Nancy Holder (author), Chiara Di Francia (artist), Amelia Woo (artist), Laurie Foster (inker), Sandra Molina (colorist), and Saida Temofonte (letterer): *Mary Shelley Presents* (Kymera Press);

Superior Achievement in a Young Adult Novel: *Clown in a Cornfield* by Adam Cesare (HarperTeen); **Superior Achievement in Long Fiction:** *Night of the Mannequins* by Stephen Graham Jones (A Tor.com Book); **Superior Achievement in Short Fiction:** "One Last Transformation" by Josh Malerman (*Miscreations: Gods, Monstrosities & Other Horrors*) (Written Backwards); **Superior Achievement in a Fiction Collection**: *Grotesque: Monster Stories* by Lee Murray (Things in the Well): **Superior Achievement in a Screenplay**: *The Invisible Man* by Leigh Whannell (Universal Pictures, Blumhouse Productions, Goalpost Pictures, Nervous Tick Productions); **Superior Achievement in a Poetry Collection:** *A Collection of Dreamscapes* by Christina Sng (Raw Dog Screaming Press); **Superior Achievement in an Anthology:** *Black Cranes: Tales of Unquiet Women* by Lee Murray and Geneve Flynn (Omnium Gatherum); **Superior Achievement in Non-Fiction:** *Writing in the Dark* by Tim Waggoner (Guide Dog Books/Raw Dog Screaming Press); **Superior Achievement in Short Non-Fiction:** "Speaking of Horror" by Tim Waggoner (The Writer).

The Life Achievement Award: Carol J. Clover, Jewelle Gomez, Marge Simon

The Silver Hammer Award: Carina Bissett, Brian W. Matthews

The Mentor of the Year Award: Angela Yuriko Smith

The Richard Laymon President's Award: Becky Spratford

The Specialty Press Award: Crystal Lake Publishing

The 2020 Shirley Jackson Awards, usually presented in person at Readercon in Quincy, Massachusetts were instead given on Sunday, August 15, 2021, in a pre-recorded ceremony as part of Readercon 31. The jurors were Aaron Dries, Chịkọdịlị Emelumadu, Joshua Gaylord, Tonia Ransom, Mary SanGiovanni.

The winners were: Novel: *The Only Good Indians* by Stephen Graham Jones (Gallery/Saga Press); Novella: *Night of the Mannequins* by Stephen Graham Jones (A Tor.com Book); Novelette: *The Attic Tragedy* by J. Ashley-Smith (Meerkat Press); Short Fiction: "Not the Man I Married" by R. A. Busby (*Black Petals* Issue #93 Autumn, 2020); Single Author Collection: *Velocities: Stories* by Kathe Koja (Meerkat Press); Edited Anthology: *Black Cranes: Tales of Unquiet Women*, edited by Lee Murray and Geneve Flynn (Omnium Gatherum).

The World Fantasy Awards were presented in Montreal, Canada, on Sunday, November 7, 2021. The judges were Tobias Buckell, Siobhan Carroll, Cecilia Dart-Thornton, Brian Evenson, Patrick Swenson.

The Lifetime Achievement Awards: Megan Lindholm and Howard Waldrop

Novel: *Trouble the Saints* by Alaya Dawn Johnson (Tor); Novella: *Riot Baby by Tochi Onyebuchi* (A Tor.com Book); Short Fiction: "Glass Bottle Dancer by Celeste Rita Baker (Lightspeed, April 2020); Anthology: *The Big Book of Modern Fantasy* edited by Ann and Jeff VanderMeer (Vintage Books); Collection: *Where the Wild Ladies Are* by Aoka Matsuda, translated by Polly Barton (Soft Skull Press US/Tilted Axis UK); Artist: Rovina Cai; Special Award—Professional: C.C. Finlay for *The Magazine of Fantasy and Science Fiction*, editing; Special Award: Non-Professional: Brian Attebery for Journal of the Fantastic in the Arts.

Notable Novels of 2021

Later by Stephen King (Hard Case Crime) is the first novel I've read by King in some time, and I love it. It's engaging, brisk, chilling, and moving. A boy is blessed (or cursed) with the power to see the recently dead and communicate with them, causing trouble and trauma as he learns to deal with the power it gives him.

My Heart is a Chainsaw by Stephen Graham Jones (Saga Press) is a magnificent novel about Jade, an unhappy young woman about to turn eighteen, living in a working-class community along a lake that's threatened by the rich families who have developed their own community across that lake. Jade is obsessed with slasher movies. She relates everything in her life to slashers and she believes that a slasher has been revivified in classic slasher fashion to wreak vengeance on those who wronged them. And she knows exactly who will be the final girl in this real life drama. Jade's voice is one of the best things about the book.

The Drowning Kind by Jennifer McMahon (Scout Press) is an engrossing novel about a social worker who returns home to a small town in Vermont after her beloved but estranged sister drowns in the family pool. The pool is fed by a spring rumored to have both healing powers and a curse. Switching back and forth between 1929 and 2019 the reader discovers the problematic history of the spring.

The Burning Girls by C. J. Tudor (Ballantine Books) is a suspenseful supernatural/crime novel about a troubled, single-parent Vicar who is reassigned from Nottingham, England to a small town, after the previous Vicar hanged himself. The new Vicar is accompanied by her fourteen-year-old daughter. The village is known for its tradition of commemorating the burning of Protestant martyrs five hundred years before, and the disappearance of two young girls thirty years previous to the novel's beginning. The teenager begins to see ghosts of girls burning, and her mother receives threatening notes and effigies of twigs representing the burning girls. Secrets abound, and several really good twists.

Near the Bone by Christina Henry (Berkley) is a powerful mix of supernatural and psychological horror. A young woman lives on a mountain with a brutal, possessive man who totally dominates her every action. Things rapidly change when the woman discovers a mutilated fox near their cabin, heralding the existence of something they'd never encountered before—a monster. In addition, three strangers show up, challenging everything the young woman had believed to be true.

The Lost Village by Camilla Sten translated by Alexandra Fleming (Minotaur) is an unsettling first novel translated from the Swedish. A young documentary filmmaker is haunted by the mystery of a mining town in which the entire population disappeared overnight, sixty years previously, except for one woman stoned to death, and a baby. Even though some of the details seem a bit far-fetched once the spell of the book has worn off, it's a very good read.

King Bullet by Richard Kadrey (HarperVoyager) is the final volume of the terrifically entertaining and popular Sandman Slim series of dark urban fantasy about James Stark, a Nephilim (part angel, part human) who is forced to fight monsters in Hell and then escapes to Los Angeles. A dangerous virus is running rampant and King Bullet, a new villain, has come to town to wreak havoc on the city, the world, and all of Stark's friends and loved ones. And it seems as if it might be personal.

The Last House on Needless Street by Catriona Ward (Serpent's Tale) is a fascinating, complex tale about a recluse who is obviously mentally ill, a girl, and a cat. A wild card is added when the sister of an abducted child believes she has found her sister's abductor eleven years later.

Madam by Phoebe Wynne (St. Martin's Press) initially seems like your traditional plot of a heroine going to teach in a private school and becoming caught up in intrigue. While that certainly *does* happen, the more one learns of this venerable institution for young women hidden away in the Scottish Highlands, the more ghastly and terrifying and threatening to the protagonist the events become.

Chasing the Boogeyman by Richard Chizmar (Gallery Press) is a fascinating look at a serial killer terrorizing a small town. Told in first person by journalist and horror writer Chizmar, the reader is kept off-guard as to whether the novel is based on real events or not. A suspenseful, emotionally resonant look at small town life and the impact of horrible events on the inhabitants.

Tidepool by Nicole Willson (Parliament) is an entertaining gothic with tentacles. Young woman goes to the small town where her beloved brother vanished while attempting to persuade the town to allow development by their business-minded family. What secrets are the townspeople hiding and why?

Whitesands by Jóhann Thorsson (Headshot Books) is a powerful debut thriller about a detective—broken by the disappearance of his daughter—who returns to duty after two years, facing a gruesome domestic murder that erupts into utter strangeness.

Rovers by Richard Lange (Mulholland Books) is a well-executed, supernatural western revenge drama about two vampire brothers making their way across the American west in the '70s, a brutal vampire biker gang calling themselves the Fiends, and a bereaved human father searching for his son's killers.

Come With Me by Ronald Malfi (Titan Books) is a terrific crime novel with hints of the supernatural about a man whose wife is killed in a random shooting. Once she's gone, he finds a motel receipt among her belongings that hints at secrets that she kept from him. A very well-written page-turner.

Revelator by Daryl Gregory (Knopf) is a terrific novel taking place in the mountains of Appalachia, where a family's females commune with their personal god and and what happens when one daughter turns her back on her responsibilities. It's also about moonshine, government buyouts, paternalistic men, and strong women.

Also Noted

The Girls Are So Nice Here by Laurie Elizabeth Flynn (Simon & Schuster) is about two former friends returning to a college reunion and being sent increasingly threatening messages calling them to task for something they did their freshman year, ten years earlier. *The Second Bell* by Gabriela Houston (Angry Robot) is about a girl in an isolated community born with two hearts, thus branded a striga (witch) and ostracized. Her mother works to protect her, but upon becoming an adult, the girl rebels. *Creatures of Passage* by Morowa Yejidé (Akashic) is about a Washington, DC taxi driver with a ghost in her trunk, and who is herself haunted by the murder of her twin brother. *The Birds* by Frank Baker (Valancourt Books) is a novel written in 1936, and was relatively unknown before Alfred Hitchcock's film. The author threatened to sue. This is the first edition with hundreds of changes and corrections by the author. With an introduction by Hitchcock scholar Ken Mogg. *All the Murmuring Bones* by Angela Slatter (Titan Books) is a fine dark fantasy about a young woman, one of the last members of a prosperous family whose deal with the mer entailed sacrificing one child per generation to the sea in exchange for keeping their ships safe. Familial secrets and lush writing make this dark fairy tale a total success. *The Cottingley Cuckoo* by AJ Elwood (Titan Books) is a dark tale about a care worker beguiled by a manipulative resident at the facility in which she works. It's clever and sinister and speaks to a longing for magic. *Queen of Teeth* by Hailey Piper (Strangehouse Books) is an sf/horror novel about a woman who develops a vagina dentata, possibly as a result of experimentation by a powerful pharmaceutical company when she was still in the womb. *The Queen of the Cicadas* by V. Castro (Flame Tree Publishing) is about the aftermath of the brutal murder of a Mexican farmworker in 1950s Texas. A wedding is set to take place on the farm where the atrocity took place, setting in motion a series of events that awakens an Aztec queen who seeks more than revenge. *Boys in the Valley* by Philip Fracassi (Earthling Publications) is about what happens at a remote Pennsylvania orphanage at the turn of the twentieth century when a group of men arrive and their presence corrupts the young inhabitants. *Darling* by K. Ancrum (Macmillan) is a young adult, dark retelling of *Peter Pan*, with Wendy being spirited away by Peter to Chicago. *Wendy, Darling* by A. C. Wise (Titan Books) is another dark retelling of *Peter Pan*, this one for adults, in which Peter takes Jane, Wendy's daughter, to Neverland. *Somebody's Voice* by Ramsey Campbell (Flame Tree Publishing) is a psychological horror novel about a true crime writer, who after ghostwriting the memoir of an abuse survivor, begins to realize that his subject's memories may not be accurate. *Children of Demeter* by E. V. Knight (Raw Dog Screaming Press) is about a sociologist who investigates the mysterious disappearance in 1973 of almost twenty-five women and children from a hippie commune. *Lincolnstein* by Paul Witcover (PS Publishing) is about the assassinated Abraham Lincoln, brought back to life by a forgotten technology in order to finish his presidential agenda. But the resurrected Lincoln has his own agenda. *Dream Girl* by Laura Lippman (William Morrow) is about a novelist, who after an accident, is confined to a hospital bed and receives a call from a woman who claims to be the protagonist of his most successful novel. Is she real, is he under the influence of the drugs he's been given—or is he developing dementia? *A Still and Awful Red* by Michael Howarth (Trepidatio Publishing) is about a young girl living in Hungary, who in 1609 goes to work in the castle of the Countess Elizabeth Bathory. In *The Shape of Darkness* by Laura Purcell (Penguin Random House), a Victorian silhouette artist living in Bath, England is shocked to realize that several of her former clients have been murdered, and is determined to discover why. *Mirrorland* by Carole Johnstone (Scribner) is a thriller about twins with dark secrets. Cat refuses to believe her estranged twin sister El has drowned while sailing, and returns to the home in Scotland where they grew up and where El and her husband Ross moved back to. *The Unwelcome* by Jacob Steven Mohr (Cosmic Egg Books) is about a women haunted by her abusive ex-boyfriend and estranged from most of her friends. When she joins some of them at a secluded cabin in an attempt to reconcile, the ex follows. *In Darkness, Shadows Breathe* by Catherine Cavendish (Flame Tree Publishing) is a gothic about two women haunted by the same entity, and who are drawn back and forth from the past to the present. *When the Reckoning Comes* by LaTanya McQueen (HarperPerennial) is about a black woman's return—after ten years—to the small Southern town in which she grew up and left because of a traumatic experience at a haunted plantation where horrific acts were committed. *Ghost Finders* by Adam McOmber (JournalStone Publishing) is about an Edwardian agency of ghost finders who investigate ghosts and other types of supernatural phenomena, often putting themselves in danger. *Blue Hell* by Greg F. Gifune and Sandy DeLuca (JournalStone Publishing) is a short novel about two people who end up in a mysterious apartment building that serves as a halfway house for the lost and desperate. *The Route of Ice and Salt* by José Luis Zárate and translated by David Bowles (Innsmouth Free Press) is a retelling of *Dracula* by a Mexican writer. Originally published in 1998 in Spanish, this is its first English publication. With an essay by Poppy Z. Brite. *Revival Road* by Chris DiLeo (Bloodshot Books) takes place in a suburban town where a dead child wakes up in the morgue and a religion-obsessed neighbor is convinced it's God's work, while others are equally convinced it's evil. *Midnight in the Chapel of Love* by Matthew R. Davis (JournalStone Publishing) is about a man who thought he escaped from the dark secrets of the town he grew up in, but is forced to reckon with them upon his return for his father's funeral. *Children of Chicago* by Cynthia Pelayo (Polis Agora) is a modern retelling of the pied piper, that opens with the discover of three brutally murdered teenagers in a Chicago park. One of the detectives brought in recognizes similarities to her sister's murder years before. *Bela Lugosi's Dead* by Robert Guffey (Macabre Ink) is about a horror movie aficionado's obsessive search for a legendary test reel of Bela Lugosi auditioning for *Frankenstein*, which became one of Boris Karloff's most iconic roles. *Mr. Cannyharme* by Michael Shea (Hippocampus Press) is a never before published adaptation of H. P. Lovecraft's "The Hound," written by Shea in 1981. *Whisper Down the Lane* by Clay McLeod Chapman (Quirk Books) is about a man who has re-invented himself after he was accused of awful deeds during the "satanic panic" thirty years before. *Shutter* by Melissa Larsen (Penguin Random House) is a debut about a young woman, who, thrown for a loop by the death of her father, moves to New York and is given a unique opportunity to be in an indie film that will shoot in a cabin on a private island off the coast of Maine. *The Final Girl Support Group* by Grady Hendrix (Berkley) is a humorous horror novel about six survivors of a massacre who meet with a therapist for more than a decade. Then, one of them misses a meeting.

Infinity Dreams by Glen Hirshberg (Cemetery Dance Publications) is a novel in stories about a couple who gather mysterious things for clients with esoteric tastes. Now retired and living in isolation, they are approached by a young journalist for an interview. *My Sweet Girl* by Amanda Jayatissa (Berkley) is a dark thriller about a Sri-Lankan-American woman who searches for the killer of her roommate while preserving her own secrets. *The Book of Accide*nts by Chuck Wendig (Del Rey) is an sf/ horror novel about a couple who grew up in Pennsylvania coal country and left. However, when they return with their son, dark magic begins to infuse his soul, endangering him and everyone else. *Good Neighbors* by Sarah Langan (Atria) is about harrowing events taking place in suburbia in the near future, as seemingly normal families turn on each other at the drop of a hat. *The Death of Jane Lawrence* by Caitlin Starling (St. Martin's Press) is a gothic horror story taking place in post-WWII England. A woman enters into a marriage of convenience with a respected doctor, calculating that it's the only way she can continue to remain independent and work, as she wants. But she soon realizes that there are secrets being kept from her. *Sixteen Horses* by Greg Buchanan (Flat Iron) is a dark thriller debut that begins with the discovery of sixteen horse heads on a farm. A veterinary forensic expert and a local detective race to find out what's going on as strange and deadly incidents continue to pile up. *Billy Summers* by Stephen King (Scribner) is a thriller about a topnotch hitman who only kills bad guys, but now wants out. However, he has one more job he needs to finish. *Red X* by David Demchuk (Strange Light) is a dark novel about the disappearances of vulnerable men from Toronto's gay village, and an investigation into a pattern that seems to be impossible in its longevity. *Closing Costs* by Bracken MacLeod (HMH) is a suspense novel about a couple, who soon after moving into their dream home are faced with a home invasion that threatens to unravel their secrets, as well as their lives. *Reprieve* by James Han Mattson (William Morrow) is about four contestants who seek to win a cash prize if they can endure the "horrors" of a full-contact escape room. A man breaks in and kills one of them. *Cracker Jack* by Asher Ellis (Bloodshot Books) is about a master safe cracker, who is forced to come out of retirement in order to pay medical bills for his stepson. The safe he's committed to cracking has something locked in it other than money—something dangerous. *Getaway* by Zoje Stage (Mulholland Books) is dark thriller about two sisters and a friend with whom they've lost touch, who go backpacking in the Grand Canyon for a week to rekindle their friendship. Then their supplies start to disappear.

MAGAZINES, JOURNALS, AND WEBZINES

It's important to recognize the work of the talented artists working in the field of fantastic fiction, both dark and light. The following created dark art that I thought especially noteworthy in 2021: George Cotronis, Jessica Fong, David Ho, Adrian Borda, Paul Lowe, Vincent Chong, Tomislav Tikulin, Olga Beliaeva, Stefan Koidl, Serge N. Kozintsev, Giuseppe Balestra, Danielle Harker, Randy Broecker, Afarin Sajedi, Nikolina Petolas, Tod Ryan, Harry O. Morris, Dan Quintana, Jana Heidersdorf, Armando Veve, Ksenia Korniewska, Richard Wagner, Paul (Mutartis) Boswell, Kim Jakobsson, Jason Van Hollander, Rohama Malik, Omar Gilani, Kealan Patrick Burke, Lynne Hansen, Colin Verdi, Ryan Lee, Dave Wachter, Dan Sauer, Kathleen Jennings, and Ben Baldwin.

Rue Morgue edited by Andrea Subissati is a reliable, entertaining Canadian non-fiction magazine for horror movie aficionados, with up-to-date information on most of the horror films being released. The magazine also includes interviews, articles, and gory movie stills, along with regular columns on books, horror music, video games, and graphic novels.

Dead Reckonings: A Review of Horror and the Weird in the Arts edited by Alex Houstoun and Michael J. Abolafia published two excellent issues in 2021, both filled with reviews, commentaries, and essays about prose works, music, and movies.

The Green Book: Writings on Irish Gothic, Supernatural, and Fantastic Literature edited by Brian J. Showers is an excellent resource for discovering underappreciated Irish writers. Two issues were published in 2021. Issue 17 is made up entirely of fiction and poetry by Oscar Wilde, Katharine Tynan, and others. Issue 18 contains a selection of profiles from *The Guide to Irish Writers of Gothic, Supernatural and Fantastic Literature*. It also included a profile of the great illustrator Harry Clarke, whose most famous work might be the illustrations for *Tales of Mystery and Imagination* by Edgar Allan Poe.

Lovecraft Annual edited by S. T. Joshi is a must for those interested in Lovecraftian studies. The 2021 volume includes wide-ranging essays about the author's work, life, and philosophies plus book reviews.

The Dark edited by Sean Wallace is a monthly webzine that publishes dark fantasy and horror. In 2021 there were notable dark stories by Dey Rupsa, Clara Madrigano, Carlie St. George, Gabriela Santiago, Dare Segun Falowo, Frances Ogamba, Hannah Yang, Eliot Fintushel, Aimee Ogden, Octavia Cade, Ifeanyichukwu Peter Eze, Carrie Laben, Kay Chronister, Suzan Palumbo, David Tallerman, H. Pueyo, Y. M. Pang, Ernest O. Ògúnyẹmí, Matthew Cheney, Steve Rasnic Tem, and Jelena Dunato.

Not One of Us edited by John Benson is one of the longest-running small press magazines publishing horror. It just changed from publishing fifty-two pages twice a year to a quarterly schedule with thirty-two pages in each issue, and contains weird and dark fiction and poetry. There were notable stories and poetry in 2021 by Michael Kelly, Andrin Albrecht, Colin Sinclair, Mary Crosbie, Patrick Barb, Sydney Sackett, Francesca Forrest, Jennifer Crow, William H. Wandless, and Steve Toase.

Black Static edited by Andy Cox published two double issues in 2021, as the publisher winds down the magazine. There were no reviews or columns in the first double issue but notable stories by Stephen Bacon, C. R. Foster, Neil Williamson, Jo Kaplan, Tyler Keevil, Zandra Renwick, Ashley Stokes, Rhonda Pressley Veit, C. R. Foster, Mike O'Driscoll, Alexander Glass, and Sarah Lamparelli. The Lamparelli is reprinted herein.

Corridor edited by Christian Sager is a welcome entry into the print realm of horror magazines. The first issue has five stories, six graphic stories, and a couple of essays. It looks good, but I'm not convinced the oversized format works—it's a bit cumbersome. I was especially impressed by the stories by Nadia Bulkin, Kristi DeMeester, Corinna Bechko, and Christian Sager.

Southwest Review Volume 106 Number 3, Autumn celebrated Halloween with an issue guest edited by Andy Davidson, full of dark fiction and poetry. There was notable fiction and poetry by Sara Tantlinger, Joe R. Lansdale, Clay McLeod Chapman, Keith Rosson, Kristin Cleaveland, John Horner Jacobs, Ingrid L. Taylor, Matthew Lyons, Nadia Bulkin, Peter Adam Salomon, and Gus Moreno.

Supernatural Tales edited by David Longhorn has long been a reliable venue for interesting short stories. This year was no different, with notable work in its three issues by Jane Jakeman, Carole Tyrell, Clint Smith, Katherine Haynes, Stephen Cashmore, Sam Dawson, Kathy Hubbard, Victoria Day, Michael Chislett, Peter Kenny, Jon Barron, Tim Jeffreys, and Mark Nicholls.

Nightmare edited by Wendy N. Wagner is a monthly webzine of horror and dark fantasy. It publishes stories, articles, interviews, book reviews, and an artists' showcase. There was notable short fiction in 2021 by Stephen Graham Jones, Adam-Troy Castro, Maria Dahvana Headley, Orrin Grey, Desirina Boskovich, Flo and John Stanton, Sam J. Miller, Steph Kwiatowski, Marc Laidlaw, Eileen Gunnell Lee, Gordon B. White, Ben Peek, Stephanie M. Wytovich, A.T Greenblatt, Gillian Daniels, Nelly Geraldine García-Rosas, Michael Kelly, Ally Wilkes, B. Narr, Laur A. Freymiller, Juliana Baggott, Joanna Parypinski, E. A. Petricone, and Donyae Coles.

Weird Horror edited by Michael Kelly published two issues, with regular columns by Simon Strantzas and Orrin Grey, book and movie reviews, and fiction. During 2021, there were notable stories by Joan Mark, Kristina Ten, Gordon B. White, Saswati Chatterjee, Donyae Coles, Josh Rountree, Theresa DeLucci, and Jack Lothian.

The Horror Zine edited by Jeani Rector is a monthly EZine that has been publishing online for twelve years. It features fiction, poetry, art, news, and reviews. Each issue include reprints by well-known writers with new stories by newcomers. There was a notable story by Garrett Rowlan.

Dread Imaginings edited by Bill Hughes was a website featuring fiction. It closed April 2022, but during 2021 there was notable fiction by Barbara Brockway, Catherine Luker, Lena Ng, and Kristina Ten.

Two podcasts regularly publish horror: *Pseudopod* edited by Shawn Garrett and Alex Hofelich, and hosted by Alasdair Stewart is a weekly show that's been broadcasting readings of original and reprinted stories since 2006. *Tales to Terrify* is another weekly. It's been broadcasting readings of originals and reprints since 2012 and is hosted and produced by Drew Sebesteny.

MIXED-GENRE MAGAZINES AND WEBZINES

Uncanny edited by Lynne M. Thomas and Michael Damien Thomas is a monthly webzine publishing fantasy, speculative, weird fiction, and occasionally horror. It also includes poetry, podcasts, interviews, essays, and art in the mix. In 2021 there were notable dark stories by Eugenia Triantafyllou, Tananarive Due, Sam J. Miller, John Wiswell, and Fran Wilde. *The Magazine of Fantasy & Science Fiction* edited by Sheree Renée Thomas is one of the longest running sf/f/h magazines in existence. Although it mostly publishes science fiction and fantasy (with non-fiction columns and book reviews), it also publishes very good horror. During 2021, the strongest horror stories and poetry were by Alan Dean Foster, Rob Costello, Lora Gray, Robin Furth, Natalia Theodoridou, K.A. Teryna, T. R. Napper, and Jenn Reese. The Furth is reprinted herein. *Bourbon Penn* edited by Erik Secker is one of the best, regularly published small press magazines, mixing horror, sf, and weird fiction. It's supported by a Patreon and is well worth the investment. The best horror stories in the three 2021 issues are by Simon Strantzas, Louis Evans, Hamdy Elgammal, William Jablonsky, A. C. Wise, Charles Wilkinson, Chelsea Sutton, and Anthony Panegyres. The Wise is reprinted herein. *Underland Arcana* edited by Mark Teppo is an interesting new quarterly webzine/magazine of weird fiction, much of it dark. In its first year it published notable dark fiction by Nina Kiriki Hoffman, Rebecca Ruvinsky, Louis Evans, Jonathan Raab, Jon McGoran, Nathan Batchelor, Lexi Peréz, Tori Fredrick, H. L. Fullerton, Jon Lasser, Christopher Hawkins, Josh Rountree, W. T. Paterson, Vera Hadzic, J. A. W. McCarthy, and Forrest Aguirre. *The Deadlands: A Journal of Endings and Beginnings* edited by Sean Markey is a new monthly magazine of speculative fiction, poems, and some horror essays. In 2021, there was notable dark work by Patrick Lofgren, G. V. Anderson, Natalia Theodoridou, and Jordan Taylor. The Anderson is reprinted herein. *Weirdbook* edited by Doug Draa published one issue in 2021. It served up a generous helping of prose and poetry, although there's usually more dark fantasy than horror. There was notable horror by Jan Edwards, Stefano Frigieri, Tim Curran, Chad Hensley, and Kyla Ward. *Vastarien: A Literary Journal* edited by Jon Padgett is a weird and dark fiction and non-fiction enterprise taking inspiration from the writings of Thomas Ligotti.

There were two issues published in 2021 with hefty helpings of fiction, and a bit of poetry, including notable work by Rhiannon Rasmussen, Simon Strantzas, Michael Canfield, Shenoa Carroll-Bradd, Deanna Knippling, S. R. Mandel, John Claude Smith, Erica Ruppert, Samuel M. Moss, Liam O'Brian, Emer O'Hanlon, Carson Winter, Sara Tantlinger, Stephanie M. Wytovich, Georgia Cook, Christi Nogle, Kurt Fawver, Michelle Muenzler, and Frank Oreto. *Penumbra: A Journal of Weird Fiction and Criticism* edited by S. T. Joshi published its second issue, with eleven new stories, two classic reprints, eight poems, and ten non-fiction pieces. There was notable fiction by Shawn Phelps, Darrell Schweitzer, Ramsey Campbell, Ngo Binh Anh Khoa, Geoffrey Reiter, and Mark Samuels. Tor.com edited by multiple in-house editors and consultants publishes science fiction, fantasy, and horror. In 2021 there was notable horror by Tegan Moore, Ian Rogers, Richard Kadrey, Catherynne M. Valente, and Glen Hirshberg. The Rogers and Hirshberg are reprinted herein.

ANTHOLOGIES

Cthulhu Deep Down Under Volume 3 edited by Steve Proposch, Christopher Sequeira, Bryce Stevens (IFWG) is an anthology of ten new Lovecraftian stories by Australian writers. There are notable stories by Alf Simpson, David Conyers, Alan Baxter, and Julie Ditrich. With an Introduction by Cat Rambo and an afterword by Jack Dann.

The Half That You See edited by Rebecca Rowland (Dark Ink Books) is an anthology of twenty-six new stories on a theme so loose that it's difficult to discern. Despite that, there are notable stories by Elin Olausson, T.M. Starnes, Nicole Wolverton, Alex Giannini, Matt Masucci, and Douglas Ford.

Uncertainties Volume V edited by Brian Showers (The Swan River Press) is a strong entry in this annual series of weird, often dark tales. This volume features twelve new stories, the strongest of which are by John Langan, Eóin Murphy, Ramsey Campbell, Aislinn Clarke, Inna Effress, Deirdre Sullivan, Carly Holmes, and Nina Antonia. The Murphy and the Holmes are reprinted herein.

Beautiful/Grotesque edited by Sam Richard (Weird Punk Books) is a mini-anthology of five stories created from a story prompt of the title. The best are by Roland Blackburn and Katy Michelle Quinn.

Fright Train edited by the Switch House Gang (Haverhill House) is an anthology of fifteen horror stories on the theme of trains. All but three are new and the best of the originals are by Bracken MacLeod, Lee Murray, and Stephen Mark Rainey.

Railroad Tales edited by Trevor Denyer (Midnight Street Press) is a second anthology of stories on the theme of trains. This one has twenty-three, all new but three. There is notable work by Simon Bestwick, Catherine Pugh, Gayle Fidler, Gary Couzens, Michael Gore, Saoirse Ni Chiaragáin, and George Jacobs.

The Bad Book edited by John F.D. Taff (Bleeding Edge Books) contains thirteen original twisted bible parables, each with a story note by the author. The most interesting tales are by John Langan, Philip Fracassi, Hailey Piper, and Sarah Read.

What One Wouldn't Do edited by Scott J. Moses (self-published) is an all original anthology of twenty-nine stories on the vague theme of what lengths a person would go to . . . whatever . . . survive? Seek revenge? In any case there are notable stories by Nick Younker, J. A. W. McCarthy, Tom Reed, Cheri Kamei, Shane Douglas Keene, Eric LaRocca, Christi Nogle, and Jena Brown.

Terrifying Ghost Stories edited by Gillian Whittaker (Flame Tree Publishing) is a generous helping of almost fifty stories, including those in the public domain, reprints from contemporary writers, and some stories published for the first time. The strongest of the eleven new stories are by Lyndsay E. Gilbert and Michelle Tang.

Great British Horror 6: Ars Gratia Sanguis edited by Steve J. Shaw (Black Shuck Books) features eleven previously unpublished stories, ten by Britons and one international guest contributor. There are notable stories by Brian Evenson (the guest), Muriel Gray, Stephen Volk, Steve Duffy, Helen Grant, and Lucie McKnight Hardy.

The Alchemy Press Book Of Horrors 3: A Miscellany Of Monsters edited by Peter Coleborn and Jan Edwards (Alchemy Press) is an all-original anthology of sixteen monster stories. The best are by Ralph Robert Moore, Tim Jeffreys,

Steve Rasnic Tem, Garry Kilworth, and Simon Bestwick. The Bestwick is reprinted herein.

Walk Among Us, Vampire: The Masquerade (HarperVoyager) consists of three novellas based on the roleplaying game *World of Darkness*. The novellas are by Genevieve Gornichec, Cassandra Khaw, and Caitlin Starling.

Sisterhood: Dark Tales and Secret Histories edited by Nate Pederson (Chaosium, Inc) has sixteen stories—all but one new—by women about female cults of different types. The best of the new stories are by Gemma Files, Alison Littlewood, and Kali Wallace.

Humans are the Problem: A Monsters Anthology edited by Willow Becker (Weird Little Worlds) features twenty-two original stories about monsters taking their power back from humans. There are notable horror tales by Christi Nogle, Gemma Files, Cory Farrenkopf, Patrick Barb, Sarah Read, Georgia Cook, and Philip Fracassi and a very good non-horror tale by John Langan. The Files is reprinted herein.

Were Tales: A Shapeshifter Anthology edited by S. D. Vassallo and Stephen M. Long (Brigid's Gate) features twenty-seven stories and poems (one reprint) and one non-fiction piece on the theme of shapeshifting. There are notable pieces by Theresa Derwin and Stephanie Wytovich.

Attack from the 80s edited by Eugene Johnson (Raw Dog Dreaming Press) is an all original anthology of twenty-two stories embracing '80s pop culture steeped in blood and cheesiness. There are notable stories by Mort Castle, Stephanie Wytovich, Weston Ochse, Lee Murray, Stephen Graham Jones, and Grady Hendrix.

In Darkness, Delight: Fear the Future edited by Andrew Lennon and Evans Light (Corpus Press) is an all original anthology of twenty-two sf/horror stories. There are some notable stories by Ben Lawrence, Tim Curran, Max Booth III, Dominick Cancilla, and Phil Sloman.

The Mammoth Book of Folk Horror: Evil Lives on the Land edited by Stephen Jones (Skyhorse Publishing) is a mix of classic work by writers such as Arthur Machen, M. R. James, H. P. Lovecraft, Algernon Blackwood, contemporary reprints by Karl Edward Wagner, Dennis Etchison, Ramsey Campbell, and others plus nine originals. The strongest of the new stories are by Maura McHugh, Simon Strantzas, Michael Marshall Smith, Steve

Rasnic Tem, David A. Sutton, and Jan Edwards. The Smith and Strantzas are reprinted herein.

Terror Tales of the Scottish Lowlands edited by Paul Finch (Telos Publishing) continues to explore different parts of the United Kingdom, with fourteen dark stories (all but two, new) and the always worthwhile interstitial material by Paul Finch. The strongest stories are by Steve Duffy, M. W. Craven, Reggie Oliver, S. J. I. Holliday, William Meikle, and S. A. Rennie. The Duffy is reprinted herein.

Nightscript VII edited by C. M. Muller (Chthonic Matter) is a reliably readable annual anthology of weird, usually dark tales. This year it includes nineteen stories, all of them quite good. But the best were by Gordon Brown, Douglas Ford, Timothy Granville, Alexander James, Tim Major, Elin Olausson, Joshua Rex, Clint Smith, Ashley Stokes, David Surface, Steve Toase, and Charles Wilkinson.

Blood and Bone: An Anthology of Body Horror by Women and Non-Binary Writers edited by A. R. Ward (Ghost Orchid Press) has twenty-one new stories. The best are by Victoria Nations, Evelyn Freeling, Varian Ross, and Kristin Cleveland.

Tales of Yog-Sothoth edited by C. J. Phipps (Crossroads Press/Macabre Ink) contains six new Lovecraftian novellas. (Not seen.)

Beyond the Veil edited by Mark Morris (Flame Tree Publishing) is the second volume of an annual series of unthemed horror stories. This volume presents twenty new stories, with notable work by Gemma Files, Matthew Holness, Christopher Golden, Aliya Whiteley, Toby Litt, Lisa L. Hannett, Stephen Gallagher, Nathan Ballingrud, Lynda E. Rucker, and John Everson. The Golden and Holness are reprinted herein.

Wildwood: Tales of Terror and Transformation From the Forest edited by William O. Simmons (Shadow House Publishing) is a reprint anthology of fifteen classic stories—with an introduction by the editor.

They're Out To Get You Volume One: Animals and Insects edited by Johnny Mains (TK Pulp) is an all original anthology of thirteen stories about non-human creatures getting revenge on humans. A few of the stories come across as farce rather than horror but there are notable dark stories by Aliya Whitely, Ray Cluley, Steve Toase, Paul Finch, Charlotte Bond, Amanda DeBord, and Victoria Day.

Giving The Devil His Due edited by Rebecca Brewer (Running Wild Press) is a charity anthology dedicated to the Pixel Project's Anti-violence against women programs and contains sixteen stories about revenge against abusers of women. Four are reprints. The best of the new ones are by Nicholas Kaufmann, Kaaron Warren, Jason Sanford, and Lee Murray. The Warren is reprinted herein.

Violent Vixens: An Homage to Grindhouse Horror edited by Aric Sundquist (Dark Peninsula Press) has fifteen tales about violence and the women who suffer from it and sometime inflict it as revenge. There are notable stories by Gwendolyn Kiste, Mark Wheaton, Buck Weiss, Sarah Read, and Matt Neil Hill.

Hymns of Abomination: Secret Songs of Leeds edited by Justin A. Burnett (Silent Motorist Media) celebrates the work of Matthew M. Bartlett, whose weird, dark fiction seems to have hit a chord in other purveyors of weird and dark fiction. The book contains twenty-one stories and fourteen pieces of interstitial material, all related to the fictional Massachusetts village of Leeds. The most interesting are by Brian Evenson, Peter Rawlik, John Langan, Jon Padgett, John Linwood Grant, Farah Rose Smith, Gemma Files, S.P. Miskowski, Scott R. Jones, Christine Morgan, and Jonathan Raab. Two micro-fictions by Jonathan Raab are included herein.

The Jewish Book of Horror edited by Josh Schlossberg (Denver Horror Collective) is an all original anthology of twenty-two horror stories encompassing Jewish themes and history. There are notable stories by Daniel Braum, KD Casey, Richard Dansky, Elana Gomel, Simon Rosenberg, Brenda Tolian, Emily Ruth Verona, and Lindsey King-Miller.

When Things Get Dark: Stories Inspired by Shirley Jackson edited by Ellen Datlow (Titan Books) is an all original anthology of eighteen varied stories of dark fantasy and horror inspired by and in tribute to Jackson, author of the classic story "The Lottery" plus the novels *We Have Always Lived in the Castle* and *The Haunting of Hill House.* Some of the contributors are Kelly Link, Elizabeth Hand, Carmen Maria Machado, Josh Malerman, Richard Kadrey, and Joyce Carol Oates. The story by Laird Barron is reprinted herein.

Body Shocks: Extreme Tales of Body Horror edited by Ellen Datlow (Tachyon Publications) is an all reprint anthology of twenty-nine stories exploring the range and meaning of body horror—from Michael Blumlein's hate letter to

Ronald Reagan, the horrors of extreme fashion by Christopher Fowler and Genevieve Valentine, and twenty-six other stories.

The Little Book of Horrors: New Translations of Classic French Tales by J. D. Horn (Curious Blue Press) collects eight tales of horror by Prosper Mérimée, Guy de Maupassant, and others.

The Year's Best Dark Fantasy and Horror Volume 2 edited by Paula Guran (Pyr) contains twenty-three stories, two of which overlap with my own picks.

Mixed-genre Anthologies

Worlds of Light and Darkness: The Best of DreamForge and Space & Time Volume 1 edited by Angela Yuriko Smith and Scot Noel (Uproar Books) features twenty stories reprinted from the two magazines of the subtitle and includes science fiction, fantasy, and horror. The British Library's publishing arm has been bringing out a series of anthologies and collections containing classic and hard-to-find gothic, horror, and weird stories. In 2021, they published: *Crawling Horror: Creeping Tales of the Insect Weird* edited by Daisy Leaf and Janette Leaf with stories by Lafcadio Hearn, H.G. Wells, and others; *Minor Hauntings: Chilling Tales of Spectral Youth* edited by Jen Baker with stories by Ellen Glasgow, M. R. James, F. Marion Crawford, and others; *Dangerous Dimensions: Mind-Bending Tales of the Mathematical Weird* edited by Henry Bartholomew with stories by H. G. Wells, Robert Heinlein, Frank Belknap Long, and others; *Weird Woods* edited by John Miller with stories by Marjorie Bowen, Arthur Machen, Edith Nesbit, and others; and *Heavy Weather: Tempestuous Tales of Stranger Climes* edited by Kevan Manwaring including stories by Edgar Allan Poe, Robert Louis Stevenson, Herman Melville, and others. *Prisms* edited by Darren Speegle and Michael Bailey (PS Publishing) presents nineteen science fiction, fantasy, and horror stories. There are notable dark stories by Michael Marshall Smith, E. Catherine Tobler, Kristi DeMeester, Lynda E. Rucker, A. C. Wise, Richard Thomas, Paul Meloy, Tlotlo Tsamaase, J. Lincoln Fenn, Brian Evenson, and Nadia Bulkin. *Voices in the Darkness* edited by David Niall Wilson (Macabre Ink) is an unthemed anthology of five new stories and a novella. Notable horror by Nadia Bulkin, Elizabeth Massie, and Kathe Koja.

New Maps of Dream edited by Cody Goodfellow and Joseph Pulver Sr (PS Publishing) has nineteen original stories influenced by the weird and dark dream mythos of Lovecraft. I admit to not being much of a fan of stories with their focus on dreams but for readers with an interest more in the visionary than the horror of the "dreamlands," this might be your cup of tea. There are a couple of notable, darker stories by Kaaron Warren and Scott R. Jones. *There Is No Death, There Are No Dead* edited Aaron French and Jess Landry (Crystal Lake Publishing) is an anthology of fourteen stories—all new but two—centered on spiritualism. Some of them are horror, some are simply quirky. The best of the dark ones are by Laird Barron, Gemma Files, David Demchuk, Lee Murray, and Helen Marshall. *December Tales* edited by J. D. Horn (Curious Blue Press) is a half reprint/half new anthology of twenty-two ghost stories. The best are by Lisa Morton, Reggie Oliver, Kate Maruyama, and Glen Hirshberg. *Under Twin Suns: Alternate Histories of the Yellow Sign* edited by James Chambers (Hippocampus Press) is an all original anthology of twenty-two weird and/or dark stories and poems inspired by the Robert W. Chambers classic *The King in Yellow*. The most interesting pieces push against the theme. There's notable work by Linda D. Addison, Kathleen Scheiner, Tim Waggoner, Steven Van Patten, Carol Gyzander, Patrick Freivald, Kaaron Warren, and a novella by the late Joseph S. Pulver, Sr. *Tales From Omnipark: 18 Strange Stories Of a Theme Park That Might Have Been* edited by Ben Thomas (House Blackwood) is an intriguing idea and includes all new fantasy, horror, and a wee bit of science fiction. Although a few of the stories are too similar in feel, among the horror there are notable contributions by Brian Evenson, Gemma Files, Maxwell I. Gold, and Orrin Grey. The Evenson is reprinted herein. *Songs of the Northern Seas: An Anthology* edited by Mark Beech (Egaeus Press) is a mixture of thirteen new dark, weird, and melancholy tales, all taking place on the northern seas. There are notable stories by Alison Littlewood, Colin Fisher, Leena Likitalo, Stephen Clark, Helen Grant, Lisa L. Hannett, and Sean and Rachel Qitsualik-Tinsley. *The Black Dreams: Strange Stories From Northern Ireland* edited by Reggie Chamberlain-King (The Blackstaff Press) is an excellent anthology with fourteen new stories that take place in Northern Ireland. Most are weird, some exceedingly dark, and a few could be characterized as contes cruels. There are notable stories by Ian McDonald,

Jo Baker, Sam Thompson, Michelle Gallen, Reggie Chamberlain-King, John Patrick Higgins, and Gerard McKeown. The McKeown is reprinted herein. *Dreamland: Other Stories* edited by Sophie Essex (Black Shuck Books) is an intriguing anthology of mostly surreal, dream-like stories, all by female identifying writers. The best dark ones are by Priya Sharma, Nicole M. Wolverton, Giselle Leeb, and Sam Hicks. *Professor Charlatan Bardot's Travel Anthology to the Most (Fictional), Haunted Buildings in the Weird, Wild World* edited by Charlatan Bardot and Eric J. Guignard (Dark Moon Books) is a clever (perhaps a bit too clever) anthology of twenty-seven mostly dark fantasy tales of haunted spaces around the world. Treated as a travelogue, the volume includes maps, illustrations, short stories, and some flash. There are notable horror stories by Kaaron Warren, Clara Madrigano, Terry Dowling, Weston Ochse, Jeffrey Ford, Ramsey Campbell, and Octavia Cade. *Chilling Crime Short Stories* edited by Josie Karani (Flame Tree Press) contains thirty-seven stories and excerpts. Ten are appearing for the first time and one was a 2021 audio podcast. There are only a few horror stories—the best of them are by Steve Toase, Robert Ford, Tyler Jones, Alexes Lester, Michael Penncavage, and Michel J. Moore. The Toase is reprinted herein. *Unburied: A Collection of Queer Dark Fiction* edited by Rebecca Rowland (Dark Ink) has sixteen new stories of sf, dark fantasy and horror. There are notable stories by Felice Picano and Sarah Lyn Eaton. *Shadow Atlas* edited by Carina Bissett, Hillary Dodge, and Joshua Viola (Hex Publishers) is a fascinating anthology of original stories, poems, "letters," other kinds of entries that all take place in the Americas. Discovering and analyzing historical secrets and mythologies and folk tales. Not all are dark, but they are usually pretty mysterious. The notable darker pieces are by Christina Sng, Josh Malerman, Annie Neugebauer, Stephanie M. Wytovich, Owl Goingback, Warren Hammond, Mario Acevedo, Colleen Anderson, Kay Chronister, Sarah Read, and Tim Waggoner. *Stokercon 2021 Souvenir Anthology* The Phantom Denver edition edited by Joshua Viola (Horror Writers Association/Hex Publishers) is the hefty souvenir book created for what became an all virtual convention as a result of Covid. Full of fiction and poetry, essays, and author interviews, the fiction is all centered around Blucifer, the famous thirty-two foot tall blue horse with red eyes that welcomes visitors to the Denver Airport. *Shoot* edited by Rachel Knightly was sponsored by Green Ink Write 2021, which raises money for Macmillan Cancer Support in the UK—It's an all original anthology of eighteen stories and poems, each inspired by the story prompt "shoot." There are notable dark stories and poetry by Charlotte Bond, Lisa Morton, Paul Tremblay, Stephen Laws, and Roz Kaveney. *Black Sci-Fi Short Stories* edited by Tia Ross (Flame Tree Press) is part of the publishers Gothic Fantasy series and includes twenty classic and new stories of sf, fantasy, and horror. With a foreword by Temi Oh and an introduction by Dr. Sandra M. Grayson. (Not seen.)

COLLECTIONS

More single-author collections than ever include multiple genres, which I love, but makes them difficult to categorize. So using my best judgment, I've separating "collections" from "mixed-genre collections." The collections I consider "mixed-genre" are below this grouping.

To Drown in Dark Water by Steve Toase (Undertow Publications) is a strong debut collection of twenty-six stories, by a writer whose stories I've reprinted several times in previous volumes of *The Best Horror of the Year*. Six of the stories appear for the first time. One is reprinted herein.

Fit For Consumption: Stories Both Queer and Horrifying by Steve Berman Lethe Press contains thirteen weird and/or horrific stories, one new.

The Strange Thing We Become and Other Dark Tales by Eric LaRocca (Off Limits Press) is a powerful debut collection of eight startling stories that occasionally touch on taboos, by a relatively new writer. All but one of the stories are new. Highly recommended. One is reprinted herein.

The Harbor-Master: Best Weird Stories of Robert W. Chambers edited by S. T. Joshi (Hippocampus Press) is part of the Classics of Gothic Horror series. The volume presents twelve stories, including some of the stories from Chambers' most famous collection *The King in Yellow*. Joshi provides an introduction to the book and background material about each story.

Finding Yourself in the Dark by Steve Duffy (Sarob Press) is the author's fifth collection. It showcases twelve weird tales that are often horror, four of them new. One story won the Shirley Jackson Award for Best Novelette, another was reprinted by me in *The Best Horror of the Year Volume One*.

Sacred and Profane: Seven Strange Tales by Peter Bell (Sarob Press) is the author's fifth collection. All of the seven excellent stories are published for the first time.

Scream to the Shadows: Twenty Darkest Tales by Tunku Halim (Penguin-Random House-SEA) is a retrospective of this Malaysian writer's horror. The collection is divided into several thematic sections: supernatural, psychological, techno-horror, stories about graveyards, and stories influenced by dark Malay myths and legends.

In that Endlessness, Our End by Gemma Files (Grimscribe Press) is the author's fifth collection of weird and horror. It includes fifteen stories, one new. Files is one of the finest practitioners in the field and if you're not familiar with her work, it's time you are.

Hollow Skulls and Other Stories by Samuel Marzioli (JournalStone Publishing) is the author's debut, and includes thirteen stories, three of them new.

Dancing with Tombstones by Michael Aronovitz (Cemetery Dance Publications) is the author's third collection, and features sixteen stories and one novella, all published between 2009 and 2020.

Eyes in the Dust and Other Stories by David Peak (Trepidatio) is an impressively strong debut horror collection by an author whose work has appeared in a variety of journals and small press anthologies. One story is new. Christopher Slatsky provides an Introduction.

A Maze for the Minotaur and Other Strange Stories by Reggie Oliver (Tartarus Press) is the author's eighth collection of darkly weird stories published by Tartarus, and as always it's a very fine collection. Most of the twelve stories were published in the last few years. Also included are two new ones.

Dead Hours of the Night by Lisa Tuttle (Valancourt Books) features twelve dark stories originally published between 1980 and 2017 including two reprinted in earlier annual volumes of my bests of the year. With stories notes by the author and an Introduction by Lisa Kröger, co-author of *Monster, She Wrote*.

Sometimes We're Cruel and Other Stories by JAW McCarthy (Cemetery Gates Media) is a powerful debut with twelve stories, half of them published for the first time. One of the reprints was in my *Best Horror of the Year Volume Thirteen*.

Thanatrauma by Steve Rasnic Tem (Valancourt Books) has twenty-one varied stories, four new, published by a master of quiet horror whose best work explores grief and how personal tragedy can unmake us all.

I Spit Myself Out by Tracy Fahey (Sinister Horror Company) is the author's third collection and it's a strong one. There are eighteen stories, all but six new. Fahey provides an introduction explaining her inspiration for this female-centered work.

The Ghosts of Who You Were by Christopher Golden (Haverhill House Publishing) features ten stories and a novella published between 2013 and 2020, with an introduction and story notes by the author. Two of the stories were originally published in anthologies edited by me and one was reprinted in an earlier volume of my Best of the Year series.

There Comes a Midnight Hour by Gary A. Braunbeck (Raw Dog Screaming Press) is a retrospective of fifteen of the author's short stories written over twenty-five years, including one new one.

Dread Softly: A Collection by Caryn Larrinaga (Twisted Tree Press) collects eleven stories, most of them new.

Pariah & Other Stories by Sam Dawson (Supernatural Tales) is a debut collection by an author whose work is often published in *Supernatural Tales*. It features sixteen new stories.

Empty Graves by Jonathan Maberry (WordFire Press) presents sixteen (one new) stories about zombies, by the bestselling author.

Look Where You Are Going Not Where You Have Been by Steven J. Dines (Luna Press) is the author's first collection, although he's been publishing strong dark fiction since 2004, mostly in *Black Static*. Included are eleven stories, two of them new novellas. The volume also includes Introductions by Ralph Robert Moore and Johnny Mains, in addition to story notes.

The Feverish Stars: New and Selected Stories by John Shirley (Independent Regions) has twenty-one dark stories, published between 2001 and 2021 (two published for the first time in this collection). With an Introduction by Richard Christian Matheson.

The Gulp by Alan Baxter (13th Dragon Books) features five dark novellas that take place in and around an isolated Australian town known colloquially as The Gulp.

The Complete Short Fiction of Peter Straub: Volume 1: Stories and *The Complete Short Fiction of Peter Straub: Volume 2: Novellas* is a limited edition two volume set from Borderlands Press. The two books contain a total of eight novellas and twenty-six stories.

Borderlands Press introduced the first volume of the 4th Series of Little Books— Past Masters of Horror and Dark Fantasy. Series IV will feature seminal works of many of the progenitors of the horror and dark fantasy genres. Each volume is edited and signed by a contemporary writer or editor. The first title *A Little Blue Book of Civil War Horrors,* honors the work of Ambrose Bierce, who wrote some of the most memorable stories of the American Civil War. The book, edited by Lawrence Connolly, contains twelve tales and vignettes. *A Little Yellow Book of Carcosa and Kings* by Robert W. Chambers edited by Lisa Morton contains the four stories of the King in Yellow Cycle.

We Feed the Dark: Tales of Terror, Loss & the Supernatural by William P. Simmons (A Shadow House Book), with fourteen stories, includes most of the contents in the author's first collection published in 2004 plus one new story.

Dead Relatives and Other Stories by Lucie McKnight Hardy (Dead Ink) is the terrific debut collection by a Welsh writer whose work has been published in *Black Static, Uncertainties*, and in other venues. Several of the thirteen stories are new, including the powerful title novella.

Beneath a Pale Sky by Philip Fracassi (Lethe Press) is a very strong second collection with seven stories, two of them new. One story—"The Wheel"—is especially suspenseful.

Bedding the Lamia: Tropical Horrors by David Kuraria (IFWG Publishing) is a debut collection of four stories taking place in the tropical areas of Australia, two new, one of those a novella.

The Trains Don't Stop Here by M. R. Cosby (Dark Lane Books) is the author's second, impressively creepy collection, with ten stories, half of them new. Rebecca Lloyd provides an Introduction.

Dreams for the Dying by Adam Light (Corpus Press) is a debut collection featuring eleven reprints, all revised from their original version and each with an author's note.

The Mother Wound: Stories by Jess Landry (Independent Legions) is a debut collection of seventeen stories ranging from flash fiction to a novella, three of them (including the novella), new.

Tales from the Hinterland by Melissa Albert (Flatiron Books) is an excellent collection of twelve new, sinister and horrifying fairy tales, with illustrations by Jim Tierney. Some of the tales take their inspiration from already existing stories, but they all feel fresh.

Weird Doom David J. Schow Sampler (Cimarron Street Books) collects eight stories by Schow, one that was reprinted in my *Year's Best Fantasy and Horror* series and one of them new. The volume also includes an interview with the author by John Scolari. The book is meant to be a showcase for the series of Schow reprints coming from the publishing house.

The Gypsy Spiders and Other Tales of Italian Horror by Nicola Lombardi translated by J. Weintraub (Tartarus Press) presents nine stories. The short novel of the title looks to be published in English for the first time.

During 2021, The Swan River Press, the Irish-centric press run by Brian J. Showers, published three collections of stories: *Eyes of Terror and Other Dark Adventures* by L. T. Meade, a bestselling author of the 1890s, now mostly known for her girls' school stories. But in her prime she was writing weird and dark fiction, mostly for *The Strand*. The volume includes nine stories and an interview; *A Vanished Hand and Other Stories* by Clotilde Graves, dramatist and prose writer who used the pseudonym "Richard Dehan" and was a prolific author of short stories and novels, only some within the fantastic and grotesque genres. Included are thirteen stories, an interview, and a contemporary profile; *The Fatal Move* by Conall Cearnach, pseudonym of F. W. O'Connell, collects all the stories from the author's original 1924 collection plus eight brief essays, originally published earlier. The volume has an introduction by Reggie Chamberlain-King.

Folk Songs for Trauma Surgeons by Keith Rosson (Meerkat Press) oddly has *not* been marketed nor reviewed as a horror collection but from the several stories in the book that I read (one is new), there's an awful lot of darkness here.

Exploring Dark Short Fiction #6: A Primer to Ramsey Campbell edited by Eric J. Guignard (Dark Moon) includes six stories, an author interview, biography, bibliography, and commentary.

The Village Killings and Other Novellas by Ramsey Campbell (PS Publishing) contains five novellas, one of them new, the title detective story—a take on the Agatha Christie tradition. With an Introduction by the author about writing them.

MIXED-GENRE COLLECTIONS

Rabbit Island by Elvira Navarro (Two Lines Press) has eleven surreally dark stories by a Spanish writer named one of Granta's "Best Young Spanish-Language Novelists." *The Glassy, Burning Floor of Hell* by Brian Evenson (Coffee House Press) is as always with Evenson a mixture of the weird, fantastical, and sometimes dark captured brilliantly in twenty-two stories, two of them first published in 2021. *A Sorcerer of Atlantis* by John Shirley (Hippocampus) includes a weird, fantastic short novel and novella both mixing Lovecraftian horror and sword and sorcery tropes. *Rainbringer: Zora Neale Hurston Against the Lovecraft Mythos* by Edward M. Erdelac (self-published) is a collection of eight stories, three of them reprints, featuring Hurston as a Mythos detective. *Things I Didn't Know My Father Knew: The Best Short Stories of Peter Crowther* (Cemetery Dance Publications) collects twenty-seven stories in several genres, including the powerful, harrowing horror story "Bedfordshire," that appeared in one of my YBFH anthologies. The hefty volume looks great, and includes welcome story notes by the author, but I'm surprised that there's no copyright/first publication credit page nor credit for the interior illustrations. *The Open Door and Other Stories of the Seen and Unseen* by Margaret Oliphant edited by Mike Ashley (British Library Publications) has an introduction and six stories. Black Shuck's Shadow series published four collections in 2021: *Hinterlands* by George Sandison presents a mix of ten sf, dark fantasy, and horror stories, half of them new. *Nine Ghosts* by Simon Bestwick presents eight weird/dark mixed-genre tales and a poem, two new-with story notes on each piece. *Beyond Glass* by Rachel Knightley has five strange, dark stories. *A Box of Darkness* by Simon Avery has five stories, four of them new—not horror. *The Ghost Sequences* by A. C. Wise (Undertow Publications) is an excellent collection of sixteen stories (all but one reprints) of ghostly dark fantasy and horror. I originally published several of the stories, and reprinted a couple in my Bests of the Year. *Spirits Abroad* by Zen Cho (Small Beer Press) is an expanded edition of the author's debut collection of the same title, with nine extra reprints, and one new story. A combination of sf, fantasy, supernatural dark fantasy, and horror. *Out of the Mortal Night Selected Works of Samuel Loveman* edited by S. T. Joshi and David E. Schultz (Hippocampus Press) is a revised and augmented edition of a 2004 title, adding more than one hundred pages of previously uncollected poetry, fiction, essays, and reviews. *Undiscovered Territories* by Robert Freeman Wexler (PS Publishing) featuring fourteen stories of dreamlike fantasy, surrealism, and occasional darkness, is the author's first full-length story collection. Three stories appear for the first time. Hippocampus Press published the *Collected Fiction of Ambrose Bierce* edited by S. T. Joshi: *Volume 1 Tales of Psychological and Supernatural Horror. Volume 2 Tales of the Civil War and Tales of the Grotesque. Volume 3 Tall Tales and Satirical Sketches; Political Fantasies and Future Histories. The Little Devil and Other Stories* by Alexei Remizov translated by Antonina W. Bouis (Columbia University Press) contains an overview of the late Russian writer's short fiction, with thirteen stories influenced by folk and fairy tales of his country. *Burning Girls and Other Stories* by Veronica Schanoes (A Tor.com Book) is a rich debut collection of thirteen mixed-genre stories, novelettes, and novellas, some retold fairy tales. Two of the stories are new. (Caveat, I am the editor of the collection). *Avenging Angela and Other Uncanny Encounters* by Jonathan Thomas (Hippocampus Press) has fourteen weird stories, some of them horror. More than half of the stories are new. This is the author's sixth collection. *Madam Cruller's Couch and Other Dark, Bizarre Tales* by Elizabeth Massie (Macabre Ink) collects fifteen stories and poems (and one novella), almost half of them published for the first time. *We Are Happy, We Are Doomed* by Kurt Fawver (Grimscribe Press) is a collection of sixteen weird and sometimes horrific stories, one new. With several interior illustrations by Harry O. Morris, whose art is also on the cover. *The Best of Lucius Shepard 2* edited by Bill Sheehan (Subterranean Press) contain fourteen stories and novellas and is more than 300,000 words. A must have for all aficionados of short fiction, but especially for readers of the fantastic and horror. *On the Hierophant Road* by James Chambers (Raw Dog Dreaming Press) presents fourteen stories of science fiction, fantasy, dark fantasy, and horror, two new, one of them an original novella. *Cabinet of Wrath: A Doll Collection* by Tara Campbell (Aqueduct Press) is the eightieth entry in the Conversation Pieces series of mini-collections. This one features nine stories, three new, all having to do with dolls, some of them vengeful. *Someone to Share My Nightmares* by Sonora Taylor (self-published) contains nine stories, all but two new. Most of the stories are dark fantasy rather than horror, with some erotic bits thrown into the mix. *Big Dark Hole* by Jeffrey Ford (Small Beer Press) presents fifteen vivid, weird, sometime dark stories—three of them new. Ford has one of the most fertile minds in sf/f/h and if you've not been reading his short fiction, you need to begin to do so now. *Widow of the Amputation & Other Weird Crimes* by Robert Guffey (Eraserhead Press) features four new, weird novellas by this imaginative writer. *The Grey Chamber: Stories and Essays* by Marjorie Bowen selected and edited by John C. Tibbetts (Hippocampus Press) is a collection of horror, weird, and mainstream fiction by the writer whose real name was Margaret Gabrielle Vere Long (1885-1952). It also includes her essays about Elizabethan magician John Dee, artist William Hogarth, and an unpublished essay about her own work. *Two Figures in a Car and Other Stories* by Wan Phing Lim (Penguin-Random House-SEA) features fourteen crime stories by this Malaysian writer, some of which skirt the weird. *The Burning Day and Other Strange Stories* by Charles Payseur (Lethe Press) has twenty-two stories of sf, fantasy, and dark fantasy, all but one reprints. *Unexpected Places to Fall From, Unexpected Places to Land* by Malcolm Devlin (Unsung Stories) is the second collection by this talented writer. It has nine weird and mainstream stories (one of them, new) and a new novella. *The Ghost Variations* by Kevin Brockmeier (Pantheon) features one hundred flash stories and vignettes by this always inventive writer. *Archetypes* by Florence Sunnen (Zagawa) collects twenty-one character studies of creatures such as vampires, mermaids, and mummies by this writer from Luxembourg. *Reality and Other Stories* by John Lancaster (W. W. Norton & Company) has eight stories by this mostly literary writer, half of them new. Some are dark, most are weird. Worth a look. *Mills of Silence* by Charles Wilkinson (Egaeus Press) is the author's second collection, and contains eleven stories previously published in various venues of the weird, plus one new novella. *Danged Black Thing* by Eugen Bacon (Transit Lounge) brings together seventeen stories (three collaborations) published between 2012 and 2021 of various genres by this African-Australian writer. *I Would Haunt You If I Could* by Seán Padraic Birnie (Undertow Publications) is an impressive debut of fourteen weird and dark stories. Eight of the stories are new, and all but one of the others were published in since 2018. *Alias Space and Other Stories* by Kelly Robson (Subterranean Press) is the impressive debut collection by one of the freshest voices around. Equally at home writing science fiction, fantasy, and horror. These fourteen stories, novelettes, and one novella demonstrate her range and are proof positive as to why you should be reading her. *Midnight Doorways: Fables From Pakistan* by Usman T. Malik (Kitab) is a beautifully produced debut collection of seven fantasy, dark fantasy, and horror stories by this award-winning writer— all published between 2014 and 2020. There are black and white interior illustrations for each story. *The Tallow-Wife and Other Tales* by Angela Slatter (Tartarus Press) is a very good volume of dark fantasy, with all twelve stories taking place in the imaginary city of Lodellan. Most of the stories are new and can be read as separate entities. With spot illustrations throughout by Kathleen Jennings and an Introduction by Helen Marshall. *Within Me Without Me: Dark Poetry and Prose* by Sumiko Saulson (DookyZines) collects about forty pieces of poetry and prose, some of which are new. *The Ettinfell of Beacon Hill: Gothic Tales of Boston* by Adam Bolivar (Jackanapes Press) collects twelve intertwined tales about an occult investigator in 1920s Boston. *The Sad Eyes of the Lewis Chessman* by George Berguño (Egaeus Press) is part of the "Keynote Edition" collection series, and comes as a small, attractive hardcover. It has nine stories, three of them new. *From the Neck Up and Other Stories* by Aliya Whitley (Titan) is the author's debut collection, with fifteen stories and a novella, including science fiction, weird fiction, and horror, all published between 2014 and 2020. *Antisocieties* by Michael Cisco (Grimscribe Press) is, as always, a must-have collection of weird, sometimes very dark fiction. The ten, all-new stories are loosely themed around isolation. *The Dangers of Smoking in Bed* by Mariana Enríquez (Hogarth) is the acclaimed Argentinian author's second collection, with most of the twelve stories appearing in English for the first time. Many stories are only marginally horror, but their darkness should be attractive to readers of the weird. *Under a Dark Angel's Eye: Selected Stories* by Patricia Highsmith (Virago) collects more than forty stories, two never before published. Dark dark dark. Her characters are amoral, immoral, mean, cruel. Her stories are gems of the dark. Carmen Maria Machado provides an introduction. *Among the Lilies* by Daniel Mills (Undertow Publications) is the author's second collection and features twelve weird stories, two of them new. *Unfortunate Elements of My Anatomy* by Hailey Piper (The Seventh Terrace) features eighteen stories (three new) of science fiction, fantasy, and horror focusing on LBGTQ characters. *Don't Push the Button* by John Skipp (Clash Books) includes fifteen stories, two screenplays, and two essays. Four of the stories are new. Josh Malerman wrote the Introduction.

CHAPBOOKS AND NOVELLAS

Comfort Me with Apples by Catherynne M. Valente (A Tor.com Book) is about a young woman who adores and is, in turn, adored by her perfect husband, who leaves her alone while he's on business trips—in her perfect house in the perfect neighborhood, in the perfect world. But things get dicey when she begins to notice odd things. A beautifully told, fast-moving, dark fairy tale.

Things Have Gotten Worse Since We Last Spoke by Eric LaRocca (Weird Punk Books) is a terrific, disturbing tale of two young women who begin a virtual relationship that devolves into obsession and horror.

The Goddess of Filth by V. Castro (Creature Publishing) is about five Chicana teenagers recently out of high school, who decide to hold a séance and call on a higher power to take them away from their dead-end lives. They get more than they bargained for as an ancient goddess takes possession of one of them.

Of Men and Monsters by Tom Deady (Crystal Lake Publishing) is about a woman who, in 1975, flees her abusive husband with their two teenage sons, moving to a small town in Massachusetts. Once settled in, the younger son acquires a critter ordered from the back of a comic book, that grows into a monster, but it's not as scary as the human stalking them.

Nothing But Blackened Teeth by Cassandra Khaw is a gorgeously written novella about several friends meeting for a wedding in an old mansion in an isolated corner of Japan. Here, old tensions bubble to the surface as the house awakens and supernatural creatures stir. But it's human flaws that ultimately lead to the horrific events that ensue (acquired and edited by me).

The Monster, The Mermaid, and Doctor Mengele by Ian Watson (Newcon Press) presents a new theory as to how the Nazi murder doctor survived undetected in Brazil for three decades before his confirmed death in 1979.

Roads Less Traveled Volume 1: Extraordinary Fiction and Interviews edited by Trevor Denyer (Midnight Street Press) contains new novellas by Gary

Couzens and Ralph Robert Moore plus interviews with and a bibliography of each writer. *Volume 2* contains new novellas by Rhys Hughes and Susan York.

Family Solstice by Kate Maruyama (Omnium Gatherum) is a novella about an annual family tradition centered on a battle in the basement.

With Teeth by Brian Keene (Death's Head Press) is about a group of middle-aged men who plan to start a criminal enterprise in the West Virginian woods, until they encounter the devolved vampires existing there. Also included are two reprinted stories.

Rookfield by Gordon B. White (Trepidatio) is about a mother who flees with her child to her hometown during the pandemic—when the father follows, he finds her family and the other inhabitants of the town pretty inhospitable.

Master of Rods and Strings by Jason Marc Harris (Vernacular Press) is a weird story about an obsessed protagonist, puppets, and puppetry.

POETRY

Star*Line is the official quarterly journal of the Science Fiction Poetry Association. During 2021 it was edited by F. J. Bergmann and then Jean-Paul Garnier, who took over with issue 44.3. It regularly publishes members' science fiction and fantasy poetry—and occasional horror. It also publishes reviews of other poetry magazines, collections, and anthologies plus a market report. There was notable dark poetry in 2021 by Avra Margariti, Deanie Vallone, Davian Aw, Hayley Stone, Sydney Bernthold, Karie Jacobson, Cecilia Caballero, Christina Sng, Bruce McAllister, Tara Campbell, and Kelly Blair.

Eye to the Telescope is the quarterly online journal of the Science Fiction and Fantasy Poetry Association. Issue 41, with the theme of Indigenous Futurisms, was guest edited by Tiffany Morris and had notable horror by Bill Ratner and Trevor Livingston. Issue 42, with the theme The Sea, was guest edited by Akua Lezli Hope and had notable horror by Gerri Leen, Malina Douglas, and John Muro.

The 2021 Rhysling Anthology: The Best Science Fiction, Fantasy & Horror Poetry of 2020 selected by the Science Fiction Poetry Association edited by Alessandro Manzetti (Science Fiction Poetry Association) is used by members to vote for the best short and long poems of the year, and can be considered an annual report on the state of speculative poetry. This year's volume is more than 250 pages, and is divided into two sections of Short Poems and Long Poems. It's a good resource for checking out the poetic side of speculative and horror fiction. Included is a history of past winners.

Dwarf Stars 2021 edited by Charles Christian (Science Fiction and Fantasy Poetry Association) collects the best very short speculative poems published in 2020. The poems are ten lines or fewer and the prose poems one hundred words or fewer.

Spectral Realms edited by S. T. Joshi (Hippocampus Press) is a showcase for weird and dark poetry. Two issues came out in 2021. In addition to original poems there's a section with classic reprints and a review column. There was notable poetry by F. J. Bergmann, Maxwell I. Gold, P.B. Grant, Wade German, Justin Permenter, Scott J. Couturier, Alicia Hilton, David Barker, Chelsea Arrington, Christina Sng, David Schembri, Adam Bolivar, Jordan Zuniga, and Lori E. Lopez.

Horror Writers Association Presents Poetry Showcase Vol III edited by Stephanie M. Wytovich (Horror Writers Association) is an excellent entry in this ongoing series, with notable poems by Benicio Isandro, Vince A. Liaguno, Lindy Ryan, Graham Masterton, Lisa Morton, Amy Langevin, Michael Arnzen, Stephanie Ellis, Ian Hunter, Deborah L. Davitt, KC Grifant, Jacqueline West, Kailey Tedesco, R. J. Joseph, Donyae Coles, and Saba Syed Razvi.

Eclipse of the Moon by Frank Coffman (Minds Eye Publications) is the poet's third major volume of speculative verse. Coffman is always experimenting with form, giving his poetry a freshness to his prolific work. His most interesting poems (for me) are the long ones that tell full stories.

The Exorcised Lyric by Steven Withrow and Frank Coffman (Minds Eye Publications) is an interesting collaborative book of poetry.

The Last Oblivion: Best Fantastic Poems of Clark Ashton Smith edited by S. T. Joshi and David E. Schultz (Hippocampus Press) includes approximately 140 poems, many of which are gorgeous and bewitching, and also has a brief introduction by the co-editors, plus a glossary.

Can You Sign My Tentacle? by Brandon O'Brien (Interstellar Flight Press) is a strong collection of thirty, mostly new poems combining cosmic horror with the black experience.

Victims by Marge Simon and Mary Turzillo (Weasel Press) contains reprinted and new individual poems by each poet and several collaborations in this dark collection focused on victims and their victimizers.

Oblivion in Flux: A Collection of Cyber Prose by Maxwell I. Gold (Crystal Lake Publishing) features more than fifty prose poems combining visions of the future and dark, fantastic imagery. Some of the work is new and included is a new collaboration with Linda D. Addison.

Field Guide to Invasive Species of Minnesota by Amelia Gorman (Interstellar Flight Press) is a beautiful work of twenty-one poetic, surreal bits of ecological awareness.

Dancing with Maria's Ghost: Dark Encounters with the Ghost of Maria Callas by Alessandro Manzetti (Independent Legions) contains poems influenced by the opera singer and her major roles, and plus some uncollected poetry by Manzetti on other themes.

The Smallest of Bones by Holly Lyn Walrath (Clash Books) contains tiny but haunting poems about our relationship to our bodies.

Strange Nests: Blackout Poetry Inspired by The Secret Garden by Jessica McHugh (Apokrupha) contains text on the left page, with drawings and words chosen for the poem on the right page. Remarkably it works, creating some powerful, dark poetry.

Tortured Willows: Bent, Bowed, Unbroken by Christina Sng, Angela Yuriko Smith, Lee Murray, & Geneve Flynn (Yuriko Publishing) is a terrific collection of new, mostly horror poetry by four Southeast Asian women, writing of pain, otherness, and also of the damage done by the myth/propaganda of female submissiveness by their own cultures. One poem, by Lee Murray, is reprinted herein.

K. A. Opperman had two collections of poetry out in 2021: *October Ghosts and Autumn Dreams: More Poems for Halloween* (Jackanapes Press), with a foreword by Adam Bolivar and the darker *The Laughter of Ghouls* (Hippocampus Press). Both are Illustrated by Dan V. Sauer.

Lost Letters to a Lover's Carcass by Ronald J. Murray (Bizarro Pulp) is a powerful collection of angst-ridden dark poetry.

Monstrum Poetica by Jezzy Wolfe (Raw Dog Screaming Press) is a strong collection of poetry separated into sections by a brief explanation of each type of monster covered.

Exposed Nerves by Lucy A. Snyder (Raw Dog Screaming Press) is a multi-award-winning poet. In this strong new collection of reprints and new poems, she includes horror and sf and social criticism.

The Voice of the Burning House by John Shirley (Jackanapes Press) brings together thirty weird poems almost half of them new. With illustrations by Dan Sauer.

Non-fiction

Women and Other Monsters by Jess Zimmerman (Beacon Press) is a cultural analysis of eleven female monsters from Greek mythology, and how their depiction as monsters has influenced generations of young women. *H. P. Lovecraft: Letters to E. Hoffman Price and Richard F. Searight* edited by David E. Schultz and S. T. Joshi (Hippocampus Press) presents and annotates the five-year correspondence between Lovecraft and Price initiated by their mutual acquaintance Robert E. Howard. *Fear and Nature: Ecohorror Studies in the Anthropocene* edited by Christy Tidwell and Carter Soles (Penn State University Press) features essays and analyses of using eco-horror in various media such as literature, manga, poetry, television, and film. It covers the period from Edgar Allan Poe to Stephen King and Guillermo del Toro. *Random Notes, Random Lines* by Donald Sidney-Fryer (Hippocampus Press) collects recent essays, reviews, interviews with the author and a raft of poetry, some written during his adolescence. *American Twilight: The Cinema of Tobe Hooper* edited by Kristopher Woofter and Will Dodson (University of Texas Press) asserts that the director was an auteur whose works featured complex monsters and disrupted America's sacrosanct perceptions of prosperity and domestic security. *Confessions of a Puppet Master: A Hollywood Memoir of Ghouls, Guts, and Gonzo Filmmaking* by Charles Band with Adam Felber (William Morrow) is a tell-all memoir about the four decades spent by the producer/director of films in the exploitation field of Hollywood. *Born Under Saturn: The Letters of Samuel Loveman and Clark Ashton Smith* edited by S. T. Joshi and David E. Schultz (Hippocampus Press) includes correspondence between 1910 and 1941 about the aesthetics of their own poetry and other poets of the period, discussions about rare books each of them collected, and sometimes, their personal lives. *9/11 Gothic: Decrypting Ghosts and Trauma in New York City's Terrorism Novels* by Danel Olson (Rowman & Littlefield) explores ghostly presences from the world's largest crime scene in novels by Don DeLillo, Jonathan Safran Foer, Lynne Sharon Schwartz, Griffin Hansbury, and Patrick McGrath—all of whom have been called writers of Gotham. *Adapting Stephen King: Volume 1:* Carrie, Salem's Lot *and* The Shining *From Novel to Screenplay* by Joseph Maddrey (McFarland) charts the development of each adaptation of the three novels from first option to final cut, through interviews with the writers, producers, and directors. *Writers Workshop of Horror 2* edited by Michael Knost (Hydra Publications) contains essays and interviews focusing on the art and craft of writing horror and dark fantasy by famous and up-and-coming writers. *Terence Fisher: Master of Gothic Cinema* by Tony Dalton (F&B Press) was an important director of Hammer films and this authorized biography is a survey of his work. *Capturing Ghosts On the Page: Writing Horror and Dark Fiction* by Kaaron Warren (Brain Jar Press) is a chapbook on the craft, philosophy, and business of writing horror, taking information from the multi-award winning author's essays, workshops, and articles. *The Conjuring* by Kevin J. Wetmore, Jr. is part of the Devil's Advocate series from the Auteur imprint of University of Liverpool Press and covers everything you'd want to know about the movie. *The Recognition of H. P. Lovecraft: His Rise From Obscurity to World Renown* by S. T. Joshi (Hippocampus Press) traces the original, limited dissemination of Lovecraft's fiction during his lifetime, through the '70s when his non-fiction and fiction was "discovered" by readers and scholars to the current day. *A Monster for Many: Talking With H. P. Lovecraft* by Robert H. Waugh (Hippocampus Press) is the third volume of essays, this one ranging from the influence of Sir Arthur Conan Doyle on Lovecraft to his opinions of Nobel Prize winners contemporary to his time. *Days of the Dead: A Year of True Ghost Stories* by Sylvia Shults (Haunted Road Media) collects 366 "true" ghost stories, one for every day of the year—it's a fun book to dip into whenever you're in need of a bit of creepiness. *150 Exquisite Horror Books* edited by Alessandro Manzetti (Crystal Lake Publishing) is a guide to contemporary horror, dark fantasy, and weird books published between 1986 and 2020. The choices are in alphabetical order and have been given scores by the editor. Various horror professionals also provide ten best lists (I'm included). The value of such a book is that it can point out books and writers readers have missed or want to revisit. *The Alchemy Book of the Dead 2020* by Stephen Jones (Alchemy Press) is an alphabetically organized necrology of almost 450 individuals who made significant contributions to the science fiction, fantasy, and horror fields compiled by Jones. With copious photographs and images. It's a fabulous opportunity to learn about recently passed creators who made a difference to our field. *The Letters of Shirley Jackson* edited by Laurence Jackson Hyman (Random House) is only tangentially related to horror by dint of Jackson's output of weird and often dark fiction. I only dipped into it, but it's a birds-eye view of her relationship with family and friends and writing colleagues. *Speculative Modernism: How Science Fiction, Fantasy, and Horror Conceived the Twentieth Century* by William Gillard, James Reitter, and Robert Stauffer (McFarland) is part of a long-running series: Critical Explorations in Science Fiction and Fantasy. The volume documents the Gothic and Utopian roots of speculative fiction and mentions not only the obvious writers such as Blackwood, Poe, and Lovecraft, but brings Tennessee Williams and his creation Blanche DuBois into the conversation. *Eaters of the Dead: Myths and Realities of Cannibal Monsters* by Kevin J. Wetmore (Reaktion Books) explores monsters that eat the dead: ghouls, cannibals, wendigos, and other beings that feast on human flesh and by doing so teaches the reader about human nature. *The Vampire Almanac: the Complete History* by J. Gordon Melton, Ph.D. (Visible Ink Press) is a guide to all things vampire. *The Dark Side of G. K. Chesterton: Gargoyles and Grotesques* by John C. Tibbetts (McFarland) is a critical study of the author's darker novels, stories, and essays.

Odds and Ends

The Otherwise: The Screenplay for a Horror Film That Never Was by Mark E. Smith & Graham Duff is a kind of tribute to the late Smith, who was a member of the band The Fall. In 2015 he and Duff wrote the script for a horror movie that was deemed "too weird" to film. This is a collection of handwritten notes, reminiscences, photos, the pitches made to sell the idea, and the actual screenplay.

Tool Tales: Micro fiction inspired by antique tools: Photographs by Ellen Datlow and Stories by Kaaron Warren (IFWG) is a chapbook of a project started on Facebook in which Warren wrote ten tales inspired by Datlow's antique tool collection, usually without knowing what the tool was until after the fact. Most of the tales are dark.

Spectrum: Fantastic Art Quarterly Volume One edited by Cathy Fenner and Arnie Fenner (Underwood Books) marks the return of the co-founders and co-editors of this important series demonstrating the state of the art of fantasy and horror. Instead of the usual showcase, this first issue is focused on interviews with a few artists and art directors and their work. Plus a tribute to six fantasy artists who died in 2020 and 2021, coupled with beautiful examples of their art. The Spectrum competition is also back with a call for submissions to *Spectrum 28*.

Laird Barron Bibliography Stories: 2000-2020 compiled by Yves Tourigny (Tallhat Press) includes a line or two about the plot of each story.

The Book of the Kranzedan written and illustrated by Michael Hutter, translated by Julia Eischer and Gowan Ditchburn (Centipede), is a charming little book of thirty-three surreal vignettes by a German author/artist about the Kranzedan, a creature never explained, never described. A lovely little collectible.

REDWATER

SIMON BESTWICK

Pale mist trailed over the wetland, twining through the reeds and cutting visibility to almost nil, even with the searchlight in the bows. Normally I'd set off later to avoid it, but we were entering the Floodland's restricted area, so the dawn mist helped us dodge the patrols.

The searchlight picked up hummocks of land—high ground or accumulated silt bound together by scrub grass—and scattered sections of broken wall, some still containing a door or window frame. A few buildings in the Floodland were still more or less whole, but most had collapsed as the water undermined their foundations.

"Do you think—" began Tanner.

"Shh," I whispered back.

Morg kept the *Jane's* speed to a crawl; he knew the channels and obstacles as well as anyone, but the banks and shoals could shift, especially after a storm, and I hadn't a second boat.

"All good up ahead, Bodie?" I whispered.

"Clear, boss."

I already regretted bringing Bodie along. He was a good lad, and I'd need a replacement for old Morg soon, but bringing a third crewman to balance our numbers with those of our passengers hadn't made me feel any safer. It had just given me one more thing to worry about.

"Fence up ahead," Bodie called.

"'Kay," I said. "Cut speed, Morg."

He did; the *Jane* slowed till it barely moved on the current. I peered over the side, holding the gaff pole to fend off any obstacles.

The fence was twenty feet high, made of coated wire stretched between concrete posts, but there was a lot of fence, Floodland and river to patrol, and the river cops couldn't be everywhere at once. So they didn't know about the gap between two of the posts where the wire had been cut away, just wide enough to admit the *Jane*.

Things scraped against her sides as we neared the gap; Tanner gripped the rail, looking ill. Miss Zoll and our third passenger—a bald, thick-set man she called Kolya, who so far hadn't uttered a single word—remained motionless and impassive.

Kolya had cold pale eyes and a gun under his jacket. So did Miss Zoll, probably. Tanner certainly would, but at that moment he held nothing deadlier than a smartphone, on which he was tracking a GPS signal.

Once we were through, I turned and said, "Which way now?"

He pointed; I gave Morg the bearing, and he spun the wheel.

◦

I make my living from the Floodland, setting nets and traps for fish, frogs, shrimp or crayfish, but I transport cargo, too. The river and its tributaries, both the old ones and the ones born in the flood, are the main means of transport around here now, having made the roads so unpredictable. I don't enquire too closely as to what I'm carrying. It's better if you can claim ignorance when you're pulled up by the river police, and better not to be nosy with some customers.

Sometimes I bring people into the Floodland, too: scientists taking water samples or out-of-towners wanting to gawk at it, which passes for tourism round here. I'll even take you into the restricted area, but only if you pay *really* well; it's a death-trap for any skipper who doesn't know the way. It's the former heart of the old town, where the ruins and remains lie thickest.

People have died here. They brought in bodies for weeks afterwards. And more yet were never found at all.

The people who work the Floodland have a name for the restricted area, where so many died, and while technically inaccurate, it seems to fit.

They call it the Redwater.

-‹o›-

We found the launch an hour later, steering through the reed beds and negotiating a maze of ruins clogged with silt and weed. By now the mist was clearing so we could see some landmarks.

A few seemed faintly familiar. An old, distant familiarity—it had been over thirty years, after all—but familiar, nonetheless. The house where I'd grown up in, or whatever remained of it, lay in the heart of the Redwater; I could have found my way there easily, although I never had. Nor would I today, because we'd already reached our destination.

There'd been a crossroads here once, where a B-road met the A-road to the city. The launch was near the only relatively undamaged building—an old Gothic Revival church—and lay canted on its side, half-submerged in the churchyard. Which was a relief, as I hadn't fancied donning my scuba gear on this particular outing. I had a short-barrelled revolver in my coat pocket; even with it I'd have no chance against Tanner and Kolya, but I'd have to abandon even that if I went over the side. But this was comparatively high ground, so the water was no more than chest-deep. Gravestones poked out of the water around the launch, and the top half of the church's main entrance was visible.

"All right," said Tanner. "Bring us alongside."

I shook my head. "Not happening."

He moved closer to me. "You're being paid to do a job, little man."

I ignored him and turned to Miss Zoll. "We can't bring the *Jane* that close, ma'am. There'll be gravestones under the surface. Rip our guts out."

Kolya glanced at Miss Zoll before turning his fishlike gaze on me. Miss Zoll nodded. "Very well, Captain. How do we proceed?"

"Nothing complicated," I said. "Couple of us go over in the dinghy. Any idea whereabouts your merchandise would be stowed?" Miss Zoll hadn't specified the details of her "merchandise" and I hadn't enquired, for the obvious reason that if she was approaching me to help her get it back then it clearly couldn't be legal.

"It's a small package." She held her hands about eight inches apart. "Easily thrown overboard in an emergency and retrieved later." She gave a small cold smile. "The GPS is quite precise." I'd placed her accent as Eastern European, but nothing more definite than that. Given Kolya's presence, I was guessing Russian. A *bratva* queenpin of some kind.

I considered what she'd told me. "And it'd be the Captain who made that call."

"Precisely."

"Most likely the wheelhouse, then."

I fetched a pair of binoculars while Morg dropped anchor and Bodie pumped up the dinghy. The launch looked more or less intact; a few windows had been blown in and there was minor but largely cosmetic damage to the exposed side of the hull. The gravestones had probably caught her on the other side, and torn her open.

Bodie put the dinghy over the side and climbed aboard. Tanner pocketed the smartphone and made to follow but Miss Zoll shook her head. "Not you, Mr. Tanner. Give the phone to Kolya."

Tanner obeyed, scowling. I had no idea what he was, or even what he thought he was. Too much a pretty boy to be an actual hard man: I guessed him to be some sort of petty swindler with a halfway posh background, hired by Miss Zoll to help with local recruiting. Kolya grinned at him, showing half-a-dozen missing front teeth, and climbed down into the dinghy. The inflatable sagged under his weight but stayed afloat, and Bodie rowed them over to the launch.

They were alongside in a couple of minutes, and Bodie tied on to the launch's prow. Kolya hopped aboard with surprising agility for his bulk, crouched down and peered through a shattered cabin window. I saw him frown—puzzled, if anything. Then his eyes widened a little and he straightened, looking grimly up in our direction.

"Something's wrong," said Miss Zoll.

"What?" Tanner called across the water.

For answer, Kolya reached into the cabin and lifted something out, then tossed it into the water by the prow. Bodie gave a cry of disgust and recoiled, almost tipping the dinghy over.

"What the fuck?" demanded Tanner. Miss Zoll drew in a breath.

Bobbing in the water was a human arm, severed in mid-bicep and sporting a selection of tattoos. It had been sheared through as cleanly as if a guillotine had done the job, but not by a blade. I was a fisherman, after all: even if I'd never seen damage on such a scale, I knew teeth marks when I saw them.

The morning sun had burned off the worst of the mist, but a thin haze still drifted through the former churchyard, between the protruding stones. I could see something else in the water too, something low and broad and humped. A monument of some kind? No; it glistened. And then there was a pale flicker—two pale flickers—in the upper part of that humped shape, and I realised they were eyes.

"Bodie!" I shouted. "Cut loose! Get out of there!"

Both he and Kolya looked my way. Kolya reached under his jacket, obviously recognising there was danger but not knowing where, maybe even suspecting treachery on my part. Tanner certainly did, because in an instant I was slammed against the guardrail with something cold and metallic pressed under the hinge of my jaw. "Stay where you are," shouted Tanner; I assumed he meant Bodie, rather than me. Or perhaps he'd seen the hump as well, and was addressing that. In either case, he might as well have saved his breath.

Bodie sawed at the line and motioned frantically to Kolya, who clambered over the cabin towards him. the pale flicker of eyes showed in the humped shape again; then it flattened out and shot forward, a low shiny blur that arrowed in towards the dinghy with the deadly ease and accuracy of a missile.

"Bo—" I began to shout, but Tanner shoved the gun harder into my throat.

The thing in the water hit the dinghy a second later. It burst like a balloon, with a bang and a wet slap of water. Bodie fell backwards, his mouth an O. He resurfaced, spluttering, and the thing sped on past him: it looked as if it might be about to submerge, but instead it veered back around., pointing towards Bodie.

Kolya, crouched in the launch's bow, grabbed the railing with one hand and extended the other. Bodie kicked towards the launch, reaching out, but the thing hit him before their fingers could touch.

Kolya recoiled, shouting in Russian as Bodie screamed and was dragged away from him. The Thing pulled away, letting him thrash and moan in the reddening water. I glimpsed torn pink flesh, and exposed white bone.

The Thing flew in again, breaking the surface just before it struck. It put me in mind of a gigantic pike—it had the same green, old-dappled colouration—but its pointed cone of a head was a cross between a crocodile's and a shark's, with teeth like bone chisels.

The jaws snapped shut on Bodie's face. There was a crunch, blood spurted, and I glimpsed a humped back with a crest of spines before it plunged beneath the water again, taking Bodie with it, leaving only a red stain on the surface.

Kolya had pulled a machine-pistol from under his jacket, aiming it at the water. Tanner, meanwhile, was off-guard; the barrel of his own machine-pistol had come away from my throat, so I knocked his gun-arm aside and hit him under the ribs, driving the air from his lungs, then butted him in the face. He fell back onto the deck and I kicked his gun away and stepped back, looking first at Miss Zoll, then across the water.

Kolya wasn't even looking our way, but studying the murky water. Miss Zoll had thrust a hand into the pocket of her coat and paled a little, but otherwise didn't look unduly concerned—at least, not about me. "Mr. Tanner," she said as he scrambled to his feet, fists clenched. "Enough. Captain?"

"Fine."

Tanner retrieved his gun, half-raised it. "Mr. Tanner," Miss Zoll repeated and he angrily put it away. "Captain," she said, "can you tell us what that was?"

I shook my head. The rest of me was shaking, too. "Never seen anything like it."

"I heard stories." Morg had come out of the wheelhouse, and was staring at the fading red mark on the water. "People coming out this way, into the Redwater, and not coming back. But—" He shrugged and stopped; Morg wasn't a big speaker.

"Fisherman's tales," Miss Zoll said, almost to herself.

"Bullshit," said Tanner.

Miss Zoll nodded towards the water between us and launch. "That was not 'bullshit'."

"Some kind of fish?" said Tanner at last.

"Big fucker," said Morg.

The waters were quiet now. Kolya stood waiting on the launch, looking back towards the *Jane*. "We need to get him back," I said. "And then clear out."

"Agreed," said Miss Zoll. "How?"

"Get the spare out," I told Morg. "And the outboard."

Miss Zoll called out to Kolya across the water in (I presumed) Russian. The big man nodded, stowed the machine-pistol and reached into the flooded cabin.

"You're fucking joking," said Morg.

"Morg," I said, "the dinghy."

Kolya barked something; at first I thought he'd been attacked. But then he knelt up on the cabin roof, dripping wet but clutching a plastic-wrapped package in one hand, and drew his machine-pistol with the other, watching a low flat ripple in the water.

"Morg?" I said. "When you're done, get the rifle. Miss Zoll, can you operate the anchor?"

She nodded.

"Good. We're out of here the second we're all back on board."

"What about me?" said Tanner.

I didn't look at him. "Stay put, and don't touch anything."

-◦-

We waited a few seconds after lowering the second dinghy, watching the water for any sign of movement, but all was still.

I climbed down into the little boat and tried not to think about Bodie. He'd been a good lad, whom I'd liked and trusted, and I was going to have to tell his mother what had happened. But that would wait until we were clear of the Redwater, the river police and the Floodland in general.

The water lapped at the *Jane*'s sides, still flat and undisturbed. The pike-thing had broken the surface before attacking; hopefully that was its habit and there'd be some warning if it came at me. But I remembered, too, how fast it moved.

"All right," I told Morg. "Cover me, right?"

"Got it." He rested his elbows on the rail, tucking the stock of his Second World War M1 carbine into his shoulder. It was a medium-range weapon at best, but that should be enough. On the launch, Kolya swept the machine-pistol back and forth through a 180-degree arc over the water.

The outboard motor caught on the first pull of the cord; I steered the dinghy away from the *Jane*, towards the launch. It was a clear run, up until the last few yards, where I crossed the boundary into the cemetery. I had to cut the speed right down to weave through the gravestones, and there were still moments when things under the surface snagged the hull, making my breath catch. I hadn't Bodie's touch with small boats in tight corners. I had done, once, but as my granny used to say, *old age cometh not alone, mate.* I forced myself to concentrate on the water ahead of me and not look around; I kept seeing that humped shape, ready to strike. But Morg knew what he was doing, and it wouldn't be Kolya's first rodeo with the machine-pistol, either.

I was so intent on those last few yards of water I forgot about the launch and nearly ran into it headlong, only pulling round and killing the engine in the nick of time. I looked up into Kolya's blank face. "Come on if you're coming, big fella."

He bared his few teeth in that unnerving grin, stowed the machine-pistol under his jacket and climbed nimbly down. The dinghy sagged under his weight, but once more steadied. As before, to my relief, the engine caught on the first try, and I began steering it back through the gravestones. We were almost clear of them when Morg shouted: "'Ware to your left!"

It was maybe twenty feet from the dinghy. I made out the spotted green colouring and the cold bloodless eyes in the long, bowed head, membranes flickering white across them when it blinked. Behind the head rose the hump of its back, and the bulk on either side of it resembled nothing so much as heavy shoulders.

Kolya cradled the machine-pistol two-handed on his knee, training it on the pike-thing. It moved as we reached the edge of the cemetery, the humped back flattening out and driving the head forward. Both he and Morg fired, but it was too fast: their bullets kicked up fountains out of the water where it had been. Kolya raised the machine-pistol, aiming, till I wanted to scream at him to fire, but when he did the bullets chopped up the water directly in front of the creature, and it had to veer to evade them. I glimpsed a long torpedo-like body, a pale underbelly, and then it submerged and was gone.

I opened the throttle all the way out, wanting only to get back to the *Jane*; even as I did I realised I'd made a mistake, that we weren't quite clear of the graves. There was a purring rip as a stone caught the underside of the dinghy, and it listed; Kolya yelped and swayed sideways, then leant in the opposite direction, shifting his weight to the other side of the dinghy to steady it.

By now we were clear of the stones and barrelling towards the *Jane*. The dinghy had multiple compartments; hopefully the tear had damaged only one of them. Morg was firing again, his shots kicking up the water over to our right, where that familiar low flat shape was speeding towards us. Kolya fired two short bursts at it, and another gunshot kicked up a spout of water just off our starboard bow: Tanner was firing single shots from his own machine-pistol. I couldn't decide if he was trying to settle accounts with me, or just a very bad shot.

I kept my eyes and the dinghy's bow on the *Jane*, not daring to look elsewhere. When we came alongside Kolya pulled out the package—Miss Zoll's "merchandise"—and threw it up over the rail onto the *Jane*'s deck, before raking the water with the machine-pistol as I scrambled up the Jacob's ladder.

Morg was reloading the M1; I got over the rail and grabbed it off him. "Kolya! Move your arse."

He nodded, put away the machine-pistol and began climbing, but was only halfway up to the rail when the pike-thing burst out of the water beneath him. It was the clearest view I'd had of it yet: a thick, cigar-shaped body ten or twelve feet long, tapered to a point with that monstrous head, with large fins running down the sides and a thick-ribbed tail at the end. As it rose and the jaws yawned open, the long fins—or rather two long, finned arms that had up till now blended seamlessly into the body—split away from it. A webbed claw with long, taloned fingers fastened over the crown of Kolya's head and wrenched backwards. Bone snapped, and he tumbled down into the water.

The beast's other claw lunged up and snapped shut on the railing. I back-pedalled, and went sprawling on the deck, the M1 clattering away from me.

The pike-thing hauled itself into view, jaws parted, the great fanged mouth grinning down at us. I could hear someone screaming, and turned my head to see with no surprise that it was Tanner. Morg was yelping "Fuck me! Fuck me!" over and again—understandable if unhelpful—while more usefully scrambling for the rifle I'd dropped.

Miss Zoll didn't look happy about events at all, and for the first time her composure looked a little frayed, but at the same time she was a long way from outright panic. In fact, she'd drawn a large sleek automatic from her coat pocket and was aiming it at the pike-thing.

It was a big, heavy-calibre weapon, bucking in her hands as she fired. Two shots hit the monstrosity, one punched a hole in its shoulder, spilling blood, while the other caromed off its skull and bared the white bone. Its head swivelled towards her and it roared: the sound was somewhere between a bullfrog's croak, amplified about a thousand times, and a maniac's laugh. Then it grabbed the rail with its other claw-hand and dragged itself up, exposing its pale, slightly sagging underbelly. Two more rounds from Miss Zoll's gun thudded into its white paunch but it hardly seemed to notice them.

At least its lower half was still fishlike, I thought; that would surely give us an advantage, out of the water. But as if to spite me, its lower body split in half, and the halves moved. One swung over the rail, and a webbed, long-clawed foot slammed down on the *Jane*'s deck, at the end of a long, finned leg. Like the arms, they knitted together seamlessly when used in the water, but could apparently separate at will.

I heard Tanner screaming in blind panic as the Jane's deck tilted, the boat lurching as the pike-thing heaved itself aboard, more than twice the height of any of us. Knives for fingers, chisels for teeth: I couldn't exactly blame Tanner for his soiling himself.

Its new shape was more or less manlike, other than the head and the hunched, spined back. I saw three or four pulsating slits on either side of its head, like a shark's gills. It looked little more than annoyed by the damage we'd done to it so far. I saw its gaze shift to Morg, who lay frozen on the deck, his fingers not quite touching the M1.

"Oh fuck," Morg said, very clearly.

It took a step towards him, and that was when Miss Zoll shot it in the throat. For some reason it seemed to really feel that one; it reared back, gargling and roaring in pain. Perhaps there was a weak spot there after all.

Morg lunged and caught hold of the M1, coming up on one knee as the creature twisted towards Miss Zoll. He was aiming at the neck. And he might have got it, too, except that Tanner broke into a wild, panicked run for the hatch that led below decks. The creature whirled and came at him, and Tanner, screaming, fired the machine-pistol.

Unlike before, he fired the weapon full-auto, emptying the magazine into the pike-thing—or trying to. Unfortunately, unlike Kolya, he was no expert with the machine-pistol, and sent bullets spraying wildly all across the deck. I dived and sprawled full-length to avoid them, as did Miss Zoll, but Morg wasn't so lucky. He was hit at least twice in the back, dropped the M1 and fell forward.

The monster, though, had taken at least half-a-dozen hits, even if none of them seemed particularly damaging, and the *Jane* juddered as it loped across the deck, planks splintering under its webbed feet, and bore down on Tanner. He had time to scream once, before the jaws snapped shut. The pike-thing reared up and shook Tanner like a rat; the lower half of him flew over the railing, hit the water and sank.

By then I'd reached Morg. I could see the wounds in his back and the size of the blood-pool that had spread out around him and I knew already that there was nothing to be done, even though he was still moving feebly and making sounds. If the creature hadn't have done the job for me I'd have killed Tanner myself. But it had. And so I knelt in Morg's blood, shouldered the M1 and screamed, "Hey, you ugly fucking cunt!" at the pike-thing's back.

It swivelled and came at me, head down. I was right about the throat, I realised; it was lowering that heavy, bone-armoured skull to shield that one weak spot. I shifted my aim and hoped for the best; I was a decent shot and the range was close, but it was a moving target and the *Jane* was shuddering again as it moved.

Near enough was good enough, though; when I fired the shot scored a line along its ugly snout before ploughing into an eye. The monster bellowed and— just as I'd hoped—it reared up, its head flung back, trying to escape the pain.

Baring, as it did, its pale and already bleeding throat.

The M1's magazine held fifteen rounds, of which I'd fired one. I emptied the other fourteen in what must have been near-record time, and nearly every one hit its mark. Tiny holes appeared in the pike-thing's throat, rapidly merging into a single ragged wound as a dozen or so bullets hit home within an inch or two of one another.

A thick dark jet of blood spouted, then a third and a fourth.. It swayed, legs bowing, and bellowed again, but the sound was weaker now. Its eyes flickered white, then stayed white, and it toppled backwards, over the far rail and into the water. A fountain of red and white flew up and rained down on the deck.

Morg was still alive; I could hear him trying to talk. "Oh fuck. Oh fuck," he said.

I took his hand. "Morg." I couldn't think of anything else to say.

"Oh fuck," he said, and died.

◄◦►

I covered him with an old life-jacket and sat back on my heels, feeling more alone and lost than I could recall since the aftermath of the flood itself, all those years ago.

"I'm sorry about your friend," said Miss Zoll. "Both your friends."

I nodded and went to the far rail. I didn't say the same to Miss Zoll because Tanner and Kolya hadn't been her friends; at best, Kolya had been an employee, and I doubted Miss Zoll had mourned a death in a very long time, if ever. The pike-thing lay face-down in the water, which had turned scarlet along the length of the *Jane's* port side; it gave a last twitch and was still. "Well," I said. "You got what you came for. Right?"

There was a pause, and then she shrugged. "Yes. I did."

I nodded, then gestured towards the huge carcass. "You could probably get a small fortune from any museum for that thing, too."

"I don't think so, Captain. This will be more than enough."

"Fine by me." I briefly considered trying to take the corpse in tow, but it would be hard enough sneaking our way back without lugging that thing after us, and I didn't want to overtax the *Jane* after the battering she'd just received. Half the deck was smashed to splinters and she was listing badly; Miss Zoll was going to have to sully her hands pumping out water all through the homeward trip. "We'll get going, then."

I went to the wheelhouse, reloading the M1 as I went. I was surprised how steady my hands were. Turning my back on Miss Zoll didn't worry me, not yet. She still needed me to get her out of the Floodland. Back on dry land might be a different matter.

The *Jane* had drifted slightly; Miss Zoll had pulled up the anchor earlier, as instructed. It was just a matter of getting the old girl started and steering her home.

The motor coughed into life, to my relief, as my biggest worry had been that the engine might have been damaged in the recent free-for-all. I coaxed the boat forward, brought her round—

—and in our path: a line of low spiny humps with white blinking eyes.

◄◦►

Whether it was the sound of the fight, the blood in the water, or some knowledge of their fellow creature's death, a whole pack of the pike-things had come running. Or swimming, anyway.

From what I could see, most of them were built along the same lines as the creature we'd just killed; some were a little smaller, but even so, just one of the fuckers had damn near wrecked the *Jane* without even trying. When the first of them arrowed in towards the *Jane*'s side I brought her round as fast as I could; there was a judder and a howl as the creature's momentum carried it head-first into the boat's propellers. The engine spluttered and I thought we were about to lose power, but she quickly regained her old rhythm.

But having swung the boat around, I saw they hadn't come at us from only one angle. An irregular ring of humped, spined, white-eyed shapes surrounded us, scattered through the stagnant water, reed-beds and ruins. There were even some in the cemetery itself, dotted among the headstones.

Tanner's machine-pistol fired behind me, then again, and again, before stuttering to a halt.

"Everything all right, Miss Zoll?" I asked.

There was a clatter of metal, the snap of a bolt being pulled back. "That rather depends on you, Captain."

For the first time there was a tremor in her voice, and who could blame her? We'd nowhere to go; we were surrounded by open water, and every inch of it was infested with the monsters. Trying to ram our way through them would be pointless; they'd board the *Jane* or tear her apart. Might as well try to ram my way through the side of the church—

"Grab onto something," I shouted and opened the *Jane*'s throttles.

I felt a pang as the boat shot forward but there was no choice. I'd build a new *Jane*. Boats could be replaced. People couldn't; especially not me.

"What the hell are you doing?" Miss Zoll's composure was gone at last.

"Hold on," I shouted, and powered the *Jane* headlong over the graveyard boundary, towards the open church doors. One of the beasts darted out of our way; another tore at the hull with its talons.

"Sorry Mum," I said, before we smashed into the church.

◄◦►

I remember the rain and the flood warnings, but we'd had them before. Even the police going from door to door and telling us to evacuate wasn't new, but the heaviness of the rain was. I remember the water sloshing round the car tyres, sheeting up on either side of the vehicle, and Mum muttering to herself before smiling, far too brightly, and telling me everything was fine. Even at that age, I knew it wasn't.

We were lucky the road ran alongside a railway embankment. When the surge came, the worst of it poured into the cutting, filling it like a canal. But it flooded the road too, and the engine of the car.

Then the water and the current rose, pushing our car along like a toy. I remember Mum crying in fear, and then we ploughed into a high wall. The wall held; Mum popped the sunroof and climbed out, then held me up so I could reach the top.

She was trying to work out how to climb up after me when another surge hit, sweeping both her and the car away. They were there, and then they were gone. I glimpsed the car's upturned wheels before they sank, but I never saw my mother, alive or dead, again.

Later on, the road collapsed where it crossed the railway tracks, taking the old station building with it. The storm began slackening off after an hour, enough that they could send rescue choppers in. One of them found me, about five minutes before I'd have passed out from the cold and slipped off the wall.

They never found my mother, or if they did she became one of hundreds of anonymous corpses in a mass grave. All I had to remember her by was her name.

◄○►

"Captain. Captain!"

Miss Zoll was shaking me. Blood ran down my face. She stepped away from me, out of the cabin. The machine-pistol fired: something roared, choked, fell silent.

The *Jane*'s motor was still running, but she was wedged fast in the church's doorway. Wood creaked and cracked as her hull began to give. I grabbed the emergency flare-pistol and a torch. The cabin windows were already broken;

I smashed out the remaining glass with the butt of the M1 and scrambled onto the bow. "Come on!"

"What the hell are you doing?" she shouted again. Then: *"What?"* as I jumped into the water.

It wasn't even waist deep; the church's floor was slightly higher than ground level outside. The place stank of decaying vegetation; the air was stale, dank and cold. Rotting pews broke the water's surface, but nothing else. I switched on the torch and waded down the aisle. Cursing, Miss Zoll floundered after me. Bellows and sounds of splintering wood rang and echoed behind us; movement felt maddeningly slow, the water fighting us every step.

I climbed into the chancel, which was just about clear of the water, and made for a wooden door off to one side, hoping I was remembering the church's layout correctly. The door was green and slippery with moss and mould and fell apart as I pulled it open: behind it, as I'd hoped, was a flight of stone steps.

Miss Zoll fell against me, almost knocking us both down. She was bedraggled, her expensive clothes soaked, her hair a wet, tangled mess, but she'd regained her old composure. She'd lost the machine-pistol; in its place she clutched the heavy automatic.

The creatures were howling as they tore the last remnants of the *Jane* apart. "This way," I told Miss Zoll, and we started up the stairs.

◄◦►

"This?" she said. "This is your great idea?"

The belfry was devoid of bats, at least: the wooden louvres that had screened it were long gone, leaving four stone columns and the parapets connecting them. It was a skeletal structure, and when I looked at the vaulted stone ceiling overhead, it seemed disturbingly flimsy.

I stared out, towards the old railway cutting. "I can see my house from here."

"What?"

"Doesn't matter."

The church bell was still in place, green with verdigris. I rapped on it; dull growls echoed up from below in answer.

"They know we're here," she said.

I nodded. "Can't get up the stairs, though. Too bulky."

"A stalemate. So what now, Captain? Wait for the floodwaters to drain away in a hundred years?"

"No." I sat on the parapet, leaning against the column. "Something a bit faster than that."

Miss Zoll lit a cigarette and offered me one. I hadn't smoked in years, but decided I'd be lucky if I lived long enough to worry about any ill effects. I drew on the cigarette and coughed, but took another drag all the same.

"Well?" she said.

"Simple enough." I took out the flare-pistol. "This."

She frowned. "Who'll see a flare out here?"

"The river police."

"The river—" She was losing her composure again, but this time from anger. "The police? Are you insane?"

"They're the only people who patrol the Floodland," I said. "And they keep an eye on the restricted area. They might even send a chopper." That image brought back a few memories.

"And this?" She took the package—her "merchandise"—from her pocket, before stowing it away again.

"Won't come up. This was a sightseeing trip that went wrong. Out-of-towner with more money than sense, wanting to see the restricted area."

"We are *not* going to the police."

"Then we're back to waiting for the waters to go down on their own."

She glared at me. I waited. "All right," she said at last. "Do it."

I leant out of the window, aiming upwards.

A webbed claw swept towards my face. I fired the flare-pistol and fell backwards, almost sliding through the hole in the floor below the bell.

Miss Zoll shouted something and fired her pistol. A pike-thing hung between two of the stone columns, trying to haul itself through. She shot it in the throat again, and it sagged and fell away.

I crawled to the parapet, retrieving the M1, and peered over the side. Three or four of them clung to the side of the tower, long claws digging into the stonework, crawling up.

"Shit," said Miss Zoll, looking over another parapet; I guessed she'd seen the same sight there. "So much for their not being able to follow us. How are you for ammunition?"

"One full magazine in the rifle, and a .38 snub-nose with five rounds."

She muttered something in Russian and crossed herself, then gestured with her pistol. "I have five shots here, seven in a spare magazine. Also—" there was a click and a five-inch steel blade flashed in her free hand "—I have this."

I had a knife of my own, in my boot, but I couldn't see what use that was. At least not until a pike-thing rose into view behind Miss Zoll, and she spun around and slashed it across the eye.

❧

After that it's a blur; only fragments remain. Such as how, at point-blank range, you could inflict a killing wound on one of the creatures more easily by ramming your gun directly into its throat and firing. Sometimes, anyway.

I remember my rifle emptying, and lashing my knife to its barrel to turn it into a crude spear. I remember Miss Zoll covered in blood, her eyes no longer human, as though a pike-thing had flayed her and wore her skin. I probably looked the same.

At some point I concluded the river police couldn't have seen the flare; that no help was coming; that there was an endless supply of the monsters; that all that now remained was whether we died by their hands or our own.

And then I remember the beating of rotors, the searchlight's blaze, the crack of rifle fire, and how, for the second time in my life, a police helicopter was the most beautiful sight I'd seen.

❧

I was arrested, of course, but the charges evaporated. When I came out of the lock-up, Miss Zoll was waiting.

"Thank you," I said.

She shrugged. "The least I could do. Come."

We drank coffee in a pavement café; we were in the city, miles from the river and the Floodland. Clean, hygienic, all mod cons. I couldn't wait to leave.

"I've transferred funds into your account," she told me. "It's compensation for your friends' families. And enough for you to get started again, however you wish."

"I'm grateful."

Another shrug. "Call it a bonus." She finished her coffee and rose. "Goodbye then, Captain."

"Goodbye, Miss Zoll."

I wondered if she'd tell me her real name, but she didn't. Perhaps she would have if I'd asked her; maybe she'd have told me what the "merchandise" that Morg and Bodie had died for was, too. But I didn't ask.

She studied me. "You're going back there, aren't you? To the Floodland?"

It was my turn to shrug. "It's who I am."

She smiled a little sadly. "Then I suspect you've only delayed the inevitable."

I watched her walk away, finished my coffee, and went in search of a ride home. I had a new boat to buy. And the Redwater called.

CAKER'S MAN

MATTHEW HOLNESS

They keep asking me but I can only tell you that it wasn't that kind of cake at all. It had no icing, and no candles. It really wasn't a birthday cake in any way, no matter how much he insisted it was. But my mum took it from him nevertheless, and promised him we'd eat it that night, and agreed again that he'd been right in thinking it was my birthday. Then, when he'd finally gone, she tore it up and fed it to the birds in our back garden, and told the three of us we'd had far more to eat than was wise for small stomachs. I can remember Jamie and Connie being upset about that, but I wasn't. They tell me that's because I was the eldest and had to set the example, but the truth was I was glad about it. So glad that I even got up early the next morning to watch Mum, through my bedroom curtains, examining the lawn out back. Most of it was still there on the ground.

We didn't know his name. He'd lived across the road from us for the best part of a year, Mum said, before she'd ever even spoken to him. For us children, that was an eternity, and for the longest time he was just the back of a large, grey head in the window of the house opposite ours. Jamie would sit beside me, staring at the man's strange, wild hair through our lounge window as we counted cars and burnt our arms by accident on the radiator, delighted in the secret knowledge that he could see nothing of us. Then I'd tell Jamie stories about the head, pretending it wasn't him at all sitting there, but an ogre instead, or monster. Then my little brother would start to cry and Connie would rush in, upset by the noise, and I'd try my best to turn the head into something else.

But still we'd watch it, knelt together on the sugar-stained couch our mum got to keep, studying the head and wondering why it never moved from that position, until one day the back of it opened up like a mouth with teeth and we ran into the kitchen, crying with fright. Then, because I was the eldest, I crept back to the window and saw it was a furred hat he'd been wearing, pulled forward to cover his face. And now it was up, and he was smiling at us, and waving, and I realised he'd been watching us all the time.

It was Mum who suggested we visit him one day, having learned that his wife had died unexpectedly the month before. We'd never once seen her over there, however, not even in the days following that first wave, when he'd begun beckoning us over whenever we made eye contact. From that point on, I'd started to observe his house more closely from the safety of my mum's bedroom, which was situated directly above our previous position in the lounge. I watched him on my own now, whenever Jamie and Connie played together on the far side of the house.

I'd sit in my mum's chair, peering at him through the hinged gaps in her three-way dressing mirror. At times he'd venture outside to water his front path or clip the hedgerows, and whenever he'd stop to glance up at my mum's window, which he did frequently, I'd flinch back instinctively from her mirror, then slowly summon up the courage to move back. Whereupon, he would smile up again in my direction, wave his hand, then carry on calmly with his work. Meanwhile I would sit there stunned, catching my breath and berating myself for not having kept still, yet relieved that the ordeal was over, and with little in the way of consequence.

Mum felt guilty, I think, because we'd missed the funeral car entirely, and he'd apparently attended the service alone, putting a brave face on it, he said, their friends being too old to travel down and "pack her off". So our mum took us out that afternoon to the florist in town to find him a nice bouquet, and when we pulled up outside our house that evening, she insisted we go over there to hand it to him in person. I begged her to let me stay in the car, knowing I wasn't yet allowed to be alone at home by myself, but Jamie and Connie were still rowdy from the sweets they'd eaten, and insisted on going in with her. Besides, Mum explained, appealing perhaps to a burgeoning maturity she sensed in me, it would cheer the old man up to see some children.

Before Connie had a chance to ring the bell, he'd opened the door from inside.

"Are you hungry?" he asked, beaming at my sister with a wide grin.

Connie, startled, looked up at Mum.

"Well," Mum replied, herself a little thrown, "we're having tea in a while."

"We are indeed," said the old man, making room for us to enter. "Come in, come in."

He stepped back into the darkness of his hall.

I didn't like his hair. It resembled a judge's wig up close, made up of small, white frizzy curls with two strange corkscrew ringlets dangling down, past his ears. I hoped Mum would say no, but instead she ushered us in. I held back for as long as possible, until eventually she went in before me, her hands on Connie's shoulders.

"We can only stay a short while," she said, and I wondered whether she was feeling as unsure about things as I was.

"Come in, young man," he said to me, almost sternly. As I stepped inside, he began humming an old-fashioned tune I didn't recognise.

There were no lights on in the house, but our eyes were young and sharp and I studied him closely as he beckoned me forward. His head was large and rectangular, with an unusually high forehead. His wide-set eyes were marked with broken vessels, and his flushed complexion seemed rather pronounced, as if the redness in his cheeks had been deliberately painted on. In certain places, too, his face looked like it had been dusted with a fine layer of powder.

He reminded me of an illustration I'd once seen in a history book at school. It was an early newspaper caricature, from the days when men wore wigs, tailcoats and funny tight trousers. One of the figures depicted in this particular picture had frightened me. It was a gentleman of some kind, because he'd been dressed in a frock coat and smart buckled shoes, but his head was far too large for his body and was drawn like an ogre from a fairy tale.

Although my teacher had done her best to explain that this was because the illustration was exaggerated and not a picture of a real person, I nevertheless dreamt about it for months afterwards, and in this particular context, being unable to distinguish between what was real and what wasn't, the hideous figure from the book became as life-like to me as anyone I'd ever met.

My subconscious mind was dwelling on this when the old man's eyes darted suddenly from Connie to me, and I had the uneasy impression he'd apprehended my thoughts. The motion of his head followed after, as though it were a separate entity, while his mouth remained fixed in that unnerving smile throughout our whole visit, utterly divorced from the expression above. His teeth were large and very white. Possibly false, I thought, although the neat, sizeable gaps between them looked very different from those I'd seen in other old people. In fact, they drew my attention so much that I almost failed to see his tongue was completely black.

"Liquorice," he said, sticking it out at Connie.

"It's a sweet," I said, sensing she was frightened. "Like black jacks."

He smiled at me oddly, like his eyes didn't mean it.

"Shoes off, children," Mum said. Dutifully we obliged, expecting the old man, like every other adult we'd ever met, to insist otherwise. But instead he merely nodded rather solemnly, waiting for us to remove them.

"We came round to give you these," Mum said, handing him the flowers.

He took them without comment, and at first I thought he was struck with a sudden sadness, until I saw it wasn't the flowers that were distracting him but Connie again, who was clinging to my mum's dress in an attempt to balance herself.

"We're very sorry for your loss," Mum added.

"You are?" he replied, sounding surprised.

I'd removed my shoes at last, and could feel the unpleasant touch of his cold, tiled floor beneath my socks.

"We really can't stay long," Mum said.

"In," he replied, rather shortly, pointing to an open door beside us. "Through there."

Mum held Jamie's hand, instructing me to take Connie's.

"You have beautiful children," the man said, following us into what I knew to be the lounge immediately facing ours. "I watch them every day."

"Thank you," Mum replied, taking the seat he was pointing her toward.

"This one especially," he continued, stepping between myself and my sister. "Such beautiful skin. Like porcelain."

He dumped the flowers on a small coffee table in the middle of the room, then placed both hands gently on my sister's shoulders. He turned her around slowly to face him, like she was a museum exhibit.

"Do you know what porcelain is?"

"No . . ."

"They make dolls from it. Pretty dolls."

Connie smiled.

"Would you like a pretty doll to play with, Connie?"

"Yes, please," she said, in a tone usually reserved for the family doctor.

"Then I'll send you one. A pretty doll for a pretty girl."

Mum looked like she was going to object, but remained silent.

"I'm starved," I said instead. "Can we go home?"

The old man turned to me.

"I imagine you'll be wanting a pretty doll yourself, soon enough?"

I don't think I quite knew what he meant, but I didn't like it.

"How do you know my sister's name?" I asked him coldly.

"I know all your names. You're very loud children. Shouting all day and night, upsetting my wife on her deathbed."

Mum glared at me from across the room, but I ignored her, my attention focused on the fact that there weren't enough seats for us all, and Connie and I had been left standing, close by him. I had a suspicion he was about to pick her up and sit her on his lap, so I positioned her near me, beside the door, and sat down between them.

"I'm sorry if they've been any trouble," said Mum.

"No trouble. She was a *horrid* snorer. Like a big pig."

He grinned at Jamie.

"Actually, we ought to go," Mum said, suddenly checking her watch. Relieved, I stood up.

"It's past their tea time. I had absolutely no idea."

"So soon?" he said, signalling me to sit down.

"Perhaps another day."

"I will hold you to that, Mrs. Ellis."

It was my father's name.

"Miss Radford, I mean. Slip of the tongue."

He poked his black tongue out again, this time at Jamie.

"Come on, children," said Mum, rising from her seat.

"Before you go," he said, waving her down again, "I have something for you."

He walked over to the bay window, winking at Jamie, and took three small paper bags out of an old tea chest. There was something inside each of them.

"These weren't touched."

He turned to face us, holding up the bags.

"A slice of cake for every child. A gift, from my wife's deathday party."

He emphasised the word, but unlike Connie, I didn't find it funny.

"You like birthday parties, don't you?" he asked my sister, giving her another big smile from across the room.

"Oh, yes!" she exclaimed.

"Well, a funeral is the same thing. Only it's a deathday party, instead. See?"

He walked back, close to Connie, and held out one of the bags, too high for her to reach. Finally he let her have it, then looked at Jamie. My little brother stood, excited, and ran to him.

"Wait your turn," the old man said, pulling the bag away rather sharply. Then offered it to me.

"No, thanks," I said.

His smile dipped a little.

"More for Connie."

He handed my sister a second bag, then gave her the third as well. He glanced down at Jamie, who looked like he was about to cry.

"*Share.*"

Jamie nodded, then looked tearfully at Mum, who sat there in her chair, watching us and saying nothing. She looked shocked, like she did whenever she'd rowed with my dad.

"Let's go home," I said.

"Home," the old man repeated, rolling up both shirt sleeves. "My, it's hot in here, with all these excitable children."

His arms were covered in tattoos. The one nearest me resembled a mermaid, but turned into something else when he flexed his muscles. He did this subtly, I noticed, so only I could see. It became something like those pictures scrawled in the concrete tubes we used to play in at the park. When my parents were off having one of their fights.

"Shall we arrange another visit soon?" he asked as my mum stood up again. I think she'd been sitting in something wet, because she kept feeling the back of her dress.

"Just the two of us."

She straightened it downward, over her legs, and addressed me.

"Toby, take them out and help them put their shoes on."

I nodded and moved Connie back toward the door, away from him.

"Jamie. Come on."

My brother walked past the man without looking at him, and followed my sister into the hall.

With both of them gone, the old man looked at me.

"The new man of the house."

"Excuse me," said my mother, edging around the coffee table in the direction of the door. He stepped in front of her, blocking her way.

"I'm a widower, after all," he said, his voice becoming noticeably louder. "And you've lost your husband. We might have a good deal of fun together."

"Let me through."

"You heard her!" I shouted, from behind. "Let her through!"

"How about tomorrow?" asked the old man, stepping aside.

"Stay by me, Toby," said Mum, walking past him into the hall.

"Tomorrow would be perfect," he continued, following us out. "I have so many of my wife's clothes to sort through, and I need a woman's touch."

I rattled the handle of the door.

"Would you like to try on some of my wife's clothes?" he asked, behind us. "Before I burn them all?"

"It's locked," I said, fighting panic.

"That's because," he replied softly, "I have the key, here in my pocket."

Mum held out her hand.

"Give it to me."

With an air of faint amusement, he reached into his trouser pocket, rummaged for a moment, then pulled out a small silver Yale key. He held it close to his chest.

"Here it is."

Steeling herself, Mum reached out and grabbed it from him. Then inserted it into the lock.

"I think you'd look attractive, wrapped up in my wife's dresses."

It was the wrong key.

"Or your porcelain daughter. A good many slices of cake and she'll fill out rather nicely."

Mum whirled around, pulling Connie and Jamie close to her. I stepped forward, putting myself between her and the old man.

He gave a comic sigh. "Wrong pocket."

He moved his hand over his flies and thrust it inside his other pocket. He rooted around again for a few moments, then drew out a second key, attached to a piece of grubby string. He dangled it before us, looking at my mum.

I snatched it.

As I handed the key to Mum, he reached out and pressed her stomach lightly with his hand.

"Any more?" he said.

Mum turned, unlocked the door quickly and pushed it open. As we stepped into the cold night, he adopted a friendly tone.

"Thank you for the flowers. I'll return the favour. Very soon."

Mum herded us over the road, into our drive. Behind us the man was muttering something to himself. Then he raised his voice and spoke to us, clearly.

"I'll send you a pretty doll. A slice of cake and a pretty doll."

He began to sing. The same strange, old-fashioned melody I'd heard earlier.

"A slice of cake and a pretty doll,
The Cake Man gave to me,
A slice of cake and a pretty doll,
Is all the life I'll see."

Moments later we were back inside our house. I removed my shoes on our entrance mat, felt the familiar softness of our hall carpet under my socks and swung the front door shut behind me. As I did so, I glimpsed him, still watching us from his front doorstep.

I locked him out.

Jamie was irritable all evening and didn't want his tea. I didn't feel hungry either, so I gave him and Connie their baths and read them both happy stories to get them to sleep. Eventually they nodded off, and when I came downstairs again, Mum was busy examining the slices of cake he'd given Connie. They were stale and hard as rock, so she threw them in the bin.

I left her watching television in the lounge and went up to bed with my stomach hurting like it used to whenever Dad came home. On the way to my own room I slipped into hers, which was unlit, and peeked through her dressing-room mirror to spy again on the old man's house through the curtains. There were still no lights on inside, but as my eyes slowly adjusted to the surrounding darkness, I could just make out his grey head opposite, crouched down like a monster in his horrible lounge.

⊰⊙⊱

The next time he came to us. It occurred three nights later, not long after my mum had gone to bed. The front door bell woke me from a dream, but I only rose and crept downstairs when I heard voices. My mum's was the loudest—he didn't shout at all, in fact—and she'd evidently been under the impression that it was a policeman at the door, because she sounded angry and was telling him to go home or she'd call them for real. He spoke to her politely and calmly, explaining he would do that very thing, only he wanted to give us the cake first, with her blessing, and she need only open the door for a moment so that he could hand it over. He insisted he was sorry about the other day and had been up all night baking it for us because nights were now unbearable for him. He grew sad at night, he said, and it was all he could do to keep from despairing over there in that lonely house, all by himself.

Mum's manner grew politer then, despite her obvious exhaustion, and she told him she'd accept it from him the following morning but not before. At once he became friendly again, almost jolly, and said he'd be over first thing. But he never came.

We didn't hear anything further from him for several weeks, and I saw almost nothing of him through the gaps in my mum's mirror. Yet occasional deliveries were now left for him on his front doorstep. Supermarket carrier bags, stuffed full of shopping, which invariably disappeared whenever I'd leave the room to eat or relieve myself.

We didn't really talk about him. Mum grew distant whenever I brought the matter up and just said he was old and grieving and needed time to himself. But Jamie and Connie weren't sleeping well. The garden was too noisy at night, Jamie insisted, and Connie began talking about a man who came into her room and sat at the bottom of her bed when it was dark. I was also experiencing bad dreams, along with the return of my stomach aches, and wondered if Connie was mistaking the old man for me, as the first thing I did upon waking and realising where I was, was to go through to their rooms and listen for the sound of them breathing.

When my birthday came around, I received presents and a visit from my aunt, but nothing from Dad. Mum said his gift would no doubt arrive later that day, but I could tell she was upset. That afternoon, the doorbell rang for a second time and I rushed through to the hall, hoping his present had arrived after all. But when I opened the door, before me stood the old man.

In his hands he held something vaguely resembling a brown loaf, wrapped in a fresh, striped towel.

"Happy birthday, Toby," he said, holding it out for me to take.

I didn't say anything to him, and I didn't reach for his gift.

"A birthday cake, Madam," he said, looking at my mother, who, I was relieved to discover, had followed me from the kitchen. "For the master of the house."

"Thanks," she said, taking it from his hands.

Before she could shut the door, he began talking about the cake in some detail. How long it had taken him to bake and how thoroughly he'd perfected the recipe, working night after night, ensuring it was exactly right before bringing it over.

The cake didn't look perfect to me. Like I say, there was no icing on it, and no candles either. Mum pulled back the towel politely to take a look, and I knew from her expression that she too thought there was nothing remotely nice about it.

"That's kind," she said, attempting again to close the door.

"And I got the right day?"

She hesitated, briefly.

"Yes."

"How much of it will you eat, Toby? The whole cake?"

He laughed loudly. I didn't say a thing until Mum nudged my arm.

"Yes, thank you."

He continued to grin at me, staring into my eyes, then finally turned back to her.

"And I got the right day?" he said again.

"You did," Mum replied, swinging the door further shut.

"And you'll eat it today?"

"Of course."

"Remember to share, young man. With your greedy brother and sister."

Mum closed the door on him and ushered me away, back toward the kitchen. Then she knelt down quietly on the carpet and carefully raised the flap of our bronze letterbox. She watched the old man walk back across the road and re-enter the house opposite. Then she stood up again and sniffed the man's cake. I followed her as she took it through to the kitchen.

"Are you going to cut it now?" I asked.

"No, Toby."

She placed the cake on our kitchen top and unwrapped it from the striped towel. Then she dug her fingers inside it and tore it apart, dragging the sponge and sifting through the crumbling fragments.

She gathered the remains inside the towel, took it outside into the garden and scattered the lot over our lawn. When she came back in, she dropped the towel in the bin and washed her hands with soap.

When she looked over at me, I was crying.

"Toby, darling," she said, coming toward me. I wept into her jumper as she hugged me close. Jamie and Connie came down from upstairs, hearing me crying, and cuddled me as well, and then Mum made tea for us all. When nothing further came for me that afternoon, I went up to bed, trying hard not to be sad about my father, and fell asleep above the muffled sounds of her crying on the lounge sofa downstairs.

◄◦►

The next morning I pulled back the curtains and watched her examining what was left of the cake on the lawn below. It was nearly all still there, the birds having hardly touched it, but when Jamie got up he said he'd heard someone in the garden during the night, and when I went out with Mum to look around we discovered a pair of muddy footprints on the compost sacks Dad had left under our side-window, which someone had evidently climbed up on to look in.

"I hope you aren't feeding my cake to the birds," the old man said later that day, bending down to address us through our letterbox. We were sat around the kitchen table, picking at our food, and Mum was holding one finger over her lips to keep Connie and Jamie quiet.

"No good for birds," he said, rattling the bronze flap up and down with his fingers. I stood up then, Mum whispering at me to stop, but I ignored her and walked over rather more boldly than I felt, toward the kitchen door. At the far end of the front hall I saw his eyes staring in at me through the letterbox. Aware that I was watching, he raised his head so that I could see only his mouth.

"I've baked another cake, Toby," he said. "Let me in and I'll give it to you."

"No," I said.

"Open the door, Toby. Let me in."

I heard my mother moving up behind me.

"Go home," I shouted, suddenly angry. "We don't want your stupid cake."

The flap snapped shut loudly and the mouth disappeared. There followed a long silence, the gloomy atmosphere of the hall lit only by the sun's final rays passing through the frosted glass panes either side of the door. I heard the muffled voices of Connie and Jamie close by and realised Mum had her hands clamped over their mouths.

Then the letterbox snapped open again and something came flying through it onto the hall carpet. Mum hugged me close and told me to look after my siblings. Then silently she moved forward, by herself, into the hall.

The object was an envelope, addressed to me. She recognised the handwriting and opened it. Then threw it back down almost immediately. She wouldn't let me read it, not even later, when the police asked to see it. It was a birthday card from my father, apparently, sent in good time, but when I managed to glimpse some of the writing while they were checking the envelope for fingerprints, I saw something horribly familiar scrawled in the margin. It was the picture from the old man's arm, and there were lots of other messages in funny handwriting too, which my mum told them wasn't my father's hand, and that's all I ever knew about it.

The police didn't do much in the end, although the old man's visits stopped soon afterwards. About eight months later we found out he'd died, alone in his house.

I watched the van arrive to collect his body. It was a white transit, which surprised me, having expected, for some reason, a black hearse like the ones we'd occasionally drive past in town. They brought him out of the house in a bag and dropped him accidentally while lifting him into the vehicle. Mum said he had no relatives at all, and as nobody we asked knew what his name was, Mum searched through the local obituaries the following week, hoping to identify him. There were no accompanying photographs, but one entry referred to a former merchant seaman who'd later worked as a Punch and Judy man, while another described a retired councillor who'd once run a bakery business in the north of England.

I grew quickly bored of Mum's searching and was drawn instead to a picture on the opposite page which upset me; a photograph of what I took to be a local pantomime dame, despite it being summer, taken close-up through a funny lens. The face looked a little like the figure in my old schoolbook and I threw the newspaper out as soon as my mother was finished with it.

Jamie, whom we'd hoped might forget our old neighbour completely, instead began to point every so often to the house over the road while singing an odd little song. He claimed he'd dreamt the melody up himself, but I recognised it as the one the old man had sung to us. Jamie called it 'Caker's Man', a title Connie also adopted. Regrettably it stuck, and the old man slowly, despite my mother's best efforts, became something of a permanent family memory.

A few months later Jamie joined Connie at school for the autumn term, and the change in routine helped them both. I, on the other hand, was losing a great deal of weight and continuing to experience severe bouts of stomach pain. I kept this largely to myself, but by December Mum had arranged for someone to come to our house, explaining initially that the lady was a babysitter. It soon became apparent to me, however, that she was also my carer.

The arrangement made sense as we could no longer rely on my father's payments, and instead Mum had to find a job with extra hours. In turn, this meant she was unable to collect us from school each day. Although

I explained I was old enough to walk my brother and sister home, she wouldn't let me do it, and soon we were being driven home instead by Lucy, a ginger-haired woman in her late twenties, who had pink, rosy cheeks and wore very bright clothes.

She was funny and pretty, almost like one of Connie's new ballerina toys. Lucy made our meals, supervised our homework hours and occasionally stayed the night when my mother was working out of town. She also used to make us shriek with laughter by driving so fast over bumps in country lanes that we'd get flung in a heap onto the floor of her Mini.

Mum never told me why Lucy was really there, but one night when she was at work, Lucy took me aside and set down, on our lounge floor, a heavy and serious-looking grey binder. From it she removed several sheets of paper containing long lists of food types, which she asked me to tick in a particular order. She wanted to know which foods made me feel most ill. She also wished me to identify which of them made me physically sick, which was always cake. She said I had to draw that particular food over and over, so that eventually it wouldn't make me feel ill at all. It didn't matter if I couldn't do it now, she said, reassuring me. She promised I would soon be able to, and that I'd be so happy with the pictures I eventually drew that afterwards I wouldn't feel remotely sick at the thought of eating them.

The night after, she stayed over again and did the same thing, talking to me alone while Connie and Jamie were both asleep, asking me to draw pictures of birthday cakes, insisting I would soon be adding nice things to them, like striped candles I liked. She said I could pick whatever crayons I wanted and colour them in like I had done when I was small. I remember wondering if she realised how old I was, and when I told her how silly that would make me feel, she laughed out loud, agreeing with me, but insisting I must do as she said.

Not long after Lucy had begun staying over, I began to suffer a recurring nightmare not dissimilar to the one I had experienced when younger, only this one was more intense, taking place in an exact replica of our house. So convincing was it that whenever I woke up, I was never quite able to tell which house I was in.

It always featured me and Connie, although my sister was much older in the dream. We were in the house, but never together at the start. The ordeal would begin in my mother's bedroom. The light outside was soft and dull in the dream, like a cold afternoon, making everything inside feel dark and heavy. There was a faint pinkish tinge to the sky, like a summer storm was approaching. I sat behind my Mum's dressing mirror, watching the house opposite through the gaps between its reflective panes.

After some time, and in complete silence, a car would draw up in the street outside. It was a strange looking car, made entirely of glass, so that I could see right through it. Some nights it looked different, more like an old-fashioned carriage from a fairy tale, but I was never able to make out its driver. Having pulled up outside the house opposite, the car, or carriage, would wait there in silence for some time, completely motionless, until gradually I began to feel frightened. Then the front wheels would turn and the car would move across the road toward our house, pulling in somewhere directly below me. It was hard to know when it had completely vanished from sight, because the car became almost entirely invisible when it moved, save for reflections, usually of the house opposite, which rippled through it like a passing current.

I would hear the front doorbell ring downstairs, and sense, soon afterwards, Connie running through from somewhere behind me. I would get up from my mother's chair and leave her room, entering the upstairs hall just in time to see the back of my sister's head descending the staircase ahead of me, but no matter how fast I ran I could never catch her.

As I followed her into the front hall, I would glimpse something move from the frosted glass window beside the door, to hide, unseen, behind it. Connie and I would then stand in silence, watching the bronze letterbox intently. After a while the doorbell would ring again, followed by three loud knocks. We were both too terrified to answer, yet I was somehow aware that whoever was standing outside had a gift for me, and wanted me to let them in. I would start to dread the bronze letter flap opening, until suddenly I would hear three more knocks, this time from the rear of the house, and Connie would run through the kitchen behind me towards the door leading to our garden.

I would follow her, not daring to call out, then catch again the sight of someone in the act of hiding themselves behind our house, only this time its shape appeared to float downward from the roof, passing the horizontal window above the doorframe, to land somewhere immediately behind.

The little I could make out as it vanished from sight vaguely resembled a human face, only one that was unnaturally large and brightly coloured, like a party mask.

As Connie and I stood before the garden door, dreading the knocks we knew would come, behind us we would suddenly hear the unmistakable sound of our front door swinging open. Then I would turn and see, set in the exact centre of our hallway carpet, a perfectly round birthday cake.

Realising I'd forgotten about Jamie, and that it must be he who'd opened our door, I would be gripped with a swift and terrible anxiety, and the dream would reach its inevitable conclusion as I crept reluctantly over to the cake, which was coated with sugared icing and decorated with pink and yellow candles, and plunge my fingers inside, tearing the whole thing open. And there I would find the mouth buried within, and the two rows of small white teeth set together in a smile. And as they fell away beneath my fingers, I'd recognise them as Connie and Jamie's baby teeth, and know that the cake had been made from my brother and sister.

‹›

"Try this one," Lucy said one afternoon, leaning down beside me and holding the plate of brightly coloured fairy cakes beneath my chin. Most of them had gone already, with Connie and Jamie now looking rather ill, having gorged themselves the second Lucy had prised the plastic lid from her pink Tupperware container. She had enjoyed bringing them out, declaring the dinner she'd accidentally ruined had been saved after all.

I think that was the first time I noticed she looked different to how she'd appeared when I'd first met her. It was hard to tell exactly, and it was only when I pictured Connie's precious ballerina dolls that I realised she no longer quite resembled them in the way she once had, but she seemed a little fuller than before. Her make-up was also different, with her face even pinker now, both cheeks noticeably redder, as if she'd been painting the colour on. Her lips looked much thicker too, and were no longer pleasant to look at, forever smeared from constantly kissing me.

"No, thank you," I said.

"Go on. Just one."

"No, thank you."

"Try the smallest one."

"I'm not hungry."

She put her arm around me and leaned closer.

"You'll eat them, Toby. I promise."

"I know I will," I said, looking round at her to let her know I meant it. "Just not today."

"No, you'll eat them now."

I noticed Connie and Jamie looking at me. Like they'd also sensed the change in Lucy.

"I can't," I said.

"I made them for you, Toby," she said, close to my ear. "Especially."

I could smell her breath. It was sweet, like warm caramel. I picked up the one nearest to me; a small fairy cake with pale orange icing. It was too soft and I felt the sponge giving way between my fingers as I placed it back on the plate.

"No, thank you," I said again.

Lucy rose abruptly and took the plate away, setting it down between Jamie and Connie. Her smile had gone.

"You two can fight over it," she said, stuffing one of the remaining cakes in her mouth. Then she walked over to the pedal bin and tipped the rest in. She was right, of course. My brother and sister did indeed fight over it. So loudly that when Mum finally came home, I got the blame.

◄○►

On my thirteenth birthday I received several books. One was a collection of fairy tales from my Dad, which were all too young for me, even though Lucy insisted they weren't, and one a large history book which turned out to be the same one I'd read at school, only with a newer cover. Mum assumed it had to be the other half of Dad's present, because the book had been left on our doorstep later that day, with a note from a neighbour saying it had been opened in error.

I glanced over the road as I picked it up, thinking I could see the old man's grey head again, in the lounge opposite ours. But when I stood up I saw it wasn't there at all, and the house was still as empty and uninhabited as it had been since the day he'd died.

When I had a moment to myself that afternoon, I took the history book up to my room and looked up the picture of the strange gentleman which used to frighten me. It was even worse than I remembered, and immediately I hid the book in the lounge cupboard downstairs.

The rest of the day was miserable. Connie and Jamie were upset I hadn't been given any toys they could play with, while the shaving kit Mum bought me ultimately sat in my bedside drawer, unused, for a whole year.

The big event came later that evening, after Lucy had dropped off some shopping for us, with Mum telling me to look upon it as a "strange" sort of present. She was sorry, she insisted, but she had to work late again at very short notice, meaning Lucy was unable to look after us like she usually would. My mother had no alternative, therefore, but to leave me in charge of Connie and Jamie until she returned later that night. It was a big responsibility, she told me, but perhaps I was old enough at last.

"After all," she said, forcing a smile, "you're the man of the house."

I asked her if she could call in sick, but she refused, and when I began to play up she told me off, telling me I was being childish, then apologised and insisted there was nothing she could do.

It would be good for me, she said.

◄◦►

Before leaving for work, my mother left me detailed instructions about where the keys were, what to cook Jamie and Connie for tea, what time they had to be in bed, and finally she handed me Lucy's number in case of an emergency, which I already had as Lucy herself had once given it to me. Finally, the door was shut, locked firmly from outside, and then all I could do was watch Mum's car disappearing down the road between the gaps in her dressing mirror.

It was the middle of winter and already getting dark outside, so I immediately went around the downstairs floor, closing all our curtains and making sure there weren't any gaps.

Then I switched the radio on and made Connie and Jamie toasted cheese. I couldn't handle the grater properly and grazed my fingers, so I made a game of it with Connie, letting her put plasters on me while Jamie played on the couch with his action figures.

I'd finished their baths and we were all watching a music programme on television when it happened. I was about to send them up to bed when my brother and sister became suddenly secretive and ran into the kitchen. I continued watching the screen, distracted by the female singer who looked a bit like Lucy, when I suddenly heard a shout of "Surprise!" and looked round to find Jamie and Connie standing there with a plate balanced in their hands. On it sat a perfectly round birthday cake, covered with sugared icing, and thirteen pink and yellow candles arranged around its rim.

"Happy Birthday, Toby!" they said together.

"Where did you get it from?" I demanded, feeling a familiar stab of pain in my stomach.

"We made it, silly," said Connie.

"Mummy helped," added Jamie. "After lunch. When you were in your room. It's a surprise."

I took it from their hands and went through to the kitchen. I put it on the table and covered it with a cloth, then realised I hadn't thanked them.

"Aren't you going to have some?" asked Connie.

"No," I said.

"Can we?" said Jamie.

"Not now."

"Mummy said we could have some."

"You're about to go to bed."

"Why can't we have some?"

"Because it's bedtime."

"But Mummy *said*."

Connie was welling up. I was tired and didn't want a fuss, so I took two plates from the cupboard and a knife from the drawer.

"Aren't you going to light the candles?" said Jamie, leaning over the cake, his nose practically touching the icing.

I opened another cupboard, took out the matchbox and lit one. Connie puffed with excitement as I set one of the candles alight. Then, reluctantly, I went round each candle in turn, lighting them all.

"There," I said, watching the soft glow light up their faces.

I knew I was being horrid and felt terrible. To make things worse, Jamie and Connie began to sing to me.

"Happy Birthday to you, Happy Birthday to you . . ."

I forced myself to join in, putting my arms around them and kissing them on their foreheads.

"Why are you crying?" asked Connie.

"I'm just happy," I said, drying my eyes. I let them blow out the candles for me. As the smoke wafted between them, slowly dissipating, I picked up the knife and cut into the cake.

I examined each slice as I laid it on the plate. There was a pale layer of cream in the centre, but nothing else. It smelt very sweet.

"Are you having some?" said Jamie.

I felt another pain in my stomach, but took a third plate from the cupboard. I cut myself a small piece, held it to my nose for a moment, then sat down between them.

"You won't sleep," I warned them.

"Mummy *promised*," Connie replied.

And with that we all ate our cake. They appeared to enjoy theirs, but I could barely get mine down. Eventually, I pinched my nose between my fingers, shut both eyes and imagined it was something else. When I finally allowed myself to smell again, I had to cover my mouth, fighting to keep it down.

"Yum," said Jamie.

"Can we have more?"

"No," I told Connie, taking their plates away. "Up to bed now."

They didn't sleep, like I'd said. Instead, they were up for hours, white as a sheet, heads craned together over the toilet bowl, clutching at their stomachs. When one of them was finally sick, the other joined in almost immediately, and I spent another hour battling my own pangs while attempting to feed them the water they craved. But every time they took some down, they brought it up again almost immediately. They begged me to call for Lucy but I told them she was away and I was in charge. They cried even harder at that and when I finally had them in their beds with buckets by their sides and towels spread across the floor, they drifted into a feverish, troubled sleep.

They both had high temperatures, as had I when I checked. After I'd done my best to clean up the bathroom floor, I made my way unsteadily downstairs, put the rest of the cake in the bin and checked all the locks again. Then I fought back a fresh urge to bring everything up and staggered up to bed.

I'd just pulled my bedroom curtains across when I heard the front doorbell ring downstairs. I sat up suddenly to check the time on my bedside clock. It was past eleven o'clock and the act of sitting up almost made me sick over my covers. I climbed out of bed and crept over to my door, hoping I'd imagined it.

The doorbell rang again. It was most likely Lucy, I reasoned, checking in on us after a late evening call from Mum. But instead of going down to see her, I moved quietly into my mother's bedroom and crawled over to her dresser.

Crouched in her seat, I leant my head against the mirrored glass and peered through the gaps between.

As I looked through, I realised I'd forgotten to draw the upstairs curtains. The room, including its reflection around me, was bathed in stark moonlight, throwing the frames and edges of my mother's furniture into sharp, unworldly focus.

I sat for some time, looking out between the gaps at the house opposite, which was dark and empty still, hoping I'd hear whoever was downstairs, waiting outside our front door, give up at last and walk away. But instead the doorbell rang a third time.

I'd somehow forgotten how ill I'd been feeling. Only that the pain which had surged through my stomach was now focused instead in my head. Yet it was not quite pain—more an uneasiness of mind and a distorted sense of things, as if the room before me was shimmering in a thick haze, and I was perceiving everything through the clammy fog of swelling fever.

I stood up with difficulty and lurched over to the landing, glancing into Jamie and Connie's rooms to check they were still asleep and breathing, then sat on the top stair and edged myself downward, step by step, toward the silence and darkness of the hall below.

I saw it almost immediately, staring in at me through the pane of frosted glass beside the door, as it had done in my dream. No longer attempting to conceal itself, the dark contours of the giant head filled the pane, pressing itself against the glass as I reached the floor. Though greatly distorted, I could make out the bold colours of a vast painted face, with huge cheeks daubed red above its wide mouth.

I knelt on the carpet, unsure whether it could see me or not, feeling suddenly as small and vulnerable as Jamie or Connie. Then, in a smooth arc, like something slowly waving at me, the face moved back behind the door.

My gaze dropped to the bronze letterbox and a dreadful moment passed. With intense trepidation, I crouched on the floor, dragging my fingers anxiously through the carpet. Then the flap sprung upward.

Beyond, all was black. I could see nothing, yet smelled a sweet, saccharine odour wafting through the hole in the door. It was the unmistakable aroma of ovens, and a cake slowly rising. I felt the nausea I'd suppressed swell up again, and thought I glimpsed something move in the darkness of the gap. But what I thought was a hand, holding up the bronze flap, instead writhed and darted through the hole to lick me. As I lurched backward, desperate to avoid its touch, I saw what was slowly growing each side of the door. Blurred horribly through the frosted panes, lined with teeth, was the vast, widening smile of a colossal mouth.

I cried out for my mum and fled back upstairs toward my bedroom. As I passed along the landing I heard something like feet pattering over the roof above, and when I entered my room and threw myself under the covers, I called out for Jamie and Connie, realising I'd left them alone. But they didn't come, and as I threw back the sheets again, knowing I had to get out and save them, I saw the brightness of the full moon beyond my window, vast and white, illuminated through the nylon fibres of my bedroom curtains.

Then I heard the sound of plaster splitting as shards of paint and brickwork crumbled like powder from one corner of the wall. I stared, dumbfounded, as long, spider-thin cracks worked their way downward from the ceiling, casting fragments of the wall outward, onto my carpet. Then the moon outside began to move across the sky. Convinced the house was collapsing, I flung back the curtains and saw it looking in at me, the vast whiteness of its giant eye moving slowly from side to side like a mechanical head luring children to a terrifying funhouse. The pair of immense lips below it were stretched wide apart, the interior of its mouth darker than anything I had ever known.

Its teeth, white and monstrous, yet unbroken like the rows of brickwork they were fixed upon, shone bright in the glare of the real moon above. With a terrifying crack, the immense jaws clamped downward, biting on the wall between us, and I knew it was making its way in.

As the room fell in around me, I heard my brother and sister scream for me in the dark. Aware I could do nothing to help them, I cried out for my mother to save us all, knowing the thing was above me, its pink, painted cheeks and blood-red lips stretched into an infinite grin as it leaned down over my bed, preparing to eat me up.

Then I smelt the scent of my mum's perfume and felt her arms around me, and knew at last where I was as I cried myself to sleep.

◄◦►

Later, amid many tears, Jamie admitted it was Lucy who'd baked the cake, having handed it to him and Connie earlier that day when Mum was in the garden. Connie never spoke about her, but Jamie said Lucy had frightened them into it, although he would never say how. The police believed there was nothing in it, perhaps recalling how things had been with us, or perhaps my mother, when she'd previously reported the old man. We only saw Lucy once after that, when she turned up, accompanied by her estate agent, to view the house opposite ours.

Mum handled that by herself, and we watched our old babysitter for the last time through the gaps in our mum's dressing mirror, arguing and shouting loudly about us from the old man's drive.

We were eating our tea later that evening when Connie told us that Lucy had been wearing his wife's clothes. When Mum pressed her, my sister insisted they'd belonged to the old man who'd once lived opposite, and were the same clothes he'd asked her to put on.

"You're too young to remember that," said Mum, a little nervously. "Besides, you never saw them."

"I did," Connie said, playing with her fork. "He used to come into my room at night and sit at the bottom of my bed. Then he'd wake me up and show me pictures of her."

That's all I can tell you, except that I ate the cake, like he wanted, and somewhere it's still inside me.

BLACK LEG

GLEN HIRSHBERG

My fault. As usual.

"Documentary filmmaker," the prosecutor said, not looking at me or any of the other prospective jurors. He wasn't even looking at his legal pad, only the defendant. Even so, everyone in the room felt the weight of his glare. "What sort of documentaries would those be?"

Can prospective jurors plead the fifth? I wondered. Then I thought maybe in this case the truth really would set me free. "Ghost hunting," I mumbled. "I followed these two—"

"Ghost hunting," said the lawyer. His smile didn't even reach his mouth, let alone his eyes. And it was definitely meant to intimidate me. Or else he was just amused. "So you're not planning to make a film about this case, then?"

There it was: the moment I'd been praying for. He'd practically opened the door for me. Held it, waved me toward freedom and an early, excused return to what passed back then for my life.

But still, he aimed his gaze toward the defendant's table. The terrified kid there, a tousle-haired Latinx with his legs pumping up and down under the table. All that movement barely rippled his billowy jeans, which were three sizes too big, almost certainly some relative's, and made his whole body look like a sack full of cats on its way to the river.

The prosecutor's smirk was for him, of course.

"Why—you seeking the death penalty?" I blurted. "I could make one about him coming back to haunt you."

Which earned me a smirk of my very own, a reprimand from the judge, a lecture to the whole courtroom about the seriousness of our task and the weight of civic responsibility—the case was a contested driving-without-license; the nineteen year-old defendant had run over a birdfeeder, and we didn't know about the sort-of carjacking part yet, or the getaway vehicle element—and, to my dismay, an unchallenged seat and assigned number in the jury box.

The trial, we were told, because of backlogged something or other plus extenuating birdfeeder circumstances, would last four days.

Four days.

That first morning, at lunch break, I thought about braving the heat to find a taco truck or a shake somewhere. But even ghost hunter work had dried up in the recession, and I was hoarding every penny for my long-planned short about the tent city downtown. I had actually completed the raw footage for it, but now the project lingered in seemingly permanent post-production (meaning I still dreamed someone might fund it), and the interest on the credit cards I'd maxed out for my equipment more than doubled my monthly payments.

So I went downstairs to the jury waiting room and bought an apple from the vending machine. It cost seventy-five cents, and got pushed out of its row like a bag of chips. When it hit the metal trough from which I retrieved it, it bounced.

I found an empty table along the back wall, which wasn't hard. Everyone without a maxed-out credit card had fled for anywhere with functioning air conditioning and less aggressive apple delivery, and the remaining prospective jurors took chairs beneath the blaring flat-screen TV at the north end of the room or clustered into the corners, where at least one or two apparently managed—by turning just right, holding still—to get reception on their cell phones.

This room, I remember thinking, the edible half of my mealy apple consumed, right before he appeared. From where would I film it? In what light? I couldn't imagine the angle or the composition. What shot would capture this tile, where even the scuffs had faded, this specific type of fluorescence, which didn't buzz, didn't glow, wasn't even itself? I can't explain. There were bulbs overhead, obviously, but they weren't where the light came from, somehow. Which of these faces best communicated the way all of our faces had gone slack along the jaw, lost some essential shelf of bone that rendered them faces and not masks, collage dots for a future artist's jury box sketch?

We were all doing the same things. Or versions of the same things. Trying to drum up enough brainpower to answer the crossword clue we'd just read four times, or remember what we did for work clearly enough to do some (assuming we could get wireless), or think of anyone or anything in our lives except what we hadn't said (or in my case, had) to get ourselves sentenced here to perform a duty we knew mattered, should care about, just couldn't quite recall why. Not so much passing time as enduring it.

"You make films," the guy said, right at my elbow.

I didn't jump. I don't think I would have remembered how. I did wonder, vaguely, where he'd come from. But I want to be clear: it's true I can't picture his face. But I couldn't have pictured my own, right then.

"Some people call them films," I muttered. Took a bite of the brown side of my apple, feeling all Marlowe. Elliott Gould Marlowe.

"About ghosts."

I took him for Latinx, too, at first. I have a feeling, based on nothing but my own unthinking white person assumptions, that most people do. A little later, before I knew, I decided he was Vietnamese. Maybe Korean. I'm sure it must drive Filipinos crazy.

"I've seen some," he said.

To cover my sigh, I lifted the apple for one more bite, nearly decapitating the tiny no-color worm that poked its head—I kid you not—out of the meat, glanced around like a mini meerkat, then ducked back inside.

Setting the apple on the table, I turned it toward the guy. So the worm could hear, too. I'm pretty sure I gestured at a nearby chair.

The guy just stood there, hands in pockets. His pants were a color, but not one I know a name for. Gabardine? Is that a color a fabric? A color they don't make anymore, anyway. Fabric, either. His shirt was the same. Uniform of some kind. Long-sleeved, in San Fernando, on a 112-degree day.

"One time?" If the guy raised an eyebrow, I didn't see it, wasn't looking. But I actually don't think he moved. "I was working this school? In Van Nuys?"

"What sort of work?" I asked. Automatic impulse. Documenting. Passing time.

"Night."

Right, sure, there's a follow-up question there. But not in that room. Not on an empty stomach. I waited.

"I was walking down this hall? And right behind me, one of the classroom doors? It opened."

I waited some more. I think I even tried to make a noise, I'm not intentionally rude, except to prosecutors with smirks for smiles and my time in their hands. In San Fernando, on 112-degree days.

"Another time?"

Now I really did make a noise, some sort of aural holding up of the palm I couldn't actually bring myself to lift. Protest sound. I mean, if you're going to tell me a ghost story . . .

"I heard this pinging. Ping-ping-ping?"

"In the school?"

"No, at the hospital. There weren't even patients in it anymore, I don't know why they needed night people. Out by Chatsworth?"

"Are you asking me?"

"I heard it. Ping-ping. Out on the stairs? So I went there, and I turned on the lights. And I walked down three flights? And at the bottom, in the basement, I found two little black bug shells. And a penny."

For a second, I was absolutely sure I was being punked. My pal Gabriel, maybe, who specializes in absurdist shorts to sell to comedy cable. Or some stone-faced bailiff secretly delighting himself, because what else would a bailiff with an actual personality do for fun in this place?

"In Pacoima, one time, I was working this lot? Used cars? Behind me, whenever I wasn't looking, headlights flashed on and off."

I felt pinned to my plastic chair, to the whole room, like someone's collected butterfly. Moth, because whatever coloring I possessed had leached away hours ago. Nevertheless, I finally stirred. Flapped.

"If you weren't looking, how did you see them?"

It was a dumb question. It got the answer it deserved.

"They went on. Then off."

Sighing, lifting the apple by its wilted stem and chucking it in the streaked plastic garbage can next to the table, I stood.

"In the same lot, another time? I saw these kids over in the far corner, by Roscoe Street? But on the lot. They saw me, too, and when they did, they moved *toward* me. Then a trash can banged."

I really did think there might be an ending to that one. Or a second episode, anyway. Abruptly, I realized what this whole conversation reminded me of: the world's worst pilot pitch.

"Once?" the guy said. "At the Galleria? I came out of the bathroom on the third floor, and I smelled orange"

"Speaking of the bathroom," I mumbled, gestured at the clock, and made my escape.

He didn't follow. At the door I glanced back. He was still by my table, hands in his pockets. If he was looking at anything, it was the chair where I'd been sitting. I felt bad. I waved.

The second I was out of there, though, I forgot feeling bad about anything except being trapped here for the rest of the week. I was going to have to find a shade tree somewhere not in the jury room. Bring my own apples. I stayed in the bathroom stall until it was time to be readmitted to court.

They only kept us another hour, that day. Long enough to finish voir dire. I'd forgotten to look for my lunch companion, and I honestly believe I might never have thought of him again. But right at the end, when the judge was getting ready to have the bailiff install us, the prosecutor glanced up from his notes. No smirk. He looked as tired and trapped as the rest of us.

"The prosecution wishes to thank and excuse Alternate Number Two."

There was no ado or fuss. The judge did raise one eyebrow, and the defense attorney dropped a hand to his table as though preparing to object. But he didn't, and the moment rippled through the room and out of it. At the left-hand end of the jury box, my lunch companion stood, brushed his hands against his pants, opened his mouth. Maybe just to breathe. Nothing came out. He didn't shrug. Just moved, head down, out of the box. In the silent whoosh of air as he passed under the room's lone vent, his shirt bubbled, and his collar—half turned wrong way out, stained black where it touched his skin—bristled against his neck. Down the little aisle he went.

Even the Latinx kid, led out in handcuffs at trial's end three days later, looked less forlorn.

Maybe that's why I did it. Maybe that's why I remembered the guy at all.

All I know is, a couple weeks later, I was sitting at my tilting apartment kitchen table—which was also my desk—confronting reality. The amateur-hour paranormal series that had paid me a semi-living for three years running had given up the ghost. My last-ditch Kickstarter for my tent city doc had gotten two pledges, one each from my mom and step-aunt. My step-aunt had suggested—in the public comments, on the web page—that I offer "more practical" premiums as pledge rewards: bar mitzvah or wedding videos, say. Or yard work.

Yard work.

I could have taken the comment down. But something about my week in court—the terrified defendant, the inexorability of the case, the decision we were all helpless to avoid by the end, even though it seemed absurd, draconian, laughable except for being the opposite of funny—had put me in a confronting-reality sort of mood.

Unexpectedly, I thought about my lunch companion. Not our conversation, not anything he'd said, but him passing in front of the jury box with his head down, collar bristling. Thanked and excused. Not necessary. I realized I didn't even know his name.

I had to put down my half-peeled orange to grab my phone. Maybe that's what actually possessed me: I smelled orange.

Funny word, *possessed*.

The collar, it turned out, wasn't the only thing I remembered about the guy's shirt. I could also see the name, stitched in red cursive over the pocket. Not the guy's name, but his company's.

Look Outs, Inc.

I don't remember thinking it was funny—the two words instead of one—in the court room. But it seemed funny, now, the first thing all month I'd laughed about. It also seemed . . . I don't know. Sweet. How condescending is that?

Anyway, I laughed. Then I looked up *Look Outs, Inc.*, and called them.

The phone call was also hilarious. The first one, anyway. *Um, yeah, I don't actually know his name. But he's worked at, let me think, a hospital, a school, and a used car lot. Yes, I understand those are all places you staff. At night, he does nights. Which, ah, that's your whole business, got it. All over the whole city, huh? Valleys, too? Good for you.*

For my second call, I led with, "He sees ghosts."

Occupational hazard, the bubbly woman on the other end of the line assured me. I was about to hang up, give up, when she suddenly said, "Wait, Bulan? Our friendly Filipino? Do you mean Bulan?"

"Erm . . . yes? Did he have jury duty a couple weeks ago?"

Which is how I found myself, GoPro riding shotgun, speeding up the 5 into the never-ending mall that is Santa Clarita, California, at one in the morning on an August Tuesday night. There was a moon, big and fat and orange. For LA on the lip of fire season, the sky seemed stunningly clear. By which I mean the city lights seemed to reflect off it, as though from the mirrored underside of a dome. One of those lights really was Venus, though. I'm pretty sure.

"You'll never find him," the woman had assured me. Good-naturedly.

"Didn't you just give me the address?"

"You been up there?"

Step-aunt lived there. I knew what she meant.

"Does he have a walkie-talkie or something?"

"A what? Why?"

"For . . . you know, night watchman business. What if he sees something?"

"He calls the cops."

"Not the office?"

"Some of us have homes," the bubbly woman said. That seemed less good-natured, somehow.

It really did take more than an hour, even after I'd gotten on the right never-ending frontage road, to locate the place. On one side of the street, malls and mall parking lots fanned forever like a trick deck of cards, Gap-Vans-Guess-Boss-AmericanEagle-TrueReligion-BananaRepublic. Pull in anywhere, tap any card, you get Food Court. "Look for the Starbucks," the bubbly woman had said. Twenty minutes into my search, at the moment I was closest to sure I'd already passed what I was passing even though I'd neither turned nor turned around, I realized that had been a joke. A pretty good one.

On the other side of the street, identical faux-rock formations framed signs for subdivisions. Porter Canyon. Golden Horse Hills. The Oaks, where my step-aunt lived. The Oaks again. Unless it was the same Oaks, with separate entrances. Or the same entrance, and I'd looped somehow. My car didn't have GPS, and as usual, I'd forgotten my phone—in those days, at one fifteen in the morning, who would I have called?—but at some point I started imagining and mouthing directions.

"You have reached your—wait—in two hundred and fifty feet, turn ar—you have reached your . . . recalculating route . . ."

What neither the buildings nor the subdivision signs had were numbers. A few times, I saw painted addresses over storm drains fronting the wide, brilliantly lit, sidewalks. All of them were within a few hundred of the number I'd been given, some above, some below. None were the number I wanted. The only other vehicles I passed were cop cars. Or the same cop car. Always, every time, headed the other direction, no matter which direction I was going. Always at the same speed, like a duck on tracks in a shooting gallery.

I almost gave up and went home. Even now, I can't say what told me I'd found it. I think I pulled into the lot to turn around and head back to the freeway, which was always nearby, a traffic light and on-ramp away, as though I'd stayed tethered to it, trotted beside it all this time like its pet. *Californians*, I remember thinking. *Freeway pets.*

Facing the buildings, I saw the same stores on either side of the entrance. Vans, Banana, Levi's. Starbucks, haha, get you a frap, Madame Look Out? Then I realized there was an unmarked building between them. Long, low, stretching like a hangar way back into . . . not darkness, obviously, they've rounded up the darkness and put it in shelters in Santa Clarita.

But distance.

I'm sure half those malls have office complexes or structures like this one tucked into them. But somehow—by its facelessness, its emptiness, its, I don't know, hands-in-pockets humility—I knew this was the place.

Market Circle Business Centre. With an -re.

Did I ever actually see a sign that said that? Confirmed my guess? Was Market Circle Business Centre even that specific building's name, and not just a designation, like East Wing or Restrooms? Why do I still, even now, avoid thinking about how I knew?

Instinctively, I parked near the front of the empty, endless lot, but not *at* the front. A good ten spaces away. I wasn't nervous. I wasn't anything. Those front spaces, though . . . They just aren't where one parks. Not without the company of other cars.

As I got out, though, stepped into motionless air that was fresher than any I'd breathed in months but tasted recirculated, not so much stale as deoxygenated, I heard my jury room lunch companion's voice. Not on the breeze, not spectrally. In my memory, where it belonged: *I heard this pinging. Ping-ping-ping?*

Otherwise, I just heard silence. The suburb-built-on-desert kind, suspended over fifty-mile sidewalks next to deserted malls.

As I crossed the lot, a cop car passed, but on my side of the street this time. I don't know what made seeing it so alarming, but I almost dove back into my own car. If I'd done so, I think I might also have hid.

Why? No idea. I couldn't see the officer through the vehicle's darkened windows, and anyway, I was probably a football field away from the street. Maybe the cop didn't see me. Maybe I looked like even less of a threat than I felt, to anything or anyone anywhere.

The cop car passed. I shouldered my GoPro, and with no particular apprehension, no specific feeling at all except a wave of exhaustion, stepped over the little curb, out of the parking lot and into the mall.

For the next . . . I don't actually know how long, but I was back in my car, fleeing and weeping, by two twenty. So. Thirty minutes? Less? All I did in the time I spent there was walk the mall. The Market Circle Business Centre ran all the way down the middle of it like some sort of breakwater—break-air—and so I wandered around it, looking for a way in, or lights, or a door on which to knock. I flicked on the GoPro a couple times and filmed my shoes.

More than anything, I felt like I was traversing a soundstage. Or downtown Disney. Some places—schools, office complexes, even other malls—feel eerie with no one in them, because it always feels like there *should* be someone in them, right? Or has been, moments before. But these Southern California sidewalk worlds . . . they feel eerie because the thousands of people who pass through them leave no trace. The sidewalks are always spotless, the windows free of fingerprints. The buildings don't even feel anchored to the land. More like something assembled on Minecraft and projected. About as suggestive of current, active habitation as flags on the moon.

At one point, passing a shuttered Ann Taylor outlet, I took a turn around the back of the Business Centre, and the actual moon blazed down on me like a lighthouse beam. It hung there, seemingly right at the end of this row of shops, gigantic, ridiculous. As fake as everything else in Santa Clarita. An emoji moon pasted onto what passed out there for blackness.

I almost returned to my car. I felt ridiculous. Instead, I pointed my GoPro straight into the light and kept going, figuring sooner or later I'd find a door to knock on, a way into the Business Centre. When I lowered my camera, I glanced right, wanting a glimpse of my own reflection in the window glass just to confirm I was actually there, and saw a woman.

She was just standing in the center aisle of the Foot Locker outlet, which wasn't dark, had to have had at least some lights on. She was old, or older: white curly hair, pince-nez, some kind of dark-colored necklace that seemed to trap light more than reflect it. The little beads weren't uniform, looked mottled or cracked.

Like beetle shells, I remember thinking as I passed. I didn't stop moving, barely had time to process. But somehow, I noted the necklace. And the way the woman had her arms folded across her chest. She was holding a pair of blue Skechers. Also, she was crying.

It didn't even seem strange. Not right away. Why shouldn't she be in there, straightening, restocking?

In a beetle necklace. Crying.

I glanced back in her direction. Just as I did, the store lights went out. In the instant *after* I saw her face, which was right at the window, pressed hard against the glass so her nose slid sideways.

That stopped me. Held me pinned to that placeless place.

I laughed.

"And right behind me, one of the classroom doors? It opened . . ."

Turning my attention back to Business Centre, I focused again on finding an entrance. Eventually I did, around the far side, where this wing of shops emptied into yet another acre of parking lot: one door, heavy, metallic, and locked.

Had I seen even a single window in the Business Centre before then? Why not? What could the dedicated workers who presumably staffed this place possibly be doing in there, and why do it in the middle of the mall?

There was a moment, right around then, when I thought I might have stumbled onto something. A film the Kickstarter crowd might actually fund, and incidentally get my tent city project out of post-production in the process.

I knocked on the door.

Desert breeze kicked up, surprisingly strong, whipping across me and into the mall behind me. Past the Foot Locker outlet. In my mind—*only in my mind*, I did not see this—the old woman lifted away, tumbling over the sidewalks and out of sight like a plastic bag.

The second time I knocked, I got an answer. From behind me.

I don't even remember the sound, couldn't begin to tell you what it was, am not even sure there *was* sound; it could have been vibration underground. A temblor, they happen all the time out there, never really stop, as though the whole planet has Parkinson's, is slowly shuddering itself and us to pieces.

So maybe I just felt, didn't hear. Maybe it wasn't in response to my knock at all.

Whatever. I was too busy whirling, fumbling my GoPro up to my face and turning it on—from protective instinct, not directorial—and so I saw what I saw through the lens.

I've played the footage back a thousand times since then. I still can't say. Neither can anyone I've shown it to. Is that a dragonfly passing? Wrong-color hummingbird? What you see is what I saw: a streak of black in the air, right at eye level, like a smear on the lens itself.

Or a contrail.

Behind me, the door knocked.

Real sound, not vibration; I definitely heard it. I didn't whirl—I'll admit it, was afraid to, scared I'd find *old woman face pressing right into mine with her breath in my nose, in my mouth*—but I turned. Slowly. Lowering the GoPro, mostly because I'd lost my sense of how close I was to the door and didn't want to bang it.

The door banged. Much louder. Four knocks, rapid-fire, *rat-a-tat-tat.*

I did what you do when someone knocks, what instinct and civilization has trained us to do: I reached out my hand. Right before I touched metal, the door *drummed. Pound-pound-pound,* double-fisted, surely. I kept expecting the metal to shudder in its frame, but it was heavy, thick, gave no visible sign.

Hoisting the GoPro again, I got it almost to my face, felt more than saw movement to my left, darted my eyes that direction.

She was maybe fifteen feet away. The woman with the necklace. Except it was a different woman. Same necklace, totally different person. Young, black hair in a ponytail, blouse and shiny shirt-vest bright pink. Skechers blue, and on her feet. Less *Ringu* monster than K-pop star. At least until the necklace twitched. Shuddered to life all at once, like plugged-in Christmas lights. The shells sprouted legs.

The moon switched off.

I wasn't consciously filming, wasn't even thinking, just recording sensation in my brain. But where did the light come from? How did I see the coyote?

They're fair questions. I can't answer them.

It loped out of the Restrooms corridor right at the end of the mall across the sidewalk from me. It didn't trot toward the woman, didn't yip or bare its teeth. It just stood, working its mangy mouth, which dripped. The least surprising living thing there, really. Assuming it *was* living. And actually there.

Wind whipped up again, too hot for the night, hotter than the air should have been, and it reeked. Dead skunk. Breath mint. Old orange.

I wasn't thinking any of those things, then. They're what I've pieced together since. Or, right, maybe invented. When I'm in comfort-myself mode, I decide I invented it.

Because otherwise, that reek was combined breath: The coyote's; the woman's/women's; and her beetles'.

The ground buzzed like a cell phone receiving messages Or a million seventeen-year locusts erupting out of the Earth all at once. I looked down, staggered sideways. The coyote humped up, slunk to its left, but closer. Circling me. Hemming me in. Or herding me toward the woman, who'd gone old again, though still in the K-pop vest. Her necklace seethed on her collarbone like crabs on rock.

Or one big crab.

I turned to run, wasn't even considering which direction, and finally noticed the Business Centre door.

The open door.

Everything stopped. It was pitch black inside, or at least I thought so at first. In retrospect, though, that moment was like the first glance up past streetlights into night sky. It takes a while. What we like to call stars coming out is really just our eyes adjusting. Finally seeing what's there.

Still. There definitely weren't any lights *on* inside. Just a hallway, long and shadowed. Doors took shape, all of them windowless, all of them closed. A water fountain. And then, way down at the end—or not the end, maybe just at the lip of even darker shadows—I spotted my guy. Bulan.

Even in the jury assembly room, even while he was talking, I'd barely bothered to look at his face. I recognized him now by his slump. The fit of his uniform shirt. Same one, I was sure. He had a flashlight in one hand, not switched on. Half-peeled banana in the other.

Did he recognize me? Even today, I wonder. Do they allow him recognition?

In the most mournful, pathetic way—as though at the window of a plunging plane—he lifted the banana and waved.

I stepped into the Business Centre, started forward, and a curl of shadow, like a stray black hair, rose out of his collar and burrowed along his neck. The shadow had bristles. A spider leg. Beetle leg. Same as the legs sprouting from the old woman's shell necklace, seething in place rather than crawling.

Not beetles, I realized. Not crabs.

Ticks.

Somehow, I kept myself moving forward. At least until I saw the rest of them:

Streaks of black filled the air between us. A woman—that woman? One of them? Both?—shimmered into existence, blinked out, blazed back again. The coyote appeared—just its mouth, then its tail, its slinky shoulders—hovering. Hunching in place. There/not-there/there. All of it swirling maybe halfway down the hall like an eddy in a river, with more black streaks radiating from it, swirling off it like mist. Right before the whole thing balled together—coiled—I realized it wasn't like a river at all. It was too contained. Too *intentional*.

More of a moat.

It exploded toward me. Coyote/women/bristle-shadow legs, and I dropped the GoPro, stumbled, grabbed the GoPro, and ran.

Left Bulan there. Ran.

Not because I'm a coward. Not only. They weren't . . . after him. Or they already had him. To the extent I thought anything, that's what I thought.

I think it still.

I wonder if he even saw them. If, for him, it was always more like looking up from the bottom of a pool. Seeing lights flicker. Hearing pings.

I don't remember sprinting to my car. I don't remember wind, light, sound, shaking earth, anything. I don't remember the drive. Somehow, I wound up on my step-aunt's porch up in The Oaks, clutching the cocoa she'd made me, babbling at her as she sat in her robe and bare feet on her porch swing and stared out at the identical houses across the way and around her. At some point, for some reason, I heard myself talking about my uncle, who'd refused morphine all the way to the end, and died screaming so loudly that we could hear him all the way down in the family waiting area. I was describing winces and tears on nurse's faces. One nurse in particular, a young one, Elysia, who'd always smiled at my step-aunt and put a hand on her shoulder.

I didn't know about the Diwata yet. I learned about them later, on one of those days when this all resurfaced. By then, I'd given up trying to find Bulan—he'd quit, I'd been told, vanished, no one even seemed to have a record of his last name—and instead just rooted around hopelessly on the internet. The Diwata are Filipino fairies. Or a Tagalog name, anyway, for fairies who spirit you away. Claim you for their own. Won't let you leave.

Were they what I saw? How would I even begin to know?

The only thing I know is Bulan's raised hand, holding banana. Those slumped shoulders. *The prosecution wishes to thank and excuse.* My lonely step-aunt, and that nurse touching her shoulder. The people and moments that attach to us as we pass like ticks, burrow in, make us sick, separate us, but also, just maybe, form the only reliable bridge we'll ever have between ourselves and anyone else. Their hard shells the path we traverse on our way through woods we all walk to someone else's porch, so we can sit and tell the story of how we got there.

THE OFFERING

MICHAEL MARSHALL SMITH

Always the same. So yes, I guess it is a ritual. Or it's become one. We land. We take a cab. We buy what we need at the store on the corner. We make what we think we need to make.

Then we wait.

◄◦►

"So, I hope it is all clear? You are happy?"

I smiled brightly at the petite Danish lady standing neatly in front of us. "It is, thank you. And we are."

I said it quickly, because I've known my wife more than long enough to be able to tell when she's unhappy by posture alone. Heck, I can tell when Lauren's not-happy with my eyes closed. We don't even have to be in the same room.

"Lovely," the woman said. Then looked momentarily wary. "Oh, I forget one thing. The shower? Please don't use it."

"Excuse me?"

This was Lauren, and you could have cut a cube of her tone and dropped it in a glass of scotch to bring it down to exactly the right temperature. A little below, actually.

"Just for tonight," the woman added hurriedly. "There was a leak in there? It was fixed this morning. It needed . . ." She mimed someone doing something—caulking, I assumed. Or spaying a cat. "I don't know this word? It will be perfect now. But it needs to dry. I'm sorry. Tomorrow morning, it will be great."

"No problem," I said, though it kind of was. After a long day of travel I wanted a shower. Lauren has a tendency to cruise straight through into the evening—especially when we're all still a little vague as to what time zone we're in—and so was less likely to actually care, but I had a sense this might be the One More Thing that could push her over the edge. "And thanks for waiting to let us into the apartment," I added, firmly. This was tactical, to remind my wife that our three-hour flight delay at Charles de Gaulle airport had put the woman to some inconvenience.

"It was no trouble. And now I say to you, enjoy!"

She waved at us—which seemed odd, as we were barely two yards from her—and backed into the narrow hallway outside the apartment. I smiled and nodded and gently closed the door as she pattered away down the staircase.

There was silence for a long moment, broken only by the sound of rain on the windows.

"For fuck's sake," Lauren said.

"How come it's okay when *you* say that?"

This was Jon, our son. Fourteen, but already an inch taller than me and increasingly the go-to in the family when it came to manhandling excessively large and heavy suitcases up and down stairs, not that I'm saying that Lauren habitually overpacks.

I made a face to suggest now wasn't the time, and looked around the kitchen. "It's . . . nice," I said. "Characterful."

Lauren shook her head curtly. "No it isn't."

"Oh it is," I persisted. "It's 'funky.' Right?"

And it was. Or at least, I wasn't sure how else to describe it. The Airbnb was on the third and top floor of what seemed like it might previously have been a small warehouse, flanked by others on a narrow and nondescript street in Christianshavn, a canal-crossed and bounded district of Copenhagen, alleged to be only about ten minutes from the central and more tourist-centered part. Christianshavn too was supposed to be 'funky,' and it was on this basis that Lauren had booked the location, though the closing minutes of the Uber from the airport had more strongly evoked a minor industrial town in Illinois, or Soviet Russia. Of course the wind and rain and dark, low skies weren't helping—nor the fact that, when we'd left our previous Airbnb that morning, Paris had been sunny and charming and generally Parisian in that way only Paris can really pull off.

The Airbnb itself was extremely . . . *compact*.

A single room on this level, divided into a trendily-designed but small kitchen area, dominated by a large steel fridge up against a concrete pillar that demarked the further space, which held a table and chairs but had no room for a couch. A walled cube had been carved out of this level to hold the bathroom, which was strange, but there wouldn't have been room for it anywhere else.

A steep and narrow set of stairs led up to where Lauren and I were supposed to sleep, an area that was probably the living area when the owners were home (this was increasingly clearly their primary and probably only residence, and we'd been requested to say—should anybody in the building ask—that we were "looking after the place" for them). A mattress bed had been placed on a raised platform there, somewhat artfully. A metal step-ladder led up to a tiny sleeping loft into which Jon was going to have to cram himself.

It was fine. Really. Well, mainly.

Many plants. White walls, cozy slate and wood in the kitchen. Lots of books wedged into shelves and on windowsills. A few black and white photos showing a good-looking couple in their early thirties (Anders and Maja, the welcome note said)—the female half of which had just shown us around the place. The bathroom, though tiny and currently sub-functional, had a serious design thing going on, including a modishly tarnished mirror. Tons of character overall, the kind of place you'd remember with great fondness if you'd rented it for a year with your crazy but gifted girlfriend, right after you left college. And were Danish.

For two middle-aged Americans and their hulking teenage son? Far less ideal—even if it hadn't been following hard on a spacious and generally fabulous predecessor, on the stylish and discrete Place de Valois (two turns off the Rue St. Honoré, and barely four minutes's walk from the Louvre).

All of this was clear to the naked eye, and not easy to spin otherwise. I glanced at Lauren, however, and saw she wasn't actually pissed any more. Just starkly disappointed. And vulnerable. I'd been busy at work before the trip, and so she'd researched and made every single one of the bookings—planes, trains, cars, and lodging. She felt responsible.

"I like it," I said. "And you know what I always say. You have to wake up in a place to really get the measure of it."

"You do always say that," Jon agreed. "And it's always dumb."

I smiled, covertly, because I understood that he was, in a rare moment of teenage empathy, picking up on Lauren's unhappiness and trying to lighten the mood. The social tools of the young are seldom subtle, but they sometimes work nonetheless.

"Come on," I said. "Let's go explore."

◄○►

Several hours later we returned to the apartment in significantly better spirits. I kept up a kind of manic, court jester-style cheerfulness as we battled over the windswept bridge to the center of town, which looked like it might be interesting were it not spitting with rain and getting dark. Jon slipped into a double-act with me, peppered with undermining comments that finally got Lauren reluctantly smiling as we slogged our way back and started exploring some of the side streets of Christianshavn, lined with narrow stone houses and more ex-warehouses.

Wikipedia had in the meantime informed me that the ground we were walking on was, in a sense, artificial—commanded to be built upon thousands of wooden piles driven into the bay by King Christian IV (hence the district's name), in the early 1660s. The inclusion of water channels had protected it from devastating city-wide fires more than once, saving a bunch of genuinely 17th century buildings and making it one of the oldest surviving sections of the city.

Once you'd got your eye into the architecture, and its presumably traditional lack of garish signage, it became evident there were bars and restaurants dotted along the streets, up little flights of stairs, or down in basements, not going out of their way to advertise their business to passers-by. Eventually we cautiously made our way down into one of them, ready to back out immediately if we were committing some kind of cultural *faux pas*. It was warm and cozy, and we were greeted with immaculate English and affable locals and good beer, and I ate a beef dish with salty little boiled potatoes and sour cream and capers and a ton of dill that was honestly one of the best things I can ever remember eating. Lauren and Jon dined successfully too, and when we walked burping back up the stairs, though it was still windy and now fully dark, we found the rain had finally stopped.

Back at the Airbnb, Jon went upstairs to lurk in his attic to watch YouTubers blather on about trivia and to interact on Instagram and Snapchat with his homies back in California—all the things young people enthusiastically do in order to fail to be where they are, now.

Yeah, I know I'm old.

I was standing at the kitchen counter, trying to figure out the coffee machine in order to combat the extra beer or two I'd allowed myself out of relief that the evening had turned out okay after all, when I heard Lauren say something.

"Seriously?"

I turned to find her in front of the open fridge. The shelves were dotted with various fridge-style things, jars and pots of unfamiliar foodstuffs with unfathomable names—and the door was lined with organic-looking cartons and bottles of liquids. Only the middle shelf was empty apart from one thing.

"She did warn us they'd left their stuff," I said, still firmly in it's-all-great mode. "And said to help ourselves, and just replace anything we use."

"I know. I heard her. And that's kind of fine, but this? Really?"

I came closer and saw that "this" was a bowl containing a mealy pale gray sludge. There was a beige skin over the surface, caused by a day's hardening in the cold interior. And what looked like a pat of butter, resting on the top. "What even is that?"

Lauren leaned forward, peered at it. "Porridge, I think. They left a bowl of porridge, Bill. In the fridge. Porridge. Why would they do that?"

"I'm sure they just forgot."

"I'm going to throw it away."

"I wouldn't."

THE OFFERING   ◄◦►   81

"Why on earth not? We're here for three days. No one's going to want four-day-old porridge."

"They might be planning on sneaking in here tonight, in the dead of night, and eating it all up."

Lauren sniggered. "What?"

"Well, come on. This is obviously their actual home. They Airbnb it once in a while to make working capital. I'm betting they're couch-surfing at a friend's while we're here. Or standing in the garden shivering. Come on—let's look."

Eyebrow raised, Lauren followed me to the back of the room. Whereas the front gave an uninspiring view of the narrow street, the rear showed something that our hunched wanderings earlier had suggested was a feature of the area.

The backs of a higgledy-piggledy collection of tall and pretty old houses—some timber-framed—and small warehouses. In between was a small, enclosed patchwork of open spaces, with a few little trees and a bench and a sagging picnic table: the whole rather damp, and overshadowed, but possibly nice in the summer. A communal garden, basically, which (according to our host's instruction leaflet) we were welcome to use. Currently deserted, of course.

"Maybe they're hiding in the bushes. Let's go down and surprise them. We could be helpful, take the porridge. They must have left it for someone."

"You're an idiot," Lauren said, yawning massively. She walked past the fridge and shut it without further action.

◄◦►

I woke at 3:00 a.m.

It wasn't the first time. When Jon was little I used to blame him for my vacation jetlag, as he'd refuse to even try to go to bed until late, and then flamboyantly oversleep, and repeat this pattern for days, force-mapping the rest of the family onto his messed-up schedule. But now he either adapted more quickly or else suffered in silence like a grown-up. Five nights into the trip, I was still suffering. He was, meanwhile, snoring above.

Though I'd crashed out at ten, I woke soon after midnight, then again at 1:30 a.m. Both times I managed to drift back to sleep fairly quickly. Not going to happen this time, I could tell. Especially not while sharing a bed (or, more accurately, lying on a mattress) that was a good deal narrower than the California King we had at home. Lauren has a tendency to hog the bed. She naturally says the same of me. It's probably just that whoever's asleep gets the lion's share of the real estate.

I lay there stoically for a while, then sat up.

The air was cold. I could hear light rain against the windows, but not see it, as Lauren had lashed a pair of towels over them before we turned in: none of the windows in the apartment had curtains. Presumably the owners liked being woken by the light, marrying their schedules to the natural seasons and local environment, or some-such hipster claptrap.

I knew I was committed now, and carefully slid out my side of the bed. Doing so silently, and getting around the concrete pillar in the middle of the small room without in the process tumbling down the opening to the stairs, was not a trivial undertaking—and by the time I'd managed it I was wishing I'd never started. But the one thing that will usually get me back to sleep is a cup of tea, made English-style with milk, sipped slowly while trying to think sleepy thoughts. And so I persisted.

One of the eccentricities of the apartment was that (unlike most such places in Europe) it had no electric kettle. After padding downstairs I put a pan of water on the stove, and prepared to wait, just like the early settlers.

It took a while to heat, and I wandered into the other part of the room, until I wound up in front of the windows Lauren and I had looked through before coming to bed.

The interstitial garden space looked even gloomier in the dead of night. A few dots of illumination within the surrounding buildings, a light or two in stairwells, one in the apartment of one of those people who are up in the night, for whatever inexplicable reason. All you could see was a variegated gloom, confusingly and intermittently high-lit by a glints from the edges of wet leaves on branches flicked around in the wind, slicked down by rain. The weather app on my phone suggested it'd be better tomorrow. I hoped so. I wasn't sure I had enough manic cheerfulness to get us through a whole day.

I was reflecting vaguely on how informal spaces are a telling indicator of the people who live near them, reflecting their values and cultures in concrete form—I'd noticed earlier that there was not a single instance of graffiti down there, just as people in Copenhagen appeared unthinkingly confident that they could leave their plentiful bicycles propped up against walls and lamp-posts, unlocked, without fear of having them being stolen—and starting to feel sleepy, when I found myself moving closer to the window, peering into the darkness.

I wasn't sure what I'd seen, at first. If I'd even seen anything at all, or how I could have. It was very dark. Only those glints off leaves gave the space any definition.

I squinted against the rain, the window glass exuding enough coldness to chill my face. Then I saw movement.

Only of some low branches, a few feet off the ground.

But this revealed a figure.

It was small. Unless my sense of scale was off—and it could have been, because I was looking downward at an angle, through a window that was misting from the body temperature air coming out of my nostrils and mouth—the person down in the garden could only be about three feet high, maybe three and a half, tops. A child's height, though from the momentary glimpse it didn't seem like one to me. The build was wrong. Neither spindly, as kids that size can be, or fat. More kind of . . . portly. The subliminally quick look at it didn't give me enough time to try to make out the face, though I came away with an impression of a thick nose, heavy brows, and . . .

Suddenly I realized I could hear a bubbling sound. Then a loud hissing noise. From behind.

The pan of water on the stove was boiling over.

By the time I'd run over to take it off the heat, and hurried back, whatever shape I thought I'd seen in the bushes below had gone. Most likely it had never been more than an illusion created out of rain and shadows. No one in their right mind would be down there in that weather, in the middle of the night, just standing there.

I made the tea. Took it upstairs and drank it slowly in bed, listening to the breathing of my wife, and the faint continuing snore of my son up in the sleeping loft.

And before long, I was asleep myself.

⟨◦⟩

I woke to an empty bed. Bright sunlight and slivers of blue were visible in the gaps around the towels up at the windows. From below came a tuneless humming that I knew could indicate only one thing—Lauren was in reasonable spirits.

I pulled on sweats and navigated down the narrow steps. My wife was in one of the chairs, studying a guidebook. She pointed her coffee cup to indicate there was more in the kitchen. I could hear the sound of falling water.

"Jon's in there," she said. "And I'm forced to admit, the shower kind of rocks. There's barely room to get dressed afterward but in terms of providing warm water from an elevated source, it delivers convincingly."

"Excellent." I poured coffee and went to the fridge for milk. As I removed the carton, I noticed something missing. "You didn't eat it, surely?"

"What? Oh, the porridge. Obviously not. It's in the trash—which, incidentally, they'd left half-full. Seriously, Bill—I know you're all about respecting people's spaces blah blah but leaving that gunk in the fridge is not okay. We're paying over three hundred bucks a night for this hovel."

"Fine." I headed toward the bathroom, hand raised to knock.

"Bad idea," Lauren advised. "He's kind of grumpy this morning."

"On a scale of one to ten?"

"We're gonna need some bigger numbers."

"Oh. Guess I'll leave him be."

"I really would."

I picked up the trash from where Lauren had left it near the door, and took the bag downstairs.

⊰◦⊱

The staircase emerged onto a kind of covered cobbled passage at ground-level which suggested horses had once been led through it. This gave out onto the communal garden, where—the Airbnb instructions indicated—trash receptacles were to be found. This proved to be true: they were all neatly corralled together in a little roofed structure in the center.

After I emerged, I looked around for a few minutes. It was hard to imagine that this area had once been sea, part of the bay. But I guess it had been this way for over four centuries, far longer than all but a couple of the cities in the USA—older by a couple of years, for example, than the earliest scraps of New York. Where once had been water was now land. Where I stood had once been a little farm holding, perhaps, long ago. A place where people lived and died and grew things according to the old ways, etc. The earth is what you make it, in the end, and this place felt real and old.

Then I remembered what I thought I'd seen in the middle of the night. The memory felt very insubstantial, as they generally do in daylight. I'd been tired, and thought it certain it'd merely been a trick of low light. Nonetheless, on the way back to the passageway I paused, squinting up against the sky, judging an approximate position in relation to the window of our Airbnb, three floors above.

Then turned.

Some branches, and a bush, to one side of a low portion of fencing semi-marking this little courtyard off from similar portions presumably associated with the other buildings. At ground level, a little flower-bed.

Even my untrained eye could tell it was there for the cultivation of culinary herbs. As I walked closer and bent forward, I could smell mint and a hint of dill, the latter especially strongly. The Danes appeared to go nuts for the stuff. And there—

I stopped, squatted down.

A couple of dill plants had been bent near the bottom of their stems, and in the wet soil by their bases was something that looked a lot like boot-prints. About six inches long. Couldn't be actual boots, because there was no impression of sole marks, which all shoes or boots had, didn't they? And they were too small.

"Who are you?"

I straightened up fast, to see an old woman ten feet away, near the back entrance to one of the other houses. Her skin was gray and her face looked like an apple that had been left on a shelf for a very long time.

"Excuse me?"

"Is not a hard question. Who *are you*?"

"My name's Bill. We're . . . looking after an apartment for a few days," I said. "For Anders and Maja?"

She looked back at me coolly. She didn't believe me, that was clear. "You are English?"

"American."

"Even worse. You people don't know how to 'look after' anything at all," she said, and turned and went back indoors.

⟨◇⟩

When I got upstairs it was clear Lauren hadn't been kidding about our son's mood.

In general Jon's pretty easy to live with. Sure, he thinks both his parents are dumbasses a lot of the time (and is not shy about hiding it), and he forgets to pick up his plate or towels or used Starbucks cups, like, *ever*—but he does his own laundry and he's smart and good company much of the time, and genuinely funny. But every now and then, wholly unpredictably . . . well, he's a teenager. Like cats, they are free spirits, unsusceptible to human control.

As I got up to the door of the apartment, I could hear him being very teenage indeed—and also heard Lauren coming right back at him, as she sometimes will. About six months ago, in a heated and unguarded moment in the midst of family strife, I observed that sometimes it was like having two teens in the family. I won't say that again. Ever.

By the time I'd done what I could to diffuse or derail the argument (Lauren had, despite her own warning, eventually knocked on the door to the bathroom asking when Jon would be out, been informed he'd be out when he was ready, had inquired as to how long that might be, been told it would be when he was goddamned ready, and it had escalated from there) and showered and got dressed and encouraged two sullen people out the door, the old lady in the garden had slipped my mind.

It only took a few minutes for Lauren to cheer up. All it really needed was a chance for her to privately express the opinion that our son was occasionally an asshole, and for me to agree. She has done the same for me when arguments fall the other way.

Jon also seemed to level out after a blood sugar adjustment, and was tolerant about touring The Museum of Design, though even I got to the point of thinking 'Oh, yet another stylish chair, cool, cool.' But then we had lunch at Nyhavn, a touristy stretch of 17th century buildings and restaurants on a canal, and somewhere during the process, we lost him.

His phone had started pinging, and—though we've made it clear a million times that phone use during meals is Not Okay—he disappeared into it. I asked him to stop. He said it was important. I asked which of his friends were involved, trying to open up a conversation, and was told it was none of my business. My response was a little terse.

During this exchange, Lauren reached out and touched my arm, which further annoyed me. It sometimes seems that her getting into it with Jon is merely judiciously firm parenting, whereas when I do the same thing it's me being oppressive, or uncool, or basically an asshole.

I fairly gently shrugged her hand off, but my irritation was obvious and so suddenly I was at loggerheads with her too.

Jon stood up and said he was going for a walk.

"Where?" I asked.

"Just, around. Does it matter?"

"We'd like you to be with us."

"So I can listen to you bicker? No thanks."

And with that, he strode off—having unlocked that most infuriating of teenage achievements: blaming parents for being in an argument that you've caused yourself.

Lauren shrugged and told me to let him go. We settled our disagreement, basically by me letting that go too, and paid.

—◇—

We spent the next couple of hours wandering the streets around Nyhavn, along the river and up and down further canals. I couldn't help missing Jon. He'd gone off by himself for a while a couple times in Paris—albeit in more cheerful moods—so this wasn't an unknown state of affairs. But it was still pretty new. Last time we came to Europe, only two years before, it wouldn't have happened. He'd still been at the stage where not only did we feel the need to keep an eye on him at all times, but he wouldn't have wanted to be without our company. We were his world. Kids simply don't get how hard it is for parents to keep up, to move with the times, to engage with the person who exists now, rather than unconsciously behaving as if they're still that child of three, five, seven years ago. Nor will they understand, until they have kids of their own, that to a parent, that little boy will always be there, like the sea-bed under old streets.

Nonetheless, it was nice for Lauren and I to have some time together, and we spent a while in a Christmas-themed store choosing a tree decoration, something we've done on our travels for many years. I was drawn to a little wooden tableau of three muted-colored, half-timber houses, with the word COPENHAGEN on it (not least, as experience has shown that as the years pass it's not always easy to remember where every single decoration was acquired), but Lauren became set on a small, gnome-like figure with a beard and bright costume. It was a little kitsch for my taste, with a bright red tunic and cheeks and nose, and the carved wood of the face made the brow and nose seem rather brutal, even unfriendly, but as Lauren is the parent in charge of Christmas decorations—and she seemed very drawn to it—I was happy to go with her preference.

"Aha," the woman at the register said. "The Nisse. Very Danish, very old. Means 'the little relative.' The guardian of the land and the home. A good choice for Christmas, I think!"

I left Lauren chatting with her and wandered back outside onto the canal to watch the world going past. It was bright and sunny and for a few minutes I felt truly as if I was on vacation.

Half an hour later, when we started needing coffee, I took a look at Find Friends on my phone and saw Jon had found his way to the main shopping area, ten minutes' walk away.

"I'm going to text him," I said.

Lauren nodded, looking a little relieved.

I sent a suggestion that we meet up at the Espresso House (evidently Denmark's version of Starbucks) in the center. I received a brief acquiescence, and Lauren and I set off in that direction.

We met up, and things were okay. Nobody apologized, as such, but we re-engaged, hung out, saw a few old buildings and statues and other things.

Later we stopped off for dinner at a fun place overlooking the river, and we had nice food and a good time, and there was laughter.

I'm glad about that.

-◦-

I was up early the next morning, a sign I'd finally aligned with the local clock, as I'm generally awake a good hour before the rest of the family.

I made coffee, considered taking a cup to Lauren but decided to let her lie in—it seemed like she'd had a more troubled night than me, and I'd woken briefly at one point to hear her moaning gently in her sleep—and to grab the prized first slot in a shared bathroom, before the floor's damp and the air humid and the mirror fogged with condensation.

It's an indication of my immense self-control that I didn't as a result wake both my own family and everyone on the entire block. Instead of yelping when it turned out the shower was freezing cold, I merely flinched so massively that it nearly put my back into spasm.

Muttering darkly, feeling as if I'd been slapped in the face by the universe, I stepped back out and fiddled with the controls, assuming one of the others had messed with them, but to no avail. There was no hot water. For god's sake.

I boiled a saucepan, brought it to the bathroom, and mixed it with cold to effect a sink bath and shave. Then, still shivering from the shock of the water (it hadn't been merely 'not warm,' but felt like it'd dripped straight off a glacier), I considered what to do next.

Both Lauren and Jon would want showers. Should I call the Airbnb owners? It was only a little after eight, and thus on the early side to bother people (though in my head I could hear Lauren arguing 'Screw them, their shower doesn't work'). It was also unlikely that they'd be able to have a plumber here within the hour, so it wasn't going to solve the initial problem. But should I call them anyway?

I decided to think about it, with a cigarette.

I don't smoke much anymore. I scaled down heavily once Jon got old enough to start to hate the fact that I did, and confident and independent enough to express this feeling. But once in a while, yes. I had a pack purchased from a tabac in a Paris backstreet. I had coffee, too.

No one else was awake, and I'd just been doused in freezing water. I was owed, right? Hell yes.

That is how the logic of nicotine addiction works.

I quietly unlocked the door to the apartment, and headed downstairs to the communal garden.

◄◦►

I was sitting at the bench with some coffee left, and was considering whether to go for broke and have a second cigarette—though it was overcast, and a little cold—when I heard a clanking sound. It was coming from a narrow stairway that led to below ground level on the left side of the building.

A short, bald, and thick-set man of about sixty emerged, holding a wrench. I put two and two together. "Excuse me?"

He stopped walking, very suddenly. "Yes?"

"Are you . . ." I hesitated, trying to work out how to phrase it simply, though every Dane I'd encountered for far seemed to be able to speak perfectly good English. "The hot water. Upstairs. It's not hot."

"I know." He held up the wrench, as if to underline his awareness of the situation. "I'm working."

"Do you know when it will be fixed?"

He shrugged. "Today, I hope. It needs replacement. Aha."

This last was to another and much taller man, who'd just entered the garden via the cobbled passage. He was carrying a large metal cylinder which, though it did not look new, certainly seemed like the kind of thing that would be usefully involved in furnace-related repairs.

The first man said something to the second, in Danish. The taller man smiled, held the rusty cylinder in my direction. "We fix."

"Great," I said, nodding very cheerfully.

They went to the staircase and disappeared back underground. I shelved plans for a second cigarette, realizing that I'd better head upstairs and break the news.

As I stood, I saw a face at a window on the second floor of the building. After a second I recognized it as the old woman from the previous morning. She opened the window.

"What did you do?"

"Excuse me?"

She thrust her gnarled finger angrily at me. "You did this. What did you do?"

"Did what?"

"The house is broken. What did you do? Or what *didn't* you do?"

"I'm sorry—I have no idea what you're talking about."

"Fix it. Or he will fix *you*."

And with that, she slammed her window shut.

-◇-

The team was predictably unhappy about the lack of hot water, and seemingly also willing to blame me for the problem—but that's how families roll. They won't necessarily kill the messenger, but they'll most certainly give him a hard time.

They made do, and forty minutes later I waited in the hall for them to leave so I could lock the door. Jon came out second, and stopped as he passed me. His face set.

"Asshole," he said, and stomped down the stairs.

I was so taken aback that all I could do was stare after him. He hadn't been joking. That was clear.

I locked the door and followed. By the time I got to the bottom and out onto the street, Lauren was looking glum. Not just because of now heavily-overcast skies, or the drizzle.

"Where is he?"

She indicated with her head. I saw Jon's back, already up at the next corner and moving fast. "What the heck?"

"He smelled smoke on you."

"Oh. *Shit.*"

"If you're going to do it, you at least need to eat a mint or something afterward."

"I'm forty-five years old, Lauren. I'm a grown-up. It's my life."

She looked at me. "Not just yours, though, is it?"

"What does that mean?"

"You're his dad."

I looked back toward where Jon had gone. At first I thought he'd disappeared, but then I spotted him by his hoodie, now nearly three blocks away and crossing the street by the bridge. I'd have to run pretty fast to catch up.

"Let him calm down," Lauren said.

I took a step in that direction, thinking maybe I should just do it. Catch up with him, try to talk. I didn't.

⭤

He didn't respond to a couple of texts, including one inviting him to meet for lunch. I knew he'd be able to eat if he wanted to, as everywhere seemed to accept contactless payment and his phone was set up for it. So I let him be.

Lauren and I walked. And we looked at more things. It was okay. The weather slowly got worse, however, and though the streets we toured were attractive, it was starting to feel rather like just more of the same. I kept track of Jon's whereabouts meanwhile. He seemed, like us, to be wandering aimlessly around—though on different tracks.

Eventually the drizzle became heavy enough that it seemed pointless to keep battling against it, and we ducked into the nearest Espresso House.

We sat at a corner table, not saying much, Lauren flicking through Facebook on her phone, me watching the street through a window frosted with condensation.

After a while I zoned out. It was late mid-afternoon, the time when residual jetlag will come and wrap you in its fuzzy embrace. I came to suddenly at the sight of something outside.

A very short, burly figure in a rustic coat, stomping past, as if furious. Something about it made me feel uneasy, and I reached forward to wipe a little of the moisture off the window. The guy had gone.

But I saw someone else, and stood quickly. Lauren looked up. "Where are you going?"

"Jon's out there. I'll go get him."

It was now raining properly. Jon seemed directionless, adrift on the corner as if unsure where to go. I walked up to him, put my hand gently on his shoulder.

He jumped. "Christ, it's you."

"Yeah," I said. "Look, come into the coffee house. I'm sorry, okay? I shouldn't have smoked."

"Whatever. You want to kill yourself, be my guest."

"You don't mean that. I hope."

"No, of course I fucking don't."

"Jon, please don't use that kind of lang—"

"Fuck you, dad. Me using bad words is the problem here? Asshole. You *promised* you'd stop."

"I know. I know. Look, Jon—it's raining. Come inside."

He resisted for a moment, then strode past me and into the Espresso House. I waited a beat, taking a deep breath, knowing there was work to do here, that it would require a lot of patience, and that I was not actually in the right.

As I turned to follow him, I thought I saw something across the intersection, behind the sheets of rain. A little above a child's height, but stocky, with a beard. But it was only the shadow of someone's coat, hurrying down the gray street.

◄◦►

Jon bought himself a coffee and joined the table. That's another weird thing about them getting older. Sure, the money was coming out of my account, so I was paying, technically. But there wasn't a little kid standing beside me anymore, asking for what he wanted and being pleased that his dad had brought it into being for him. Maybe even saying thanks. Apart from my financial role, the transaction was now his. I was now just some other guy standing in the coffee shop.

I caught myself having these thoughts and told myself: *woah, lighten up.*

He joined our table. There was some conversation, mainly between him and Lauren. I stayed out of it for the most part, wanting to avoid simply re-igniting the same argument. She asked where he'd been and what he'd seen, and received monosyllabic answers. Then his phone buzzed and he fell straight into some protracted interaction on that—plugging his earphones in for good measure.

I sent a silent but sincere beat of hatred toward the creators of social media, especially those designed to addict teenagers, and looked out of the window at the rain.

◄◦►

We waited until it had slackened off a little, then set off for home—in the hope that the hot water had been fixed so Lauren and Jon could have showers before our last evening meal in Copenhagen.

Jon walked a few yards ahead, earphones still in place. After a couple of attempts to engage him in light conversation—both met with a heavy sigh, yanking one (but not both) of his earphones out, a bored and monosyllabic reply, and immediate replacement of the earphone)—I kind of lost it.

"Jon," I said. "For god's sake. I'm trying to chat to you here."

"I'm listening to music."

"You can do that anywhere. And it's unbelievably antisocial. This is supposed to be family time. We're on vacation. Together."

"I don't even want to be here."

"Bill," Lauren said, quietly—but two days of trying to keep things nice had crept up on me to the point where I wasn't listening. "Seriously, Lauren. This is *not okay*."

"I know, but—"

"You know what's really not okay?" Jon said to me. "You *smoking*."

"Christ's sake. I know, and I'm sorry."

"So stop."

"I'm *trying*."

"No, you fucking aren't. If you were *trying* then you wouldn't buy any more."

"It's not as simple as—"

"Yeah, it really fucking is."

"Jon, will you *stop* swearing at me. It is *not* okay."

He looked at me. There was something in his eyes I'd never seen before. Someone who wasn't a kid any more, but almost a grown man. Both lived inside his head, I knew that, but right now I was only seeing the man, and he was furious. "Fuck you."

And with that he started to walk off.

"Jon," I said, still angry but suddenly stricken too. "Just wait, okay? We'll go back together."

"I don't want to be with you."

Anger took the upper hand in my soul again, in an instant, like some horrific emotional tag-team. I stormed after him. "Oh yes? And *then* what, genius? You're just going to stand outside the place and wait for us in the rain?"

"I've got the other key, dumbass."

He made a face, smeared with something else I'd never seen before. An expression of insolent pity. He yanked the keys out of his pocket and jangled them in my face. "See?" he said. "I don't need you anymore."

Then he plugged his earphones back in again and strode off into the wind.

"Fuck you then," I said, quietly. "Fuck. You."

I took a few deep breaths, then turned to see Lauren standing in the rain twenty feet behind, looking small and sad and alone. "I'm sorry," I said, when I got to her.

She shrugged. "It's not your fault."

I wasn't so sure. "Let's give him some time."

She gestured eloquently at the climactic conditions.

I pointed across the street at a bar.

◄◦►

We gave him an hour. A couple of beers and some talk about the next chunk of the vacation—four days in London—brought us both back to a point where we knew we'd be able to deal with Jon more positively. Then we walked back to the Airbnb.

I let us into the apartment. The second set of keys was lying on the kitchen counter. The bathroom was empty, however, and showed no sign of having been used.

I looked at Lauren. She mouthed the words "good luck."

I went up the narrow stairs to the upper level, and stood at the bottom of the steps up to the sleeping loft.

"Jon, I'm sorry," I said.

There was no reply. I wasn't surprised.

"You're right about the smoking," I went on. "And I'll try harder. And I know that, in a lot of ways, you maybe don't need me anymore. Or you feel that way, at least. Me *or* mom. I get that. But I hope you still want us. Because we want you. We love you."

Still no reply.

I put one foot tentatively on the foot of the ladder. He didn't tell me to go away. So I climbed up.

He wasn't there.

◄◦►

This is our seventh return trip.

I can hold something of a conversation in Danish now. It's useful for talking to older people. They're the ones who know the old stories, and they're the ones who believe me.

Like the woman in the community garden. It was her that we first encountered when we ran out of the house into the rain that night, desperately searching for our son. This time she was neither angry nor rude toward me.

Instead, when she learned why I looked so scared, and why Lauren was crying, she looked sad. "Sometimes the guardian's punishment is too hard," she said. "And maybe it's not even your fault. They should have explained to you."

She wouldn't elaborate, not that night at least. She went back indoors and would add nothing further. To me, or to the police, who I know did their best. They looked for Jon for months. The case is still open.

The old woman's dead now. Another neighbor told me when we came back last year.

◂o▸

Lauren's hair is gray.

We book the same Airbnb every year, for five days. I think the owners believe it's some kind of way of honoring what we lost. A ritual of remembrance.

They don't know about the bowl of porridge we make and leave in the fridge, or that we make sure to put a big pat of butter on it, as I now know is traditional.

They don't know that it never works.

Or that I don't smoke any more.

◂o▸

On every trip, each morning when I wake, I keep my eyes closed for a while, and listen. Hoping to hear a noise from the sleeping loft. Any kind of noise.

A quiet snore, or the sound of someone turning over. Some sign that my little boy is back. That he's up there.

But he never is.

FOX GIRL

LEE MURRAY

in a former life, in another time
a fox girl departs from the land of jade
in a former life, in another time

to a distant cloud where fortunes are made
nine obedient wives, all refugees
a fox girl departs from the land of jade

amid ugly tongues and eyes that won't see
one hangs herself in her husband's kitchen
nine obedient wives, all refugees

carves up her child like boning a chicken
what kind of woman would kill her daughter?
one hangs herself in her husband's kitchen

leaps to her death in the Chinese quarter
the husband sucks on an opium pipe
what kind of woman would kill her daughter?

the neighbours all say she wasn't the type
so quiet, she barely uttered a word
the husband sucks on an opium pipe

so quiet, she barely uttered a word
in a former life, in another time
she wasn't from here, we couldn't have heard
in a former life,
in another time

SHUCK

G. V. ANDERSON

No one, not even Bridget, could remember how it started, and yet by the winter term, it was common knowledge that she'd taken over the old smoking area and, for a price, would answer one—just one—question about the death of her friend, Samantha. Year Nines were especially bloodthirsty. Balancing on the threshold between childhood and everything after, they demanded to know things like: Did her brains wash off your parka afterwards? Did she die right away? Did you *actually* see her head come off?

Bridget charged an extra 50p for that last one.

The teachers knew she traded in gore and often skulked in the car park adjacent to the smoking area during lunch—wraiths, lost against the tarmac in dark grey coats, just *waiting* for an opportunity to lecture her about unhealthy grieving habits, but Bridget was doing just fine, thanks. In fact, it helped to break the crash down into a nod yes or a shake no, to mythologize—and not only helpful, but lucrative. Sammy had been a practical, worldly girl; she would have approved of Bridget's enterprise, even if it came at her own expense.

Today, though, the car park was haunted by another specter. She watched as something dark slinked behind the head teacher's Ford Escort—something shaggy and quadrupedal and vaguely canine. Bridget clenched her fists, knucklebones undulating into place beneath her skin. It didn't reappear, the dog, but to see it at school . . .

Too close. She'd have to kill it after all.

Can you kill Death?

A welcome distraction in the guise of a Sixth Form boy came sidling up to the smoking shelter. "Hey, Fridge."

"Hey, Mardy."

He was rolling a cigarette. "Busy?"

"Piss off," she said mildly. "You've had enough questions out of me."

"Not everything's about Sam, babe." Mardy licked the Rizla's edge, sealed it, and offered her the first smoke. Crud ran under and all around his nails. She refused. She hated the taste of cigarettes—she might as well shovel ashes straight into her gob—and Mardy knew that, but he was the sort of person who always offered.

He lit his cigarette and sat next to Bridget, their thighs touching. She was pretty sure Sammy wouldn't have approved of *this,* which, if she was being honest, was rather the point. The only thing spoiling her triumph—the worm in the apple, the shit in the pool—was that Mardy kept calling her Fridge. Frigid Bridget.

"I know you're not frigid," he'd said teasingly, the last time they'd been alone. His hand snaking up her skirt, fingertips twanging her knicker elastic. "It just turns out you're a stone-cold bitch, giving up someone's last moments for money."

"She would have given away mine for less," was Bridget's knee-jerk reply, and then, angry at herself for letting an ugly truth slide out—always a risk when you were grieving a girl like Sammy—she'd called him a wanker and told him to get off her coat. By the time she saw him again, the fire in her gut had gone out, and now she couldn't even remember its warmth.

Frigid Bridget, the stone-cold bitch. Fine. Whatever. As long as she could shoot straight, it wasn't the worst moniker to leave school with.

"My dog had her litter," said Mardy. "Did you want one of the puppies?"

"Not really," Bridget replied, slipping her scarred right hand into her pocket. She'd been scared of dogs ever since a Jack Russell took a bite out of her when she was small. It was one of her earliest memories. Other people, when they thought of dogs, conjured up caramel eyes and wagging tails; all *she* could think of was the flash of snapping teeth. To her mind, it made perfect sense that Death would take this shape—they both trotted at your heels, deceptively docile for years and years, until one day . . .

"They're all gums, though," said Mardy.

"The mum isn't."

Mardy smiled. His teeth were the same yellow as good, salty butter. "Okay." He shrugged. "I was just asking in case you wanted to, you know, come over."

"Are ditches not good enough for you anymore?"

"Oh, don't get me wrong, they're cleaner than my sheets. *Definitely* your parka. But, ah, actually, my mum wanted to say hi."

This tore her attention away from the creature lurking behind the Ford Escort. Mardy had never invited her home. They were each other's sordid little secret. Bridget liked it that way. She thought he felt the same. After all, who wants to be seen dating *Fridge*?

"Do *you* want your mum to say hi?"

He shrugged.

"You're not half selling it."

"Forget it, then." He flicked away the cigarette, barely done. He enjoyed the prestige of being Someone Who Smokes at School more than actually smoking. There were sweeter flavors. His look turned sly. "Do you want to skive instead?"

By *skive*, he meant *find somewhere quiet and fool around*. And she wouldn't even be expected to do anything—she never touched him. She'd tried to once, but was too self-conscious of her scars. Better, easier, faster to lie back and concentrate, pretend she was alone. Sammy had said sex was supposed to be *fun, dummy*, but Bridget found herself worrying too much about the faces she pulled, the sounds she made. Whether or not she had a double chin. What Mardy thought about while he was down there. Sammy? Other girls, other boys?

Bridget—well. Bridget just thought about Death.

"I can't today." She told him she was on, which was a lie.

"We don't have to do stuff every time."

He was hurt, she realized. Good: let him hurt. "What else is there? *Talking*? I hate football, you hate Nirvana."

He gestured past the school to the PE grounds. "You used to play football."

"Sammy used to play football. I played hockey. Dick," and she stomped off instead of untangling the dreaded knot of jealousy, guilt, and self-doubt in her breast, woven as tight as any string of fairy lights. Sammy had tangled them expertly. She'd done it when they'd stood in their PE kits by the side of the gym, waiting their turn at badminton, and Bridget's eyes had lingered a little too long on Mardy. Sammy had put her hand down the waistband of Bridget's shorts, tugging *out* to demonstrate the snug fit and *down* to reveal her stretchmarks—which Sammy, of course, didn't have.

"Mardy doesn't go for dumpy girls," she'd said, and everyone within earshot had sniggered.

◄◦►

The alchemy between two people is never perfect—it can't be—but normally there are pressure gauges. Checks and balances. Other hobbies, other people in orbit around the nuclear pair. With Sammy and Bridget, one nasty, the other reticent, there were no such distractions. Left to curl up on themselves like ingrown hairs, the girls calcified into something mean and bitter. An animal that bites itself as often as grooms.

In the last months of Sammy's life, they'd finally begun the messy process of pulling apart. Sammy started hanging out with other girls. They called her Samantha, which felt classy. They passed tampons under the toilet stall doors to each other, and as a rule, anyone else caught short on the loo with stained knickers around their ankles who dared call out for a pad got slung with palmfuls of pearlescent liquid soap out of the wall dispensers. When it dried, it looked disgustingly like spunk. No doubt these new friends indulged Sammy's worst tendencies, but Bridget didn't have to care. At last, she'd gained some distance, a little autonomy—which was exactly what made the night of the crash so unfair. They no longer had any right to be out together; it was a trip for old times' sake, and not even a good one! Now Sammy was dead, and it seemed Bridget would never escape her.

They'd been speeding home on Sammy's moped after seeing a gig in Great Yarmouth, Bridget riding pillion. Her small stature, which Sammy had often sneered at, ended up saving her life: shorter than her friend by a foot, the sheet of metal that slammed into Sammy's face when a haulage lorry jackknifed in front of them merely grazed the scalp of the girl perched behind her.

Everything was a blur now, but she was sure . . . Well, reason conspired to twist things, but there had been flat, empty fields either side of them for miles until the last second, when Bridget was certain she'd caught sight of a monstrous dog on the grass verge.

Black fur matted by peat.

Two red, very round eyes.

Sammy didn't see it. She was watching the road and the lorry ahead, the corrugated metal sheets that would shortly kill her bouncing loose in their bindings. But Bridget saw the creature, *smelled* it, and recognized Death.

This was fen country, after all. If you're born and raised in Norfolk, you can't help but carry Shuck in your bones.

⟨◦⟩

Bridget jerked upright. Marshland slid past the window, sectioned off and made sensible by dikes and culverts. Just now, there had been a huge, hunched shadow. On the verge. Like before. Guts cold, Bridget grasped the emergency brake and pulled.

"Stop the bus!"

The driver braked so hard the back end of the vehicle swung round. The other passengers shrieked and made a grab for anything that would make them feel safer—the seat in front, their belongings. Bridget staggered up the aisle to the door, shaking hard. The driver was on his feet.

"What the bloody hell was that for?"

Bridget's face greyed. "I just . . . I need to get off."

He was all too happy to jettison her by the side of the road. She bent double over the tarmac, letting the wind snatch away the stringy bile hanging from her mouth. The bus continued along its backcountry route without skidding or blowing a tire or spontaneously exploding, despite the premonitory prickle of her scalp. Nor was there a dog, though she found fresh scorch marks among the nodding heads of saxifrage.

The clouds were lined with sickly yellow by the time Bridget arrived home, her feet soaked through from overgrown grass. She lived with her Grandpa

Frank in a squat stucco-finished farmhouse hidden by trees, half an hour from anywhere interesting. As she approached, something about the air felt rank.

She turned into the drive, heart jolting her ribs.

Shuck was waiting for her on the front step. He *engulfed* the front step—there was no way past him. Her school, her bus, now her home, closer and closer. The crash should have done for her. In the smallest of increments, Death was trying to amend his mistake.

Bridget hauled in a breath. "Oi!"

Shuck's attention narrowed.

She cast about for a projectile, grabbed a large rock that had broken off the boundary wall, and chucked it at the dog. It thumped him in the ribs. A smaller animal would have sprung out of the way. His matted fur simply absorbed the impact.

His ears swiveled back. He bared his teeth and pushed off the front step as if to start towards her.

"Don't you dare," she yelled, throwing another stone. This one caught him on the muzzle. He didn't even flinch; the red eyes stared throughout. A third hit his neck. Then the porch light flicked on, and the encroaching dark was burned away. Shuck melted into the Norfolk twilight, and warmth flooded the gravel as Grandpa Frank popped his head outside.

"Is that you shouting, Bridge?"

She pushed past him grimly. He smelled of engine oil. "I thought I saw someone hanging around. You need to start locking the bloody door, Grandpa."

"Mind your language, eh?" He scratched his whiskers with nicotine-colored fingers. "You're late."

"Bus trouble," she replied, which covered a lot of ground. She left her wet shoes on the porch. The walk had worn out the toes of her socks, so she pulled those off too and dumped them straight in the kitchen bin. Then she threw herself upstairs.

"Hey, dinner's waiting for you!"

"Be right there."

She spent precious little time in her room anymore, and it had taken on an anonymous quality—the Soundgarden and The Verve posters were gone, living on as pale rectangles in the paintwork. There were no childish knickknacks dangling from the ceiling. After the crash it had been easier to strip everything away and start again; but she hadn't, yet. Started again. The bed linen was blue, an old set of Grandpa Frank's. The other linens in the cupboard, either Sammy had slept in over the years or they'd *been* Sammy's. She wasn't ready to pick through that minefield. And no photographs had graced the nightstand since she was young. It was too eerie to see her mum smiling cheerfully, ignorantly from inside a cheap Woolworths frame. In the same way it was eerie for Sammy to have jerked her head at the haulage lorry and said as they kicked off, "Wouldn't want *that* to fall on you."

Pretty soon, the lorry's contents would be slicing her to ribbons. The subtle fingers of Death plucking an unsubtle chord.

Bridget groped under her mattress. She felt the long, hard double barrel of a shotgun. Grandpa Frank's shotgun. It had a walnut stock and two round, unblinking black eyes, good for staring down something big. She'd fetched it from the shed.

Just in case.

◄◦►

The window on the landing overlooked the front of the house. Bridget spent her nights perched on the sill, the break-open shotgun dangling from the crook of her elbow. The vigil, while comforting, was an impotent gesture—the only shells she'd found in the shed had been badly stored. Moisture had corroded the casings. If, by sheer luck, they still slotted into the chamber, the powder inside was almost certainly ruined, to say nothing for her aim. Her mum had taught her to shoot a long time ago, but they'd fired at clay pigeons in their own time, in good light.

Death would come by night and he wouldn't wait for her to shout, "Pull!"

While she kept watch, Grandpa Frank snored, oblivious, and that was a comfort, too. Her mum had slipped away, you see, unwitnessed by all except the early hours—terrifyingly easy in every way Sammy's demise wasn't—and since then it had played on her mind that Death could seep undetected like rot.

Whenever her eyes threatened to close, she prowled the dark house noting every hazard: exposed wiring, glimpses of Victorian wallpaper, the old boiler. Invisible. Innocuous. Well, a dog can nuzzle as well as bite. Sometimes, before retiring to her post on the landing, she would slip her cold feet into Grandpa Frank's wilted army boots and stand a while on the gravel drive. Test the air for the smell of singed undergrowth.

Doing just that, she saw a pair of eyes burning in the murk. No huff of vapor gave him away—but then, she reasoned, Death had no need to breathe. She brought the shotgun up. Her pulse jumped in her fingertips, unsteadying the barrel.

"Come on then, Cujo," she muttered, sounding much, much braver than she felt.

But Shuck was in a voyeuristic mood that night and ventured no closer. They stood off until the sun broke over the tree line and the red eyes resolved into bike reflectors abandoned in the grass.

Bridget laughed bleakly, a sticky film of plaque dulling the gleam of her teeth.

She walked into town later—she couldn't bring herself to trust the bus—and purchased two boxes of shells from the Outdoor Store. The man behind the counter was a friend of Grandpa Frank's, so the sale was made on a knife-edge—on the one hand, he knew the family to be responsible gun owners; on the other, Bridget looked like she was one bereavement short of a breakdown.

"All right, love?" he probed.

"Yeah," she replied, setting the coins atop the counter, "just finishing my Christmas shopping. My granddad wants to take me shooting over the holiday," gambling that his friendship with Grandpa Frank was the distant kind that wouldn't elicit a phone call.

"Keepin' well, the two of you?"

"We're fine." Not reassuring enough for him to release his grip on the shells. She switched gears, cranked a smile. "We're good. Cheers. I'll tell him you asked."

Her purchase complete, Bridget stamped out of the store. Thank God for shoe chains; brown slush had frozen into rigid wrinkles overnight and made a rink of the pavement. The high street looked pitiful—the council had strung lights across the road that flashed in a cheap artifice of movement: holly-wreathed bells flicked left, right, left, right; a tree illuminated itself from the bottom up. And the window displays, so inviting by night, bordered as they were with spray-on snow, stared haggard and hungover at the locals as they passed by. Too early for the cafés to open; too early for much at all except the gritting lorries and the troublemakers.

Too crisp and sober by far for Shuck. Safe, then, to linger.

Bridget watched someone dress a mannequin in the Oxfam shop's window. The slip dress they were pinning into shape skimmed the knees. Slinky, in a bubblegum-and-butterfly-hairclips kind of way. It was something Bridget would have liked to test drive, if the spaghetti straps didn't practically forbid a bra and the satin didn't cling quite so much around the middle.

A boy yelped, "Try it on for us, Fridge!" Bridget tucked her chin and looked around. Mardy was there with his mates, but it wasn't him who'd shouted; he was already smacking their arm and coming over to her, his hands thrusting into the pockets of his bomber jacket. His cheeks were pink as if they'd just been pinched.

"Hey. Spending your hard-earned money?"

She drew the plastic bag containing the shells behind her. The Outdoor Store didn't brand its bags, but its contents were visible up close.

"Maybe."

He nodded at the slip dress in the window. "Were you going to try it on?"

Bridget shrugged. The last time she'd strayed from softened plaid, jeans, and Doc Martens, Sammy had laughed in her face.

But Sammy wasn't here anymore, was she?

"It's not the kind of thing I wear," said Bridget quietly. "It wouldn't suit me."

It was Mardy's turn to shrug. "You'd look great."

She glared at him, and he met it. No smirk played around his mouth, except the one that said he didn't know how to proceed when girls refused compliments—she could see his mind working out where to tread next. Backtrack or push forward? A joke? Either way, his expression was genuine—vaguely baffled, even—and his friends were jeering, calling him back, yet he ignored them. It was all the affirmation she needed. Bridget set her shoulders and strode into the charity shop. She asked the assistant to unpin the slip dress, please, she'd like to see how it fits, feeling quite outside herself. Once the curtain was drawn across the door to the changing cubicle, she had to brace herself against the wall for a moment and let her brain catch up to her racing pulse.

She set the bag down and peeled everything off except her knickers and socks, then dropped the dress over her head and scrutinized her reflection.

She hated it immediately.

Why was her skin so pallid? She disappeared against the satin. Why were her thighs wider than her hips? Why did her knicker-line have to protrude? You had to create the illusion of going commando in dresses like this; everyone knew that. And why was the thermostat set low enough in here to harden her nipples? She folded her arms across her chest, shame burning the back of her sinuses.

The curtain suddenly clinked aside and back into place. "Told you you'd look great, babe," whispered Mardy.

Her breath caught. She covered her face with her hands. Her voice dripped mortification. "Oh my God, get out."

He giggled. "The manager will see me." He was so close that he couldn't *not* put his arms around her waist—there was nowhere else for them to go. He bent his head to hers, the smell of chewing gum mixing with tobacco and his own faint musk. "Are you going to buy it?"

"Are you actually taking the piss? I want to *burn* it."

"Why?" Mardy drew back as far as the cubicle would allow and appraised her. She felt his hands wander down to pinch at the hem, check its length. "It's nice. Different. You *do* want it, babe. I saw the way you looked at it in the window."

She replied, "It looked better on the mannequin," but what she meant was, *it would look better on Sammy.* How tired she was of having to navigate the crater that girl had left behind.

"Er, no." His hand cupped her bum. "Can't do this to a mannequin."

She snorted and said, "You're an idiot." He shushed her and drew her face into his chest to stifle her response, and they stood like that for a long moment. His heart beat through his jacket, sure and steady against her forehead, and his fingers slowly curled into her hair as a different mood took hold. Their exhalations were too loud in the tiny space. She felt movement in his trousers. The response from between her own legs? Nothing.

"You need to go," she whispered.

The curtain twitched. He sighed. "She's standing right there. I'm going to get a bollocking."

"You should have thought about that earlier."

He shifted. His tone changed. "What are the bullets for, Fridge?"

They both looked down. Amid her discarded clothes, the plastic bag had spilled its secrets.

"Shooting," she said.

"Shooting what?" Easy question, easier lie, and yet Bridget couldn't think of one—rabbits, birds, beer cans, anything would do except this strange, guilty silence. The longer it stretched, the angrier she got. Mardy lowered his voice. "Shooting *what*?"

"Oh, myself, I don't know," she snapped. "Can you get out now, please? I've asked twice."

Without a word, he dashed for the door. The manager yelled at the back of his head, and the look she gave Bridget then, you'd think she'd stepped in something. "Leave, before I call the police!" Bridget didn't need telling twice; she was already jumping into her jeans. She ran from the shop the second she was decent—still, after all that, wearing the slip dress. Flustered with embarrassment, she hardly felt the cold. At the next alley, she flung her bag and bra down and started buttoning up her top.

Mardy was already there, getting his wind back.

"Are you *okay*, Fridge?"

He said the word with such delicacy, as if *she* was the cornered dog about to bite.

"Fridge?"

"My name's Bridget," she fired back, "and I'm *fine*."

"Sure? You just said you were going to blow your head off."

"It was a joke, Mardy." She shoved her arms into her coat sleeves and zipped up the front with a quick, sharp rasp.

"A really bad one."

"Well," Bridget served—buttons askew, bra swinging from her hands, she found herself shouting without knowing why—"I'm grieving, so."

"Yeah," he volleyed, "you've been through shit, I get it. But this whole attitude, like you're the first person to lose a friend, is getting really fucking old, Fridge."

Lose? *Lose*? Sammy wasn't a set of *keys*.

She wasn't a friend, either. The feelings would be cleaner, surely. The grief would be simple, with no savage relief muddying the water. She'd never had the courage to ask anyone after the crash: *Is it okay if I hated her?*

"Have you ever seen," she said, voice trembling uncontrollably, "someone you know turn into meat?" Her eyes looked like glass: glistening, even the whites. She held up a hand to stop his reply. "She was meat, Mardy. Roadkill. Her clothes were the only thing that looked human." She gasped for air that wouldn't come. "No one should ever have to see that."

Mardy started forward. "You're having a panic attack."

"Don't touch me."

She charged past him into the dull grey of the street. The scattering of people there murmured to each other—look, it's the girl whose friend died in that awful crash—and Bridget turned her back to them, gritting her teeth. How long had Sammy been dead? Long enough, and yet somehow Bridget was still being defined by her.

She hadn't helped matters, of course. She hadn't broken new ground, only kept to the grooves Sammy had carved for her. The same choice of college, the same clothes, the same stomping ground. Even the same boy. A rat in a cage pressing the same old buttons, a slave to dopamine. No more. She passed a beggar, a collection tin for the PDSA, a wishing fountain, and she threw coins their way until she had nothing else left to give.

⟨⚬⟩

They sat for dinner, she and Grandpa Frank, at the tiny kitchen table. He couldn't abide chat at mealtimes, so they ate in near silence; their spoons scraped the bottoms of their bowls and their mouths worked gingerly around the microwaved lasagna. However, it was companionable. Grandpa Frank didn't ask much of her—he never had. Not the most paternal of men, he simply got on with his routine as if she'd never come here, as if she was passing through. Sometimes he asked about school. Exams. Never sex or the sanitary products in the bathroom. Never Sammy, for which she was grateful. And each night, when he finished his meal, he would rinse his bowl and spoon and set them to drain, pop open a can of Coke—a sole concession to sugar—and plant a whiskery kiss on the crown of her head without saying a word.

Tonight, she grasped his hand as he made for the living room. He glanced down and frowned.

"I'm heading straight up," she said.

Grandpa Frank gestured with his Coke. "*Generation Game*'s starting."

"It's the eighteenth."

The date of the crash. Always the date of the crash. He needed no further explanation. He muttered something gruff about time passing and patted her shoulder. "Sleep well, then."

"You too."

Off he went in search of his leather recliner, clearing his throat with a cough. The TV murmured to life. She sat unmoving for a while in the darkening kitchen, until she heard Grandpa Frank scrunch up the can of Coke like he always did when he was done. She scraped the rest of her meal down the sink and washed her bowl and spoon, placing them neatly on top of his, and helped herself to a swig of milk and a Wagon Wheel. By the time she padded to the living room, the half temazepam she'd crushed into his food had done its job.

She didn't allow herself any guilt as she tucked a rug around his legs. The shotgun had a bark to it, and she didn't want to startle him.

She loaded the shells by touch in the hallway. On that dim winter's evening, electric light felt like an imposition. Plus, it would suggest wakefulness to anyone lurking outside, and—she snapped the gun closed with a grimace— Bridget wanted Shuck to let his guard down. She wanted to be close enough to hear a whimper when she pulled the trigger.

The gravel out front was rimed with frost. Every step sent cracks whisking across the skein of ice, as if the house perched upon water. She paused to listen when the ground finally turned to noiseless grass. The cold ached against her eyeballs. She heard the distant hush of tires on tarmac and the ticking of the clock in the house behind her, but nothing organic—no crickets; they perished in autumn, singing lullabies to their eggs—nothing living except her own breath and her own blood throbbing in her ears.

She tiptoed between grass and stone. Years of Sammy jumping out and scaring her by shouting *Woof!* in her face had trained her to expect surprises; she didn't blink twice when a dark shape skittered along the tree line, snapping twigs in its wake. Her glove was too bulky for the trigger guard.

She bit it off and readied a finger, wincing as her scar met the burn of cold steel. The gun bucked, spitting shot. The boom echoed, then crackled as shot tinged off the trees, before silence restored itself. Already, she knew she'd missed; the peace was too thick, loaded. Watchful. She glanced back toward the house. She knew Grandpa Frank lay within, and yet its windows stared gauntly as if plucked out. As if the structure had stood empty for years. It was quite a distance away, further than she'd realized. Had she given Shuck room to double past her?

Her lips peeled apart, skin splitting. "Shit," she whispered shakily. How could she be so stupid?

Frost dampened everything—feeling, fear, even adrenaline. With a sense of unreality, Bridget lumbered stiffly around the garage, stepping through undergrowth, to check the back of the house. After that, she would go inside. Warm up.

Bridget?

She hesitated, pinned between the wall of the garage and a holly bush. The voice had come to her as if from underwater.

She looked over her shoulder towards the front drive.

Bridget!

Two red lights.

She whirled around to face them. Fired.

The lights fell; something heavy hit the gravel, gurgled. Steam lashed the sharp air. The wind brought iron with it. She stared, shotgun limp in her hands. A strange, twisted protuberance spun in the air, round and round, accompanied by a fast click-click-click.

Like . . . like a bicycle pedal and chain.

Bike reflectors.

Mardy.

She'd shot Mardy.

Halfway to his side, her legs gave out. She wailed an approximation of his name and her voice broke, ripped by grief. Starlight picked out the speckled texture of his torso: he glistened like ground beef. She crawled towards him; she touched his wounds, expecting to sink her fingers inside him, but found him peppered with something coarse and dry. And he stirred, conscious! She gasped; at that range, buckshot should have torn him apart.

"Bridge," he breathed.

She touched his face. It was a wonder he *had* a face. The man at the Store—he must have swapped out the shells, given her rock salt instead. Dangerous, but not always lethal. Less than useless against a creature like Shuck. She threw the shotgun aside in despair.

"Mardy," she whimpered. "I'm so—so sorry."

"I heard a gunshot."

She sobbed. Of *course* he'd been on his way to check on her. Of *course* Mardy would do that. She'd fired into the trees and probably hastened his coming.

Her chest hitched. "I need to go and phone an ambulance."

When she turned around, Shuck was standing over them.

Her hand moved for the shotgun—idiot; it was unloaded, and what were the shells in her pocket going to do, exactly?—but Shuck got there first. A streak of white teeth. Splitting pain. She screamed herself hoarse, but of the two souls nearby, one lay dying, the other lay drugged. No one was coming to help. He yanked her into the murk of the trees, and she tried not to look at her arm as the dog's teeth degloved it, but she felt every bone in her wrist grind to dust, and thought she would pass out.

Past the trees, across a ditch into open marshland, Shuck came to a halt and dropped her ruined arm onto the pale, frozen grass. Each green blade was encased as if by glass—a field of sparkling teeth, their tiny points reflected in the sky far, far above. A lower jaw, an upper jaw, and the fens a wet tongue between them so flat as to discern the curvature of the Earth.

It struck Bridget, then, that she had been brought across some boundary. That although he'd let go of her, she'd never left Shuck's mouth.

She lay sprawled on the ground for some time, if time could be measured here. Ice crystals formed on her lashes. Slowly, the wilds returned. A raft spider tiptoed beside her head; a fen cricket burrowed into the rich soil; a pair of dappled curlews gracefully dipped their downturned bills amongst tussocks of cocksfoot and red fescue as the giant dog curled around her and licked warmth into her cheeks. His breath was foul.

Will you never learn?

A tired, resigned sort of hatred settled in her limbs. Her head lolled away from him, a million teeth stabbing her cheek. Several yards and several lifetimes away, blue lights flashed on the side of the road. A police car. An ambulance. A jackknifed haulage lorry. If she concentrated, she knew she would recognize the smoldering remains of a moped. Of the smear that had been Sammy, she saw nothing.

A woman in a high-vis jacket was loping in Bridget's direction, the beam of her torch sweeping the smoking debris, searching. Bridget watched her advance for an age; she watched for so long that by any reasonable physics, she should have been found, but for all the woman walked, she came no closer.

Oh, Bridget's body was found, certainly. But *this* moment was only a simulacrum of that one. A holding pen. A threshold between life and everything after.

Heartsore, as she always was when the truth rushed back in, Bridget turned away from the crash. She had been here many, many times. Had failed to move on many, many times. At least her end was calm. Private. She'd crawled far enough away from the accident to find a little tranquility, which turned out to be a blessing and a balm when she surfaced raw from every failure. What must it have been like for Sammy to return to this moment, that wretched, inhuman state, again and again as she reconciled with her own Death?

Not for the first time, resentment softened into a resemblance of grace.

Shuck lay his muzzle upon his front paws and looked at her pityingly.

You tried to kill me again.

Until she accepted him, she was stuck on a loop. Playing infinite projections over which she had minimal control. This, he had explained. Meanwhile, the world continued on without her. While she was lucid, she asked, "Grandpa Frank?"

Is still safe and well. Mardy, too, though I don't know why you fixate on that boy. He thinks of you not one bit. Her face crumpled at this. The Mardy she always conjured was not the Mardy she'd known. Shuck snuffled at her neck. *Peace, child. It is the way of things. Are you ready to try again?*

Bridget shook her head. She grasped a handful of his greasy scruff, tight enough to imprint the sensation of a fist onto her mind. Something to anchor her, force a reckoning. Something to give her courage for the next attempt. "I need a minute."

A minute, a millennium. He sighed, nostrils flaring close to her face like the twin barrels of a gun. *I can give you all the time in the world, Bridget.*

THE HUNT AT ROTHERDAM

A.C. WISE

always believed my father would be the one to take me on my first hunt. However my elder brother Cecil was the one beside me as the carriage pulled into Rotherdam's wide, circular drive.

"Try not to be nervous, Trev." Cecil patted my thigh awkwardly.

I peered from the window at the expanse of Rotherdam Hall. It was every bit as imposing as I'd imagined, made more so by the lowering sky framing the roof's peaks and valleys.

"I promise you, it's not half as bad as father's stories, and it'll all be over one way or another within three days." There was more resignation than conviction in Cecil's voice as he reached past me to open the carriage door.

"No sense dawdling." The tightness of Cecil's jaw and the way he moved, the point of his cane viciously attacking the stone drive, left me wondering if his leg pained him especially here. After all, it was during a hunt he'd received his wound, and yet he sought to reassure me?

Generations of men in my family, going back to my three-times-great grandfather, had come to Rotherdam to hunt. All the young men of a certain age within a thirty-mile radius did the same. I wouldn't escape my fate by wishing things otherwise.

I followed my brother up the wide, shallow steps to the front door. Demure statues of women stood to either side of the entry. Incredible skill showed in the delicate veils covering their faces and the merest hint of features visible underneath. A chill ascended my spine.

The head butler greeted us with a bow, taking our coats and hats. Another servant took our bags, indicating we should follow him up the grand staircase. Rotherdam's interior proved just as oppressive as its exterior—dark polished wood, jewel-toned carpets, and portraits glaring out at me from the walls. The eyes of patriarchs followed me, brows angled in judgment, marking me as one who didn't belong.

Cecil and I were given rooms beside one another. In mine, I found a wash basin and a pitcher of fresh water, of which I availed myself. The décor and furniture were as heavy as the rest I'd seen, drapery the color of a good claret surrounding the bed and pulled tight across the windows. Thinking to let in a little light, I twitched the curtains aside and was dismayed to find my room looked out over the very woods where we would hunt tomorrow.

Twilight had already begun to gather, a bruise pressed against the clouds. I couldn't shake the vision of pale shapes moving between the shaggy trees and I yanked the curtains closed again. A knock at the door adjoining Cecil's room with mine startled me, and I unlocked it from my side.

"I need your help with this blasted thing." Cecil held out the silken length of his tie, his collar undone. Despite being the elder brother, he'd always been hopelessly clumsy in such matters.

"Aren't you ready yet?" Cecil eyed me, still in my travel clothes, as I sighed and took possession of his tie and collar, setting them right.

"Unlike you, I am fully capable of dressing myself quickly and impeccably." I affected a haughty expression, lifting my nose. Cecil responded with mock sourness.

"Well do it, then. Cocktails start within half an hour, and I'm desperate for a drink."

Cecil retreated, and I dressed quickly. As I emerged to meet him, a bang drew my attention at the far end of the hall. I turned to see the same servant who had carried our bags struggling to lift a dropped trunk, while the butler stood nearby berating him. The man to whom the bags presumably belonged made to help, but the butler steered him away, frowning.

The man belonging to the trunk was blond and slightly rumpled from travel, giving him a roguish air. He looked up, either by coincidence or perhaps sensing my gaze, and flashed a smile. My cheeks warmed, and I was immediately grateful for the hallway's dim lighting. Cecil took my shoulder, guiding me to the stairs. This time his sour expression did not dissolve into a grin.

"Do at least try to pretend to take the hunt seriously." Cecil spoke into my ear, leaning on me as we descended the stairs. "Even if you don't catch anything, give the appearance of effort."

At the bottom of the stairs, Cecil gave me a significant look. Voices and laughter drifted from a room to our right. It struck me that Cecil had volunteered to accompany me in order to shelter me. I could only imagine how the weekend would go if my father were indeed at my side. Gratitude and guilt flooded me, and I stood straighter, vowing not to give my brother occasion to regret me.

Drinks were pressed into our hands and we were pulled into a swirl of conversation and bodies. Cecil introduced me to our host and his wife, and then in rapid succession a dozen others whose names I promptly forgot.

I watched the young men who, like myself, had come to Rotherdam for their first hunt. They spoke loudly, their claims brash, either nerves or genuine excitement. Too many had eyes that spoke of hunger, and I looked away, turning my attention instead to the women.

There were few enough—our hostess, the wife of a retired colonel who was a peer of our host, and a sister-in-law who had survived her husband, our host's brother, and now lived at Rotherdam Hall. They reminded me of the veiled statues outside, speaking with their heads bowed, their lips scarcely moving. I had the feeling that their true conversation occurred telepathically, that they only spoke the occasional word aloud for the sake of decorum.

I tried not to let my gaze stray to the door too often, wondering after the man I'd seen in the hall upstairs. When he appeared just as I happened to look up, I nearly dropped my drink. Dread and hope gripped me simultaneously as he worked his way around the room, introducing himself.

"First hunt, eh? Harrison, but you might as well call me Harry."

My mouth went dry, but I managed to shake the proffered hand, only imagining it lingered a moment longer in mine than was strictly necessary.

"Trevor. Yes. First hunt." I took a sip of my champagne, too quickly, coughing, and Harry thumped me on the back.

"We'll muddle through together then." His eyes flashed, achieving the effect of a wink.

I was spared the need to reply when the bell rang announcing dinner. Course after course appeared, all meat, bleeding and on the edge of raw. My stomach twisted. I watched our hostess, who had perfected the art of moving food about her plate to suggest consumption, though I never once saw her put a morsel to her lips.

I could not deny her loveliness, but nor could I deny the eerie, otherworldly quality to her beauty. Her black curls were perfectly coiffed, her dark clothing chosen to blend with Rotherdam's walls, features sculpted from wilder stuff to match some Platonic ideal. Ropes of jet beads dripped from her throat and ears, and two thick, silver cuffs circled either wrist. I thought of chains.

After dinner, the men were ushered one direction, and the women disappeared in another. Brandy and cigars were brought round. I wanted the night to be done, the whole weekend done, my hunt failed, and Cecil and I our way back home to my father's disappointment.

"Remember, lad, don't venture onto the grounds after dark. That way lies certain death." The retired colonel threw his arm about Harry's shoulder jostling me without ever noting I was there.

Face florid with drink, the colonel leaned closer to impart more advice, his gray moustache fairly tickling Harry's cheek, and I felt a brief stab of envy. Harry tossed a look my way pleading for rescue. I froze, arrow-shot. My head, already made light by the endless wine at dinner, and now the brandy and cigar smoke, spun.

"Steady on." Cecil caught my arm, speaking through gritted teeth. I couldn't tell how much of my brother's grimace was on my account, and how much because his leg pained him.

I'd only seen his scar once, a jagged line like a lightning strike, made by a savage claw. If it had not been for my father, Cecil surely would have bled out on the forest floor.

At last we were released to our beds, and I helped Cecil up the stairs. I could not resist one last glance from the window. The moon shone unnaturally bright, throwing every detail of the forest into sharp relief. I saw then, distinctly, the shapes I had imagined before.

Low and white and long, they crept along the ground like mist, winding between the black trunks of trees. They poured themselves like things liquid and boneless. Every terrifying story I had ever heard about the hunt came back to my mind. Tomorrow we would face those things, their uncanny eyes, their howling voices, and their hunger for blood.

◄◦►

Dawn came too soon, rising gray and pearled with moisture. We were roused by a great pounding, fists banging on doors. Then all was a flurry of bundling into our warmest clothes and rushing outside. I had the brief thought that I might slip away amidst the chaos, but reminded myself that if I brought shame on myself, it would fall on Cecil too.

Fog clung everywhere, making me feel I had stumbled onto a journal page—bold ink lines for the trees drawn on cream-white. I tried not to think of what the fog hid.

We moved as a group, holding close for a moment before fanning out. I immediately regretted the loss of others around me, even the brash and bragging ones. I thought at least Cecil might stay with me, and I wondered if our host had contrived to separate us. Not just my brother and I, but all of us.

The hunt had its traditions after all, and it wouldn't do for two men to catch the same bride.

I moved cautiously, hoping to find a spot to remain unseen until the hunt came to an end. I had no intention of taming one of the wild ghouls of Rotherdam's forest to be my wife, beyond having no interest, the practice was barbaric.

Oh, I knew all the reasoning—how much happier the women were once caught, raised from the status of mere beasts by virtuous marriages to good men. Without the hunt, they would wander forever, wailing and haunting forests and moors, bringing unwary men to ruin.

The image of our hostess came to my mind again, roped in her jewels. I thought of my mother, my sister-in-law, and the scar on Cecil's leg.

A low, whuffling sound came from my left. A dim shape, sniffing the air. Shadows bruised its eyes, and deep within, I caught a hint of moss and stone, the color of the forest itself. Thin lips surrounded a mouth full of teeth. Nostrils drank angrily at the air. Hair, long, ropy, and tangled, dragged through the leaf mold, making a horrible sound as the creature swung her head from side to side.

Hunting.

I squeezed my eyes shut, praying she hadn't seen me, praying my scent wouldn't catch in her terrible nose. Fear sweat rolled from me beneath my layers of wool. A hand clapped itself across my lips, and a shout lodged in my throat as another pulled me roughly away.

I was spun, pressed against one of the trees, the hand still in place so I tasted the salt of the palm on my lips. Harry's eyes met mine and he lowered his hand.

"Our first hunt is a rousing success so far, wouldn't you say?" Again, that flash of grin, cutting through to the heart of me.

Even though he'd removed his hand from my mouth, his body still blocked mine against the tree. If anything, he leaned closer. I scarcely dared breathe. His scent mingled with wet bark, dripping pine.

"Jolly good thing I was here to save you, eh?"

"I hate this." I'd meant to hold the words back, but they were there, blurting themselves free.

Harry's eyes widened. He didn't move. My pulse thundered. I took a breath, and plunged on.

"It's horrid and barbaric. These things—"

"Brides," Harry interrupted me.

"Women," I spat back. "There has to be a better way."

I imagined what he must see. A coward. A deviant. The curved blade of Harry's smile returned, gentled, but no less wicked, no less dangerous. Perhaps more so. It left me flayed.

"I agree," Harry said, voice low. "The hunt is barbaric. Do you know, once they're caught, the women are locked in attics? Sometimes it's months or years before a wedding occurs, and even a marriage isn't a guarantee. I had an aunt, my uncle claimed she had returned to her old ways, reverted and gone feral . . ."

He let the words hang, a look of disgust crossing his face.

"That's terrible," I murmured, trying for the appropriate amount of sympathy, to convey my full agreement and shed the awareness of his body against mine. "Surely it can't be like this everywhere?"

"No." This time, Harry's expression was a grimace. "There are places where men fish their wives from the sea. There are forests where they hunt, but not wraiths, deer and bear and foxes, animal brides whose skins are stolen and locked away. I've heard of things like our ghouls, but raw and bleeding, women with entrails hanging from their waists, creatures who feed on unborn children, and drowned things pulled from rivers and ponds."

I shuddered.

"But we are Rotherdam men, and for us it's misty moors, attics, and the hunt." Harry shrugged, then his expression flickered, almost calculating. "What would you have instead? Romance? Courtship?"

I thought he meant to tease me, but I found sympathy in his gaze, and perhaps even hope. My breath stuttered. He placed a hand against my jaw, so that he must feel the pulse thudding in the hollow of my throat.

"Matches made for love?" His thumb traced my lower lip. "Or desire?"

Had his body not held me up, I would have fallen. I couldn't believe his boldness. I opened my mouth, perhaps to object, but his lips replaced his thumb so swiftly I scarce had time to register it. Dizzy, I let his tongue explore mine, clutched at the front of his coat as he slid his hand to the back of my neck and gripped it firm.

"Better?" he asked. Harry's face was flushed; I imagined mine must be pure fire.

"In some ways, yes." I let out a shaky breath. "Worse in others."

I would have spoken again, but a sound caught my attention. A bride watched us from between the trees. Harry started back, hand straying toward, but not touching any of the weapons or restraints we all carried.

The woman's eyes locked with mine; I thought of storms wracking the heath, lightning-struck oaks. Panic shredded the last of my nerve, but the woman made no move. She put a finger to her lips, and melted back into the mist.

All three of us were spared.

Then a shout and a ruckus went up from deeper in the woods, followed by a ragged cheer. One of our party had captured a bride.

◦

The woman howled and thrashed, hands bound, as a group of three men, the colonel and our host among them, led her back to Rotherdam Hall. I caught Cecil's eye. To his credit, he held my gaze, ashamed, but his posture clearly said he believed nothing could be done. This was the way of things, and always had been.

My blood boiled. Words rose to my lips, but Cecil moved closer and placed a hand on my arm. Sorrow tinted his gaze. I held my tongue, but my heart sank as I watched our hostess and the other women take charge of the chained bride. They spoke low as they led her up the stairs, a hushing sound like wind through pine trees, a language meant for her ears alone and not mine.

"This is horrible," I gripped Cecil's arm. "We must leave."

"One more day, then we'll go home." Chagrin in his voice.

Another realization struck me - he would be the one to bear the weight of my father's disappointment should I return brideless. Cecil was the elder, the one upon whose shoulders the family's future rested. Though he had never said as much aloud, I suspected my father knew my true nature. It was Cecil's duty to see me sorted and out of the way where I could not damage the family name.

I swallowed around the lump in my throat and nodded, though my eyes stung. One more day wouldn't kill me. And at least Harry would be there as well.

◦

Another night of rich food, brandy, and cigars. Where the first night's dinner had been all reminiscence of hunts past, and advice solicited and unsolicited, the second night's meal was decidedly celebratory. The successful hunter, who I learned was the retired colonel's nephew, was toasted repeatedly. The women— our hostess, the colonel's wife, and the sister-in-law—had been excused, or perhaps banished to tend to the new wife-to-be. Would they murmur comfort in their forest voices, or would they tell her to run far, far away?

Another dawn arrived, this time dripping with rain. I bundled myself as best I could, but still the weather bit at me as I trudged outside. Cecil excused himself, pleading important correspondence, but I could tell his leg pained him.

I tried to contrive a way to stay near Harry, but again, we were all separated. Misery gripped me. Rain fell into my eyes, steady, relentless drops wearing at my clothes and my mood.

I only had to endure a few hours, and then we could return home. And I would never see Harry again.

The thought struck me as a blow. Perhaps if I were bold enough, I could find my way to him tonight. My mind lingered over the possibilities, and as I stepped around the trunk of a tree, I found myself face to face with a bride.

In my haste to flee, I tripped. Pain jolted from my tailbone up my spine as I struck the ground, and damp immediately soaked my clothes. I kicked at the leaf mold, but my heels slipped, finding no purchase.

With supernatural swiftness, the bride was upon me. She caught my ankle, holding it in a grip like iron, nails pricking my skin even through my boot. Breath left me. Had I wanted to, I couldn't even have screamed.

Eyes like rain-wet stones watched me. I tried to imagine her features reshaping themselves into something soft, demure. Slowly, she removed her hand from my leg, making certain that I marked that she was letting me go.

"Sister." The word emerged rough, from a throat unused to human speech, the edges grating.

She jerked her head, long ropes of hair swinging, and I looked behind me to Rotherdam Hall.

My throat dried, though the rest of me was soaking wet, and I fumbled the words more than once before getting them out.

"I'll help you," I said. "If I can."

⊸⊹

A foolish promise, perhaps, but what else could I do? I loathed the hunt. I wanted to see it ruined, but I could not rip the tradition out by its roots. Still, perhaps I could spoil at least one wedding.

I knew I wouldn't sleep, so it was nothing to slip from my bed and creep down the stairs. I found my way to the kitchen where a door let out onto the side yard. I had arranged no signal with the bride; I could only hope she would be waiting. I had no clear idea what she meant to do, or how I might help, but even though my heart pounded, I was determined.

I pushed open the door, stepped into the yard, and took a single breath of the night air before a shadow fell upon me. Two. I yelped, struggling, and when I finally sorted my limbs free, I found Cecil and Harry gaping at each other and me. Evidently, they had both been watching for me.

"Trevor." Cecil spoke first, his tone warning.

"Look, I can—" Movement near the line of trees froze us all.

Cecil lifted his cane as if to use it as a weapon. The bride emerged from the forest, tall and pale and terrible in the moonlight. Her hair hung like a shroud, and at this distance, her features were but smudges of shadow.

"Get back." Cecil and Harry both tried to push me behind them. Cecil shot Harry a sour look, Harry looked in turn amused.

I stepped free of both of them.

"I promised her my help." I lifted my chin, defiant.

From his initial shock, Harry's expression cracked into a grin and he slugged my upper arm in approval. Cecil, however, frowned.

"What do you mean?"

"I mean, I'm going to help her free her sister, and if you're not going to help me, I suggest you get out of my way."

I'd never stood up to Cecil as such before. I'd never had the need. I adored Cecil, looked up to him. And over the weekend at Rotherdam, I'd come to realize just how much he had kept me from the worst of my father's moods. Still, on this, I would not budge.

After years of following in his shadow, that I had suddenly grown a spine and taken action on my own probably surprised him more than anything. Cecil shook his head. He clearly thought me foolish, but he wouldn't stop me.

"Perhaps you'd best return to bed," I told him. "If I'm caught, you'll have plausible deniability."

"No," Cecil said after a moment, his expression grim. "You're right about . . . everything."

I wondered again about my sister-in-law, whether she remembered anything of her former life. Cecil was a gentle soul; perhaps it was no accident he had yet to produce an heir. Perhaps it was his own small act of rebellion against our father, the system of the hunt, and a way to apologize to his bride all in one.

I lifted my arm and waved toward the trees. The bride glided forward, sniffing a question as she reached us, gathering the scent of Cecil and Harry. Her lips curled.

Unchecked, untamed, I'd heard it said a bride could tear a man apart as easily as a scrap of lace.

"My brother," I explained in a whisper. "And my . . . friend. They're here to help, too."

I held open the kitchen door. Cecil had explained to me during our carriage ride that wards protected Rotherdam and kept the brides from entering or leaving. Perhaps she needed nothing more of me than a way in, but I followed as she moved deeper into the house, Harry and Cecil close on my heels.

We climbed to the top floor and found servants' quarters and one room with an iron bar and padlock closing the door. The bride's expression curdled in disgust, lips peeling back from her teeth. She reached for the barred door, then drew back, the tips of her fingers smoking. More wards. Beyond the door, I heard the drag of chains.

"Keep watch," I murmured to Cecil.

"How will we get it open?" I turned to Harry, speaking my gnawing despair aloud.

The bride's hands twitched impatiently and she glared. If denied what she'd come for, would she turn on us instead? I imagined Harry's flesh rent, blood soaking his clothes. Had I doomed him? Had I doomed us all? But Harry merely winked.

"Ah This is where I come in." He reached into the pocket of the smoking jacket he'd thrown over his sleepwear, producing a tied bundle, which he undid to reveal lock-picking tools. "Never travel without them."

He knelt, setting to work. The bride paced behind him, and I willed Harry to go faster. I heard the satisfying clunk of the lock undone, and simultaneously, the terrifying sound of a door creaking open further down the hall.

The colonel emerged, and time slowed to a molasses thick crawl. Our perilous mission hung suspended in the safety of the dark as the colonel busied himself stuffing the hem of his shirt into his trousers. A frightened maid peered out from her door, clutching the front of her nightgown where the buttons had been torn.

She let out a squeak of alarm. The colonel's head snapped up, and he fixed us, moustache working furiously.

"What it the meaning of this?" He took a thundering step toward us.

The bride fairly shoved Harry out of the way, and through the open door, I saw her sister caught in a slant of moonlight. Her hair had been braided, her skin washed. A chain circled her ankle and ran to a ring fixed to the floor. Already, she looked different, less.

"How dare you interfere with my family's property? I shall raise the alarm. I—" The colonel's blustering advance halted as suddenly as if he'd run into a wall.

Between one moment and the next, three shapes solidified from the shadows so I couldn't tell whether they had always been there, or simply appeared—our hostess, her sister-in-law, and the colonel's wife.

Before either Harry or I could see to the chain holding the captured bride, her sister had crossed the room and snapped it as though it were nothing.

"You can't . . ." The colonel's words ran out of steam almost as soon as he opened his mouth.

His wife laid a hand on his arm, and I swear I saw him tremble. Our hostess turned, gaze flicking once to the brides behind us before landing on me again.

"Go now."

Simple words, but they carried the power of a storm, relentlessly pounding the moor. Even supposedly tamed, I could hear the lashing, howling wind in her voice. Her eyes were black, fathomless, and despite the demure way she kept her lips closed, I knew her teeth were still sharp.

She bowed her head, and I could not see whether her expression glittered with hunger or shone with regret as she turned to stand shoulder to shoulder with her sisters, moving toward the colonel as one. All I knew was that I didn't want to see what came next.

"Come on." I grabbed Harry's hand, trusting the brides to follow or make their own way free as I ran for the stairs.

Cecil no longer stood guard, and I hoped he'd followed my earlier advice and returned to bed where he could claim innocence. However, as Harry and I burst from the front door and onto the circular drive, we found Cecil waiting, a carriage and two horses ready.

"I took the liberty of procuring transportation." His expression was wry, amusement pulled in a veneer over sorrow, despite his best efforts to keep it hidden. It took my breath away.

In this moment, my hand in Harry's, warm palm against palm, Cecil thought he was losing me. I couldn't say what the future would hold, only that I would not be welcome at Rotherdam any time soon, and perhaps never again in the world it represented. I let go of Harry's hand, throwing my arms about my brother so I nearly unbalanced him. He staggered back, only my embrace keeping him from falling.

I kissed his cheek, then turned back to Harry. I had no right to expect anything, and my heart stuttered on hope in the instant before his hand landed in mine. He squeezed my hand once before taking the driver's seat while I climbed inside.

Just before Harry cracked the whip and sent us galloping away, a scream echoed out from the upper reaches of Rotherdam Hall, followed by the keening sound of wind, though the night was utterly still. I thrilled and my blood ran cold. I vowed never to forget that sound - gruesome death and bloody vengeance rolled all into one.

DANCING SOBER IN THE DUST

STEVE TOASE

The inside of the masks are rough with nails and wire. I push my hand inside. Raw metal snags my skin, adding new blood to old. I place the head-mask to one side and take the leg piece out of the wooden trunk. Built from cardboard and skin it has been made heavy with plaster of Paris and encased bandages that healed no-one. I lay it in position, followed by the arms and body piece. The gauzed eyes stare at me, daring me to try on the outfit. I ignore its challenge and continue to empty the crate.

⊷⊶

1. *Der Schlaffman (The Sleeping Man) Outfit, 1923, Gypsum, Cardboard, House Paint.*

Der Schlaffman is a costume made to be worn during the dance The Dream of the Still Sea. *While the dancer appeared on stage wearing the costume, the first act is for him to be sewn into the outfit. The stitches run up the back, across the slash representing the mouth, and through the eyes reducing visibility to very narrow slits. The dance is then performed purely in response to the location of sounds performed by the second dancer representing* The Still Sea.

◄◦►

By the time I have finished, ten costumes are laid out, radiating from where I sit in the museum attic. I count three times just to check. Six are too small for me to wear. The others would fit, but not comfortably. Comfort was never intended to be part of the performance. At the bottom of the empty crate I find three files of papers bound with cheap red string. I do not open them in case the words within animate the masks and they prevent me from leaving this room of grey light and dust. Cradling the documents to my chest I climb back down the metal ladder, leaving the costumes prone upon the wooden floor like sacrifices around a king. It doesn't feel right to crate them once more.

◄◦►

The curator walks up to the desk, where I sit with choreography plans and costume designs spread out around me. He is a small unkempt man who hovers before he speaks. He reminds me of a bird who waits until the killing is done.

My first instinct is to shuffle the papers away. To hide them from sight, but they are obscure enough in their language. By the time I make my decision it is too late. He picks up a piece of yellowed paper and turns it over to better see in the light of the archive's high windows.

"Die Schiedler Tanzen," he says, putting the document down and picking up another.

"You know of this?" I say. I shuffle the papers as if looking for something and conceal two pages. He picks up another, adjusts his glasses and sighs.

"Of course, Frau Armstrong. We have records of all that is held within the archive. These were donated by the police when they finished their investigation. Of little value apart from morbid curiosity. No artistic merit."

"Morbid curiosity?"

"The Schiedler Tanzen were husband and wife. Their approaches were unconventional and not to everyone's taste. Not to anyone's taste, even in the febrile atmosphere of the Expressionist movement."

In my head I see the costumes still laid out on the wooden floor several storeys above us. Smell the painted cardboard dulled by dust. Feel the iron scratch against my skin. My hand goes to the scab on my wrist and I resist the temptation to scrape it off.

"Do you know where I can find out more?"

The curator looks toward the floor then back up at me and nods toward the door.

"Not here," he says and turns his back on me.

I slide the papers into my rucksack, and leave. The curator will not interfere with the costumes. They will stay where they are until I return for them.

‑‑o‑

2. Der Tod Von Tieren (The Death of Animals), Outfit, 1927, Gypsum, Roofing Nails, Fur From Unknown Animals, Mummified Meat From Unknown Animals, Papier-mâché

Der Tod Von Tieren was only used for one performance, offending even the decadent tastes of the audiences at the time. Little detail remains of the chore-ography, (the diagrams are highly stylised), but they seem to suggest that a live animal was used during the course of the show.

‑‑o‑

The microfiche reader is rarely used anymore and it takes time for the librar-ian to find first the machine itself and then the roll of newspaper records.

"We have a project to digitise our archives," the librarian says, leading me through the corridors of paper. "We haven't got that far back yet. Are you sure you cannot be more precise about the year?"

I cannot. My only guide is the date of the last document in the files. I do not remove them from my bag until she leaves me alone.

It takes all afternoon to find the notice of their deaths, searching through year after year until I find the column hidden within a morning edition of the city's main paper, removed by the time of the evening edition. Once I have the date I visit the police station to find out the address.

‑‑o‑

The police are still housed in the same building they were in the 1920s, a vast arc of windows and wall painted the same green as their officer's uniforms. The entrance smells of vomit and regret, and I step around two recently released drinkers who are only suffering their hangovers until they have enough energy to drink once more.

Inside, I hand the receptionist my print-off and wait while they disappear to return with a police officer whose rank I do not know. He holds my piece of paper in his hand, low to his side like a knife.

"What's your interest in finding this building?" he says, without introducing himself.

"I'm a theatre historian. Dance mainly. I saw a photograph of one of their costumes online, and I was intrigued."

"We've had people trying to find the address before," he says, then goes silent.

I lean on the counter, my rucksack heavy on my back as if its weight is pushing me to ask the next question.

"And did you give it to them?"

"They were ghouls. Wanting to do murder tours. We don't need that kind of tourism."

"That's not my interest," I say, and hand him my university ID hoping he does not look at the date. He hands it back, writes something on a piece of paper and pushes it across to me. His handwriting is neater than I was expecting.

◄◦►

3. *Das Tier Unter der Erde (The Beast Under The Soil), Outfit, 1921, Wire, Clay, Glass, Stones, Concrete*

There is no evidence Das Tier Unter der Erde was ever used in a performance. Although the files found contain both choreography and sheet music for a short piece involving the 'mask' no contemporary accounts exist of a dance involving the outfit. The costume is incredibly heavy (weighing in at 13 stone) and would have been far too restricting to perform in for very long.

◄◦►

Apart from graffiti on the outside walls, the house looks like it has been untouched since the 1920s. It stands alone on the outskirts of the city, hidden within a copse of overgrown blackthorn trees. The river runs beside the fence, water shattering against the tumbled stones of a broken weir. In its shudder and shift I hear music and pause to make notes, before returning to the task in hand.

Although the shutters are rotten and askew I can see no signs of entry, so make one, wrenching damp wood away from soft plaster. There is no glass in the windows.

Inside is dark. I think about widening the gap in the window to allow in more light, but something about the house suggests that it does not want to be lit by the sun. Instead I find my lighter in my pocket and let that guide me through the broken rooms.

There is no floor. I am tempted to blame that on thieves following the abandonment of the house, but everything else is in place. I say that as if the rooms are crammed with furniture and crockery. This is not the case. Stepping along the exposed beams, I walk into the second ground floor room. The two hammocks hang from the ceiling, swinging from the breeze caused by my movement through the door. For a moment I expect Jochan and Sabine to sit up, annoyed to be disturbed, but there is nothing in the hammocks except dust and dried blood. I walk over and push the nearest one, letting it swing back and forth. The dirt of eighty-years slips through the bullet hole like sand through an hourglass.

◆

*4. Lawine (Avalanche), Outfit, 1920, Gypsum, Copper Wire, Lime
    Paint, Razorblades*

Lawine is the earliest of the eleven known costumes attributed to Die Schiedler Tanzen. The attention to detail is exquisite, with finishing touches that are lacking from their later outfits. For example the stitching on the gloves, and the detailing on the face show a degree of care that seems to be missing from subsequent costumes. It is noticeable too that Lawine is much lighter than their later outfits and that the interior is not as raw, with padding in place to cushion against any sharp edges left by the production process. The razorblades have all had their edges dulled, though it is noticeable that when the costume was repaired (possibly for the brief reprisal of the dance for the disastrous 1926 retrospective), that the lost razorblades were all replaced with sharp ones. Examination during recording found many rusted due to the presence of blood.

—◦—

The upstairs of the building is barely used, with dead pigeons covering most of the floor, mummified and still. I step my way through the corpses to reach the single cabinet on the other side of the room. I'm not surprised to find it is older than the 1920s, and broken. Poverty meant that even the one piece of furniture they allowed themselves would have been scavenged from the streets. I open the doors, just to make sure, even though I know that nothing will be inside, and then tip the whole thing over onto the carpet of dead birds, turning my face from the rising cloud of dust. I reach into the cavity beneath the floor, until moments before hidden by the cabinet. The box is heavier than I expect and it takes all my effort to lift it out and carry it back down the broken stairs. It smells of rotten meat and sealing wax. I resist the temptation to open it straightaway and leave the house to its ghosts.

—◦—

5. *Der Wartende Mann An Der Kreuzung (The Waiting Man at the Crossroads), Outfit, 1925, Sackcloth, Iron Nails, Iron Barrel Hoops, Wooden Splinters, Bottle Glass, Tar*

At the time of the performance Der Wartende Mann An Der Kreuzung (worn during the dance by Sabine) was interpreted as taking its inspiration from Voodoo, and particularly the rituals surrounding Baron Samedi. When this was suggested in a local newspaper, Sabine is supposed to have flown into one of her characteristic rages, threatening to burn down the printing press responsible for producing the publication. No other clues to the inspiration were left by the couple, so only supposition is available to us. However, the most fitting interpretation has recently been put forward by Dr. Helen Canterbury, during the conference that preceded this exhibition. Dr Canterbury pointed out Sabine's grandmother was born in the North of England and would almost certainly have been familiar with folklore surrounding criminals gibbeted at crossroads. This seems far more in line with the other themes in Sabine and Jochan's work.

-◇-

I leave the box unopened in my room and return to the museum, ignoring the temptation to stay and just open the lid a touch. To reach inside and feel the texture of the costume. I control myself like all good dancers should, and leave.

The curator looks up as I knock on his open door. He carries on reading for a moment and puts his book to one side.

"Come with me," I say and do not wait to see if he follows. I hear him shuffle in his chair as he rises, then smell the reek of aftershave as he falls in step behind me. We climb through the museum in silence until we reach the ladder up into the attic.

"After you," I say and wait until he climbs, placing each foot with care as if preparing himself for a betrayal. He is not looking in the right place for treachery.

Once he is inside, I follow him up and stand aside as he turns on the overhead bulb. The light glares down, the dull costumes waiting upon the wooden floor like skinned clowns.

-◇-

6. Die Frau Der Weiden (The Woman Of The Willows), Outfit, 1929, Copper Wire, Stones, Gauze, Velvet Curtains

One of the last costumes Sabine and Jochan made, Die Frau Der Weiden is also one of the most elaborate. Each length of copper wire has been knotted to create some kind of approximation of willow branches. The detailed choreography found in the archive accompanying the costumes shows the complex performance was designed to create sound and not just movement. As with all the later costumes designed by Die Schiedler Tanzen the interior provides no padding or protection for the dancer, and the sharp copper wire would have been incredibly uncomfortable for the performer. Indeed, one contemporary report describes visiting the backstage area after the performance to find Jochan's body covered in slashes, blood seeping down to collect on the floor.

-◇-

I can tell by his posture, by the way his shoulders slump, that the curator has no interest in my find. He turns to face me and shrugs.

"You found the costumes then?"

"You knew these were here?" I say. He looks me up and down as if searching for some glitch or error that might explain me.

"Of course. I told you before. We have records of all material we hold within the museum. We just choose to—" he pauses while searching for the right word. "Emphasise some of our collection over others. No-one is interested in this amateurish fancy dress."

I nod, because I know that what he says is true for himself. Unless it is chipped marble or dusty oil paint, then it will find no place within his exhibitions.

"I will ask you to please pack them away, and in future not enter areas of the museum that are off limits to visitors."

"I'm not a visitor," I say. "I'm a researcher."

He pauses halfway down the steps, just his head and shoulders above the hatch, looking like he is emerging from the earth.

"You are a visitor. You are not accredited by an academic institution recognised by our organisation, and you will do well to remember that I only allowed you to have a certain amount of freedom as a favour to an old friend. An old friend, I might add, who only had the vaguest of recollections of you."

He disappears out of sight and leaves me with the ten costumes of Die Schiedler Tanzen, but all I can think about is the eleventh waiting for me.

◄○►

7. Hügelgrab (Burial Mound), Outfit, 1924, Soil, Clay, Moss,
   Grasses, Stones, Sacking

Hügelgrab seems to represent a changing point in the approach of Die Schiedler Tanzen. Here is where we first see seams left raw enough to raise welts on skin, due to the movement of the ill-fitting costume during the marathon 5 hour performance. In some ways the chronology of Die Schiedler Tanzen's costumes represent an abandonment of skill through time, as if the shedding of detailing was part of the intention.

Although known about in private circles for a long time previously, it's believed that the performance of Hügelgrab was the first time that Sabine Schiedler's violent rages played out in such a public forum.

◄◦►

In the attic I cannot resist the temptation and strip, leaving my clothes beside me in an untidy pile. I take my time. There are many decisions to be made. The costume must be big enough to fit, and it must be in good enough condition that I do not have to worry about damaging the fabric. These narrow my options and I choose Der Tod Von Tieren.

Even though the meat has mummified over the decades I still feel I can smell a hint of rotten flesh as I pull the sleeves onto my arms, and step into the leggings. There is no flexibility. No allowance for knees and elbows. I pause, remove the arm pieces and slide the mask over my head.

The weight sits on my shoulders, grinding welts into my collarbones. Slipping on the arm pieces once more I pick up the fur covered gloves and flex my hands until my fingers are in place. The points of roofing nails scratch their way into my palms, and through the discomfort I wonder if they reroute the destiny hidden in the lines there.

I have no urge to dance or to move. I can barely keep standing in the outfit. Inside the mask is raw, the gauze used to carry the gypsum roughly cut and inward facing. If I turn my head to see better out of the narrow eye slits my cheeks are cut many times and blood collects in my mouth. I cannot tell if the iron taste is from the wounds or the rusted metal. I am so engrossed in my own discomfort I do not notice the curator behind me until it is too late.

◄◦►

8. Waagen (Weighing Scales), Outfit, 1923, Metal strips, Heavy weights increasing up to 14lbs, Meat hooks (rusted), Leather straps, Buckles, Wine bottles, Rough hemp sacking.

Waagen was most certainly one of the most extreme performances by Die Schiedler Tanzen and may reflect the deteriorating mental state of both Sabine and Jochan. In contrast to many other performances, the choreography involved the dancer (in this case Jochan) dressing in the outfit on stage. First the basic clothing is worn and strapped up at the back, then the iron strips are affixed to the arms, preventing them moving from a crucifixion pose. On the end of the metal strips were rings through which the meat hooks were threaded. Once this was done Sabine placed the mask over her husband's head. Many witnesses recorded that this was the most disturbing part of the performance. Extending from the mouth and each eye was a single glass wine bottle. Apart from this the mask was featureless. It did not take a leap of imagination to imagine what would happen to Jochan if he fell, unable to use his hands to break his descent.

Then, over the next ten minutes Sabine suspended increasingly heavy weights from each side of his outstretched arms. There seemed to be no pattern and no attempt to 'balance' the distribution. Waagen was performed three times and on each occasion was halted by worried members of the audience, concerned for the wellbeing of Jochan. Sabine's rage at these interruptions was only matched by her husband's.

—⟨o⟩—

"Whatever my personal feelings about these particular items of our collection, that does not give you licence to wear them, like, like . . ." he stumbles, his anger overcoming him. "Some toddler rummaging through a dress-up box."

I am still stood as Der Tod Von Tieren. He seems unsettled by my appearance, as if I am the dead animated by cardboard and Papier-mâché. My face hidden, I smile at his discomfort.

"Outfits such as this are made to be worn, not locked away. Die Schiedler Tanzen did not put so much work into their costumes for them to be forgotten."

He looks me up and down. I notice his hands are clenched into fists by his sides. I smile again.

"You will take the costume off, and you will leave the premises."

"And if I say no?" My voice sounds muffled.

"Then I will bring the authorities to eject you from the premises," he says, but there is uncertainty, as if in that sentence he is acknowledging he is no longer an authority. He is used to compliance. From artefacts. From visitors. From colleagues. My resistance unnerves him. Only the pain stops me laughing at his growing awareness that he is a fallen king. I undress in front of him, taking my time to put on my own clothes. This time he sees my smile, and turns away to stare into the darkness of packing crates and forgotten artefacts.

-‹o›-

9. *Der König der Küste (The King of the Coast), Outfit, 1928,*
   Sacking, Metal Funnels,

Papier-mâché, Sand, Rubber Tubing
   This late costume was very simple and eyewitnesses reported that at first they thought it represented a new direction for Die Schiedler Tanzen. Jochan appeared on stage in what appeared to be a comical outfit. Light and loose the sacking juxtapositioned with the regal name suggested some kind of comment on poverty and wealth. However, as the performance progressed, the audience became more and more disturbed.
   Sabine joined her husband on stage, carrying a large bag of sand. With no other music or real choreography she began to use the funnels to pour the sand into the clothing, until the weight was so great that Jochan was no longer able to move. Then, using the tube and funnel affixed to the mask, she poured in dirty seawater, presumably into the mouth of her immobilised husband until his stomach held no more and the water and vomit fountained onto the stage.

-‹o›-

Back in my accommodation I sit on the edge of the bed and stare at the box for half an hour before lifting the lid. I wish I was more versed in the rituals of saints. The Church must have liturgies for exposing holy relics, but having never taken holy orders I do not know such words. Instead I sit in silence, and when the moment feels right I open the lid.

The mask is on the top. I lift it out and hold it up to the light. It is obvious straight away that it is far too small for me to wear. I cannot deny I am a little disappointed, but as long as it is worn then everything will go as it should.

There is little decoration. The eyes are gauzed, so that the performer can see the reactions of the audience. I reach inside, and catch my hand, blood collecting in my sleeve. I am not the performer for the dance to come. Yet it is fitting that I, the one who brings this performance back to the waiting world, is the one who it takes a price from first.

Next, I remove the tunic and hold it in one hand, gauging the weight. Again, the beauty of the costume is in the lack of adornment. The simplicity. All the detail is hidden on the inside, away from the gaze of the audience. The only way for those who watch to know what is hidden is in the movements of the dancer. The interpretation.

I lay out the whole outfit on the floor. Each piece as well made as the last. Sitting beside it, I run my hands over the plain fabric and sigh. It's hard not to be disappointed that someone else will bring life back to such an exquisite piece of tailoring. I pick up my bag and leave to visit the museum for the last time.

—◦—

10. *Moderne (Modernity) 1922, Outfit, Papier-mâché, Cement, Rubble, Glass*

Although Die Schiedler Tanzen later themes veered more toward the esoteric, their earlier work suggested a tension between the emergence of a modern world and their discomfort with those changes. In Moderne, one of their earliest known performances, Die Schiedler Tanzen expressed this in the discordant orchestration and awkward movements. Moderne was responsible for the initial interest from audiences in their work, an interest that seemed to fade over the decade.

—◦—

If I hadn't left a note with the address of my accommodation I doubt the curator would have ever found me. Though he knows I have stolen Lawine, he is surprised when I open the door wearing the costume. He walks past me, into the room and waits for me to shut the door, holding his hands behind his back, face toward the floor.

He is lost for words, but only for a moment.

"As soon as I leave here, I will be contacting the police."

"And yet you didn't bring them with you," I say. I like the sound of my voice inside the costume. I imagine that my words rustle the metal stitched to the outside.

"We have matters to discuss first."

"The eleventh costume. The one believed to have never been made, or worn," I say. I point to the floor, the rusted razorblades rattling along my sleeves.

"Take off that outfit, donate this one," he says, sweeping his hand toward the mask. "And we'll call an end to the matter."

"I thought you weren't interested in amateurish fancy dress."

"I'm not," he admits, and I admire his candour. "But hidden things and lost things will bring attention to the museum and attention brings funding."

"And that's all you care about? Funding?"

"All I care about is the museum. And what do you care about?"

I pause for a moment, and really think about the answer. Give it some time and consideration. He kneels down and runs a hand over the front of the mask.

"The performance," I say.

The sleeves of Lawine are baggy enough that he does not know about the presence of the iron bar until it makes contact with the back of his skull. I try not to break the skin, but there is a small cut and for a moment I have a few nerves that it might ruin the performance.

Carefully I slide him into the costume. It is not easy. He is a dead weight. Soon though he is ready and I wait for him to wake up.

It is hard to tell at exactly what point he realises he is the star of the show. There was no chance for him to rehearse so all his choreography is improvised. The buckles that hold the sleeves to the thighs make it difficult for him to stand and as he does the razorblades and nails inside the mask press down into his skin. I listen to them grind rather than cut through his skin and muscle, and for a moment I imagine I can smell scorched bone from the friction. As he sings, the blood soaks through the plain white fabric. Die Schiedler Tanzen never named the outfit, but I think I shall call it Die Blumen.

By now he is upright and his full weight is on the blades in the feet of the tights. He stumbles, trying to reach the door, but every gesture increases the intensity of the performance. Die Schiedler Tanzen designed the costume perfectly. None of the blades cut his tongue, so he is able to provide his own accompaniment throughout. Eventually he is tired out from all the work he has put into the choreography and collapses to the ground. When I lift the mask from his face he wears the marks of his strenuous performance. I am saddened that the costume is only suitable for one show, but now I have seen the dance as Die Schiedler Tanzen intended, I'm sure that I will be able to recreate it many, many times.

◄o►

11. Unknown, 1930?

It is rumoured that at the time of their deaths Sabine and Jochan had been working on a costume that was to be the culmination of their performances throughout the decade. However, though their notes, diaries and sketchbooks have been very thoroughly researched, there are only hints of such a costume.

Soon after their final public show, the bodies of Jochan and Sabine were found. The conclusion of the police at the time was that Jochan was shot first while he slept and Sabine then drowned herself in the river beside the house. The final costume was never found.

THE GOD BAG

CHRISTOPHER GOLDEN

I never knew where she got the idea for the God Bag. In the waning days, when my mother's memory turned into a source of constant pain and confusion, I asked my brother and sister about it, but neither of them knew the origins of the threadbare velvet thing, or even when she started stuffing prayers into it. The earliest any of us could recall Mom mentioning it was shortly after she and Dad divorced. I guess I'd have been around seven years old, which means my brother, Simon, would have been nine and Corinne, our sister, about fifteen.

"I'll put it in my God Bag," she'd say.

I remember the look in her eyes when she talked about it, as if she assumed we all knew exactly what she meant. I honestly don't recall if she ever explained it to me or if I figured it out through context clues, but the gist was clear—when Mom was troubled, wrestling with something in her heart, or when she'd lost something and needed to find it, she'd scribble a prayer on a scrap of white paper, fold it up and stick it into the God Bag.

Reading that, you might assume we were a religious family, but I wouldn't go that far. Corinne, Simon, and I attended Catholic schools from first grade up through high school graduation, but we were never regular church-goers, not even when our parents were still married. Dad's religion was self-indulgence; bars were his church, women and alcohol his communion. Mom had a more eccentric sort of faith. She burned St. Joseph candles, had psychics read her tea leaves, was devoted to the predictions of her tarot cards . . . and she had her God Bag.

Years passed the way they do, and occasionally I'd remember the existence of the thing, but only as a funny anecdote from childhood. College came and went, I built myself a sustainable career as a graphic designer, I married Alan Kozik and we found a surrogate to carry our baby, which made us dads. Being gay complicated my relationship with my mother, but I'd heard worse stories and we all survived the turmoil. She loved Alan, and she loved our daughter Rosie even more. Her first granddaughter—it meant everything to her. Yes, my siblings were older, yes they'd had their own weddings, yes they'd had children of their own, and Mom loved each and every one of them. But Alan and I had the only girl, the only granddaughter. Any resistance my mother had to the idea of me being married to a burly, bearded guy who liked to hold my hand just about every minute of the day . . . that went out the window when Rosie came along. From then on, Mom acted as if she'd never had an issue with me being in love with a man. I still nurtured some resentment, but I let it go the best I could. Why fight the tide of joy?

Joy.

It never lasts.

We began to notice Mom's memory failing a year or two before the dementia really dug its claws into her. For a long time, her lapses seemed mundane enough, but when it began to really fail, there could be no denying it. One week it manifested in simple things like misplacing her phone or forgetting plans we'd made, but soon after she would finish a phone call with Corinne and then call her back half an hour later with no recollection of the earlier conversation.

Mom despised going to the doctor. She hated for her children to know her personal business, including her health. She held onto this weird intimacy as long as she was able, but eventually Corinne insisted she be allowed to accompany her to the doctor, and the news was grim. Smoking had done more damage than we imagined, and in ways we had never anticipated. Yes, Mom did have a tumor in her lungs, but it was small and slow-growing and far from her biggest concern. She also had COPD and end-stage emphysema, as well as vascular dementia. Decades of smoking had narrowed the blood vessels in her brain and in her extremities, and the blood that did flow wasn't carrying nearly enough oxygen.

Every day, it would get a little worse. Eventually, either the constricted blood vessels in her brain would cause a stroke or her blood oxygen level would fall so low that a heart attack would kill her. She would stop being able to draw in enough breath to keep herself alive.

Meanwhile, the dementia ravaged her in other ways. She had never been a healthy eater, but now she tended to forget or lose interest in anything but draining cans of Diet Coke and crushing butts out in the same stainless steel elephant ashtray she'd been using for forty years. Loose, dry skin hung from her arms and legs and her hair remained in constant disarray. Her moods had always been mercurial, and now they ranged from near-catatonia to pure joy, from loneliness to rage, sometimes in the space of minutes. She had delusions, mostly harmless, a way for her unconscious mind to fill in the vast, empty spaces in her memory.

"Oh, it's up on my bed," she'd say of the memoir she claimed to be writing, or a book she thought she had given you, or records of some improvised bit of personal history. Photographs of a trip to Ireland that I'd taken—a trip she insisted she'd been on with Alan and me. She had photographs to prove she'd been there "up on my bed."

She'd never been to Ireland in her life.

On a Tuesday morning in late August, I took the day off work to bring her for an MRI. We knew what the results were likely to be, but in order to get Medicare and the local elder services to give her the coverage she needed, we had to jump through the hoops. I hated doing it, but not as much as Mom hated having to go. Even at her most confused, even when her memory turned to smoke around her, she still understood that visiting doctors at this point was futile. Nothing we did could keep the train she was on from crashing, but we had to keep Mom going to her appointments and try to remind her to take her medications, because that was the only way to be sure Medicare would cover the costs of what was to come.

My mother wanted to stay in her home, to live out her last days there, and we were doing everything in our power to grant that wish. Soon that would change.

Something would happen, some household accident, some injury or emergency that sent her to the hospital, and then the whole paradigm would shift.

But that Tuesday had been quiet. Just me and Mom. I brought her a couple of glazed doughnuts—one of the few things she would eat—and then drove her to the MRI appointment. She didn't complain, even seemed in good spirits, but then she had always loved the summer and the sun. Eighty degrees, windows down, I drove her to the doctor's office and checked her in. As I sat in the waiting room reading the historical novel I'd brought along, I kept losing my place on the page, worried by how long it was taking and whether the staff might be having difficulty keeping her on task. But when it was over, the nurse walked my mother out to me and the two of them seemed to have become fast friends. As horrible as she could be, Mom also knew how to charm strangers when she felt like it.

We drove home with the music up loud and the sun shining. Shortly after two o'clock, I pulled into her driveway and killed the engine. She'd gone quiet, slipping into that numb, hollow mood that came over her so often now. No matter how bad her memory might be, how confused, she knew that arriving home meant I would be leaving soon and the shadow of that knowledge darkened her features.

I helped her up to her room, cracked her a fresh can of Diet Coke, and chided her when she tried to light up a cigarette. I had always hated the damn things, and now more than ever. For twenty years she had remembered not to smoke in front of any of her children, but now even that was slipping. She crinkled her eyes and gave me a pouty look, but she put her cigarettes aside.

"I wish you didn't have to go," she rasped in her gravelly voice, pausing every few words to catch her breath. "I get so lonely."

The words were familiar now, but no matter how often I heard them, they carved my heart out.

"I know. But I'll see you again in a few days. Corinne's visiting you tomorrow, and tonight you'll see the nurse. Who's on Tuesdays? Sylvia?"

"Yep, Sylvia. Yes." She nodded, brows knitted gravely in an attempt to communicate confidence. I knew the expression well—it meant she had no idea which nurse would be working tonight, helping her bathe, keeping her company, keeping her out of trouble.

The bedroom wasn't hoarder-level disaster, but it was close. Stacks of books and documents everywhere, pill bottles, a hundred antique knickknacks that would have to be sold eventually but none of which my mother would part with, even now. Especially now. Her Queen bed looked more like a nest, with too many pillows, blankets, and two different comforters, both of them with stains I didn't want to think about, no matter how many times they had been washed.

Mom slept alone on the left side of the bed, the right side piled up with bags of Cheetos and mini-Reese's cups, cigarette cartons, her checkbook and bills that Corinne would take the next day to make sure everything was being handled properly. Left to her own devices, Mom would either not pay the bills or overpay someone she didn't actually owe. There were notebooks she had scribbled in, some DVDs Simon had brought for her to watch, and sticking out from beneath a dirty pink sweatshirt, a familiar faded blue velvet with gold tassels.

"Mom, is that the God Bag?"

The question confused her. She frowned as if remembering what the God Bag was to begin with, then she glanced at it and nodded. "Of course. I have a lot of prayers these days. If I'm going to die, I want to make sure I get a good reception on the other side."

I laughed, but it wasn't funny. Once I would have reassured her, told her she wasn't going to die anytime soon, but even she knew her time was limited.

"I didn't realize you still had this," I said, studying the bag.

It was a royal blue, faux-velvet, drawstring thing with obscure origins, but I assumed it had originally held a bottle of fancy scotch or brandy. Mom's generation had given bottles of alcohol as holiday or housewarming gifts when they couldn't think of anything more personal. The drawstring was a golden, corded tassel. The God Bag had seen better days, but it still served its purpose. The latest couple of notes jutted from the overfilled bag.

"Are your prayers ever answered, Mom?"

I don't know why I asked. Truly, I don't. The words skipped over the thinking part of my brain, went right from the impulse to my lips, and the moment I spoke I wished I had kept silent. If the prayers she put in her God Bag had been answered, she wouldn't be lying in her bed waiting to die.

But her eyes widened a bit, glinting with a clarity I hadn't seen in them for months. "Always," she said, laser-focused on me. "They're always answered. You're happy, aren't you? You and Alan and Rosie?"

Her voice didn't rasp or falter. Her gaze felt sharp, her focus weighted. She almost never remembered Alan's name now, didn't mention him until I mentioned him first. I didn't think it was her old Puritanism returning, just the rockslide of her memory carrying Alan over the cliff into obscurity. Right then, though, I could see she remembered everyone, everything, with utter clarity.

"You prayed for me and Alan?"

"Of course I did. I wanted you two to have a family. I wrote it down and put it in my God Bag, and I got my only granddaughter."

She smiled when she mentioned Rosie. As she always did. Her life had been a series of resentments and vendettas, a terrible example for me and my siblings and for our children, but in her imagination she and Rosie shared a bond, and I never had the heart to shatter the illusion.

"Well," I said. "I'm grateful."

I started to open the drawstring. "Maybe I should put my own prayers in here."

Mom ripped it from my hands. "Get your own God."

I held my breath, worried she would topple over into one of her rage moods, but once she had the God Bag tucked against her chest, she seemed comforted, and in moments her eyes glazed over again. Whatever had prompted her outburst, it had passed.

"I'm going to get you something to eat. Some of that chicken salad from yesterday." I had been perched on the edge of her bed. Now I stood and left the room, her words echoing in my head. Of course she had meant to say "Get your own God Bag," not "Get your own God." She missed words all the time, or mixed them up, and that was obviously what had happened here. Even so, I felt a cool prickle at the back of my neck as I went down to the kitchen.

Get your own God.

The joke was on her. I didn't believe in anyone's god, and I certainly didn't have one of my own.

I went down to the kitchen, which held its own nightmares. It felt like a relic from another age, maybe the galley in a ship found adrift at sea with all hands lost. When had she last been down here to get some food on her own? Some of the plates were set out on the counters. Several knives crusted with dried peanut butter were in the sink. There was a home health aide that helped with such things, but it wasn't fair to always leave it to her, so I reminded myself to run the dishwasher before I left.

I fixed Mom a chicken salad sandwich—on a hot dog roll, because it was easy for her to handle and she wouldn't have eaten an entire sandwich anyway—and carried it upstairs on a small plate with a handful of grapes. I hadn't been gone much more than ten minutes, but I could smell cigarette smoke and she had turned up the TV nearly to max volume.

"Your lunch, madame!" I announced as I entered the room.

The cigarette had already been stubbed out in the ashtray. She'd taken maybe three puffs. She lay in bed, her head slightly tilted, mouth open, eyes closed. If not for the wheezing labour of her breathing, I would have thought she had died.

She dozed off fairly often in those days. Fifteen, twenty minutes, sometimes as much as an hour. I glanced at CNN on her TV to check the time and decided I would wait for her to wake. I hated the idea of disturbing her almost as much as I did the idea of her blinking back to consciousness and finding herself alone. Would she even remember that I'd been there? I wasn't sure, but I didn't want to leave without being able to say goodbye. Just in case.

I set the plate with her chicken salad roll amidst the debris on her nightstand and turned the volume down. My phone lay dormant in my pocket and I knew I could kill time on Twitter or playing Wordscapes, but I figured I would just sit in the chair at the end of her bed and watch the news for a while, let my mind rest.

Then I saw the God Bag again. Such a strange artifact from our family history, as if someone had dredged up a long-forgotten photo album. I knew it was private, and yes, it felt like an intrusion even when I was reaching for it, but my mother was dying and soon enough we would all be rooting through the detritus of her life. Her mind, the person she had been, was already being erased, and given how tenuous our relationship had often been over the years I could not help myself from wondering.

I dug in, sifted around at random, and pulled out a folded piece of white paper. When I unfolded it, I found her familiar scrawl and realized this one had to be at least a couple of years old—written long enough ago that her handwriting remained crisp, with the confident loops and flourishes I associated with the younger version of my mother.

A better job for Simon, she'd written. Just those five words, and the date—10/11/17. I smiled as I studied the words, barely a prayer, more of a wish. I tried to remember how long ago my brother had quit working for the German company whose CEO treated his employees like they were competitors in some kind of reality show, where they were judged on loyalty, forced-enthusiasm, and the ability to come to work and feign good health even when they were sick as dogs. The job had been withering Simon's soul, but he'd been afraid to talk to headhunters for fear someone would tell the boss and he'd be fired. Now he worked at a Boston tech firm whose office culture was the polar opposite and I could see the difference it had made in him, both physically and mentally. I wondered when he had gotten that job. Early 2018, I thought, and it made me smile again as I realized Mom would have taken the credit. She'd put the wish in her God Bag and it had come true. That would have made her incredibly happy, to believe she'd had a hand in changing Simon's life for the better.

Mom's breathing grew worse as I sat there. I glanced around in search of the inhaler she was supposed to use twice a day, but it was nowhere in sight. The nurse would find it later, but as I watched my mother I was reminded of the first weeks after we'd brought newborn Rosie home from the hospital. Alan and I had put her cradle in our bedroom and I remembered lying awake at night, listening to her breathe, terrified that she would stop.

It's strange the way life echoes. Strange and terrible.

When I felt confident Mom wouldn't die in the next five minutes, I dug back into the bag and pulled out more of the folded prayers. *Family trip to Florida* was in there. So were three versions of *I want Corinne to move home*, from back in the days when my sister lived in Arizona. *Someone to paint the house* was among the more mundane wishes, along with *A better car* and *I pray for my back to feel better*.

Some of them were a bit more vindictive. Mom had a history of suing people for just about anything, particularly if she herself had done something wrong and decided that pretending to be the injured party would get her out of it. There were negligent injury lawsuits and real estate lawsuits. When my grandmother had died, she'd ended up in a legal fight with her siblings over the will. As I dug through the God Bag, I found half a dozen notes wishing for victory over her enemies. Some of them were court cases but there were other, more petty disputes.

Kill the raccoons. That one made me catch my breath with its cruel brevity. There had been raccoons on her property for ages. Sometimes they became brave and rooted through the trash or found a way into the garage and clawed at mouldy old boxes of things Mom should have discarded decades ago. For that, she had prayed for God to kill them.

"Jesus Christ," I whispered, staring at that single creased sheet of paper.

I folded the raccoon-murder-wish again and tucked it into the God Bag. There were so many of them. The dates ranged over the course of many years. Nearly all the prayers had been written on white paper, but I was intrigued to find that some of them were red. No other colours that I could see, only white and red. I began to unfold the red ones.

A kidney, said the first one. It had been written in black marker, the lettering somehow shakier than the others. Thick and blocky, though. Determined.

My diamond.

Annabeth.

The cottage.

Cosmo.

I confess that at first none of them made sense to me, not because I didn't understand the references but because they broke the pattern. Mom had fought uterine cancer years ago and during surgery the doctors had discovered that one of her kidneys had been badly damaged. I couldn't remember the details, but I knew they'd had to remove it. Had there been damage to her remaining kidney? Had she feared she might need a kidney transplant, which would explain her wishing for one?

About a dozen years before, she had lost her wedding ring on the beach in Florida, so that one made sense.

Annabeth had been her closest friend for nearly forty years before they'd had a falling out and Annabeth had moved to New Mexico to be with her son and his family. Warm and funny, with a wicked sense of humor, I'd always loved Annabeth and had been sad to see their friendship destroyed. Shortly after she had moved to New Mexico, she'd had a bad stroke. Annabeth survived—as far as I know she was still in New Mexico—but the stroke damaged the language center of her brain, making it virtually impossible for her to have an ordinary conversation. She could still write, though not with the eloquence she'd once had, and had sent letters to Mom several times. Whatever had happened between them, it must have been awful, because my mother never even opened those letters. She put them in the garbage.

The cottage had to refer to the one up in Maine. My father had inherited it from his parents, but Mom had gotten it in the divorce—she said because we kids loved it so much, but we all knew it was just one way for her to hurt him. He had it coming, of course, but from that point on I could never feel completely comfortable there. When she'd reached her early seventies, Mom had started to falter financially. She made bad decisions, took risks, got into a few real estate deals with men she should not have trusted. Without telling us, she mortgaged the cottage until it was underwater, ended up in a court battle to try to save it. That would have been around 2009.

Cosmo had been her dog. An adorable little terrier who mostly liked to sit on the sofa next to her with his head on her lap. She loved the little fellow, scratched behind his ears, fed him, even took him out for a stroll up and down the sidewalk in the days when she could still manage that without having to stop every twenty feet to catch her breath. A UPS truck had struck him. The injuries had been enough to kill him, but not quickly. When Mom had been told he might linger for days, she'd had to make the tough decision to put him down.

I stared at the red prayers, trying to figure out what I found so odd about them. Yes, they were even more succinct than the wishes written on white paper. Instead of *Save Cosmo*, she had just written his name. Instead of *Let me find my diamond* and *Help Annabelle get well*, she'd written only *My diamond* and simply *Annabelle*.

I started opening white prayers again and when I came to one that said *A happy and healthy baby girl for Tom and Alan*, I swore softly to myself. Obviously her wish hadn't been the reason we had Rosie—Alan and I had wanted a baby, a family—but I had thought it was entirely a delusion when she had given herself credit. Yet some part of her dementia-stricken mind had remembered writing this prayer down, and she certainly had asked God for a granddaughter. No wonder she put so much faith in the ridiculous bag.

I stared at that prayer again, touched by the kindness of Mom's wish but also deeply frustrated by the way it had fed her constant need to be in control. I loved her, but her narcissism and passive-aggression had been poisoning that love since the day I was born. As I folded the paper and began returning the various wishes to the bag, the answer struck me—the reason the red prayers made me uneasy.

How had she known?

The red prayers had not been granted. If God really was out there listening to Mom's prayers, able to read or intuit the wishes she placed into her God Bag, then he had ignored the ones on red paper. Actually, much worse than ignoring them, he had done the opposite of what she'd prayed for. You want your diamond back? No. You want to make peace with your best friend? She'll move thousands of miles away and nearly die. You want your dog to live? How about I make him die in agony instead?

Shuffling again through white prayers, I couldn't have said if most of them had been granted, but there were certainly some that God or fate had granted her—that family trip to Florida, a better car, and a granddaughter. A happy life for me and my husband and our daughter. I wasn't ready to credit Mom's God Bag—or the existence of any deity—for our happiness, but the difference between the prayers written on white versus red paper seemed clear.

I stuffed the others back into the bag, but I held onto a red one. Unfolding it again, I stared at the single word there—*Cosmo*. Beneath it, Mom had scrawled the date, as she had on all of the rest. The 12th of July, seven years before.

I couldn't breathe for a moment, staring at the date.

Alan often teased me about how poor I'd always been at judging chronology. A vacation we'd taken ten years earlier would seem only a few years ago. I knew the year we'd married only because I had memorized it. Some dates stuck in my mind but that 12th of July wasn't one of them—I might've been doing just about anything that day. The next day, though . . .

The 13th of July was Alan's birthday, and that particular year had been his best ever because that day we'd gotten the phone call that the agency had found us both an egg donor and a surrogate willing to carry our child. That was the day we learned we were going to have a baby, be a family.

Our joy had been slightly diminished by the phone call I received from my mother that night telling me Cosmo had been hit by a truck, that he'd lingered for hours before she'd had the vet put him down.

I stared at the red paper in my hand and the date on it. The day before Cosmo had been hit by the car. Why had Mom been so worried about him—worried enough to put a prayer into her God Bag—the day before he'd been hit?

"She wrote it down wrong," I whispered to myself. That had to be it. She'd simply gotten the date wrong.

Her bedclothes rustled. Her legs jerked beneath the spread.

"Put that back," she rasped—more of a growl.

I snapped my head up and met her eyes. She didn't look at me, only stared at the red paper in my hand, the bag on my lap. Then she jerked forward, tangled in the sheets, spindle-legs bare as she crawled toward me.

"That's not yours!" she cried. "Not yours!"

The mad look in her eyes made me think she didn't recognize me, not in that moment. But maybe she did, and the fact I was her son didn't matter at all. She thrust out a hand but out of reflex I jerked away from her.

"Give it to me! It's *my* God. Mine! Give me the fucking bag!"

"Jesus, Mom," I said, tucking the red prayer back into the bag and cinching the drawstring.

She snatched it from me with more strength than I'd seen in her for months, then held it against her chest and collapsed at the end of her bed, chest heaving as she tried to catch her ragged breath. When she started to cough, I saw red-flecked spittle on her lips, hideously brown mucus that only hinted at the rot in her lungs.

"I'm . . . I'm sorry . . ." she managed to wheeze.

Exhaling, I began to reply, hoping to offer her some comfort, but then I saw her apology hadn't been meant for me. She'd been speaking to the bag, holding it against her chest as if it were her only love. She'd gasped out her regret, but it had been offered to a faded faux-velvet sack instead of to the son she'd just shrieked at. She'd been talking to God.

Her God, anyway. She'd made clear she didn't think he belonged to me.

I'd had enough for one day. Pointing out the sandwich I'd made for her, I waited for her to settle back under her covers, confirmed that she had the TV remote control, and made my departure. I needed out of there, away from the smell of cigarettes and my unbathed mother. I wanted fresh air to clear my head, but even when I had gotten into the car and driven away, windows open to let the breeze blow in, my mother's screeching voice lingered, as did some of the things she had said.

Get your own God.

❖

Weeks passed. I visited every few days as her mind and body continued to deteriorate. The God Bag had vanished, though I knew it must be under the bed or in her closet. I thought about it often, usually in times when my own mind ought to have been quiet, out for a run or in the shower, but I didn't search for it. Mom had been deeply upset when she saw me holding it, and I decided there was no point in agitating her further.

But her words still lingered, as did the savage, desperate gleam in her eyes when she screamed at me to hand it over. And the prayers themselves, the folded scraps of red and white paper, and the dates. I never brought it up to Alan—he had lived with me through a lot of the pain my mother caused us both over the years, and now he watched as I had to process the war between empathy and resentment that was going on in my head. The last thing I wanted was to have him think I was losing my mind. What else would he think, after all, if I told him the dark thoughts I'd been having about the correlation between the white prayers and the red ones?

But the dates on those paper scraps—the one about Cosmo and the one wishing Alan and I would give Mom a granddaughter—they made the back of my head itch, and late at night when I couldn't sleep, sometimes they gave me a chill. I wondered about the other paper scraps, about what would happen if I matched the dates on the red prayers with the dates when she lost her diamond, or when Annabelle got sick, or when she'd lost her court battle up in Maine and the family cottage along with it. I wondered if I looked back far enough, if I could find earlier batches of notes from the God Bag, if I would find red paper scraps where she'd written down *My marriage* or *My ex-husband*. Had she chosen these things to sacrifice?

The concept of a God who loves you unconditionally and doesn't ask for anything in return except your faith and love—that's a product of the modern world. Old gods—even the early Christian god—demanded offerings and sacrifices, blood rituals, slaughtered lambs. In the Old Testament, God told Abraham to murder his son in the name of the Lord. Abraham was about to do it, too, before God said, *Hang on, Abe. I was just fucking with you. Did you really believe I wanted you to cut your child open and let him bleed out just for my entertainment, just to make me feel good about myself? To prove you love me? Yeah, okay, maybe I did want that, but now that we're here and I see how sharp that knife is, I guess it's enough that you, his father, were willing to murder him for me. And that Isaac will live the rest of his life knowing that. I guess that's sacrifice enough . . . for today.*

And the Old Testament God was far from the only cruel, bloodthirsty, needy fucker. Most of those old gods—and demons, let's not forget them— were happy to bring a little magic to your life, answer your white-paper prayers, if you had the right red-paper sacrifice to offer up in return.

The more I thought about it, the more absurd the whole thing seemed. There were no gods, not in those ancient, violent days, and not today. My stress and anxiety had combined with a dying old woman's dementia and obsession to turn simple coincidence into heinous divine intervention.

On a Sunday afternoon, nearly a month after the incident with the God Bag, I went to spend a few hours with Mom. She found it difficult to concentrate on much of anything by then, but she always liked watching New England Patriots games, so I thought I'd keep her company. I figured she would ask me the same dozen questions she asked every time we spoke and I would give her patient answers, and then she'd ask them again and I'd be a little less patient, but I'd still indulge her. That was the way it had been going lately, and at least that day we would have the football game as a distraction.

That was the plan, anyway.

Just after one o'clock, I walked into her room. As usual, the volume on her TV had been turned up much too loud, but when I saw she was sleeping, I left it that way. Even over the blaring voice of the announcer and the roar of the stadium crowd, I could make out the guttural rattle of her breathing, shallower than ever.

She lay with one skinny leg uncovered save for a thick purple woolen sock that bunched around her tiny ankle. The God Bag lay beside her, but its contents had been spilled onto the floor next to the bed, a small mound of white paper, sprinkled through with the occasional slice of red. I'd had my phone in hand, scanning Twitter for the day's insanities, but now I set it on the nightstand, knelt by the pile of prayers, and began to sift through them.

From the corner of my eye, I noticed a little pile of scrap paper to my left, as if it had fallen off her bed and slipped down beside the nightstand. I pushed my fingers into that space and pulled out a little stack, mostly white but a handful of red pieces, too. On her nightstand I spotted a stubby little pair of scissors and a few thin strips of the red paper, as if someone—the home health aide, perhaps—had indulged her by cutting it up for her, then scissoring off the uneven edges.

A tightness formed in my chest.

Shuffling through the mound on the floor again, I spotted only her old handwriting, back when she could still write in cursive and remember the dates. There was nothing new in that stack, at least not at first glance.

I rose to my feet and stared down at her. The God Bag lay in a pile with a cigarette carton, a bag of fun-sized Milky Ways, and a faded pink sweatshirt stained with chocolate and Diet Coke and things she spit up when she couldn't find a napkin close at hand. I stared at the bag. The drawstring was loose, the bag deflated so that it looked empty, but when I noticed the black Sharpie lying on top of the sweatshirt, I thought she might have written a final prayer.

On television, the action halted. The referees huddled for a conference to see what penalties they felt like calling. In my mother's bedroom, I reached for the God Bag and snatched it off the bed. As if sensing its absence, Mom groaned and began to cough in her sleep, breath hitching. Her lips, I noticed, had turned a deep blue.

I reached into the bag and pulled out a scrap of paper.

White paper.

I unfolded it. Mom had used the Sharpie to write a sentence, and though the letters were poorly formed and some forgotten, I could make out her prayer. *Want my mind back.*

The words, stark and jagged against the white paper, cut me open. My left hand rose to cover my mouth. Tears welled in my eyes and I lowered my head, the prayer dangling in my right hand before I let it flutter to join the rest of the old prayers on the floor.

"I'm so sorry," I whispered. "You didn't deserve this."

She began to cough again, worse than before. I watched her strain to breathe. Simon and Corinne and I had agreed to cooperate with Mom's wishes on this. Machines might keep her alive a bit longer, but by then she would have wanted to die. Thinking of my siblings, I realized I should probably call them. Mom might have months to live yet, but in that moment it certainly did not seem likely. She looked paler than ever, and though her cheeks reddened from coughing, her lips darkened and the bags beneath her eyes seemed to be turning blue as well.

Gasping, Mom opened her eyes. I could see in them the profound shock of a woman who understood, truly, at last, that she was going to die. She had prayed to get her memory back, when what she ought to have prayed for was the ability to breathe freely. But it was too late for any of that. The years of oxygen deprivation had already done too much damage to her brain and lungs and circulatory system. How many mini-strokes or mini-heart attacks had she already had?

"Mom," I said. "It's okay."

What else could I say?

In spite of her panic and the blue tint to her skin, she spotted the God Bag dangling in my right hand and her desperation seemed to grow. Her fingers scrabbled at the bedsheet and she tried to reach out for me, or for the bag.

"It's okay. We're all going to be all right," I told her. "You shouldn't have to be afraid to go. It's okay."

I moved toward her, and my shoe pushed over the mound of prayers. I remembered today's wish, that final scribble. She'd finally admitted to herself what had been happening to her, and she had turned to her old faith. I looked down at the pile now spread across the floor and saw the red prayers again, and the pattern returned to me. The method to her madness. The white prayers, and the red ones.

Her coughing continued, but grew thinner. She managed to speak my name, and I decided the hell with it. I could not stand there and watch her die, no matter what Simon, Corinne, and I had agreed. That conversation had taken place in a time when none of us imagined we would be standing by her bedside when it happened. I couldn't just stand there and keep telling her it was okay.

"I'm sorry, Mom. I'm going to call an ambulance. You shouldn't . . . I can't just . . ."

Words failed me. I felt the tears on my face. I reached for my phone.

As I did, she made another weak grab for the God Bag. I wanted to scream at her, to tell her to forget it. No gods were listening to her. She was dying, and no amount of bizarre faith would save her. Her lunacy could not give her the oxygen she needed or fix her brain.

She stared hungrily at the bag. A dreadful idea occurred to me, a sickness in my gut. I opened the bag and reached down inside. Yes, there was another prayer in there, a folded slip of paper. Even before I drew it out, I knew what color that paper would be.

Red, of course.

I dropped the bag to the floor. When I unfolded the prayer, my heart filled with hatred. In her childlike scrawl, in thick black Sharpie, my mother had written my daughter's name—the name of the granddaughter she had always wanted, the child whose birth had given her such joy. In exchange for getting her memory back, she had offered up Rosie.

On the nightstand, my phone began to buzz.

It was Alan calling me.

On her bed, my mother's eyes cleared. I saw her blink in surprise as her fear abated. She tried to get control of her breathing.

"Mom?" I said.

When she focused on me, I saw the recognition there. The calculation and intelligence.

"Tom," she said. "Help me up. Get the nebulizer and . . . look around . . . for my inhaler . . ."

It seemed impossible, but I couldn't deny what I saw in her eyes, the clarity and knowledge there. My phone had stopped buzzing, but only seconds later it began again, vibrating on the nightstand next to my mother's overflowing ashtray. Alan was calling me again.

I picked up my phone. Tapped to accept the call.

"Hey, honey, I'm with my mom. Can I—"

Alan cut me off, but I couldn't understand a word he said. He wailed into my ear, catching his breath, *trying to tell me.* The only word I was sure I'd heard was "Rosie."

I looked down at the red prayer in my hand.

My mother saw my face, looked at the letter, and the new clarity of her mind filled in the rest. I saw her understand what she had done, saw the moment of realization, of horror.

She tried to scream. Gasping, wheezing, face and lips darkening further, she reached for me and slid out of her bed, sprawling in the pile of red and white prayers.

I ended the call with Alan. It wasn't fair to him. He should have been able to share his pain with me. But I couldn't give him that just yet.

Numb, I slipped the phone into my pocket, turned, and walked out into the hallway. Once I'd left the bedroom, I couldn't hear my mother's struggles anymore. Not over the volume of the television set.

Downstairs, I sat in the chair where she'd spent decades smoking herself to death.

My mother had wanted to die at home, and I decided to grant that wish.

All of her other prayers had already been answered.

THE STRATHANTINE IMPS

STEVE DUFFY

People always tell the truth around a campfire," she said.

"Does this count, technically?" I said. She'd moved away from the bonfire, far back into the shadows, and I'd followed her there.

"Very good point," she said, and smiled. So the things she told me, as the fire burned out and the noise of the festival faded away, and the short summer night wore into dawn—all those things I had to take on trust, and I pass them on to you with that caveat. Some of them can be looked up in the newspaper morgues; some you can Google. The rest, you'll either believe or you won't. To begin with the checkable things:

Amanda's father was the scion of one of the biggest and most prestigious publishing houses in the UK, heir to a large family fortune which he inherited when his parents died within a month of each other in 1969. Forbes, an only child, was then just twenty-eight. He'd been married to a fleetingly fashionable clothes designer who'd left him in between bereavements. She died too, a few years later, in a motorbike smash-up in Goa.

Forbes, left with sole uncontested custody of two children, Amanda (six) and her brother Euan (coming up three), lost no time in ceding day-to-day control of the firm to the board, engaging the first in a series of identikit nannies, and abandoning his Chelsea town house for the old family estate in Scotland. There he embarked on a chemically-assisted journey of inner exploration that derailed him entirely from the whole of the outside world.

There wasn't much room for passengers on board Forbes' voyage. Occasionally, guests would descend on the estate, visitors from London, hippy princelings and princesses, bearded troubadours and their gauzy gorgeous girlfriends, but for months on end the family were used to going without anybody's company but their own. Amanda's childhood played out like a summer holiday that lasted all year round, a storybook world of no school and deliciously safe adventures in the walled grounds of the lodge.

"Dad used to come out of the library once or twice every week," she said, "make a great thing of playing with us, banging drums and leading us around the house like some sort of crazy ringmaster. Or else he'd turn up at breakfast and get us to tell him our dreams, and he'd write them down in a journal. Most of the time it was just us and whichever Twinkle was around at the time," 'Twinkle' being Forbes' generic name for the succession of child-minders that passed through Strathantine Lodge.

The high turnover in Twinkles may have owed something to the lodge's location, tucked away amongst ten thousand forested acres eight miles from the nearest village. The greater inaccessibility of its laird, holed up in the library with his £1000 stereo and his medicinal-grade trips, possibly also came into it. For whatever reason, none of the Twinkles stayed much longer than a season, and so there would always be a lingering sense of impermanence at the heart of Amanda and Euan's dreamlike childhood. Otherwise, they might have thought that nothing would ever change, or would ever have an end.

⟨◇⟩

The lodge was so amazing (*said Amanda*). You've no idea. It was like a dream house that made itself up as it went along, a mad little castle in Bavarian gothic dropped on the Ayrshire coast. I'm not sure the family nuttiness began with Dad, you know. Anybody who'd build a place like that can't have been quite right upstairs, and it actually dates back to some stuffy old millionaire in the nineteenth century. All that dosh must have gone to his head, delusions of Glamis and Walter Scott and God alone knows.

There were terraces and gazebos, turrets and battlements where the piper used to play, at least one folly in the grounds, and a boathouse where a miniature steamboat lay in its own wreckage. Inside, there was a great hall and a minstrels' gallery, it goes without saying, and on every floor rooms led on to rooms, rooms without end, each one different, each one more crazy than the last. We might have found Miss Havisham in one, and the brides of Dracula in the next, and Sleeping Beauty lying on a four-poster in the one after that. There was a big hydro pool in the basement, drained for decades, and unwashed stained glass windows like glimpses into long forgotten stories. Dad was cooped up in the library, happy enough so far as we could tell, and we were wandering around with Twinkle, or more often without her, left to our own devices. This was how we grew up, if you can call it growing up. As if Dad had been dropping the acid, but we were all of us having the trip. Those were lovely, lovely days, and we were so happy: up until the summer of 1976.

That was the heatwave summer, remember? The big drought, baking hot week after week, nothing but sunshine, not a cloud, not a sniff of rain. The lawns were dried to straw, and the whole forest felt combustible: everything smelled of dry pine and crackled like tinder. We were tanned little savages, running around half naked most of the time, and we only put our togs back on when Dad had some guests come to stay for a week or so, round about the middle of July.

His name—you'll love this—was Alge. I didn't know then if it was a given name or a nickname, or his surname, or something he'd just made up for himself. Twinkle and I called him "Algae", because we both thought he was a bit scummy. The woman with him, Lettice, was kind and quiet, and I liked her a lot more. It was as if she existed wholly in Alge's shadow, though, and she hardly ever came out from it except with us kids. She befriended us straightaway, and we let her join the club. Not Alge, though.

There was something about him I found absolutely off-putting. If Dad had taught me anything it was to be accommodating of all different types of people, so it must have been something quite marked for me to react that way. It might have been nothing more than his looks. Alge was a podgy little man with a round piggy face and thick round specs, a long thin hank of receding hair on top and a straggly handlebar moustache. He wore the same loose cheesecloth shirt with a waistcoat over it every day of his visit, and he always smelled of sweat barely masked by patchouli. So yes, it might have been his appearance, but I don't think I was quite as shallow as all that.

There was his manner as well. Twinkle instantly marked him down as a perv, and that was spot on, I think: he would touch you, quite casually it would seem, but for just an instant too long, or in a way that didn't feel right. He would show a little too much interest if he found us on our own. He would tell us stories that were supposed to be funny, but somehow weren't. Kids have a radar, don't they? It's not always switched on—it wasn't ever on with Euan, he was everybody's friend—but when it is, it's very accurate. I made a point of never being alone with him, and particularly never letting him be alone with Euan.

Luckily, Alge stayed up in the library with Dad for the most part. He was doing research, he said, after a trip to Marrakech he and Lettice had just taken. He called it a "pilgrimage", of course: none of Dad's lot ever just went on a holiday. He showed us slides he'd taken of Morocco, and it looked a wild place, the last place on earth, perhaps, but a beautiful place. But there was always a subtext at play, some ulterior motive. I remember even during the slide-shows, he would linger overlong on the naked street boys dancing on rooftops and beaches, draped across couches, sunlight and shadow.

Euan missed most of this, of course, so I took it on myself to keep us both out of Alge's reach. We'd pass the day playing cat's-cradle with Lettice, or folding paper fortune-tellers, or singing songs with her taking the difficult harmony parts. I showed her all around the estate, told her the stories we'd made up about things, and generally treated her like one of our Twinkles. I was keen to drag her out of the house for rambles, but she never seemed to want to be very far away from Alge. It was as if she needed always to know where he was, every hour of the day and night. At first I thought that was just soppiness or timidity on her part, or romantic obsession, which I found pathetic. Thinking back now, it's clear she had other reasons.

One day, I took Lettice up on the battlements to look out across the estate. The firth was absolutely placid, with hardly a ripple on the flat blue sea. The lawns and the terraces were uniformly brown, parched soil showing through in the places where we ran and played our games. Even the pines on the hillside were lifeless, like dried flowers in an arrangement. Twinkle had gone into town on her bicycle, a trip she made once or twice a week, usually with Euan on the handlebars. Alge, so far as I knew, was in the library with Dad. There wasn't even the cry of a gull to disturb the silence.

"It's paradise," Lettice said, stretching back to sunbathe on the sloping leads. She sighed happily. "Does all of this belong to you?"

"Well, not everything," I said, trying not to sound too proud. "All of the shore, and from the line of those trees over there to the folly on the far—"

I broke off. On the path that led up to the woods, two figures were heading for the treeline, walking briskly, hand in hand. One large, one small. Even at that distance I could see that it was Alge and Euan.

I glanced back at Lettice. She was looking where I was looking, and if I hadn't already been spooked, I would have been now. Under her peeling sunburn she'd gone white: absolutely blanched out with panic. It came to me that she'd been expecting something like this all along, that this was why she'd been so nervous. It hit like a gut punch: to realise that Lettice had been on her guard ever since she'd been here, that she'd been more worried about Alge than I'd been.

Seconds later we were both running downstairs. I knew Strathantine like the back of my hand, but that afternoon I ran from room to room, finding only locked doors, unopenable windows. The mazy layout of the lodge, the very architecture, seemed to be working against us. Finally, I dragged Lettice after me to the back morning room where the French windows opened with a stiff creak, and we ran out into the stillness of the afternoon. The hot blank void seemed to swallow up any noise we might have made, otherwise I would have screamed Euan's name.

Ignoring the path, I set off across the lawns. I knew the trail doglegged through the woods, so I reckoned this short-cut would head off Alge and Euan before they got any distance into the trees. Behind me Lettice was running full-tilt up the gravelled path—she was an ungainly sprinter, her elbows stuck out comically as she ran, but she was covering the ground fast enough.

I slipped between the trunks of the firs, and the close low branches scratched ruby-red tracks across my skin. I wiped the blood off, and I could smell it on my hand when I held it up to my nose. Just for a moment, I wondered if something else might be picking up its scent. It was the weirdest thing: I'd been running wild in these woods ever since I could remember, and I'd never known a minute's anxiety in them, nor anywhere on the estate, for that matter. But that afternoon on the path, I felt as if I was being watched, and by something that wished me no good. I couldn't see it, but it could see me; that was how it felt.

I shook myself like a dog shaking off water, trying to clear my head. There was no sign of anybody until Lettice, her chest heaving with exertion, came pounding along the path. Euan and Alge should have been somewhere in between us, but we'd lost them.

I suppose the panic I saw in her face must have been there to see in mine as well. I was about to say something when Lettice put a finger to her mouth. She lifted up her head and—of all the unlikely things—she snuffled at the air. At first I thought this was ridiculous: was she going to sniff them out like a lurcher? But then I realised what it was she was smelling. From in amongst the trees there came the rich, decadent scent of burning incense.

"Be quiet," Lettice whispered to me, and gestured for me to follow. We stepped off the path on to the drifts of fir needles beneath the trees, heading down towards the banks of the stream, following our noses.

The stream ran in a little gully through the wood, around the back of the house and down the terraces in little landscaped waterfalls into the firth. It had dried to a trickle in the heatwave: normally we'd have been able to hear it clearly from the path, but I remember there was no sound of water that day. But after a few more steps, we could hear Alge's voice. "They're all around us, Euan," he was saying.

Again Lettice put a finger to her lips, and I stopped. She raised a hand, made sure I was following her lead, and tiptoed forward. I followed behind her, so nervous I was actually trembling.

"You know, I think they've been in this place forever. It's been a special place, long before there were people. It belonged to them before we came and took it over. The air is thick with them, if you could only see. If you could only summon them. It's a knack, like any other. I can teach you how, Euan, would you like that?"

I couldn't make out what Euan said in response. He sounded as if he was out of breath from running. Alge spoke again, softly, crooning:

"They're always waiting to come to you—you just need to learn how to let them reveal themselves. All you have to do is be in the right space, stare into the fire, breathe in the smoke, and you have to *want* to see them, and they'll always be there. They wrap themselves in the flames, do you see? In the smoke and flame. Stop dancing now. Stop dancing and come to me, and look into the flames. *Azhar nafsak ya tifl allahab* . . ."

I could see them through the canopy of the trees, pinned in a bright shaft of sunlight. They were sitting on the bank of the stream with their backs to us. Alge had cleared a circle about six feet wide, scraped it clear of fir needles and old branches and piled the debris into a little cone in the middle of the circle. The smoke we'd smelled back on the path was coming from several joss sticks stuck into the soil, one either side of him. Alge's right hand was out of sight, but his left hand lay on Euan's shoulder.

"The djinn, Euan. Just as I told you. They'll writhe up out of the flames, naked and beautiful, and you'll see them. Once you see them, they'll always be with you. You'll learn to summon them—watch!" Alge took his hand from Euan's shoulder and reached down into his pocket. He produced a small glinting item: I couldn't make out what it was at first, but then I heard the scrape and grind of wheel on flint, and I realised it was a Zippo lighter. He touched it to the kindling, and I saw flames licking out.

The sight of fire broke the spell. I ran towards them, yelling—and I can still hear myself, how childishly outraged I sounded—"You stupid idiot!" I pulled Euan away from him, and kicked the mess of kindling into the stream. "You could have caused a forest fire! In the middle of a drought! How can you be so *stupid*?"

Alge just sat there, staring at me with a slack grin on his fat face. "*Aljaniu qadim*," he was saying to himself, under his breath. "*Aljaniu qadim*." I dragged Euan away, and stood with both arms protectively around him, glowering at Alge. Just as Lettice dodged between us and began to stamp on the smouldering remains with her wooden Dr Scholl's clogs, I saw one further thing, something I could scarcely begin to process. But it set me to running.

I ran all the way home, half dragging, half carrying Euan. There was no sound from behind us, and nobody followed us out of the woods. "Are you all right?" I asked Euan, but he didn't say anything. He looked dazed, as if he'd barely woken from a long deep sleep. My mind was running in every direction, and I wondered what had been in that incense.

As we broke clear of the trees I heard the honk-honk of the horn on Twinkle's bike. She was turning the corner of the drive around the side of the lodge, and I waved to her with both arms. We met each other by the open French windows, where I tried to explain what had happened. Twinkle lifted Euan up, turned him from side to side and examined him. Calmly, he submitted to the manhandling, still saying nothing. I could see she was panicking, and I thought, had everybody except me realised the truth about Alge? Had everybody been waiting for this to happen?

Not everybody, it seemed. When Twinkle and I took Euan up to Dad and told him everything, he took it all in with a show of polite interest, as if he was listening to one of Alge's rambling tales of old Morocco. Once we'd run out of breath he nodded sagely and said, "We've all got a lot to learn from Alge, you know."

"*Dad!*" In all the years of his comparative failure as a father, I'd never been so angry with him. "Dad, he had his flies unzipped!" There it was, the thing I'd hardly allowed myself to think about until I'd got Euan safe away.

He just looked at me with that bland incuriosity that was his unvarying response to the world and its events, the indifference that made me so mad. "Did he? Well, it's a warm afternoon. Perhaps he was going to take a dip in the stream. Perhaps we all should."

"Don't be *stupid*, Dad," I pleaded, but he was smiling at me, as if by insulting him I'd somehow lost the argument, and that was that. Twinkle did something then that shocked me: I'd almost forgotten she was in the room with us, but she announced herself by tendering her resignation on the spot. She'd barely lifted her voice except in song for all the months she'd been with us, but now she let it all go. She told Dad exactly what she thought of him, of life at the lodge, and most particularly of Alge. I was so proud of her.

"You need to get your head out your arse and look after your children, and you need to kick those weirdo friends of yours into touch," she concluded, and then Dad did something that I now think burned the last of the bridges between us. He simply turned away and ignored her, and he would not speak another word until we all left the room, defeated as always by the sheer inertia of his beatitude.

I spent the rest of that day in my bedroom with Euan. He was unusually quiet, and seemed happy to read or to just lie on his stomach on the bed, staring through the wide-open window as the warm honey light of the setting sun filtered through the room. Lettice came knocking at the door, but I wouldn't let her in. I said we didn't want to talk to anybody; I wasn't used to lying, and I'm sure she heard that in my voice.

Later that night, my stomach still knotted up from hunger and from fear, I heard the sound of car wheels on the gravel drive. Outside, Alge and Lettice's Bentley was pulling away from the house. Dad was standing in the drive, waving them off. After their tail lights had vanished round the corner he turned back towards the house, but I'd already pulled back from the window.

⟡

Twinkle stayed on at Strathantine for the best part of a month. I don't think she was working out her notice: I think it was more out of concern for us, and I'm not sure Dad even paid her for those last few weeks. One day, some friends of hers arrived in a mini-van, and she took her leave of us. There were tears on my side as well as on hers; she pressed a thin piece of card with a scribbled phone number into my hand, and hugged me so tightly it made my ribs creak. Euan submitted to her embrace without returning it, then politely waved goodbye, in that flat affectless way that had become the norm with him since the encounter in the woods.

Euan was a real worry by now, and Dad was no help whatsoever. It was as if they were both retreating into their own unreachable space. Of course Dad had begun that trip a long time ago, probably before we were born, but Euan went practically overnight from being a bright, lively child into a pale and passive ghost of himself. "Dad, he's so withdrawn," I pleaded, but all he'd say was: "Euan is an old soul. He's finding his own centre. You should be prepared to let him travel on his own road. You can't make the journey for him"

Old soul or not, I was horribly concerned for him, not least because I knew that dealing with this situation was more than could reasonably be expected of me. I was, I suspected, a pretty old soul myself, but I was still just a thirteen-year-old kid on her own. I tried my best to look after my brother, having no other option but to play the grown-up. Someone, I felt, had to care enough to guide him on that road, no matter what Dad said.

In a sense my job was all too easy. Euan ate the food I prepared; he came for walks with me, trotting by my side like a stolid little gundog; he required no great effort on my part by way of entertainment. He read his books, he watched the portable TV in his bedroom, and for hours on end he'd gaze out of the windows at the Scots pines behind the house. But he didn't chatter all day the way he used to: there wasn't the incessant string of babble at my elbow, the endless questions and endearing observations. He hardly spoke at all. This wasn't Euan travelling on his own road; it was Euan stuck down a dead end.

I desperately wanted to get him some help, but Dad was inflexible, not to say inert. He ignored everything I had to say whenever I tried to discuss it with him, leaving me with no other option but to carry on trying my best. To what end, though? I tormented myself with the possibility of running away. I think I might have done that, if the prospect of reality hadn't always been so distant from us. Never having seen it for myself, I hardly felt there could be anything real outside the walls of the estate. Where might we run to? On my mental map of the world there was only white space. It defeated me before I could even begin to think about it. I just couldn't do it; though it would have been better for all of us if I had.

One Friday at the end of August, the heatwave finally broke. I remember the black thunderheads massing out to sea, the incredible smell of the first raindrops on the parched Ayrshire countryside. The sound of the thunder was such a relief: it was as if a new dimension had appeared in the Flatland world of the drought. Even Euan seemed to rally for the first time in weeks, kneeling on the bedroom windowsill with the rain splashing in his face, watching as the lightning ripped and stabbed across the night sky. Then the next morning dawned grey and overcast, and he retreated into the new normal of unresponsiveness and passivity.

The first weeks of autumn were as damp and dull as the summer had been Mediterranean. Only into the second half of October did the sun come back, lower in the sky now, all but heatless, and accompanied by strong gusting westerlies. Dad stayed shut away in his library; I took him a meal up each day, which was left on its tray as often as it was eaten. I was allowed to phone the village shop and place an order for a food delivery each week. The van driver became our main contact with the outside world, and like the postman he came only as far as the gatehouse of the lodge. When I asked about a replacement for Twinkle, Dad said he was considering the matter. What was there to consider? It was just another of the unknowns I had to deal with.

I cleaned and dusted around the place as best I could, but in practice I concentrated on the areas we actually lived in. I found dustsheets, which

I made good use of, and soon all the big rooms were shrouded and silent as we retreated to a handful of manageable spaces, like nervous squatters in someone else's house. Outside, after each autumn storm, the estate workers would come to tidy up the parkland, clearing away the fallen branches and stacking them into a resinous bonfire for the beginning of November.

Now and again, the phone would ring, and when I picked up, there was only silence on the line. It was sometimes the case that Dad was too far away—inside his head or outside the lodge—to answer the telephone, and often he unplugged his extension; actually, very few people rang us at Strathantine Lodge. Sometimes, Euan would pick up. Once, I found him sitting with the phone to his ear with a faraway look in his eyes, and when I took the receiver from him I heard, unmistakably, Alge's voice. Instinctively I let the phone fall with a clatter, then retrieved it only to bang it down hard on its cradle. When I'd recovered my breath I told Euan never to answer if it rang again. He looked at me with that same heartbreaking remoteness, and said nothing.

October was wearing on, and each day the dusk fell a little more quickly. All summer I'd relished the contrast between the dark coolness inside the lodge and the glaring blast-furnace of outside; now, I found myself leaving the electric bulbs on in the few rooms we used, or lighting fires in the grates. It felt as if the gloom and the chill were outward manifestations of what had become of our family, and I wanted to fight against them as best I could.

Early one evening, I was looking for Euan. I hadn't seen him since I'd made him lunch: I'd spent the afternoon doing housework, and now it was time for the evening meal.

"Euan?" I called, standing in the middle of the great hallway. The sun was down, and what light there was barely picked out the bones of the mullions in the high narrow windows, but I moved through the shadows with the confidence of familiarity. There was nothing to scare me in all that crazy old pile of a lodge; or there had never been anything.

I ran upstairs and checked the bedrooms, his and mine. No sign of him, apart from the crumby plate that had held his sandwich. I came back down the creaking oak staircase and turned left, heading for the kitchens.

As I passed the phone nook in the hallway, I noticed the receiver was off the hook, dangling from its cord. I was about to replace it when I heard voices coming from the earpiece. Or no, a voice, one only; quiet and furtive and only too familiar.

"Never call this house again!" I screamed at Alge, and slammed down the receiver hard enough (I hoped) to make his ears ring. But who had he been speaking to? Dad was a creature of his library; he just wouldn't have picked up the downstairs extension. There was only one other possibility. And listening now in the re-established silence, I thought I heard something from the kitchens.

The builders of the lodge had tucked away the staff and their various functions in a miniature wing all to themselves. To reach the kitchens you passed through a back parlour where the housekeeper used to hold court, in the days when there had been more staff than inhabitants. This back parlour was approached through a corridor with stone flagging, which opened on to a broad low-ceilinged space. An inglenook fireplace with the family shield in oak above it was flanked on either side by great high-backed settles made cosy by heaps of plump cushions. It was a favourite place of ours: to be sitting there with Euan and Twinkle when the fire was lit felt as snug and companionable as anywhere in the whole house.

But Twinkle was long gone now; and yet, as I paused at the end of the corridor, I could hear voices.

From where I stood I could see only the back of the nearest settle: the fireplace was recessed into the wall to my left, and the settles shielded it from view. The room was unlit, with only the flickering of the flames in the grate to set the shadows at play. The voices, like the firelight, were coming from the deep heart of the inglenook. Had I lit the fire down here? I was sure I hadn't, and it was not a thing that would have occurred to Euan, or so I thought. Dad, needless to say, would never think to do anything so practical.

Still I could hear the crackling of the fire, and mixed in with it, I could hear whispers. They were as soft as the flames that licked away at the logs, and in my heightened state of nervousness they seemed to me just as dangerous. They reminded me of the sound of Alge's voice on that summer afternoon, drifting through the trees, whispering words in some foreign language. But who were those words being whispered to?

The answer came when I heard Euan's laughter. He hadn't laughed much since Alge's visit, but I recognised his happy snigger immediately. How could

I not? It had been at the centre of my world for so long. The voice seemed to respond, or perhaps it was only the rustling of the flames, and that's what made me break cover and dart around the side of the settle.

There was Euan, quite alone, silhouetted against the firelight as he knelt on the stone surround of the inglenook. He seemed not to hear me at first, and I called his name. He turned slowly, almost reluctantly, I thought.

"Euan, who was with you?" I asked him.

He just looked at me, and said after an uncomfortable pause, "What do you mean, Mand? There's no-one here."

"I thought I heard voices . . ."

"Oh, I might have been talking," he said, and turned back towards the fire.

And I felt at that moment that I was going entirely crazy, and I did not walk out of the parlour, I ran.

It's a terrible thing to be forced to consider, especially when you're only a child: the proposition that you might be going out of your mind. And I had nobody to help me through it. All I had was Dad, and I ran to him without the faintest expectation of help or even consolation. The library, ten times as large as the back pantry and three times as high, was likewise lit by nothing more than a log fire. Dad was sitting in his armchair with his feet up on a low table piled with books and papers. He opened his half-closed eyes as I burst in and said "Well?" His voice was lethargic and somehow long-suffering, as if I was in the habit of disturbing his journeys in the higher void.

Now I was here, I didn't know what to say. In some sort of horrible fast-forward I imagined myself telling him my fears, pouring it all out as you might do to a parent who actually cared, and I supplied for myself the languid scorn with which he'd answer me. All I could manage in the end was to ask: "Were you on the phone just now?"

"On the phone." He gave it exaggerated consideration, as if to emphasise the banality of the question. "No; no, I wasn't. Were you?"

"I picked it up," I said, trying to talk around the lump in my throat. "It was that friend of yours."

"I have many friends," he said serenely, and I thought, *lucky you*. "Which friend in particular?"

"You know," I said, and when he shook his head I said, "Alge."

"Alge?" He gave a little snigger, without any real mirth. "Oh, I don't think so, Amanda."

"I know his voice," I insisted. "It was him."

"That surprises me." Still his voice was low and even.

"It's not the first time—he's been ringing on and off since he was here with Lettice. He's been talking to Euan."

"And he phoned just now?"

"Yes!" I was sure of that if of nothing else. "I think he was talking to Euan again."

He didn't answer me. Instead, he reached for the table, selected a newspaper from the pile, and handed it wordlessly to me.

It was a copy of the Evening Standard from the previous week, folded to a quarter-page article. Over a photo of a wrecked and burned-out car, the headline read CRASH COUPLE IDENTIFIED.

"Read it," my father invited me. I got as far as the first paragraph, and then I had to stop, because I thought I was going mad again.

"The driver of the Bentley that burst into flames on the Chelsea Embankment at the weekend has been identified as Algernon 'Alge' Venables, poet and contributor to various journals of the so-called counter-culture. Mr. Venables was the driver of the car, and his passenger is said to have been Miss Lettice Barkley, his partner. The identities of the couple were established at post-mortem, the blaze having been so fierce as to render them unidentifiable by the usual means . . ."

I couldn't read any more. I was biting my lip so hard that I drew blood, or else I think I would have fainted. The taste of the blood filled my mouth as I let the paper drop to the floor.

"Poor Alge." If there had been anger or bitterness in Dad's voice, that would have been understandable; likewise, grief. It would have been the natural response. Instead, he said, "I don't think it was him on the phone just now, do you? No matter how badly he wanted to talk to Euan."

I couldn't answer. I had to believe what I'd heard on that phone line, even if it meant I was crazy after all. But Dad was still speaking.

"Amanda, don't you think you're getting slightly obsessed with being a mother to your brother?" In that same tone, he continued: "You know, if you really want a wee bairn of your own to play mummy with, you could always go down to the village dance on a Friday night. I'm sure there'd be plenty of the local lads who'd oblige." He looked at me quizzically over the top of his granny glasses, and I had to run again. But where to? Only to another wing of the prison, a shuttered room where I could lock the door and cry behind it, and nobody would ever hear me.

◦►

The weeks after that were unbearable, and yet I didn't have a choice in the matter. I had to bear it; someone had to look after Euan. I feared for him in every possible way: I felt as if I was all that stood between him and something I couldn't even put a name to. All I could see was its shadow, that was all, its silhouette against the firelight.

Through it all Euan remained unreachable. Later that same evening, when I asked him if he'd been on the phone, he smiled distantly and said "I picked it up, yes." I asked who he'd been talking to, and he said, "Oh, no-one." So much for that.

Dad, though, showed signs of coming out of his shell a little as October came to an end. The high winds of autumn had brought down all the loose branches in the woods, and a few of the rotten older trees besides, and the bonfire on the old tennis courts was piled a good twelve feet high. The Strathantine bonfire was a local custom, probably the only one of which Dad approved. It was certainly one that he fostered: each Guy Fawkes' night all the local children were invited to the burning and encouraged to make masks, and sweeties and sparklers were laid on at the laird's expense. Dad would give a little lecture about ancestral fire ceremonies held at the waning of the year, and nobody would pay him the slightest bit of attention, and then the fire would be lit and everyone would have a grand time.

This year I was looking forward to the bonfire more than ever. For the first time since Twinkle left there would be outsiders around the place, if only for an evening, and it didn't really matter who they were, they would be other people, real living individuals. Dad constructed a poster that might have advertised a gig by Pink Floyd at the Roundhouse in '67, and I was sent on my bicycle to pin it up in the village shop. Even Euan bucked up, or seemed to: he spent hours with papier-mache and poster paints, designing masks for bonfire night and tossing them into the fire because they "weren't right", apparently. When he finally came up with one he considered appropriate, I wasn't allowed to see it. I took this as an encouraging sign of individuation.

The night of the fourth was clear and cold: the moon was waxing gibbous, and there were only stray wisps of cloud. I was a long time getting to sleep that evening, and I ended up going down to the kitchen to get a glass of milk. As usual, I didn't bother with a light, and when I passed through the corridor into the back parlour I was surprised to see the low flicker of firelight in the hearth. Nobody had been in the back parlour all day, so far as I knew, but a small pile of kindling was alight in the fireplace. As I looked at the flames they smouldered out into wisps of acrid smoke, and the parlour was swallowed up again in darkness. Behind me in the corridor, I heard the patter of bare feet on flagged stone floors, and what might have been the stifled sound of laughter.

Guy Fawkes' day came in bright and cold, a thin nagging wind that tore the last of the clouds from the sky. I spent the day making chocolate crispies and toffee apples for the evening's celebrations, and Dad went out and played the part of a responsible adult with the gardeners as they made the last structural adjustments to the bonfire. Euan was with him, and I took all this to be a good sign.

By half past four the sun was dipping into the sea: I watched it go down, like a great beacon out on Ailsa Craig. For once, Dad actually came and ate with us in the back parlour. It was the last time we were together as a family, and I can hardly bear to think of it now. At six, we went to open the gates and lit the braziers to guide our guests, and by seven there were fifty or so villagers and their children gathered happily around the pyre, the adults in their scarves and gloves, the children in their home-made masks.

A polite cheer greeted the appearance of Dad, on the once-yearly occasion of his wearing of the kilt. He looked, as usual, both embarrassed and amused. I glanced around for Euan, but I couldn't spot him among the masked children clustered around the eats. "Welcome, feasters," Dad announced, his quiet voice straining to be heard above the ambient chatter. "Welcome to the closing of the year gone by. Welcome, imps," and the kids obligingly whooped and squealed, "welcome to the fires of Samhain."

He held aloft the resinous torch, and then touched it to the nearest brazier. The fire bit into it eagerly, and he lifted it again, before thrusting it into the heart of the pyre.

In no time at all the bonfire was alight, and the people around it oohed and aahed and began to clap. Dad imposed a steady beat on the applause with his rhythmic clapping and stamping, and began to sing in a high piping voice:

Circle of light, circle of sound,
Circle of ancestors, gather around,
Come to the fire, come to the light,
Come to the dance on a Samhain night!
Summer is out, winter is in
Samhain night and the veil is thin
Come to the imps as they dance the old round
Come to the bonfire, come out of the ground!

Some of the children took up the chanting, and soon they were weaving in a laughing, skipping conga line around the bonfire while the adults waved their sparklers and clapped gloved hands. Tigers, lions and monkeys, dogs and cats and hares, their masks brought to life in the dancing of the firelight. Dad beamed at them like a priest well pleased with his congregation.

Usually I would have been in amongst them, circling the fire. At this moment, though, I was starting to worry about Euan. The imps had danced past me three or four times, yet there was still no sign of him. Was he with the adults? I decided to climb the side of the hill till I could look down from above and see everybody all at once.

The hillside ramped sharply by the side of the tennis court, and soon I could see everything; but I still couldn't see Euan. The emotional fatigue of the last few months had left me constantly on the edge of panic, and I could feel that formless fear rising again in the pit of my stomach as I squinted through the mounting shower of sparks. Behind the bonfire, away from the circle of light, lay the dark bulk of the lodge.

Not entirely dark.

Up on the battlement where Lettice and I had once basked in the summer heatwave, there was a gleam in the darkness; a lit torch, being swung in circles. I couldn't see from that distance who was swinging it, but I knew it had to be Euan.

For a second time and space seemed to become inverted, and I was simultaneously staring down from on high at Euan, running towards the woods in the glare of the hammering sun, and squinting up through the bonfire blaze in the here and now. The same panic that had overtaken me on that July afternoon came back, redoubled, and I ran once more towards the danger. Dad saw me, and he called out, "Amanda!" but I was already halfway to the lodge.

Inside was dark, and I fumbled for the lights. Nothing. I snapped the switch up and down, but the power was off. As I've said before, I didn't need light to find my way around the house, and I was off running again, dodging the furniture in its dustsheet shrouds, those dull and hulking ghosts who shared the lodge with us.

As I clattered around the echoing wooden gallery, making for the staircase that gave access to the battlements, I thought I could smell smoke, and I tried to remember which rooms I'd lit a fire in that day. None on this floor, I was certain. There was dad's library, but as always he'd have locked the door behind him on leaving. The question was far back in my mind, though, because all I could think of was Euan.

At the top of the spiral stairs, the door to the roof was open wide. It wasn't just the exertion that choked off my cry of "Euan! Euan, are you there?" Panic takes you by the throat and by the pit of the stomach and most crucially by the brain; it pummels your body while it stops your mind from putting two and two together. A case in point: there was nowhere to hide on the battlements, and very soon I realised that Euan wasn't up there. Far below the bonfire imps sang and laughed and shouted, and for precious seconds I was totally incapable of working out what to do next. Into the stunned silence came a whisper. *He came back down before you could make it up here*, said the Sensible Amanda who'd been pushed out of my consciousness. *You need to go back down and look from room to room.*

And, more insistently, *find out what's that burning smell.*

At the foot of the spiral staircase there was no doubt about it: the smoke was thick enough to catch at my throat. I think if there had been any light I must have seen it. Light was coming from the minstrels' gallery, though: the big tapestry that took up one whole wall was on fire. The flames had taken hold of the old thick material, the stag and the hounds being eaten up along with the hunters and the trees. *Oh Euan*, I thought, *no . . .*

Fire at my right. I swivelled round to see a figure with a torch, a small figure, racing along the corridor and darting into one of the bedrooms. Again my mind seized up. I didn't know whether to run outside and sound the alarm or chase down Euan and rescue him. The speed at which the tapestry was burning left me only one option: I had to make sure Euan was safe.

When I burst through the bedroom door the four-poster bed was already ablaze. Keeping my distance, moving around the walls, I checked out the whole of the room. No Euan. How could it be? I hadn't seen him come out again. The answer was in the small connecting door, which I discovered by falling backwards through it.

The door led to a bathroom, tile and porcelain, non-combustible. A further door opened to the next bedroom, which was already on fire. I managed to skirt around the flames and reach the door to the hallway. Back in the direction of the gallery, that small shape with the torch was silhouetted against the orange glow of the burning tapestry, and I thought I could hear laughter down the corridor. "That's not Euan," I thought, even as I raced towards it. "That's not his voice." But I thought I knew the voice from somewhere; and again I got a flash of that afternoon, back in the woods, standing next to Lettice while strange murmurs drifted through the pines.

Long before I could reach it, the figure was gone. I came up with a hard thump against the banister of the gallery, and what little breath I had was knocked out of me. Across the gallery, on the farther side, the figure was moving. It paused and turned to face me, as if we were playing a dreadful game. Instead of Euan's face, I saw the frozen features of a mask.

The papier-mache was painted red, with blue and yellow swirls running up and down it. It had huge white eyes with round staring holes to see through, and it must have been a trick of the firelight, because for a second I thought that behind those eyeholes there was real fire.

"*Euan!*" I couldn't help it. The scream was dragged out of me.

And I swear there was a reply, from somewhere back in the corridor; I thought it was my brother's voice, crying out my name.

The figure on the far side of the gallery laughed again. I could hear it even from a distance. "Amanda!" it called, and I couldn't tell if it was the voice of

Alge, dead in a blazing car on the Embankment, or the voice of Euan, who I loved so much, or the voice of something that has no voice in the rational world except the crackle of hungry flames in dry tinder.

I looked back down the corridor, but the fire was already out of the bedrooms and surging along the walls and ceiling towards me. Euan's voice came again, or so I thought; this time it was from below, somewhere in the great hallway, and I pelted down one set of stairs while the masked figure danced along the parallel flight on the other side, touching its torch to the draperies and paintings as it went. Everything was burning.

I ran from room to room calling for Euan, but I couldn't hear him any more. The sound of the fire was loud now, the roaring of a beast set free and feeding on the dry dust of centuries. Outside I could see people, come down the hill from the bonfire and clustering at the windows to see what was going on. I screamed to them to look for Euan, and ran on. Some of those faces looked like the mask of the creature upstairs, and then when I looked again it would be just another of the village children, close up to the glass, watching me as I ran and screamed.

As on that day back in the summer, the very bricks and mortar of the rooms seemed to be working against me now. Several times I ran head-on into a closed door I'd thought was open, or a wall where I thought there was a door. I picked myself up out of sheer desperation and stumbled on, trying to keep my mind clear, covering my face with one arm to keep from breathing in the smoke.

Back in the hall, I heard voices from upstairs again. Without stopping to look I ran for the stairway, but when I was halfway up a whoosh of flame at my feet sent me staggering backwards, arms flailing for balance, feet unable to find the steps. I must have landed on my head, if I ever landed at all and I'm not still falling, because that's my last memory of childhood and of home; the sensation of falling, and there being nothing to stop me.

◄◦►

The next I knew I was lying on the lawns, high up on the terraces, barely conscious, pressing myself flat against the damp chilly grass as if I might fall off the surface of the earth into the void above. The lodge was fully ablaze, flames streaming from the windows, black smoke blotting out the moon and stars. Dad was by my side, not holding my hand or stroking my head, just staring at the conflagration with all the concern of a curious passer-by. "Amanda," he said, when he saw I'd come to. "You're all right—just a bump on the head."

"Where's Euan?" It came out as a scream, and Dad flinched as he always did from conflict.

"They're doing their best," he said, turning back to the fire. "You see, they can't go in there. The firemen. It's past that now."

And gravity came unstuck, and I fell off the earth's inert surface.

My memories start up again in a patchy sort of way the morning after, when I woke on a sofa in the gatehouse of the lodge. Again, Dad was with me; again, he told me that they hadn't found Euan. All the memories of the night before hit me at once with the force of a boxer's punch; I started sobbing and I didn't stop. Dad didn't leave my side through it all, but there was no reassurance in his presence. He told me I was lucky they'd found me and brought me out, but for my part I wished they'd left me inside, with my brother, where I belonged.

We stayed on at the gatehouse for a week while the fire crews searched the rubble of Strathantine Lodge and the police took statements out of nothing more than habit, it seemed to me. They were unable to determine the source of the fire, which had taken hold with unnatural rapidity. They were unable to say if an accelerant had been used, or who might have had a motive to do such a thing. Worst of all, they were unable to find any trace of Euan, or of anybody else that might have been in there. The fire had taken every clue.

In the end, there was no active requirement for us to stay on the scene; nothing except the sucking, aching absence of my brother, the hopeless draw of the smoking ruins. Dad had been in touch with the family firm, who wired us money to buy a change of clothes and a second-hand car. We set out for Dad's old pad in Chelsea, and all through that long journey I don't think we spoke about anything that mattered. The space between us was unbridgeable.

The flat had been kept in good order by cleaners who came once a month. Dad unlocked the front door and let himself in, as if only that morning he'd stepped out for a stroll down the Kings Road to Alge's place, perhaps, for one of their adventures. "Are you coming?" he asked, when I didn't follow him.

"I thought I'd get us something for dinner," I said, and he smiled vaguely. "Aren't you the sensible one," he said, and turned away, for the last time as it happens.

I didn't bother with dinner. Instead, I found a phone box and used up the last of my change calling the number I'd kept safe in my pocket all this time, written down on the inside of an old Rizla packet. Then I waited in Sloane Square like one of London's dead-eyed street waifs, until Twinkle emerged from the underground and carried me away.

I spent the next decade roaming round the country with Twinkle and her traveller friends, living in caravans and draughty farmhouses and sometimes old buses with the seats ripped out, learning the way the world worked, making friends with other outcasts just like me. It wasn't easy; I kept having spells in which everything became too much for me, and once or twice I almost fell backwards down that staircase for good, but the travellers helped me through as best they could, and here I am, more or less reconciled, the best Amanda I can be given what I had to work with.

Dad never came looking for me. After I phoned and told him who I was with, but not where I was, he set up a bank account and fed monthly payments into it, and in this way he washed his hands of the last of his encumbrances. I didn't miss him much, but I did miss Euan, I missed him horribly. I miss him still.

And on nights like tonight (*she said, staring at the embers of the bonfire*), you know, I still look for him in the flames. I always, always look for him. I never see him, but sometimes there's that other face, the face of papier-mache, the one I wish I'd never seen. If only I could have looked behind the mask that evening, just to be sure, you know? Just to be sure.

THE QUIZMASTERS

GERARD MCKEOWN

Cycling home that afternoon, my biggest concern was whether it might rain. I had just passed Glarryford, with a ten-mile ride ahead of me back to Ballymena. Wished I'd taken a coat, like Mum had suggested. As a muddy old Ford Fiesta crawled up on the left of me, I thought I felt the first spit of rain. *There* was a car that needed a good burst of rain. Would it be heavy enough to clean the dirt off it though? Also available in white, even though it was blue. I looked up at the heavy grey sky and waited for another spit.

"Excuse me," the driver, a beardy-looking hippie in sunglasses that didn't suit the weather, said, leaning his head out of the window. "Am I close to Ballymena?"

"Keep following this road," I said to him. "Turn left at the end and keep going straight. That'll take you into Carniny. That's you on the outskirts of Ballymena."

"Very good," he said. "Is Liam Neeson from Ballymena?"

He had an English accent. This was the sort of question I'd have expected from an American tourist, in a car too big for the road, honking at me *to get outta the frickin' way.*

"He is," I said. "There's no statue or anything though."

"Can you name anyone else famous from Ballymena?" he said. Ballymena is an odd place for a tourist to go; it's not scenic, and there are no tourist attractions worth talking about.

"Eamonn Loughran? He was a world champion boxer. Not sure what his weight class was. Lost his belt there a couple of years ago and hasn't fought since."

"Very good," he said, like that was his catchphrase. "What weight division did he fight in?"

"I just said I didn't know."

"Well take a guess."

I squeezed my brakes to stop. The hippie had his foot on the brake just as fast.

"Guess," he said, not mentioning that we'd stopped.

"Welterweight?"

He motioned with his head at the road in front of us. I obediently began peddling at my previous speed. The Fiesta trundled alongside. The hippie stuck his head back in the window. That's when I clocked someone in the passenger seat. The driver stuck his head back out.

"Very good," he said in an enthusiastic tone, as if he was a true TV quizmaster who could turn on the charm when the cameras were rolling, as if me stopping had been forgotten. "Who's the MP for Ballymena?"

I knew where this was going; he was leading up to ask my religion. I could give the wrong answer, say I didn't know, but these two would make their own minds up anyway.

The best chance I'd have of getting away was if they stopped the car to get out. I'd throw the bike over the hedge and hope the field wasn't too bumpy to ride across.

"What's with your questions?" I said, hoping I could bait him into stopping the car.

Whoever was in the passenger seat said something to him, but I couldn't hear it.

"Do you know the answer?" the quizmaster asked.

"I might."

"You look too young to vote. I don't think you know it. You might as well take a guess though."

"Ian Paisley."

"Very good," he said. I'd half thought of giving him a wrong answer just to hear what his catchphrase would be then.

"Ballymena's not the name of the constituency," he said. "Do you know what that is?"

I noticed his accent slip when he said Ballymena. He pronounced it Ballamena, like a local would. He was from somewhere in Northern Ireland. His beard was probably fake too.

"Do you know this one?" he asked.

I did know, and I only knew because my dad insisted we watch the news every evening, at a time when my schoolfriends were watching *The Fresh Prince of Bel-Air*, *The Simpsons* or, fuck knows why, *Boy Meets World*. Dad loved to shout at the TV when some politician he didn't like was being interviewed.

"North Antrim," I said.

"Very good," he said. "Be a bit quicker with your answers now. Quickfire. Quit this stalling. What party is Paisley the leader of?"

"The DUP."

"Which stands for?"

"Democratic Unionist Party."

"Very, very good," he said, adjusting his catchphrase as if he knew it needed refreshing. "Is politics a subject you know a lot about?"

"Not really," I said, getting ready for them to jump out of the car. "I keep myself pretty neutral."

"That's sensible. Here's a sports one," the quizmaster said, his accent slipping again. "Who's the most capped player for Northern Ireland?"

"Surprised you're not asking me how to spell John."

"Quick now. Do you know?"

"J-O-N."

"Ha ha," he said. "Quit your time-wasting and answer *my* question."

His tone when he said *my* implied an importance to the questions, something beyond this weird set-up, that I wouldn't be able to guess, and he wouldn't explain unless he had to.

In the distance I heard a tractor. At our speed, there was no way we were catching up to it; it must have been coming towards us. When they pulled aside to let it pass, that's when I'd jump the hedge into the field.

"Pat Jennings," I guessed. Him and George Best were the only Northern Ireland players I knew.

The tractor, a big red Massey Ferguson, came puffing out the end of a lane and turned down the road away from us. Even at its slow speed it pulled quickly ahead. I turned back to the quizmaster, who'd been watching me watching the tractor. His grin seemed to acknowledge he'd known what I'd been thinking, as if he'd read the change of emotions on my face at every step of my failed plan, from hope to despair, through flickers of disappointment and anger as the tractor did the opposite of what I wanted it to. Needed it to.

The quizmaster ducked his head back into the car and spoke to the person on the passenger side. I tried to get a look at whoever was sitting there, but in the overcast afternoon, they were in shadow. I couldn't even make out their shape clearly, whether they were male or female.

"Very good," the quizmaster said. "It was Pat Jennings. Most people go for George Best."

Most people? Had they done this before? I couldn't just wait to see where they were going with this. Next time he ducked his head back in, I was going to ride for it. I changed up a gear to make it easier to accelerate.

"What was that you did?" the quizmaster asked.

"That one of your questions?"

"If you like. You'd better give me the correct answer."

"I changed gear. There's a bit of a hill coming up."

"No there's not," he said. "Don't get any ideas about riding off."

I maintained eye contact, without agreeing or disagreeing.

"We can do more than run you off the road," he said.

I didn't want to ask what the more was, but the fact he had admitted this much, that running me off the road was an option, proved I was right to feel unsafe.

"What's your strong subject?" he asked, again in that friendly TV host tone.

"Dunno. Music, Films, TV shows," I could hear in my voice that he'd shaken me.

The guy in the passenger seat said something to the quizmaster. I knew it was a guy by the tone of his voice, but I couldn't hear what he'd said.

"Okay," the quizmaster said, sticking his head back out of the window. "Who plays Joey Potter on *Dawson's Creek*?"

My surprise at being asked a question about something as unexpected as that silly show, snapped me momentarily out of the fear I'd been feeling, then plunged me back into it and held me down deeper. For the first time, my legs shook with adrenalin. I thought I was about to cry.

"What?" I said. My mouth was dry.

"Who plays Joey Potter on *Dawson's Creek*?"

I almost started to laugh. "Katie Holmes."

"Ten out of ten," the quizmaster said. "You're a lucky fella."

"What?" I said, knowing as soon as I'd said it that I shouldn't have challenged him saying lucky.

The quizmaster glanced ahead of him. I realised he'd barely looked at the road since he pulled up beside me. The guy in the passenger seat must have been watching for oncoming traffic.

"Stay in school," the quizmaster shouted before they sped off.

I squeezed my brakes and stopped abruptly. Without realising it was coming, I vomited over the handlebars. Stringy orange saliva hung from my mouth, strands of it resting in the treads of my front wheel.

A fresh wave of panic hit me, as I realised they might turn and come back. I cycled on, hoping to come across a house, a phone box. Somewhere I could tell someone. Somewhere I could feel safe. Only, I wasn't exactly sure what had just happened. Sure, the man had threatened me, or been threatening, by telling me they could run me off the road, or do more than that, and the mysterious guy in the passenger side had been creepy, but really what could I tell the police? They asked me some questions and drove off. I picked up speed, hoping not to see that muddy blue Fiesta coming back for me.

I heard the shot before I saw the body. I knew it was them. It didn't sound as far ahead as I'd expected, and even after the quizmaster had threatened me, I hadn't thought he'd meant with a gun. Even the suspicion of it would have sunk me so deep into fear, the shock of it would have killed me before they'd taken aim.

My shaking hands threatened to fly off the handlebars, but the danger of cracking my skull on the tarmac forced me to hold steady. I squeezed my brakes but going slower felt more uncertain. I started to peddle, then sped up, not processing why, or that I shouldn't. A wave of what I could only describe afterwards as morbid curiosity overcame the instincts that should have been protecting me. I felt strength in my arms as I gripped the handlebars. I didn't even slow down for the corner, and even though I took it as wide as possible, I almost came off the bike.

Again, another clear straight road stretched out in front of me. The combination of a signpost ahead, the clouds, and a distant house made the sight seem like a messed-up face. Like it was grinning or something. As if it was someone from the newly opened McDonald's in town wishing me to have a nice day.

In the road ahead I clocked a bike lying on its side, but no sign of the rider. I stopped beside it and looked around, wondering about the gunshot and if they'd taken the owner with them.

"Who plays Gunther in *Friends*?" a woman's voice said. "Who plays Gunther in *Friends*?"

The voice sounded impatient. A body lay crumpled in the long grass beside the fallen bike. I stepped off my bike, laying it on the edge of the grass, and tried ignoring the unsteady feeling in my legs.

"Who plays Gunther in *Friends*?" the woman said.

I'm not sure if she noticed me, as she stared upwards at the heavy bags of potential rain crowding the sky. She was wearing a baggy top, like a waterproof jacket, black like a bin bag. I wasn't sure if I should touch her to feel for where she'd been shot. I'd heard you were supposed to put pressure on the bullet hole, or tie your shirt round it like in the films, but I froze with my hands held in front of me as if I was about to do something with them.

As my shadow hit her face, her eyes flicked but didn't connect with mine.

"Who plays Gunther in *Friends*?" she said, more frantic than before.

"I don't know," I said. I could picture the actor who played him, his peanut-shaped head bright like a lightbulb, but I didn't have the first clue what his name was. That would have got me shot.

"Who plays Gunther in *Friends*?" the woman repeated, her voice sounding close to crying, her breath catching in her chest, like sobbing, as if she was dragging every breath into her lungs.

"Gunther," she said, alternating with each breath. "*Friends*."

"Gun," she said, fighting for breath. "Gun."

I hadn't even time to make the connection before her speech dissolved further.

"Gu . . ." she said. "Gu . . ."

The last attempt at a word caught in her mouth as the 'u' drew out into a long rattling exhalation. All sound from her stopped. Sirens were the next thing I heard. For all the good they did.

The police never caught The Quizmasters, as they came to be known. The details I gave the police were useless, a blue Ford Fiesta, very muddy. In my panic, I'd forgotten to note their number plate. Others did, and the plates were fake. As fake as the quizmaster's beard and English accent. There were three other survivors. Two passed the quiz, while another survived the shooting. There were five deaths in total, including the cyclist I'd witnessed. Because guns were involved, paramilitaries were suspected, but the different organisations all put out statements saying they weren't connected.

One local newspaper, in bad taste, printed the quiz questions from the survivors. I refused to speak to the paper, so they must have got mine from the police. I'd kept the question about Gunther to myself. Not telling the police, the woman's family when I went to her funeral, or the counsellor I saw afterwards when I started getting panic attacks every time I left the house. I didn't know who played Gunther and could have answered only a few of the questions put to the other survivors.

I couldn't watch *Friends* after that, and it's on everywhere, even still, though the series has long finished. That show will never die, first being repeated endlessly on Channel 4 for over a decade, to being repeated endlessly nowadays on Channel 5. After that, it will move to a smaller channel, something like Dave, or UK Gold. And I'll come across it when I'm channel-hopping, perhaps even seeing one of James Michael Tyler's 148 appearances as Gunther. I might even gather enough nerve to watch Gunther harmlessly long for Rachel, a girl he will never get. The character and the actor both innocent parties. Neither knowing their connection to the slaughter of three cyclists and two pedestrians between Coleraine and Ballymena on that unlucky overcast day.

That small secret nugget of knowledge being only mine, is the tiny, but present, burden I carry for not being able to hold that woman's hand, or offer her comforting words as she died, but also a reminder that I'm only here because of a small set of lucky questions.

Every time I flick on the television, the possibility of seeing Gunther haunts me.

ALL THOSE LOST DAYS

BRIAN EVENSON

1.

I only ever visited OmniPark twice. The first time, my parents insisted we go. My father was—in his own words—a "science buff," and my mother was the kind of spouse who felt it her duty to wholeheartedly support whatever her husband suggested. My older brother and I were, I suppose, mildly intrigued by the park, about the things my father and the glossy brochure he had picked up somewhere suggested it contained. We might even have been relatively enthusiastic, right up to the moment we discovered the park was in West Texas, nearly fifteen hours away by car.

"Come on," my father said when we groaned, "we'll make a family adventure out of it. It'll be fun!"

That first time was a lot like most of the other vacations my father schemed up for us. It started with a long hot drive from Utah down to Odessa in a station wagon whose air conditioning my dad kept turning off during the most sweltering stretches of road. ("Engines are prone to overheating on days like this," he'd remind us as we gasped for air). Sometimes he'd even turn the heater on and then tell us—"Science in action here, boys!"—how that drew heat off the engine. And no, we couldn't roll down the windows, because that increased drag on the car and gave us bad mileage. "If I can stand this," he'd announce from the front seat, casting half-glances back at us as sweat poured down his face, "then you can too."

By the time we reached Odessa, a little past midnight, we were all soaked through and exhausted. We checked in at a little no-name motel on the edge of town; the kind of place people rent more often by the hour than for a night or two. My father had gotten a deal on it, and saw himself as outsmarting the town somehow by not staying closer to the park and paying more. The room's air conditioning was scarcely more functional than our car's had been.

Mercifully, the night cooled off around three in the morning, letting me fall into a dreamless sleep. I only woke when Dad pulled the curtains open and flooded the room with sunlight. He was already dressed and ready to go, Mom too, and couldn't understand what was keeping both me and my brother.

2.

What can I say about that first visit that hasn't already been discussed on countless message boards and blogs? We visited all seven of the Realms. We rode all the rides. We ate lunch—not at one of the sit-down restaurants, obviously, but at the cheapest snack stand Dad could locate on the guidemap.

Was it a fun day? Yes. A little strange, not quite like anything I'd experienced before. Sure, fun, yet a little *off* somehow, too. I remember moments of amazement—a few of awe, even—and moments of exhaustion and boredom. A few times I laughed out loud at how hokey an effect seemed, but a moment later I'd become convinced this was all part of a larger plan: I'd been meant to laugh and relax so as to be caught off guard by what followed.

Our parents' constant presence—by which I mean my father's— made it hard to truly lose ourselves in the experience. Half the time my father was expounding on the scientific principles behind a ride and its Realm, while the other half he spent pointing out what he saw as factual or design errors. By that age, we'd learned it was better to let him run on: if we cut him off or told him we already knew what he was telling us, he'd be bluntly offended and would feel the need to give a lecture on respecting your parents. Better by far to nod along and zone out.

By late afternoon my brother had had enough. To be honest, so had I. My brother, though, was older than me, seventeen, which meant he'd been putting up with dad for two years longer. I could tell by the way he was fidgeting and scowling that he was on the verge of saying something that would ruin Dad's mood—which would, in turn, ruin the day for the rest of us.

We were in the Realm of Time, strolling through the garden of the ersatz Victorian mansion, when Dad's veneer of patience began to crack. He had stepped a few paces away to scrutinize a display of statues holding antique timepieces, and was complaining to anyone within earshot that there was no replica of a water clock—that a whole class of ancient timepieces was missing. When no one paid him any attention, his mood began to darken.

It darkened further once we entered the mansion itself and climbed one of the grand staircases leading to the upper rooms. The mansion's library, filled with leatherbound volumes titled with time-related wordplay, struck him as possessed of a levity inappropriate to serious scientific endeavor. As he inspected some of the most obviously fictional fossils and "far-future" artifacts I saw his nose wrinkle.

"This whole place is ridiculous," my father announced. "We're skipping the Time Machine ride."

"Why?" my brother asked. I could hear the edge to his voice. "We walked through the rest of this Realm. We should do the ride."

"Why? Because time travel is impossible," said my father.

"Says who?" my brother shot back.

"It's just a ride," I said quickly. "It's probably fun even if it doesn't have much to do with science. Why don't Sam and I go on it quickly and then we'll meet you and Mom downstairs at the Conservatory Parlor." That was the snack shop just below. "You can get ice cream," I added. Dad loved ice cream.

My father hesitated a moment, torn between the thought of enjoying ice cream without having to buy any for his children and his ever-present compulsion to control us. When Mom took his hand, he sighed. Finally he nodded.

"One ride only," he said. "And it's either ice cream or the ride. See you downstairs in twenty minutes."

3.

Even after Dad departed, my brother remained in a bad mood. Bad enough that at first I wasn't sure if he'd snap out of it before we had to meet up with Dad again. If he didn't, we'd have a real problem.

We trekked down the tiled hallway from the library to the laboratory, arriving just as a man with thick glasses and wild gray hair took his place at the front of the room and clapped his hands to attract our attention.

The small crowd hushed and listened as he explained how we were about to undertake a great journey—through time rather than space. We would be the first humans besides himself, he claimed, to experience not only the distant future but the full extent of time. He gestured to a wall that had slid silently open to one side of us, revealing a series of wood-paneled vehicles studded with brass knobs and buttons. These, he claimed, were time machines, carefully preset for appropriate destinations. He encouraged us to choose one and step aboard, adding a warning that the voyage was a risky one, and he could not be held responsible for any hazards encountered during our journey.

"Only the truly adventurous need apply," he said. "The meek should feel no shame in leaving this path untrod."

Each vehicle held two people, and so naturally my brother and I clambered together into one and pulled the lap bars down to lock us in place.

4.

The ride itself was, more or less, your average carnival attraction. We began by gliding down a tunnel shot through with lights and lasers, the vehicle shaking and spinning, eerie sounds rising chaotically all around us. After a minute or two, we emerged to find ourselves—so the instrument panel claimed—in the year 802,721 AD, beneath a pale-red artificial sky. Clicks and whirrings surrounded us as strange elf-like creatures, meant to be the far-future descendants of humans, swiveled and bent to their tasks in the same endless cycle. They were Eloi—a name I later realized OmniPark had taken from H. G. Wells' *The Time Machine*. They were, obviously, animatronic creations, and functioned far too jerkily and repetitively to be convincing.

"Dad would have hated this," I said.

My brother gave a short barking laugh.

I should have realized that, as with the other rides, this strangely unconvincing moment may have been entirely intentional—a ruse meant to trick us into dropping our guard. Our vehicle suddenly twisted and slipped down into what felt like a dark underground tunnel. The light had dimmed to a deep magmatic glow. The tunnel itself had become uncomfortably humid and warm. The Eloi we had seen above were gone now, replaced by hairy gray-skinned humanoids that a subreddit would later inform me were Morlocks. Where the Eloi had been obviously animatronic, however, the Morlocks moved with startling fluidity. A particularly sharp smell, not unlike chlorine, irritated my nostrils. The Morlocks seemed to be closing in on us, and for some reason I felt genuinely under threat. The control panel of our vehicle flashed a warning and issued commands to manipulate certain levers and knobs. I dutifully focused on doing so, partly so as to avoid having to look at the Morlocks too closely.

Just when they had our vehicle surrounded and escape appeared impossible, the floor opened beneath us and we plunged down into another vortex of light and sound. This one resembled the first vortex in most ways, but something was different here, too: it seemed more real, more like something I should take seriously.

But after the Morlocks, even this plunge through the vortex felt like a respite. I turned, smiling, toward my brother, to share with him the thrill we both must have felt.

But the other side of the vehicle was empty. My brother was gone.

5.

My memories of the rest of the ride are vague and tangled. I remember craning my neck and struggling against the bar that held me in the vehicle, howling my brother's name. If I could have wormed free, I would have retraced the ride's path back in search of him. But between the darkness, the flashing lights, and the appearance of a new wave of bizarre creatures, I couldn't figure out how to release the bar.

By the time we passed through the final rooms and found ourselves back in the laboratory, I was near-hysterical. When an attendant finally unlocked the vehicle, I tried to climb out and charge back down the tunnel. A pair of attendants stopped me. I must have made quite a spectacle of myself, but when they made it clear they'd call security if I didn't leave, I finally managed to stammer out a few words about my brother's disappearance.

Once they understood what had happened, the attendants began to take me seriously. Almost too seriously: the way they sprang into action made me feel my fears had not been unwarranted. Those visitors still in the ride were rushed to the unloading dock and hurried out the exit. The ride was shut down, and all guests in line waiting to ride were sent away. While one attendant roped a "Closed for Maintenance" sign across the entrance, the other attendant—a rail-thin man with a pockmarked face—struggled into what looked like a hazard suit. Retrieving a long-handled electric cattle prod from a hook on the wall, he hurried up the tunnel, quickly vanishing from sight.

6.

He couldn't have been gone very long, probably no more than ten minutes, though it seemed much longer than that. For the first five minutes or so, all was silence. Not even the remaining attendant spoke.

Suddenly, a series of crackling noises echoed from within the tunnel —the cattle prod, I assumed. Guessing what he might be using it for, what he was driving back, made my imagination run wild.

Then I heard, as if from a great distance, a long, low howl—a sound I could not identify as animal or human.

The remaining attendant placed his hand on my shoulder, and left it resting there in a way I suppose he meant to be reassuring. I realized I had been holding my breath so as to better hear what was happening in the tunnel, and all at once I let it loudly out. The hand on my shoulder tightened, and within the darkness of the tunnel I glimpsed movement.

I saw the hazard-suited attendant, silhouetted by the coal-red lights. He was unaccompanied—or so I thought, until one gloved hand appeared from behind his back, tugging my brother toward the exit. I'd never seen my brother move like this: crouching low and glancing about nervously, gripping that gloved hand. When he emerged into the unloading area, he looked disoriented and exhausted. And that wasn't all that had changed about him. At first I couldn't put my finger on the difference until he came closer, and I saw his chin was covered in a soft, almost invisible growth of beard. Since when had my brother needed to shave? Never, as far as I knew. His face had been smooth this morning, hadn't it?

"Sam," I said. "Where were you? What happened?"

My brother stared back at me, seeming to look straight through me. The attendant released Sam's hand and began to shimmy out of his hazard suit. I reached out and touched my brother's arm. He continued to stare past me.

I shook his arm and called his name, and he blinked.

"It's you," he said, seeming to return to himself a little. Then suddenly he wrapped me in his arms and crushed me against him.

This in itself was strange: our family had never been much for physical displays of affection. I could count on one hand the number of times my brother had hugged me. But apparently his time alone in the tunnel had rattled him. No; it was deeper than that. He was changed, somehow. He smelled different, like stale sweat and grime, with a hint of that sharp scent I'd smelled on the ride.

It wasn't until he released me that I noticed that his clothing was covered in dust, and the right knee of his jeans was torn. *From falling off the vehicle,* my mind offered. He was probably lucky he hadn't gotten more badly injured.

"Why did you climb out?" I asked him.

"They pulled me out," he said.

"'They?'" I asked, but he just shook his head.

And then the attendants were guiding us speedily to the exit, and we found ourselves outside, blinking into the afternoon sun.

7.

By the time we reached the Conservatory Parlor, both Mom and Dad had finished their ice cream. Dad made a point of looking angrily at his watch. He opened with a lecture on the importance of keeping track of time, which rapidly flowed into a lecture on the importance of keeping one's promises. How could we lose track of time in a clock-filled exhibit called the Realm of Time? was the general gist. We must've done it on purpose, to spite him.

I opened my mouth to tell my father what had happened, but my brother reached out and touched my arm and stopped me.

"We're sorry," he told our father. "It's my fault. The ride made me sick. It won't happen again."

Dad drew back a little, surprised to find my brother so subservient. He seemed not quite to believe it, and then he looked at my brother more closely.

"What happened to you?" he said. "Those pants are ruined. Do you think clothes grow on trees?"

He had fallen, my brother claimed, dizzy after the ride, and had torn them somehow. I just kept my mouth shut.

Dad began a new lecture on the importance of telling not only the truth, but the *whole* truth. Under normal circumstances my brother would have fought back, but now he sat quietly, letting Dad's words wash over him, apologizing once more after my father had again had his say.

"Just don't let it happen again," said our father at last, partly bewildered and partly mollified. He gazed around the room and rubbed his hands together. "Well," he said, "What Realm shall we visit next?"

My brother begged off. He still wasn't feeling well, he claimed, and he needed to sit the afternoon out.

"If you think I'm going to run you back to the motel, you've got another thing coming," my father began, raising a finger in warning. But instead of rising to take the bait, my brother said he had no problem waiting back at the Entryway Pavilion.

"But the park doesn't close for another seven hours," my mother said, her voice creased with a hint of worry.

"That's all right," my brother said. "I'll be fine. The time will pass."

When Dad realized my brother was dead-set on sitting out the rest of the day, he launched into a lecture on the value of money—specifically money spent by one's father on a once-in-a-lifetime vacation.

I was probably the only one who noticed that an undercurrent of panic had crept into my brother's refusals.

In the end, our father succumbed. We led my brother back to the Entryway Pavilion, where he found a bench to settle on, and we left him there. At 9 pm when we returned, he was waiting at the exact spot where we'd left him, as if no time had passed at all. He looked up as we approached, momentarily perplexed, almost as if he didn't recognize us.

The next day, he refused to return to the park. He still wasn't feeling up to it, he claimed. Since my father hadn't yet paid for our second day's entry, he was only too happy to leave him behind in the hotel room. When we returned after an uneventful day at the park, we found him seated on the side of the bed, exactly where he'd been sitting when we departed. Again he glanced up in momentary confusion, seemingly unsure where he was, or what he was doing there.

The following day we drove home.

In the sweltering backseat, I tried again to tease out of him what had happened in the tunnel.

"Drop it," he said. When I probed further, he turned to me with a wild look in his eyes, a look that frightened me. Not because I felt threatened by it, but because it was clear how threatened my brother felt—by, what, he wouldn't say.

I dropped it.

8.

After that my brother was never the same. It was almost as if he wasn't all there—or rather as if he periodically sunk deeply into his body and had to be recalled to the surface when someone from the outside world tried to interact with him. His responses were slow, and often he blinked around him uncomprehendingly, failing to acknowledge people and places he had known all his life, recognizing them only after an awkwardly long delay. In those moments, I wondered if my brother had fallen in the tunnel and suffered a brain injury, or if perhaps this was more psychological: post-traumatic stress. At first I tried my best to be patient with him—but the more time passed, the more my patience dwindled. When would I get my real brother back? Who was this stranger who'd taken his place?

"What's wrong with you?" I finally demanded one afternoon when he forgot the way back from the bathroom to his own bedroom. "I know you don't want to talk about what happened in that tunnel, but how bad could it possibly have been? You were only alone for fifteen minutes."

He shot me a piercing look, fully present for the first time in days.

"Fifteen minutes? Is that all it felt like to you?" He considered me with narrowed eyes for a long moment. Then he sat down on my bed and tugged his shirt off.

"Here's what happened," he said. A purplish ragged scar ran from his hip across his chest, terminating in a deep starburst divot taken out of the meat of his shoulder. Not a fresh scar, but an old, faded one.

"That didn't happen in the tunnel," I stammered. "The scar is too healed."

"It did," he said. "I almost didn't survive."

I reached out and touched the scar, half expecting it to be fake, something he'd put on with stage make-up. But it felt real. He let me prod it for a moment and then he pulled away, snatching his shirt from the bed and tugging it back over his head.

Then he sank back into himself and shuffled off to his room, forgetting to close the door behind him.

9.

The next year did not go well for my brother. He'd been a good student, but his grades fell precipitously. Teachers began to complain of his unresponsiveness in class; his handing-in of incomplete assignments, or sheets scrawled with gibberish.

The school's guidance counselor scheduled an emergency meeting with Mom and Dad, convinced that my brother might have developed a drug habit—what else would explain his sudden decline? My father tore my brother's room apart searching for drugs, found nothing. My brother just stood by and calmly watched it happen. But if it wasn't drugs, what else could account for this sudden transformation? Mental illness? My father flatly rejected that notion, since to accept it would imply something faulty about his genes, and that premise was obviously untenable. It was easiest for him to decide that my brother had willfully given up and was simply not trying, that it was a failure of character.

My father lectured, cajoled, screamed, but nothing seemed to get through. My brother did manage to limp on to the end of the year, though, and squeak past, just barely, and graduate. The day of his eighteenth birthday, he moved out.

I didn't see him much after that. Sometimes on weekends, my mom managed to coax him over for weekend laundry and a free dinner, but during the week he was unreachable. When I pressed, he mumbled something about working for a local construction company. He made enough for a dilapidated room in a shared apartment on the edge of town, he said, and he'd managed eventually to buy a beater car. My father would often mumble about what a waste it was, him not going to college, him having given up on life, but my brother didn't seem to care. "Don't be like your brother," my father started saying to me, and before long he had developed that statement into a full lecture.

10.

So things went for the next six months, until one night, around two or three in the morning, I jolted awake, startled from sleep by a sound. At first I thought it might be a branch scraping against my window. But no, its rhythm was too deliberate. I was wide awake now, my heart thundering in my chest.

I got up and crept to the window. My brother stood outside, tapping the glass with a pebble. He waved when he saw me, as if it was perfectly ordinary for him to be standing outside my window in the darkness.

I wrestled the window open. "Sam," I whispered. "What are you doing here?"

But he was already clambering through the window and into my room. I stepped back and let him tumble through the window-frame, landing in a heap on the carpet. As soon as he'd regained his footing, he started pacing back and forth, unable to settle.

"What's wrong?" I asked. "Should I wake up Mom?"

He stopped. "If I'd wanted Mom or Dad," he said, "I would've knocked on their window. I knocked on yours, didn't I?"

"What do you need me to do?" I asked.

He opened his mouth, and then closed it again, as if he didn't know where to begin.

"Can this maybe wait until morning?" I asked.

He shook his head. "In the light it never seems like as big a deal," he said. "It's only at night that I can grasp the full extent of the problem. It has to be now."

Then he sat down on the bed and began to speak.

11.

He had started having dreams, dreams that he was still back there, that he had never left. Could I understand what he meant? How horrible it was? To think that he, or part of him anyway, had never left, was still back there?

"Left where?" I asked.

"The Realm of Time! The Time Tunnel!" he said. He had been in there, enjoying the ride, and then they'd dragged him out. Maybe he'd had one arm out of the cart a little, maybe that had been what was wrong, and either his lap bar hadn't been fully locked—or maybe they had a means of unlocking it. That was possible, because even though they weren't smart, they were crafty; he'd found that out from all those months he'd spent trying to avoid them, trying to stay alive. Because surely I could understand that what had been minutes for me had been much longer for him? And whose idea had it been anyway to build a ride that did something so dangerous—that messed with time?

"I don't know what you're talking about," I said.

He was up and pacing again, seeming to see neither me nor the room around us.

It was real, he claimed, all real. Or some of it anyway. That first room, no, that was set up to look fake so that you'd just assume the later stuff was fake, another ride. But it was much more than a ride. They had dragged him out and attacked him—I'd seen the scar, hadn't I? They'd done that, and he'd been very lucky to get away, lucky not to have been eaten.

"But who?" I said. "Who are *they*?"

"Why the Morlocks of course!" he snapped. His speech was pressurized now, too rapid. They were real, he claimed, the Time Tunnel wasn't a ride—it was exactly what the inventor had said it was: a tunnel through time. The experience that everyone saw as a simulation was in fact real. At first the Morlocks had been kept at bay by the surprise and wonder of the strange vehicles, but their hunger had eventually driven them to defeat the safeguards and pluck someone out of a vehicle, and he was the one who had been plucked. He had lived there for almost a year, hiding from them, running for his life, surviving by the skin of his teeth. "All those lost days," he said, with great despair. And then they had caught him again, and would have killed him if it hadn't been for a mysterious figure wearing a shiny suit with a weapon that sizzled with power when it touched them and drove them away.

I realized then that something was seriously wrong with my brother. He seemed not even to recognize that the person in the hazard suit who had come for him had been one of the ride attendants.

But, then again, why had the attendant had to take a cattle prod with him down the tunnel? And why had he had to wear a hazard suit?

"And the worst thing," my brother claimed, "is that something went wrong. The shining figure was able to bring me out, yes, but it could only bring part of me out. I was torn in two somehow. Half of me is still in that distant future, still fighting for his life. I need that other half back if I'm ever to be myself again."

He was, he announced, going back to the park, back into the Time Tunnel. He'd go in and try to get the other part of him out. If he succeeded, maybe things would go back to normal and he could again be the person he had been before. If he failed, well, then at least both halves of him would be together, even if they were together in a world that was more like a hell. He wanted someone to know, he said, he had to tell someone, just so at least one person would know what had happened to him if he never came back.

When he was finished, he seemed to sink deeper into himself again. And then he clambered out the window, crossed the lawn, got in his car and drove away.

12.

OmniPark security found my brother's car a few weeks later, abandoned on the ground floor of the parking structure. A police investigation unearthed video of him entering the park, then sneaking into the Realm of Time. After that, nothing.

I tried to explain my brother's story to my parents, who responded exactly as expected: Dad furious that I hadn't awakened him when my brother sneaked in; Mom hoping that Sam might have already been found and admitted to a mental facility. Of course, neither of them entertained the slightest possibility that his story held a grain of truth. In the crisp light of that autumn morning, I had difficulty believing it myself.

And that was where we left it. Two years later I headed off to college, and the summer of my sophomore year I found myself taking the long drive down to OmniPark without telling my parents. I would, I told myself, take one more trip through the Time Tunnel, just in case. Just to see if I could find my brother.

But the Time Machine ride was no more. Park Management had stripped out the old ride back in '91, to make room for "Pterry's Time Tunnel"—a ride for children. No Eloi, no Morlocks, and definitely no brother.

I went through anyway, and here and there found evidence of the old ride: the effects that claimed to be pushing the vehicles backward and forward in time were the same, and where the Morlocks had been were still bits and pieces of ruined and rusty machinery that I thought I recognized. Scratched into the side of one of these I thought I saw a crude letter "S," which might, I told myself, have referred to my brother, to Sam.

Or so I thought at the time. To be honest, it was dark and I was traveling quickly enough that I'm no longer sure that I saw anything scrawled on that machine at all.

ANNE GARE'S RARE AND IMPORT VIDEO CATALOGUE OCTOBER 2022

JONATHAN RAAB

"ELEPHANT SUBJECTED TO THE PREDATIONS OF A MENTALIST" – DIR. B.S. STOCKTON, 1921

A harrowing 47 seconds of early black and white motion photography, this film appears, at first, to be a derivation of the popular 1903 silent film short *Electrocuting an Elephant*, but is in fact something far more grotesque. A simulacrum of a large, grey elephant stands at center frame against a backdrop of a labyrinthine concrete industrial complex. Upon closer inspection, the creature is revealed to be an undetermined number of men, women, and children trapped inside a large costume of grey-painted fabric and bound together with lines of rope, patchwork thread, and cloth billowing in the wind or pressed outwards by hands seeking escape.

Each leg of the human body-assembled beast is composed of two or three tall, muscular men lashed together by pig iron chains to support the weight of the creature's bulbous body. The elephant's trunk is likewise a person wrapped in chain and dirty textile, but rail thin and malnourished, face twisted into a painful grimace or the rictus grin of recent death. The elephant's head is a globe of cloth and floppy fabric ears that bubble and pulse with the struggle of those within. Its painted-on eyes and smile are white and stupid, comical in their cartoonish proportions.

Just as the viewer's mind begins to accept the horrific contours of the elephant's construction and its nauseating implications, a black-clad figure enters from the right, movements blurred by missing frames and the degradation of the film stock. The figure raises a cloven-hoofed hand, points at the writhing mass of human suffering trapped beneath fabric and chain, and—

Well, we won't dare spoil it for you.

Agfa nitrate base film stock, acceptable condition.

Two thousand three hundred dollars.

OL' WILL'S BIRTHDAY BASH AND DITHER FAMILY REUNION – DIR. VARIOUS, 1952

A collection of disjointed, stuttering, handheld shots taken over the course of one afternoon and evening at a birthday party. The image is fuzzy and green, as if the lens were coated with a translucent slime. The film depicts dozens of malformed, asymmetrical faces over the course of its nine-minute runtime, all wearing pained, forced smiles. There are shots of a picnic table, home to open, steaming dishes of discolored, rotting lumps of meat and overcooked vegetables congealing to mush; a dog, hanged by its neck on a leafless tree, its paws still twitching; an interior countertop, home to row upon row of bottles of dark and anxious liquors; children, fleeing into a cornfield of tall, leering stalks and rows that run at angles contrary to all sane and sanitary principles of distance, horizon, and perspective; and a birthday cake, its surface full to the limit of burning candles, brought forward through a line of naked, pale bodies, whose mouths twist and lips slap in mockery of song. At its terminus, the cake reaches an amorphous, fleshy impossibility, all mouths and eyes and chipped teeth and bowels roiling beneath the surface of its repugnant, stained skin. Dare, dare to look upon ol' Will in the depths of his cups, at the nadir of his descent, within the apotheosis of his transcendent debasement! Dare! Dare! DARE!

16mm film strip on reel and in case, acceptable+.

Two hundred twelve dollars.

THREE SISTERS BOG

EÓIN MURPHY

Charles Barkley had been missing for a night and a day when Michael's father finally gave in and agreed to go into the Sisters Bog to look for him. Michael waited at the back door; an old army jacket a size too big hanging from his slight frame. It didn't zip up, not since Charles—Charlie to his friends—had gnawed through the teeth of the zip, but it was waterproof and familiar.

He kicked his wellies against the step, an unconscious imitation of his father tapping the mud from his boots whenever he entered the house from the fields. All the while Michael kept watch, eyes flicking from the gathering twilight for signs of the missing dog to the silhouettes of his parents arguing in the kitchen. He could feel time slip away in the tight knot of his stomach.

The dog, a Labrador that despite being nine years old still had the same outlook on life as a puppy, had bolted from his pen the evening before. They had searched everywhere. Up at the school, the old church, even at cousin Art's house, where he had been found the last time, luxuriating in unlimited treats and the attention of a dog starved eight-year-old.

Throughout the search, Michael's eyes had drifted to the suppurating sore at the heart of the valley, knowing that the fool Labrador had gone there in search of fearless rabbits and interesting odours.

The McAlister farm sat on the last dry patch of ground before the bog started. The clean, tended green fields of the valley floor collapsed into a swamp of twisted alder trees, bulrushes, and pools of water that could be ankle high or ten-foot-deep, and you only knew the difference when it was too late to change your mind.

The kitchen door opened and Michael's father, Seán, joined him. The shotgun in his hands was pointed at the ground, its barrel open, the breach empty of cartridges.

"A quick look, that's all." Each word carried an edge and Michael felt the guilt rise again. He should have put the lead on the dog. His father had sworn for five minutes straight when Michael had told him Charlie was missing.

He pushed past the boy, his shoulder knocking Michael against the door, and out into the twilight, his face set in a grimace. Michael hesitated on the threshold, glancing at the shotgun.

"Just in case," Seán said. "Foxes." He didn't sound convinced by his own words.

Michael nodded and followed. They trudged across the yard and into the house field, past the big stone and on to the edge of McAllister land. Neither spoke, each lost in their own mutual silences that had grown as the boy had, grown big enough now that he rarely called him Dad anymore. Michael took an occasional glance at his father, hoping for an encouraging nod or smile to take away the sickening fear that gnawed at his belly. None came. So instead of worrying at the growing and frightening distance between himself and his father, he focused on listening for the welcome bark of an excited and guilt free dog. He was still waiting by the time they reached the fence.

Double strands of barbed wire marked the boundary between McAllister land and the bog, a belt of rowan trees on the other side closing off the view of the swamp. Once past the rowan, the Three Sisters Bog took its time to emerge, like a bruise on pale flesh. The flat land, thick with lush green grass, stirred into yellow and brown hillocks, ground that had never been turned for planting. As the land twisted from managed order into chaotic nature, patches of bull rushes grew and sprouted around stunted alder trees.

Where the trees started, so did the bog.

They paused at the fence, stopping one post down from another to which the dried carcasses of crows had been hung to warn off more of their brethren.

A faint odour of rot drifted downwind towards Michael. Not enough to cover your face, but enough to wrinkle your nose. Michael was never sure who put them there.

Michael waited for Seán to put a booted foot on the lowest stretch of wire, force it down whilst he hauled up the middle strand, so Michael could duck through and then wait for his father on the other side. Instead, Seán passed Michael the shotgun and clambered over the fence. He grunted when he hit the ground, a squelch welcoming his return to earth.

Michael watched, unsure how to respond to not being helped through the wire, the shotgun held with ease in his arms.

Seán gestured and Michael passed back the shotgun and took his turn to climb over. The wire caught at his trouser legs, metal spikes punching through the denim and scratching the skin beneath. He wobbled at the top of the fence as his father watched the undergrowth for movement, probably out of habit more than any desire to shoot game. No one hunted in the Three Sisters Bog.

Michael dropped to the ground, wiping his bloodied hands on his trousers as his father waited impatiently. He pulled a small torch from his pocket while Seán popped a pair of white-skinned cartridges into the shotgun's breach.

It snapped closed with a hollow clunk.

"Right, stay behind me, follow my steps. There's holes everywhere in here and we don't need you going missing as well."

Michael nodded, swallowed, words burbling out: "What about the Sisters?"

Seán glanced into the woods, spat on the ground and back at Michael.

"The three of them will be inside by now, so don't be worrying. If we do spot one, I'll do the talking, you say nothing, understand?"

"Aye, Da."

"Keep the beam of that down and don't shout, okay? The fewer who know we're out here the better."

They trudged across the field, the ground under their feet getting wetter as they went. Michael kept the torch pointed at the ground in front of them, a single bright patch in the growing twilight. The light picked out tangled clumps of grass interspaced with puddles of black water that stretched longer and deeper the further they went into the bog.

It slouched in a long stretch between the river and the road, the ground sodden with the run-off from the mountains that pinioned the land between them.

Trees, willow and alder, had long since invaded, to the point where from the road it resembled a forest more than a swamp. Standing in amongst the trees, closed in by the mountains that loomed above in the dim light and the smell of rancid earth filling his nostrils, Michael felt this place was timeless, the same now as it had been when the Celts had farmed the valley. He watched for a flash of yellow fur amongst the low hanging branches, twitching towards every noise that came towards him.

Michael had been warned away from the Three Sisters Bog since he was a child, the story of an uncle who went in and never came out again turning the fence that separated it from the McAlister land into an impenetrable barrier that existed as much in his mind as it did in the field. Everyone in the village knew the warnings. The bog, and the things in it, were dangerous, the ground underfoot there untrustworthy. What went in, might never come out. Not even teenagers took dares to cross into the bog, sticking to the abandoned church in the hills for their transgressions.

Michael kept behind Seán, following his steps as much as possible, water squelching over the snout of his green wellies, the mud beneath sucking at the soles of his feet.

"Charles? Charlie?" he said, his voice closer to a whisper than a shout. His father turned back to him for a moment, his craggy, scar-pitted face almost indistinguishable in the dusk light. He shook his head before walking on.

Michael pushed through the trailing catkins of the stunted trees that seemed to reach out and grasp at them, their scraggly limbs catching on coat arms and hoods. The trees were sick, their trunks ringed by a thick, layered fungus, red brown plates eating into their silver bark.

It was quiet in the bog. No crows circled overhead and the gentle breeze that had been playing with the grass in the field was gone, swallowed up by the swamp. The flat dead water soaked up Michael's calls to the point that a few yards from where he stood it was if he had never spoken.

They moved deeper into the bog. Overhead, the sun slipped behind the mountains, its heat lost to the valley, and the cold rushed back to take its place from the hollows it had lurked in during the spring daylight.

Michael's breath was a faint ghost in the air.

"We can give it ten more minutes," his father said.

Michael's chest hitched and he clenched his fists.

"Fine." He stamped past his father, snapping the torch up and flashing it between the trees.

"Charlie, here boy," he shouted across the bog. "Come on, you stupid dog!"

Seán thumped after him, a heavy hand slamming down on his shoulder and squeezing.

"Stop, now." His voice was a snarled whisper.

"Charlie!"

"Stop, damn it." Seán scanned the undergrowth, looking for something. "Right, that's it, we're going."

"But Charlie—"

"Charlie'll either come back on his own or not; we need to get out of this bloody bog." Seán squeezed his shoulder harder. "Home, now."

Michael tensed, ready to run into the swamp the second Seán's hand fell away.

A song slipped through the trees and rushes, breaking the quiet with its lilting, cracked tone, the words in Irish and outside Michael's understanding. In the woods, a light moved towards them.

"Shit." Seán raised the shotgun towards the light.

A woman wound her way through the trees, untouched by their snatching limbs, a lamp held high above her head.

She grinned when she saw them, her teeth flat and perfect and yellow.

"Pat! 'Tis yourself. And you brought the young fella. I was wondering who would be out wandering the glade at this time of night."

Seán hesitated a moment before lowering the shotgun.

"Aye, it's us," Seán said, not correcting her when she used Michael's grandfather's name, "We're just out for a wee walk and got turned around a bit." He looked up at the night sky, clouds high above and unmoving. "It's a nice night."

"It is, it is." She ambled closer, one leg stiff and fighting her with every step, pushing her into a stumbling lurch that didn't slow her for a second.

She stopped in front of them, lamp held in the air, half-blinding Michael. She said nothing, waiting.

"Out for a walk yourself, Nan?" Seán asked.

The woman was old, her features lost somewhere in that timeless point the elderly used to reach, back before modern medicine and over the counter Botox, where they could be anywhere between fifty and eighty. His father had told him the three sisters had been ancient when he was a boy, and now they seemed as much a part of Coldwood as the mountains or the pub. She wore a faded, yellow dress, a pair of cracked black wellies on her feet. Nan's hair was a twisted knot that sat on top of her head, pinned in place by a clutch of hair clips that glinted flashes of rusted metal in the lamp light.

"Aye, out checking the traps for game." She lowered the lamp to her hip to show a pair of rabbits tied to her belt, the back legs split down the centre and the leather passed through bone and flesh. Streaks of blood stained the yellow of her dress.

Black dead eyes stared back at Michael. Nan grinned at the father and son.

"This pair will do for stew and the child can get the bones."

Michael looked up at his father. The man caught it and made a slight shake of his head. Don't ask.

"Well, we'd best be going back home," Seán said. "The boy's mother will be wondering where we got to."

"But what about Charlie?" Michael blurted out. "We can't go back without him." His voice rose into a shout.

"Charlie?" Nan asked, her smile twisting into a leer. "Another child?"

"He's my dog. He's a Labrador," Michael said, perhaps seeking support and hope from Nan.

Nan smiled.

"Is he about this height?" She held a hand about waist high, gnarled fingers brushing against the rabbit corpses. "A bit old for a Lab, but still bouncing like a puppy?"

"Yes!"

"We have him in the house. The youngest found him in the glade this morning." She turned back the way she had come and started to push her way through the trees. "Are yas coming?"

Michael took off after her, Seán cursing and following behind.

"Watch your step," she said. "Sometimes the glade takes a bit more than it should." She pointed to her left, the half-rotten carcass of a cow rising from the mire, empty eyes watching them as they passed.

The old woman led them though the bog, following a faint trail of flattened deer grass and moss.

"Just up the hill," she said, gesturing with the lamp towards a low rise that began in front of them.

It hunched on top of the bog, a wart of a hill with a small cottage at its apex, the three windows that faced them blazing with light. Smoke billowed from the chimney, the smell of burning turf faint and welcoming in the cold night air.

Nan huffed her way up the gentle slope, the peak of the hill no more than ten feet higher than the surrounding land. A gravel path threaded its way up to the door, ragged grass on either side filled with the detritus of children long since gone. A rope swing, devoid of a seat, hung like a noose from a tree branch, an abandoned rusty tricycle that was fatally pierced through by tangles of briars and grass sat near the door to the house. Michael never knew the sisters had children.

Seán slipped in front of Michael, the shotgun still held at the ready. He paused letting the old woman gain a few yards. As Michael passed, he stopped him with a rough grip on his elbow.

"Don't drink the tea, don't eat the food, okay? The sisters—" he struggled to find the right word, "—they can be a bit odd. You don't know what they might give you," his voice was quiet, the edge of earlier lost, softened by what felt like fear.

"Okay," Michael said.

"If they ask, say we're expected home for dinner." Seán stared into Michael's eyes until the boy nodded.

"Good lad. Let's get in and out as soon as we can."

Nan stopped at the red door, turning a brass knob on the side of the lamp so the flame guttered out, leaving them in the dark. Nan stepped into the house, turning back to wave them on.

"Christ," Seán muttered and followed after.

Michael went with him. He ducked as he crossed the threshold, the stone lintel hanging above him as if he were entering a cave. There was no hall. One moment Michael was outside, the next he was in the kitchen, its floor lined with old flagstones. A table sat under a green framed window, the surface scraped and pitted, a pot of tea and five cups sitting on it.

The walls were whitewashed, the lime an inch thick and falling in clumps like old skin. A low fire was in the hearth, turf burning in a nest of red-hot coals. Another woman sat beside it, near identical to Nan but for the apron she wore, its threads old and stained. A wooden spoon was tucked into its broad pocket, a jagged crack running from the rim into the centre, leaving a wicked edge.

"And who's this, Nan?" she asked, rising out of the chair and rubbing her hands clean on the apron.

"It's Pat McAlister and his young fella." Nan pulled the rabbits loose from her belt and tossed them over the back of a chair, their heads lolling, dribbles of blood leaking from their open mouths.

"I can see that, Nan. But why are they here?"

"They're looking for a dog," Nan said.

"Charlie," Michael said,

The second sister rolled her eyes. "There's an English name if I've ever heard one. You'll have a cup of tea."

"No thanks," Seán said, quickly. "Not before we have dinner. You said our dog was here?"

"Oh he is, he is. Sit down there, Pat." She lurched towards a dresser set against the wall, its shelves filled with tins whose labels Michael didn't recognise. "I'll see if we have any chocolate for this lad," she winked at Michael. "Boys and their sweets."

Nan pulled out a chair, nodding and smiling, "Sit, sit."

Seán sighed and took his seat, nodding for Michael to follow. He kept the shotgun across his knees. The second sister placed a biscuit tin on the table, its edges red with rust. She sat at the head of the table and picked up the teapot.

"I'll be mother," she said, teapot clinking against the cup, her hand shivering with the weight.

"Poor mother," Nan said.

"Poor mother indeed." The second sister raised her head, her blue eyes watery and shot through with blood. "She died birthing us," she said. "We had to be cut from her."

"She didn't want to let us go," Nan said.

"She didn't want to let us out." The second sister fixed Michael with a wide-eyed gaze. The fire crackled in the quiet. "She died screaming."

"She did," Nan said. "She died screaming."

Silence fell, tea glugging out of the ceramic teapot and into cracked cups stained with age. Nan passed them out. Michael took his and examined it. The cup looked as if it had been dug up from somebody's back garden, the blue pattern faded, the edges chipped and worn. Dirt crawled along the cracks in the porcelain. Flecks of loose-leaf tea floated on the top, swimming in the rainbow sheen that skimmed across the surface.

"Milk?" Nan waved a jug towards them, the liquid inside thick with clots.

"No thanks," Seán said quickly, Michael echoing him.

"How about a biscuit?" She grinned, flashing her flat teeth again and popped the lid. A musty smell rose from the tin. The biscuits bore grey tendrils of mould. Nan offered the tin and both man and boy waved a warding hand at it.

"Are you sure?"

"Wouldn't want to spoil dinner, not after all the effort the wife has put into it."

Nan gave a slow nod, her eyes narrowing just a touch. "Best to keep her happy then." She scooped a biscuit from the tin and scraped it along the metal, shedding thin lines of fur from it. With a conspiratorial wink at Michael she took a bite.

"Lovely," she said, spitting crumbs across the table.

Michael pushed the cup away, the teaspoon rattling in the saucer as it stuttered across the table top.

"So, how's the farm, Pat?"

Seán shrugged.

"Grand, grand. It was a mild enough winter and the cattle weren't too bothered by it."

"It's shocking," Nan said. "Not a decent winter's morning in it. Haven't seen its like in years. The glade barely froze."

Seán nodded and pretended to take a drink from his cup.

Beside him Michael twitched in his seat.

"What about Charlie? You said you had him."

The second sister stopped mid-slurp and lowered her cup back into the saucer. She reached for another cup, and poured greasy tea halfway to the top. Sour milk followed, until it was almost white, little dots floating on the surface like rancid clouds. Four heavy spoonfuls of sugar followed.

"The child is in the back bedroom," the second sister said. "Playing with the dog. Take her this." She slid the cup to the edge of the table.

Michael looked to his father who nodded.

"That's grand. Off you go, Michael. Be polite."

The second sister chuckled.

"Oh yes, be polite. And quick."

Michael picked up the cup and saucer, the liquid slopping from side to side as he walked in careful steps across the uneven, broken tiles of the floor to the peeling green door.

"Don't worry about knocking," the second sister called into the quiet. "She won't care; too absorbed in her games."

Michael steadied the cup in one hand and reached for the handle. The surface was rough, the silver marred with bumps, the metal corroded in odd ways that left a gritty feeling in Michael's palm. The spring inside creaked and ground against metal when he pushed it down, the door sticking a little and needing a shove to open it. Tea spilled over the side of the cup and down Michael's hand in a lukewarm dribble.

The room was lit by a table lamp on a nightstand. A single bed was the only other piece of furniture, a mound of blankets heaped on the mattress. Clutches of animal bones, arranged into the shapes of people and animals and bound with strands of blue bailer twine, dangled from the ceiling.

A hunched figure sat on the other side of the bed, a blanket pulled over her head like a cloak. She was singing to herself, the same song Nan had been keening out in the bog.

"Hello?"

The second sister cackled and called from the kitchen.

"Say hello to our guest. He's here for his dog."

The singing stopped.

"It was in our glade." Her voice was a broken version of Nan's.

"He ran away," Michael said. "He does that sometimes. I have tea for you."

She snorted. "Don't want tea." She jerked her arm back, pulling at something. Then came a familiar whimper.

"Charlie?"

The dog huffed. There was a shuffle of claws on wood.

"Stay there," she told the animal. Another jerk of an arm and a whine of pain. "You were in our glade; you belong to us."

She turned then and looked at Michael. The third sister was another facsimile of Nan. Her face was caked in make-up. Bright red patches of blush blossomed on her cheeks, the powder rippled and torn like abraded skin. Her lips were smeared in thick layers of lipstick, as if it had been applied over and over again, the previous layers never washed away. A child's approximation of how her mother would apply make-up.

"Its fur is mine, its flesh is mine, its bones are mine." She bared rotten teeth at Michael and pulled at Charlie's fur, the dog yelping in pain. "It's my dog!" she roared.

There was a thump of feet and the second sister stormed in through the door. The wooden spoon was in her hand and she started to hit the child about the head with it.

"No shouting in this house!" Every word was punctuated with the crack of the wooden spoon.

The child squealed, curling into a ball on the bed, a gnarled hand raised to defend herself.

Charlie, free of her grip, scampered across the floor and rushed against Michael's legs. The dog was cut across his snout, dried scabs and fresh blood running across the black of his nose. His collar had been torn away and tufts of hair ripped from his skin, red clots clumping together the fur across his back and haunches.

"Poor boy, poor Charlie. What did they do to you?" Charlie's tail wagged slowly back and forth, and he buried his head in the boy's shoulder. Michael placed the cup and saucer on the floor and hugged the dog to him, the fusty smell of the house, which clung to the dog's fur, in his nostrils.

"Michael, get out of there," Seán called him.

Michael obeyed, Charlie sticking so close to his leg that he had trouble walking.

Seán stood in the room, Nan beside him.

"Let's go," he said.

"They hurt him, Dad," Michael said.

"Let's not worry about that right now. We need to get home." He turned to Nan: "Thanks for your help, we'll go out the gate and stay out of the bog."

"Now just hold on there a minute, Pat." The second sister stood in the doorway, the wooden spoon held at her side, the third sister hunched child-like behind, her face covered in red welts. "You know that's not the way it works."

"What comes into the glade belongs to us," the third sister said.

Charlie whined, stepping back from the women in the doorway.

"No, he's mine," Michael said. "I've had him since he was a pup and you can't keep him just 'cause he chased after a rabbit."

The second sister ignored him, her eyes fixed on Seán.

"One of our rabbits," her voice cracked with old rage. "In our glade. The child found him and pulled him from a swallow hole; he spent the night in our cottage and," she smiled, flashing rotten teeth, "he ate our food and drank our water. He is ours. Same as anything else that comes into the glade. Ours to do with as we please."

Michael stood in the square of light from the kitchen, shaking his head, a tear of frustration running down his cheek.

"He isn't, he isn't! Dad, tell them!"

"Aye, Pat, tell us." The second sister looked from the boy to the man. "Tell him how it's always been in the valley. Tell him what happens to the rubbish that's dumped in our hedges, the animals that cross over into the glade. Tell him about the people. Tell him what belongs to whom. Tell him what happened to that wee brother of yours." She nodded towards the bones strung from the child's ceiling, some old and yellow. Michael's eyes fell on a jawbone twisting on its length of twine.

Seán rubbed at his forehead.

"We didn't think you would see us, we just wanted to find the boy's dog, please, just this once."

The second sister shook her head.

"If we let you away, then word'll get out and half the village will be tromping through the glade, getting lost in the mire, tearing up our flowers, taking what's not theirs."

"What if we make an exception?" Nan said. "The McAllister's have been good neighbours and haven't crossed into the glade in many a long year. Such courtesy should be rewarded."

The third sister roared.

"No, he's mine, he's my dog! You can't give him back!"

The second sister raised the wooden spoon and threatened her with it. Her protests subsided.

"But there has to be a price. Three of you came into our glade, we must get something in return." Her eyes fell on Michael.

"No," Seán said. "Not a chance. You can keep the dog."

"What, no!" Michael said. "He's our dog, we should just take him."

"You can try, certainly," Nan said. She went to the front door and opened it. "The glade won't be pleased though at someone leaving without our permission. Feel free to take the chance, see how far you get."

"Jesus Christ," Seán said.

"He won't be much help, the rules were made before he showed up with his doves and alms and being one with the world."

"That's Buddha dear," the second sister said. "But she's right, see how far you get. Or, we could exchange something else. A boy for passage seems reasonable enough. You and your wife can always have another."

Seán looked at Michael and shook his head.

"No, never." He raised the shotgun, closing the barrel and flipped the safety off. "We're going to leave now," he said, "down the lane and over the gate. We won't be bothering you again and I'm sorry for the trouble we've caused. But you're not taking him. Please, just let us go."

"Ach, Pat, what are you thinking? Pointing a shotgun at three old women? What will the police think?"

The sisters shifted closer.

"It's a terrible thing to do to we three," Nan said. "My heart. I thought he was going to kill us."

Seán shifted the barrel of the gun from one sister to another, always keeping Michael behind him.

The child began to weep, tears streaking through her thick make-up, all the while smiling. The second sister reached out and pushed the gun aside.

"You know that won't do what you hope it will anyway. But we're good folk, so how about a compromise?"

Nan nodded. The child shifted closer.

"What about you, Pat? We could have you. Just a night and a day. A dog isn't worth a lifetime and a boy isn't good for much. We're being fair. We've always been fair."

"I don't know,"

"If we wanted to, we could take you all. Dog, boy, and man," the child said. "The boy would be so much fun, I reckon."

The second sister smiled. "He would, wouldn't he?"

"No, it's fine," Seán said. "I'll stay."

"Then drink the tea," Nan said, "and I'll see the boy out of the glade."

Seán's head snapped up. "No, I'll go with you, to see him safe."

"Now, Pat, you know it doesn't work like that,"

He nodded and lifted the cup one handed, a shake running through his fingers. "Take him now, before I drink." Seán turned to Michael. "Tell your mother I had to stay with the sisters but that I'll be back in a night and a day."

Michael shook his head. "You can't, Dad! You have to come too!"

"Just go, okay? Get out of the house and the bog. Now go!"

"Come on, lad. I'll see you and your dog to the road." Nan put an arm to Michael's back and moved him to the door, the dog following along at his heel.

He glanced back for a moment and saw the tears trickling down his father's cheek as he lifted the cup and drank deep. Then the door closed behind him.

THE STEERING WHEEL CLUB

KAARON WARREN

Eddie sat in his car for a long time in front of his wife's house. His hands clutched the steering wheel, knuckles white. He barely blinked, and when he squeezed his eyes shut, the glare of the street lights meant there was no darkness even behind his eyelids.

He let out a breath. In the confines of the car his breath stank; whisky, cigarettes, beer, tooth decay he had neither time nor inclination to get fixed. He laughed; a short bark. She wouldn't be nagging him about that anymore, would she? Not that or anything else.

She stirred next to him.

He unclenched his hands and looked at them.

Something caught in his throat. It was the same feeling he'd had on their wedding day, when he turned around and saw her coming down the aisle, beautiful when she was usually just pretty, walking towards him to say she'd love and obey.

He momentarily felt that same sense of excitement, love, and desire.

His phone rang, his mate Gerry. "How the fuck are ya?" Gerry said. "You were ber-lind last night." He HAD been blind drunk, so much so it was only the last few hours he remembered. The irritation leading to fury.

"Mate," Eddie said, "what a night! If anyone asks, I crashed at yours. Right? Too pissed to get myself home."

Gerry laughed. "What's her name, mate?" and for a moment Eddie wished that's all it was, he'd fucked some slut and didn't want his wife finding out. That'd be easy. He'd done that enough before. He didn't even have to try; women loved his blue eyes, his smooth skin, his cheekbones. They loved his footballer muscles.

He started the car. "Thanks, mate."

Hanging up, he looked at his wife, her hands folded over her head. "Pretty as a picture," he said, and laughed. "Ready for a ladies' lunch with all your friends." She had no friends anymore; they all hated him. Fuck them. And her family were bastards; he would never have to talk to any of them again, thank fuck. A feeling rose, for a moment, a possible sadness, but he swallowed it down, necking a stubby of still-cold beer to wash it away.

Both her eyes were swollen shut, and fingermarks around her neck seemed to pulse at him.

He wasn't feeling much pain. She'd feel it. She'd suffer. She'd deserve every bit of it. He punched a song into the player, Public Image Limited 'This is what you want . . .this is what you get", a song he liked to play loud, so loud. She used to like the band; years ago they'd seen them live.

He floored the accelerator. She reached over to try to stop him, both hands grasping at the wheel, climbing on to his lap like she used to long ago, reaching for his eyes with her long fingernails, and for a moment he was back there in that time, remembered it, and so he died with an erection.

◄◦►

Alex Thompson kept an eye on the auction sites. Most of the club's memorabilia came from these places, or lucky finds at garage sales or charity shops. When he saw the steering wheel, described as carrying "visible bloodstains, fingernail impressions," he knew they needed it.

Alex had been a member of the Steering Wheel Club since its inception twenty-five years earlier. It was established as a place where men could gather and talk about cars without anyone telling them off or making them feel lesser. Over the years they'd filled it with things that made them happy:

framed front page newspaper stories about classic race wins, and photos of race winners, as well as their collection of steering wheels. The idea was inspired by a defunct English club, and they'd talk about that, the famous drivers who'd attended it, and the steering wheels that decorated the walls there. Alex's club had close to a hundred of them now; wheels from famous drivers, including the 'death crash' ones. Wheels from cars that had travelled across the Nullabor Plain, and those that had travelled the entire National Highway. They had other wheels, too, infamous ones like the wheel from a van driven by a drunken mother, in an accident which killed seven children.

All of them carried a ghost of the driver, an echo of what was.

◄◦►

Alex wore driving gloves to buy the steering wheel, and tolerated the sideways glance the two men at the auto-wreckers gave each other. They weren't the brightest of souls.

"Lucky you got permission to sell off the parts," he said.

The men laughed. "We don't need permission, mate. Once the police have done their shit and it crosses the threshold, we can do what we want with it. It's part of our charter."

Alex itched to touch the wheel with his bare hands. "You're doing good work."

"Be glad to get rid of it." Most of the car was unsalvageable. "I don't believe in ghosts, but that wheel gives me the creeps."

Alex handed over a business card. "Let me know if you get any more like it. And you're welcome to come to the club one evening as my guests. See how it all looks." It was easy to be jovial with these men. They offered no challenge to him. They admired him because of how he presented himself, clean and confident.

He kept the wheel, wrapped in a towel, in the boot of his car until he could get to the club, not wanting to touch it until it was in place.

◄◦►

The club was in an old building on a backstreet, a converted mansion that had quirky shops on the ground floor. They rented the top floor. Alex loved the smell of it; motor oil, cigar smoke, good aftershave. The foyer was tiny and really only served as a place for them to put out flyers and promote motor events. Through the door to the main bar, well lit and with converted car seats as furniture. The walls were covered with memorabilia, and in the far corner was the arcade driving booth. Alex had picked up the booth years ago when a games arcade closed down, an 'as is' game. They'd never tried connecting to sound or power, and there was something meditative about sitting in that booth. It wasn't sound-proofed but at the same time felt all-encompassing.

Alex wasn't the only one who saw, or rather felt, ghosts in the club. They didn't talk about it but some of the steering wheels carried something with them. You sat in there, positioned your hands, and you were transported, you felt what that driver felt. The exhilaration, the glorious fear.

Alex sat in the driver's seat of the game. He wanted to experience this steering wheel one more time before he swapped it for the new one he'd just bought. The existing one had come from an accident on the track, the car careening wildly out of control, crossing the boundaries and almost flying over the crowd. Eyewitnesses described it as being in slow motion, giving almost all of them time to run out of the way. There were injuries, people hurt in the rush, but just two deaths: the driver and an elderly man who had drunk himself into a stupor and, people hoped, had not known what was coming.

Alex put his hands on the wheel. The immediate sensation was a stomach-churning one, like you get on a high-flying ride at the Fair. Then exhilaration and, Alex thought, a sense of relief. The members had all felt this and between them decided that perhaps the accident was deliberate; that the driver had chosen to die.

Most of them didn't believe the steering wheel (and others before it) was haunted. It was Alex's stories, his fantasies, that made them seem alive.

The sensation had lessened. Either the ghost was fading, or his echo at least, or Alex was becoming immune to it. Either way, it was time for a new experience.

Most of the steering wheels carried little or no echo. Some carried just a shiver. Others thrust you into the last moments, embedded you in the experience. He had high hopes for his new one.

Useless Euan was the only man there. He stood with his light beer, sipping it as he always did. "How's the wife?" Euan said.

"Oh, you know. She's a modern woman. Thinks cooking and fucking are provinces of China." The joke was that nobody believed this of Alex's wife. "I've got a new steering wheel," Alex said. "You can stick around and watch it go in."

More of a command than a request, but Euan said, "Sorry to love you and leave you, need to go coach my daughter's soccer team."

Alex offered to do the coaching for him. He offered this service often. Euan said, "Err, no thanks," to which Alex said, "Your loss."

He didn't want to unveil the steering wheel until there were plenty of other members about, so with the club so quiet he ducked home for dinner. He'd been neglecting his wife, and club food was notoriously bad, frozen food cooked in the microwave. He returned to the Club after he'd eaten, expecting he'd have the chance to show off the steering wheel and fill them all in on the story of it. None of them were interested though. It seemed they were having a wake; Paul Moss had lost his brother (not in a car accident, although Alex couldn't quite gather how he'd died) and Paul was drinking to excess, joined by the rest of them. They were raucous, laughing and joking, as disorderly as these men got. Alex set aside the new steering wheel, thinking now was not a good time to present it.

A group of women arrived, perhaps summoned by Paul, and Alex enjoyed their company. He slipped off his wedding ring and played the lonely widower: Women loved that. "I miss her, I just want to hold her," he said. He had the air of a military general, but he'd never been one. Pink-skinned, broad across the shoulders but also across the stomach, he smelled of soap. He was a keen hand washer and fuss would be made if there was no soap in the bathroom, at home or here at the club.

There was no female bathroom. The rare lady visitors (always racing fans) used the men's, although the board had to draw the line at assignations happening in there. Plenty of private nooks and crannies for that stuff.

Alex didn't want to bring out the new wheel with the idiot women there. One of them climbed into the driving booth and play acted, but left it quickly, face white under her thick, ugly makeup.

"See a ghost?" Alex winked at her. She ignored him, which pissed him off. This was his club. Who did she think she was? He turned his anger into something else, though, an irresistible, passionate charm, and he wouldn't take no for an answer as he pressed her into the alcove that used to house a telephone, many years ago.

Paul Moss was crying in a corner, the drink and the grief meeting in the middle. The members stood around watching him for a while, disgusted. "Pathetic," they said. "Look at him."

Alex didn't have that last whiskey. The idea of being physically incapable, of not being able to look after his physical needs, was one that filled him with horror.

He showered at the club, wanting to maintain the moral high ground at home. He had no delusions about the hypocrisy of this but he didn't care. When once his wife had looked at him reproachfully, now she looked at him hopefully. That look made him livid; how dare she wish him a lover, a woman on the side, in the hope he might leave the marriage?

Alex got a lift home from Euan. He'd been fine to drive, had driven in that state before, but Euan was there to serve, so why not. On the way home, Alex called his wife.

"NORWICH," he said, winking at Euan, who barely suppressed a laugh.

"Nickers Off Ready When I Come Home," Euan said. The men always liked to say the actual words.

Alex didn't ask Euan in for a drink. While he knew the house would be spotless (it better be) and food ready to eat, he was so ashamed of his wife he couldn't let anyone see her.

Not anymore.

She hadn't been out of the house in what, six months? He thought even if he let her go now she wouldn't be able to. Luckily she'd been a primary school teacher so she knew how to fix cuts and abrasions. Breaks she treated with pain killers. He didn't mind her when she was on those. He could blame the drugs for her unresponsiveness.

She was sitting up on the couch, wearing one of the dresses he liked. Bottle of wine open on the coffee table, and some kind of snack. The sight of all of it relieved him. He really didn't have the energy to put her in her place tonight, if she'd done the wrong thing.

◂◦▸

The next day Alex got to the club early. A couple of members were already there, or, given the state they were in, hadn't left. It was disgusting; Alex prided himself on his appearance and couldn't understand how others didn't. It was the mark of a man.

They watched as he laid the new wheel down and stretched out with tools to take off the old one.

"That was a good one. Loved it. One of the best." This from one of the club's greatest sycophants.

"It's no Le Mans '55," Alex said. He was still on the lookout for one of those.

"What's the story on this one, Alex?"

He told them about the good man who couldn't take it any more, and about the crash that left nothing behind but this steering wheel and a tool box, and their wedding rings in the ashes. The last time they had one like this, it was the drunk mother, with all the kids in the car. They'd pulled that one out after a couple of days; even without touching it, they thought they could hear screaming. "I reckon you go first on this one, Al. You scored it, you get first go." They all nodded. Most of them don't really like touching the wheels.

The old wheel came off easily. Holding it, he got that sense of vertigo, of flying, and it made him feel a little ill. He laid it carefully on the floor outside the booth. They'd hang it on the wall later, between the Austrian Grand Prix winner and the Bathurst 500 Winner. He positioned the new steering wheel, still covered with a towel, and then fixed it in place. He really wanted the rest of them to piss off, leave him to it. He wanted privacy for this, wanted the experience, the first experience, to be uncluttered by these observers.

"Drinks, boys? I'm parched, I tell you. My shout."

That surprised them, and they trooped to the bar, where he bought them all a whisky and a beer each, before he slipped out back to the booth.

He sat in the driver's seat, breathing hard. He wasn't as young as he used to be and even this level of exertion puffed him out. He lifted off the towel and placed it beside him on the floor. There was no passenger seat but there were pedals, something he'd insisted on when the booth was being converted. He put his foot on the brake (an old habit) and placed his hands on the steering wheel.

He felt powerful. He felt his chest filling with air, his lungs inflating, and he breathed out. His muscles tensed; he recognised this, it was anger, his muscles tensing as if some kind of chemical ran through his veins, and he could feel that lessening of thought, the *forget all else* blankness he knew so well himself. His knuckles ached. His heart beat with excitement, and he felt a deep sense of rightness, of satisfaction, but then his eyes filled with tears because there was sorrow as well. If he survived this he'd never stop crying; he knew that. This was why the man had died. He wanted to stop crying.

Then something else, on top of that. It wasn't lust but he had an erection, it was a physical response, a muscle-memory action. Like the times he caught his wife sidelong, and for a moment remembered their early days, how he was taken back to those wild times and he wanted sex again.

It was that.

And speed, he felt speed, and then the coming of impact

Then orgasm

He tried to take his hands off the wheel, feeling the impact coming, not wanting to experience it, but it felt so good he couldn't.

And it was impact and orgasm and impact and orgasm and impact, until something clicked, his hands froze, and he could no longer decide for himself to take them off the wheel. In his mind's eye he could see her, the other wife, thrusting her fingers into his eyes, reaching deep into his brain

He became dimly aware of men around him. One of them was a doctor and they roused him, brought him back to life, but he couldn't lift a hand, could barely blink. He'd never experienced anything so powerful. "Elizabeth," he rasped, calling for his wife.

◂◦▸

Elizabeth Thompson heard a key in the front door and ran her hands over her hair, flattening down any wild bits. She had a roast in the oven (it was Sunday) and she'd made a trifle for afterwards. She had to start early because she couldn't move quickly at the moment; every breath hurt her ribs.

"Hello?" she heard. It wasn't Alex. IT WASN'T ALEX.

"Hello! Hello!" She tried to calm herself. She'd practised the words she'd need to use to save herself, so many times. How to get it across quickly? How not to sound insane? She'd considered simply asking for a lift somewhere, to the shops, making sure she had her handbag with wallet and passport, which he'd never taken from her, and her pills, ready to go with just that.

"Mrs. Thompson?"

What could she say? What words could she use? Two men stood in the doorway, from the Club, she thought, with their Hardie 500 T-shirts, their Peter Brock caps. What could she say to THEM, her husband's friends? Then she saw their faces; the pity, the shock, the horror, and she knew she wouldn't have to say anything at all.

The relief at not having to explain made her cry.

◂◦▸

Paul ushered Mrs. Thompson out the back door while Euan helped Alex in the front. He could barely walk and Euan didn't want to touch him. The doctor said take him home, put him to bed, but Euan wasn't going upstairs. He wasn't touching this man any more than he had to. "What sort of cunt are you?" Euan said. "Ay? Who does that to a good woman? Who does that to anyone?"

He sat Alex in an armchair. Alex grabbed his wrist, starting to regain himself, starting to remember who he was. His eyes ached; he could feel that woman's fingers in them and was sure he was bleeding, but when he haltingly reached for his face, he found tears, not blood.

◂◦▸

Euan and Paul returned that night with the steering wheel. Alex had managed to get himself a beer, and there were some crusts of bread at his feet. He was back in the armchair, fumbling with the remote, wanting to watch the racing, the race.

Euan unwrapped the steering wheel. "We all decided you can have this. None of us want it. We never have. And you're not welcome back at the club, Alex. And it'll be the nurses looking after you, not us. Not your wife."

Paul appeared from upstairs, carrying two heavy suitcases. "I think I got everything she wanted," he told Euan.

Euan placed Alex's hands on the wheel. Alex shook his head, half shook it, but then the sensation over took him and there was nothing else

◂◦▸

Alex called for help but none came. No one organised the nurses or anyone else for him.

He died and orgasmed and cried and the impact and the fingers in his eyes, and he died and orgasmed and cried and the impact and the fingers in his eyes

He called for help

He would be found. In all of it, he knew he would be found, filthy, rotting, and they'd say, what sort of man dies like that, with no one to love him?

He died and orgasmed and cried and the impact and the fingers in his eyes, and he died and orgasmed and cried and the impact and the fingers in his eyes/guilt/sorrow/death/orgasm/

He wondered who would touch the wheel next and would they feel him, too. Would he be, at least, remembered there?

The pain was worse each time, and the fear. Now he got it. How this shit could build up. How it wasn't a single event, it was a series of them, and the more of them the worse the next one would feel.

He felt the loss of the future. All he was supposed to be.

They would find him like this. That was worse than the pain and the fear, the guilt, the sorrow, the death/orgasm/death/orgasm, the blindness of her fingers in his eyes.

They would say, this nobody. This unloved man.

This powerless man.

This forgotten man.

THE KING OF STONES

SIMON STRANTZAS

Judith regretted letting Rose talk her into the car trip. It was a huge mistake; she knew as soon as she agreed to it, but there was no snatching the words back. Not without causing a rift between them. So she swallowed her regret and assured herself it would be fine. How wrong could it go? Two days later she knew, silently fuming behind the wheel, stuck in a line of traffic with no visible end. And there were still four more days of vacation left ahead of them.

The worst part was Rose appeared unfazed. She sat in the passenger seat, feet on the dashboard so Judith couldn't help but be confronted by those gnarled, twisted toes as she looked through the windshield. Rose whistled and hummed as though the two of them were strolling through a park. As though it were a bright, lazy Sunday morning at home, and there were no troubles anywhere in the world.

Judith wanted to hit something. Instead, she sighed deeply.

Rose looked up from under her sun hat.

"Don't let it stress you out, love. This is part of the adventure. Just try to relax."

Judith took another deep breath. Held it. But was overwhelmed by how much longer they'd be stuck.

"Screw this," she said. "I'm getting off the highway."

"But we're in the middle of traffic. How——"

"Just watch me."

She signaled, more out of habit than courtesy, and forced her way to the furthest lane amid a chorus of honks and curses. There, she took the car onto the shoulder and put the pedal down. Rose pressed herself flat in terror while Judith navigated the slalom between concrete walls and other cars, inches of leeway on either side. If Rose said something, Judith couldn't hear it. Not within her haze of anger. And it wasn't until they reached the exit and left the traffic snarl behind that either of them could relax enough to speak.

"That was . . . dangerous."

"It all worked out. Nobody was hurt."

Rose's calm was slow to return.

"Do you even know where we are?"

Judith didn't. She hadn't made note of the exit, nor did she see any street signs that might help them find the exit on a map. But she had a quick plan.

"All we need to do is drive around the traffic. If we follow the highway using side streets and roads, eventually we'll get to a place where whatever caused the tangle is gone, and we can get back on. Meanwhile, we get to see some more small towns and scenery. And should we end up loving a place, we'll just stay over for a night. That's the whole point of this trip, isn't it? To explore?"

"Yes," Rose hedged. "Though I was hoping we'd reach Murtaugh before we stopped. This will put us behind schedule." She took a moment to ponder the idea. "Ah, who cares? Let's just go and see what happens!"

How had they ended up together? Judith was still amazed. They experienced the world so differently. Rose with her hippie skirts and positive thinking, Judith in her black Slits T-shirt and blurry tattoos; they didn't look like they lived in the same universe, let alone knew each other. And yet when her ex-girlfriend Kim introduced them at a Bikini Kill show twenty years ago—back when Judith was writing music reviews for Idaho's second-most popular alt newspaper, and Rose was irregularly publishing her photocopied zine—Judith was blinded by a light that pierced right through her darkness. Even if she didn't always appreciate Rose, part of her knew how much she needed her. It was impossible to put into words how much.

They drove along wooded streets and past untended fields, trying to keep the highway in view as regularly as possible. When it looked to be going north, they drove north. When it appeared to veer west, they too veered west. Sometimes they saw it snake through the woods for a stretch of a few miles—always backed up with red lights—sometimes not for a long while. And eventually they stopped seeing it altogether.

"Maybe the road curved without us realizing it?"

"It's okay, love," Rose said in that supportive voice that made Judith feel like an infant. "Should we stop and ask somebody for directions?"

"Who are we going to ask?"

Rose was optimistic they'd find someone, but Judith knew they hadn't seen a single person since exiting the highway. At first it was satisfying: to not be caught in the grinding traffic, driving freely without anyone in the way, made Judith feel liberated. Even stoplights seemed foreign. But after a time it grew uncomfortable. Nobody walked along the side of the road. No one passed them, driving in the opposite direction. Nobody at all.

Even stranger, there were no houses along the streets. No postboxes or signs. There was the road and there was nothing else, not even a place to refuel if needed.

It wasn't until half an hour passed that they saw proof they weren't alone. Rose was the one who spotted it because of course she was. She grew immediately excited, dancing in her seat, and urged Judith to pull over without explaining why. Judith did so, but only because the aimless driving was starting to affect her mood for the worse. Getting out of the car, if only for a moment to stretch her legs, might fill Judith's reserves for another hour.

But Rose had seen more. As soon as the car stopped, she leaped out and jogged to the edge of the road, beyond which the ground gently sloped away. She stood there, yellow sundress rippling in the breeze, and put her hand to the brim of her enormous hat.

"I knew it," she said, pointing into the distance. "Those are peach trees!"

◄◦►

They left the car behind as they walked downslope toward the orchard. There were almost two dozen trees, arranged in three rows, surrounded by thinning woods. Rose had grabbed her camera from the trunk, so Judith did her best to tolerate the occasional pauses for photographs of drifting pink blossoms and petals. The day was nearing its warmest and brightest, and Judith was starting to burn beneath her black T-shirt. She regretted not bringing a better pair of shoes for walking through grass and dirt as she'd expected to spend most of the trip on sidewalks and pavement. Her military boots were too cumbersome, and the extra weight she'd put on since she and Rose had met wasn't helping. Besides, if Rose could handle the trek in a pair of open-toed sandals, then surely she could.

When they reached the peach trees, Rose laughed effervescently, and held out her hands as though the petals were snowflakes. All Judith noticed were the fallen peaches littering the ground. Every footstep was precariously close to rot, and she wondered if that was supposed to mean something more than it did.

At the far end of the plot, they made an unexpected discovery. Hidden from the road was one more peach tree. It had been felled at some point in the past, though it wasn't clear by what. It was much larger than the others, yet they remained upright while it lay on its side, not just toppled but uprooted as well.

"This thing is huge," Rose said. "I can't even tell how tall it was."

She paused, taking the sight in, before excitedly adding, "Get a photo of me with it!"

Judith accepted the camera begrudgingly. Waved her onward.

"I guess go to the uprooted end. It will probably be more interesting."

"But you won't see how tall the tree is." Rose said, pouting from beneath her wide brim.

Judith choked down her disinterest.

"Maybe, but you'll see how thick it is. You can count the rings. Isn't that almost as good?"

For Rose, it was.

They took measured steps around the fallen tree, careful to avoid the crown's dried branches that jutted like spears toward them. Judith reached for the massive trunk for balance and was repulsed; it was like putting her hand on a decaying wet sponge. When the two of them reached the foot of the tree, the sight was astonishing. The roots pulled from the ground were splayed like dozens of fingers, twisted and woven into gnarled knots and patterns. Untold years of weather had stripped away any loose dirt, leaving plenty of room for the spiders and insects to build permanent homes.

"What is that?" Rose asked. Judith peered around the tangled roots.

It was a small cast-iron pot, worn and weathered, sitting knee-high on a slice of tree stump. Around it the ground had been trodden down to the dirt, and there were two larger indentations that couldn't have been footprints. Judith thought they might have been made by someone's knees.

The pot appeared to be filled with black peach stones, each wrinkled and hard. Judith imagined whoever harvested the peaches would eat one on occasion, but it was baffling why they would bother saving the stones.

"Whoa . . ." Rose said, staring into the fallen tree's roots.

Judith turned, and was equally dumbstruck.

The roots had clearly grown randomly and naturally, but nevertheless they'd miraculously woven into an illusion that could be seen only when standing directly in front of the pot. The way they bent and twisted created the illusion of a man seated with eyes closed, his beard twisted into tendrils. The image was rough and gnarled, but there was no mistaking what it was. Judith stepped closer to better examine how the trick worked, but as she did the figure returned to being a shapeless collection of roots. A step back allowed the illusion to regain its shape.

"That's the most incredible thing I've ever seen," Rose said. Even Judith had to agree. "Take the photo so I can show everybody when we get home. No one's going to believe it!"

She bounded in front of the trunk, then straightened her sundress and adjusted her hat so her face found the light.

Rose's hair caught the sun and wouldn't let it go; a corona enveloping her like a halo. Judith was breathless when she saw it—a deep and sudden remembrance of how much she truly loved her. Despite the irritations and minor disagreements, she was lucky to be with her. Judith was so overwhelmed she nearly forgot to raise the camera, and when she did the lens captured the waves emanating from Rose like something by Vermeer. What the camera didn't capture, however, was the illusion of the rooted man. Even when Judith knelt down beside the pot, or tried different angles, the results were the same. The camera saw Rose, but could not see him.

"Photos flatten everything," Rose eventually said, as though the words were meant to comfort Judith, not mollify her. But it didn't help; Judith's inability to capture the illusion was too frustrating. "It's probably better this way. More special. You and I will remember this moment even if we don't have any pictures."

"I'm sure we will," she said, deciding she no longer cared. "We should probably go now. Find the highway before we lose more of the day."

"Okay," Rose said. "Just let me do one thing."

While Judith waited, Rose kicked at the rotten peaches in the dirt, looking through their scattered remains. When she found a suitably dark stone, she picked it up and rubbed it between her hands to flay any remaining flesh, then walked to the pot, knelt down in the worn spots, and laced her fingers together as if in prayer, the stone between her palms. She whispered something into her hands before dropping the stone into the pot. She then stood and let her dress fall back to her feet.

"For luck," she said.

Judith rolled her eyes.

—◦—

The return journey to the car was worse because they walked uphill into the sun. Rose still had boundless energy, taking more photographs of the peach trees and their blossoms, while Judith trudged behind wishing they'd never left the house. She couldn't help but wonder where they'd be now if they hadn't taken that off-ramp. Probably already in Murtaugh, sipping a drink on a patio.

"Hey, someone else has pulled over," Rose said, and Judith looked up to see a small truck parked next to theirs. It was old, a pale shade of blue, and two silhouetted people stood on the edge of the road looking out over it. Judith couldn't get a clear look at the pair with the sun at their backs, but she suspected they were an older couple by the shape of their shadows.

"I bet they saw the peach trees and stopped, too," Rose said. "Those blossoms really are beautiful. Where do you think they're headed?"

"Does it matter?" Judith said. "It's not like we're going to see them again anyway."

Rose stopped. Slumped her shoulders, and turned to face Judith. The look on her face was unexpectedly halting.

"Why do you have to be like that?"

"Like what?"

"Like . . . like you are. Always so negative about everything. Don't you care about me?"

"What? Of course I do."

"It affects me, you know. I try to not let it. I try to be cheerful for the both of us. I try to keep us happy. But you make it so hard sometimes. It's like you're trying to ruin things. I feel like . . . like . . . like you're emitting bad vibes or something. All this negative energy radiating from you that I constantly absorb, and I don't know how much longer I can do it. Do you get what I'm saying? I don't know how much more I can take on."

Judith didn't know what to say. The shock of Rose's confession was disorienting, and her first instinct was to question what she'd done wrong. But she hadn't done anything. She wasn't at fault.

"I don't know what you're talking about. I'm not being negative. I'm just being me. This is who I've always been. You used to tell me you liked that about me. That I wasn't fake."

"It's not about being real or fake. It's about not treating me like your emotional punching bag."

"I really think you're blowing this out of proportion."

That was too much. Rose sputtered, threw up her hands, and stormed off toward the car. Judith felt irritated; the couple on the road probably saw the whole exchange and was judging them.

She let Rose get a minute or two ahead before following. A short break would help, she thought. Let Rose cool off and regain some perspective. When Rose got nearer the car, Judith watched her wave at the couple who were standing there, though Judith wasn't sure if they returned the gesture.

◄◦►

Judith woke in the dark, not sure where she was. Opening her eyes made her head hurt, an ache that spread from the base of her neck forward, and when she tried to reach up to feel what happened she discovered she couldn't; her hands had been bound. But that made no sense. And why was it so hard to think?

Her last memory was of sweating through her shirt by the time she reached the road. Rose had been speaking to the strange couple, two women somewhere in their forties or fifties, dressed in ill-fitting clothes and looking slumped and miserable. She babbled, not giving them the chance to talk, while Judith continued to the car, having no interest in meeting strangers, not when she was already upset. Why had they chosen to crowd her and Rose instead of driving an extra few minutes up the road? The orchard had to be visible from elsewhere. Or if not, there was likely another. Orchards aren't planted in isolation. Judith had popped open the trunk and forcefully pushed aside Rose's bags to get to her own. There was another shirt in there, an extra she brought in case of emergency. The last thing she remembered was turning her back on Rose and the nameless couple to find it.

Where was she? Indoors, in a room that was dark, but not without some light coming through a window. Each blink was painful, but she forced herself to ignore it. Judging by the color of light, it had to be late afternoon, which meant she'd lost a few hours. She tried again to pull her arms free, but they were tied behind her back. Maybe with coarse rope, like something used on a farm. The air had that kind of smell, too. Earthy, mixed with dust and manure. And peaches. She smelled peaches. The chair she was seated on was hardbacked, and in the gloom she made out shelves around her. On the other side of the room was a steel sink beside a stack of crates. It was some sort of storage room.

Where was Rose?

If they hurt Rose . . .

She couldn't let herself think about it. Focus on the immediate. Her hands were tied, but her legs weren't. Could she somehow stand? Maybe get to a shelf and find something to cut herself free? She tried kicking out but the chair wouldn't budge. She tried planting her feet on the floor and leaning, but the ropes were too tight; she couldn't get enough leverage. Fits of struggling didn't loosen anything. They just tired her out.

The door opened before she could do more. Two middle-aged women walked in, stooped with dark scarves wrapped around their heads. Judith couldn't tell if they were the women from the road. She couldn't remember what those women looked like.

"Where am I? What's going on? Where's Rose?"

Her own voice was so loud it made her head throb. But the women didn't respond. The one with a lower lip that extended in a permanent pout filled a bucket in the sink while the other, round-faced with gray wisps of hair protruding from under her scarf, took hold of Judith's face and inspected it from different angles. Judith considered trying to bite the woman, or just spit at her, but with her hands tied Judith feared how vulnerable she was.

Once satisfied, the woman shuffled back to the door and opened it for a third woman to enter. This one was stern and lean, her hair tied up and as close to silver as Judith had ever seen. The new woman approached Judith and said nothing. Instead, she bent close, nostrils flared, and inhaled deeply. She ran her finger along the side of Judith's face and scowled. Shook her head. Stood up. The round-faced woman reappeared, accompanied by the pouting woman who was carrying the bucket. The silver-haired woman pointed at Judith, then left the room.

"Please, tell me what's going on," Judith implored, but there was no suggestion of understanding. Rather than answer her, the pouting woman set down the bucket and lifted out a sopping rag. She twisted out the water. The round-faced woman's arms dropped on Judith's shoulders, pinning her down. Judith screamed, but they disregarded her as they scrubbed her clean.

◦

They led her outside, still bound by coarse ropes. The sun had already ducked behind the horizon, but there was still enough light for Judith to see where she was. A small village formed by no more than a dozen hand-built ramshackle houses. The inhabitants of those houses stood in their mismatched clothes, witnessing Judith's march into the oncoming night. The pair of haggard women had cleaned her and removed her T-shirt, her jeans and boots, dressing her instead in a long yellowed gown that felt gritty against her bare skin. They did not give her shoes.

She didn't know where they were taking her. No one would answer her pleas. The realization that she'd been trapped and would not survive didn't elude her, but she struggled to keep from thinking about it. That ended, however, once she was in open air, being stared at by dozens of scrutinizing eyes. The fear took hold faster than she could contain it.

"Rose!" she screamed. "Where are you, Rose? Rose!"

The villagers looked at one another, aghast. But Judith couldn't stop screaming. It went on and on and did not stop until her pouting captor struck her hard across the face. Judith shut up immediately from shock. The woman appeared shaken, too, unsteady, while her partner stared with wide eyes. The rest of the villagers looked shocked as well, some of them mouthing their confusion. Some of those looks then shifted toward anger.

The grunts and chirps from the villagers drowned out Judith's cries. They ran toward her, a wave of unwashed people dressed in patched clothes, and she struggled to escape. But when the villagers descended, it wasn't on her but on the pouting woman.

The woman didn't try to run or protect herself. She stood stoically as they arrived, unmoved by fear or regret. When their punches and kicks landed, she said nothing. There was no sound except of meat pounded and bones broken. The villagers tore at the woman in silence while Judith, unable to watch without wanting to scream, was led away by the round-faced woman and another, taller, woman with graying black hair and pinched eyes.

Behind Judith the bloodthirsty attack did not slow or stop. When they loaded her into a rusty and puttering truck filled with crates of peaches, she could not bring herself to look back. If that was what happened to one of their own, what might happen to her? To Rose? It was too painful to contemplate.

No one spoke to her in the truck. No one answered her questions. She struggled against the hands that pinned down her arms, but couldn't shake them free. And if she could, so what? There would be nothing she could do. Nowhere she could go. She had no option but to sit there and tolerate the stench of sickeningly sweet peaches while she conserved her strength in hopes an opportunity would present itself. Were she younger, were it the days before she met Rose, when she attended rallies and raved at shows, the anger and aggression would have carried her through. When she was all wired muscle and attitude. But she'd grown older, less interested in changing the world, and become too soft and weak, too unobservant. And because of that, she'd lost both herself and Rose.

The truck pulled over to the side of the road. The sky was an impenetrable black, devoid of stars, devoid of light. Judith didn't even see the reflection of the taillights ahead until she was dragged from the truck. When she did, they looked familiar, but it took a moment to realize why. They belonged to her car. Hers and Rose's. Its trunk was open.

In the distance a group of torches burned. The round-faced woman and her tall partner yanked Judith again, directing her down the slope and toward the distant flames made smaller still by the vast darkness.

Upturned roots and branches, fallen brambles and pebbles, dug into and scratched her bare feet. This would be her end. She knew it. So much time fighting, so many things done wrong. And for what? To lead her to this moment? She'd carried so much hate and anger for so long, but it amounted to nothing in the end. It made no difference. It made nothing better.

The air stank sour of rotten fruit, and Judith couldn't keep from stumbling over the uneven ground. But the two women would not be slowed; each time Judith tripped, they lifted her and pushed her forward. Even when she hesitated, even when she fell, scraping her face on something she couldn't see, they pressed her on toward the flames.

And when she was finally pushed through the penumbrae and into the light, the crowd of villagers was revealed. Some were dressed in gowns similar to hers, both women and men, shoeless, hands together in supplication. Others were dressed as they'd been in the village, in old worn clothes, unwashed and unrepaired. She saw a man with a graying beard wearing a shirt that looked familiar, like one of hers. It had been rolled up in her suitcase, left in the trunk of the car. Judith knew what that meant and wanted to scream.

But didn't. Instead, she stopped, powerless to speak. The crowd of villagers had parted. And in their parting Rose was revealed, feet torn and bloodied, face bruised and reddened from her own hard scrubbing.

Judith let out a throaty chirp when she tried to call Rose's name. Yet Rose heard it, and her eyes alighted with hope and love and terror. Judith struggled to run to her but was held in place. The distance between them insurmountable.

Judith lashed out, but couldn't connect with anyone. The cast-iron pot waited before the fallen tree; the stump she'd seen earlier was gone, replaced by a circle of misshapen bricks and a fire. The pot hung above it from a metal tripod, the stones inside dulled by the heat.

"What do you want?" Judith demanded. "Why are you doing this to us?" And still there was no answer.

But some faces turned to her. Some opened their mouths and made a horrible wet clucking. And Judith understood with horror why the villagers had been so silent. Behind their cracked lips, behind their decaying teeth, their tongues were gone. Cut out. Only stumps of dark flesh that rolled and convulsed in the firelight.

"Judith!" Rose yelled as she struggled to escape. "I love you, Judith," she said, and began to weep.

"Let her go!" Judith screamed. "Let her go! Oh my god, Rose. I love you! I love you so much! Let her go! Let her go right now!" She fought against the hands holding her. "I'm going to kill you! I'm going to kill you all! Let her the fuck go!"

Judith screamed and screamed, but no one cared.

They dragged Rose forward to the burning pot and forced her to her knees. She sobbed uncontrollably, tears and mucus streaming down her face, her speech unintelligible. Her captors took care to position her in the worn grooves as more villagers approached, grabbing hold of her arms, her legs, her shoulders. She cried out in pain, cried out for help. But Judith couldn't give it to her, no matter how much she struggled and cursed. The villagers continued, slipping a cracked wooden yoke around Rose's neck, twisting the oiled bolts tighter until her head couldn't move. Rose's tear-strewn face was pointed toward the splayed roots of the fallen tree, and she stared directly at the illusion she and Judith had discovered an impossible few hours earlier.

"What's going on?" she blubbered, the yoke forcing her jaw shut. "What are you doing?"

"Let her go!" was all Judith could say in her manic state. Over and over again.

The silver-haired woman appeared from the crowd, dressed in a long brown patchwork skirt that just covered her bare feet. Her long tresses had been let down, her eyes glistened, and in her mottled hands she held a long pair of metal tongs. She pointed at Rose with an unsteady hand and the villagers pulled back Rose's hair, away from her face.

Judith screamed, no longer capable of forming words, becoming a primal force of rage and terror. She felt it embody her, overwhelm her, become her; an enveloping and transforming red mist of pain. With her newfound power she wrenched with all her strength and tore an arm free from her captor. And, before anyone could stop her, she drove her elbow into the tall woman's face, breaking something, and tried to claw out the shorter woman's eyes. Villagers appeared suddenly, piling onto her, trapping her arm before it could do further damage. She roared with rage but couldn't prevent what was happening. Couldn't prevent herself from being subdued.

All the while, the woman standing over Rose wasn't distracted. She lifted the heavy tongs and placed them in the cast-iron pot. By the time Judith was immobilized, everyone had stopped to watch the silver-haired woman with reverence. Everyone except Rose, who continued to bottomlessly sob.

The stones shifted and popped until the woman removed the tongs, holding a smoldering black stone in their grip. The villagers uttered a sound in unison—an indescribable low-pitched drone as though they were attempting to sing—and the silver-haired woman placed the burning stone on Rose's forehead.

Rose's scream nearly shattered the world.

Judith screamed, too. Anger flowing as she watched the villagers push down on Rose, steadying her so the old woman could add another burning stone, then another. One by one the stones were placed in a circle around Rose's head while Judith cursed and sobbed impotently. Rose no longer cried, no longer moved as the stones embedded themselves in her melted flesh. Blood streamed down her unconscious face, soaking her gown as Judith continued to rage.

She screamed until she couldn't hold a breath any longer, screamed until her throat was raw and her limbs were weak. Until she could no longer fight against the villagers bearing down on her. Then, depleted, she collapsed in the grip of her captors. All strength and rage burned away. An empty shell.

But the villagers would not allow her to fall. They held her up, striking the sides of her face until her eyes opened, and made her watch as they lifted the unconscious Rose from where she knelt and brought her to the felled peach tree. They hoisted her into the tangle of roots, her arms spread wide, her legs crossed at the ankle. Blood soaked the top of her gown black.

They pitched Judith forward, dragged her to the cast-iron pot, forced her to kneel. Hanging before her was Rose, caught in the roots of the tree, the mirage of the bearded man behind her. It was too much to bear. Judith wished she could close her eyes, but couldn't. They were locked on Rose's drooping face.

The silver-haired woman approached, her arms spattered to the elbow with Rose's blood, dragging the long tongs behind her. She stood between the pot and the tree and looked at what remained of Judith. She cocked her head, then put her hand on the side of Judith's face. Judith recoiled, tried to pull away as the vestiges of herself fled. The woman waited until they were gone before stroking Judith's face.

When she was done, she stood and inserted the tongs again into the burning pot. Judith did not move, but the villagers pinned her down nonetheless. Pinned her as the woman removed another wrinkled black stone. Judith's body tremored, but she was unaware of it.

And the woman dropped the stone onto the ground.

She held out her hand. A villager rushed to her side and handed her a full waterskin. She uncorked it and spilled the contents over the black stone. It sizzled under the stream, and when it stopped the women bent and fished the stone from the mud. She stood, and without brushing away the dirt and debris, placed it in her mouth.

There was a moment of silence before the first tremor traveled across her body. Then there was a second, forewarning the seizure that quickly followed. The woman made a choking sound, like something being pulled from the muck, and pointed toward Rose's limp body. Blood poured out of the silver-haired woman's open mouth and over her chin, followed by the squirm of a shriveled black tongue. It danced across her lips as the woman croaked a single word.

"Watch."

And Judith watched, too beaten and numb to resist. She watched Rose hanging there, her body limp, her chest heaving with troubled breaths. And as she watched she thought of nothing. Not of why this was happening. Not of the last thing she'd said to Rose. Not of all the times she'd been irritated, impatient, or angry with her. Not of all the times she wished she were somewhere else. She thought of nothing. Nothing but of Rose and how she'd failed her.

Judith wanted to speak, but there were no words.

Suddenly, Rose's unconscious body jerked. The villagers dropped to their knees. Bowed their heads.

But not Judith. She was transfixed.

Rose jerked again, and every limb went rigid at once. They stretched out from beneath her filthy gown like sticks. Her eyes opened wide. So wide. So very, very wide. As though she were trying to see everything at once.

"Oh my god," she screamed. "Oh my god!

"I can—all of—oh my god!

"All of the secrets. All of the secrets and the pains. Oh my god, I can feel them. I can see them. Oh my god.

"They're in me. Under my skin. I'm overflowing. I'm transforming.

"Oh my god. Look at me!

"Look at me now!"

She convulsed, limbs flailing, eyes rolling white. And the roots of the dead tree began to tremble, to creak. To move. They curled toward the hanging Rose, reached across and wrapped around her, one at a time. Over and over, constricting until they enveloped her, pulled her in. Took her and her crown of thorns away from this world.

"The King needs his Queen," the silver-haired woman croaked as she stood, one tired leg after the other. "And she is a vessel primed."

The woman bent down and placed something on the ground in front of Judith. Then stood and touched the kneeling woman's face.

"From their union might sweet fruit spill."

With that, the woman spit the bloodied stone back into the pot.

◄◦►

Judith knelt in front of the fire and whispered. No one held her down any longer. No one had to. There was nowhere for her to go. With Rose gone there was nothing left. Just Judith and her memories of all she'd done wrong, of all the trouble she'd caused. She knelt where Rose had, a stream of words falling from her underbreath while the villagers stood in a circle, silent and patient.

It was her fault. She'd prepared Rose. Had been preparing her since the moment they met at that show, so many years before. Primed her to suffer, to take on what wasn't hers, until it bore her out, opened a hole that needed to be filled. Judith had prepared her unknowingly for this moment. To suffer their sins, to carry them away. To be taken below as some ancient payment, some ritualistic bargain. It was Judith's fault it happened. Judith's, and Judith's alone.

The knife the silver-haired woman left lay in front of her. Its handle carved from old wood, its blade curved and thin. It did not gleam in the dying firelight. It did nothing but wait for Judith as she whispered and moaned and tried to expel everything she'd seen, everything she'd done.

But she couldn't. She couldn't relieve herself of the burden. It weighed down on her, heavier and heavier. She couldn't breathe. Couldn't do anything but be crushed by it. She was going to die there, alone amid the peach trees. Alone in the dark of nowhere. And her anger would plant itself like a poisonous seed in the soil. Grow outward. Corrupt everything until there was nothing left to corrupt. Until it was all destroyed.

Unless she unburdened herself.

She rattled off her mistakes, listed her crimes, her sins; spoke each, one after the other, until her tongue carried them all.

Then she snatched up the knife.

The blade was sharp and quick and when she was done she took the writhing length of flesh that bore what she no longer could and dropped it into the black iron pot to cook and shrivel, harden and blacken. Become a stone condensed to pure sorrow. Another piece, another rune, to summon the twin bounties of harvest and forgiveness.

But forgiveness had a price. And sometimes that price demanded forgiveness of its own. Forgiveness no one else could grant. Not the King. Not his courtier. Not even his new Queen, the gift of a village to one so much older, adorned with the purest of crowns. Forgiveness that could only come from within.

Forgiveness like that required an impossible amount of strength.

Strength Judith did not have.

So instead of forgiveness, she gave away the only things she had left to give. Gave away her burdens and her pains. Offered them up to the King as so many had before, and as many would again. The act of letting them go filled her with relief impossible to express.

She no longer had the words.

STOLEN PROPERTY

SARAH LAMPARELLI

E than was lying, though he might not have called it that. He was lying as he followed Wayne over the cresting pass, primeval Montana glaciers filling their view, the remote valley spilling before them as the thin morning air whipped through their lungs and chapped their faces. He was lying as they began their descent, switch-backing down the mountain until the scrub of elevation flowered into a thick, ancient forest that sprung up to engulf them, skittering shale giving way to a dense soil that filled the treads of their boots. He was lying when they found the bodies, two of them, split open in the brush just off their path, marked by a storm of bluebottles that stirred with their approach, the static buzz of wings filling the space between the trees.

"Bears, probably," Wayne said, his rangy figure crouched beside the man with a flexibility Ethan hadn't expected. He poked at the body with a brittle stick and the drone of insects surged. Wayne was a medical student down in Bozeman, but the easy, clinical way he examined the bodies made Ethan uncomfortable. He seemed unaffected by the shock of the discovery, the swarming bugs, the heavy, rancid smell in the air.

"Wh—what do you mean probably?" Ethan stammered. He could feel his composure slipping at the edges, his breathing gone shallow as fear clenched his gut. His eyes jumped along the tree line, searching for a tuft of fur, a lumbering shape. The raised white scar that marred the back of his left forearm started to itch, like it always did when he was agitated, and he scratched at it nervously, his head swiveling in search of danger. "What else could have done this?"

When Ethan first registered what was slicking the grass red he'd spun away, gagging and swatting at the unclean flies, but it was too late. He'd seen them. He knew they were splayed at broken angles, their skin torn and jagged. He'd seen the glimmering white of bone through the churned red flesh, like the bottom of a porcelain bowl glimpsed through a thick stew. The woman had been dressed in a neon green rain slicker, and Ethan recalled the freezing drizzle that had seeped under his collar as he'd stepped off the shuttle his first day in the park. The slicker had been shredded to pieces, and bits of bright nylon clung to the swaying weeds. She might have been blonde, but there was no way to tell with her hair caked in so much dirt and blood. At the very least she was better off than the man whose head was missing entirely. In its place, there was only a ragged neck wound pulsing with insect life.

"Oh, there were definitely bears here," Wayne said, using the stick to indicate where the bodies were torn and gouged, bringing its tip down against the woman's mangled back, the deep gashes in the man's chest and thighs, "but grizzlies can be scavengers, so there's no way to tell if they did the killing. They're getting close to hibernation, and they'll eat just about anything."

Wayne didn't turn from the bodies, so Ethan couldn't read his expression. He could only see the back of the pilled knit cap Wayne always wore pulled tight down over his ears. It was autumn, well past peak season for backpackers and tourists, and they were in the most remote part of the park with no cell signal. No satellite phone.

Wayne remained unfazed. "We can't say for certain how they died. That's all I'm saying."

"So, what? We keep going? Report it at the first ranger station we find?" Ethan couldn't control the rising pitch of his voice. He wasn't prepared for backcountry hiking. He was fit enough, sure. Years of running track had solidified the habit, made his short frame lean and strong, but he didn't know the park, didn't know what he was expected to do. All of his energy had gone into the lie, into holding up the disguise. Now, he almost wished he was back in the dank San Francisco apartment he'd fled, where only his twin brother talked about the mountains when he turned up unannounced, checking in under the guise of a friendly beer or to encourage Ethan to visit their mother up in Petaluma. He had a key, and Ethan would find him there from time to time, nursing a local IPA on the stained couch, his expensive ethically-sourced sneakers and graphic tech-company T-shirts out of place among the scavenged furniture and streaky mildewed walls.

Wayne stood, chucking the stick into the trees. He was shaking his head as he turned to Ethan. "Nearest ranger station is a two-day hike back the way we came."

Ethan felt his remaining energy evaporate. He'd been counting on letting gravity drag him along on their slow march to the valley floor before collapsing into his tent for the night.

Wayne must have seen him slump, because he gave him a long, appraising look.

"There is another way," he said. "About a mile down there's a rough-cut trail that leads out to a research station. The summer's over, so it might be empty. Worst case, we could break in. Fire up a generator and radio the rangers. Let them know what we found. We could be there midday tomorrow."

He had the steady reassuring tone of a physician.

Ethan knew the man was Montana born and made the trek up to the park every year, often spending weeks alone in the backcountry. That's how they'd met, three days earlier, huddled around their lukewarm rehydrated dinners, the only two souls at their shared campsite. Ethan could tell immediately that Wayne knew what he was doing. The way his hands assembled a camp stove, handled a knife. He moved his body through the wilderness with an ease and familiarity Ethan hoped to emulate. For a man in his early thirties, Wayne had a strangely weathered appearance—deep wrinkles creasing his eyes when he smiled—but he shared his knowledge freely, and Ethan was happy their paths had crossed. They'd been hiking together ever since, Wayne telling Ethan about the park and his life in Bozeman with his wife, Marci, while Ethan bombarded Wayne with stories from the high pressure, high stakes world of Silicon Valley tech startups.

It didn't matter that Ethan had actually been tending bar in a kitschy pub near Fisherman's Wharf since dropping out of college. Wayne didn't need to know that. He didn't need to know what Ethan had gotten involved in—what he was doing to make rent in a city that seemed determined to expel him. He hoped his hiking companion didn't notice the furtive glances over his shoulder, how he was always listening for the liquid metal sound of a magazine sliding into its well, for the heart clenching *chuck* of a slide pulling a bullet into a chamber.

Ethan's eyes crept back toward the depression in the brush. "Do you really think going off trail is a good idea? With the bears?"

Wayne shrugged. "It's not exactly off trail, and these folks—" He furrowed his brow and absently kicked a clod of dirt toward the bodies. "These folks were on the main trail when whatever happened to them happened."

Wayne had the slow, over-pronounced drawl of a native Montanan. It was the voice of a man who was at home in the mountains, and Ethan felt his heart rate slow and the clamp of his jaw relax. He gave Wayne a nod, and the two men hoisted their packs.

The gear Ethan was hauling was not his own. Well, it was as much his as any stolen property ever truly belongs to the thief. Even his name, Ethan Joseph Morris, didn't belong to him, though it was the name printed on the backcountry permit neatly folded into a Ziploc bag and stowed in an outer pocket of his rucksack. The name, and the pack for that matter, had been his brother's, but he wasn't using either any longer, so now they belonged to Ethan.

It felt strange to leave the bodies there like that, unattended and uncovered, and Ethan wondered if they would still be there when the rangers came looking. There was something nagging at him as they moved away down the trail, setting off alarms in the animal parts of his brain. It was as if there was something or someone in the trees watching them, but glancing back he saw nothing. He couldn't tell if the terrible, consuming feeling of dread was for what lay behind him or for what lay ahead.

◄◦►

Calling the trail to the research station "rough" was an understatement. It had seemed fairly well defined as they stepped off the main trail, the ground packed under foot and the debris of the forest cleared away, but it quickly became muddled and hard to follow as it juked between enormous hemlocks and cedars. Ethan knew he'd be lost in ten steps if left on his own. Wayne, however, moved through the forest with clairvoyant-like confidence, pointing out where large rocks and branches had been cleared by the researchers to maintain a trail Ethan couldn't see.

The campsite Wayne led him to wasn't much to look at either, only a small clearing with no lock boxes or wire rigging to secure their packs in the trees out of reach of any curious animals that might pick up an unusual scent. Wayne, undeterred as ever, hoisted some ropes to secure their packs as Ethan began the nightly struggle to pitch his claustrophobic one-man tent. By the time he'd finished, Wayne had set up his own tent, used his butane camp stove to boil water, had rehydrated their meals, and, to Ethan's surprise, was carefully constructing a small fire. Even Ethan knew that backcountry fires were forbidden. Large swaths of the park burned each summer, and every ranger station was papered with notices and warnings directing backpackers to avoid so much as lighting a match.

When Wayne noticed Ethan staring, he shrugged. "It's autumn. We're almost out of fire season. And it's going to be a cold night." He smirked and raised an eyebrow. "Plus, if a ranger stops by to cite us, we can tell him what we found. It's a win, win."

The sun was sinking behind the trees, and Ethan had already shrugged on more layers than any other night he'd spent in the park. He smelled the bright tang of winter on the air and was thankful for the fire's warmth. Settling onto a nearby boulder, he ate his dinner of beef and barley soup, spooning it directly from the bag it was packaged in. Glancing across the fire, he noticed Wayne covertly unfolding small, lined slips of papers from a pocket on his fleece. He inspected each and fed them one by one into the flames.

"What's that?" Ethan asked, gesturing with his spoon, his small dinner almost gone already. He couldn't be sure, but he thought he saw Wayne's jaw flex, a ripple of panic cross his eyes, but he dismissed it as a trick of the firelight. It was throwing shadows, twisting and distorting the other man's features. Hollow eyes. A gaping maw.

"Nothing," Wayne mumbled. "Just some notes Marci sticks in my gear sometimes." His dry, cracked lips split into a smile. "It's sweet, but I don't want to pack 'em with me if I don't have to."

Ethan couldn't imagine a few pieces of sentimental paper adding even an ounce of weight to Wayne's pack, but he understood the temptation to let go of anything that might weigh him down. On the shuttle he'd heard a pair of hikers discuss snapping the handles off their toothbrushes to lighten their loads. But now Wayne sat hunched and quiet before the fire, almost brooding in his reticence.

"So . . ." Ethan began, working to fill the silence, "What's Marci up to while you're out here in the woods with me?" He hoped the question would dispel the strange tension that had suddenly grown between them.

Wayne's shoulders slackened. His rough face filled with sweetness. "Oh, you know, she's a teacher so she's got the school year starting up. And Missoula's a college town, so things are probably getting a little crazy with all the students back. You wouldn't know about that, living in a busy place like San Fran." He finished feeding the papers into the fire and stared after them. Behind him the woods loomed, dark as a gullet.

"I thought you said you lived in Bozeman," Ethan said, shoveling the dregs of his meal into his mouth without enjoyment.

Wayne froze in his task. The smile that had seemed so pleasant moments before had an unsettling fixed quality Ethan had never seen before. It was full dark now, stars peeking through the canopy and there were many places the moonlight could not touch. Orange firelight licked the edges of Wayne's face, and his hat, still tugged down low, now cast his eyes into deep shadow. For the first time, Ethan began to wonder who exactly he was alone in the woods with.

"I'm doing a residency in Bozeman." Wayne's words were slow, almost like he was trying to convince himself. "We live in Missoula."

Ethan wiped his spoon on his pants and shifted his focus to the man across the fire. "I thought you said you and Marci love Bozeman."

The rictus on Wayne's face broke and he nodded, his smile calm and reassuring again. "She came out to spend the summer with me, do a little hiking in Yellowstone. Now she's back in Missoula for the school year. I'll see her on weekends, holidays. Hopefully line up my next rotation at Missoula General."

Ethan started to relax as Wayne drawled his explanation, but nearly fell backwards off his rock when Wayne straightened from his crouch without warning. He kicked the small fire apart to disperse the flames and began collecting his gear to pack in for the night in what felt like a purposeful silence. Within minutes, Ethan was alone with the smoldering remains of the blaze at his feet. He was so stunned by Wayne's sudden departure from the fireside that he sat frozen, staring at the place where the man had been. In the dirt where Wayne had stooped there was a single forgotten fold of soiled paper.

-◦-

Alone in his tent, comfortably zipped into his sleeping bag, a slim mat buffering him from the cold ground, Ethan carefully unfolded the torn page. It was covered front and back with what he imagined was a woman's careful hand, the penmanship looping in places while never truly turning to cursive. It did seem to be written by Marci, though it wasn't a love letter. It read more like a trail journal, and it was dated from only the previous week. There was a stain on the lower half that could have been dirt or blood. Ethan used the small LED clipped to his fleece to read.

> *Wayne and I decided we were done traveling with Howard as we were making the climb down from the notch. Something about him changed in the last few days. He seemed irritable one second, and then would compliment Wayne incessantly the next. It was getting too weird, and this is our honeymoon. Wayne took him off to the side yesterday and told him we needed some alone time and that we haven't been together much since his residency started. Howard seemed to understand. He told us he'd buy us a beer if we ever ran into him in Whitefish, and he took off down the trail. The only odd thing is that we heard the strangest sounds outside the tent last night. I'm used to hearing a critter or two sneaking around, but I swear I heard the sound of footsteps. Human footsteps. And we haven't seen anyone else in this section of the park. Part of me is nervous that Howard—*

There was a crunching sound outside the tent, as if a heavy boot had come down on dried twigs and leaves. Ethan clicked off the light, leaving the tent in unpolluted darkness. The steps began in earnest, making a stilted progression around the campsite. Ethan was tempted to call out, thinking it could be a ranger there to inspect the fire, but the words wouldn't form in his throat. He felt the cool air fill his lungs faster as the steps grew near, rounding the place where their fire had been. One moment Ethan was sure they were the cadenced steps of a man, but the next he would swear they were the lumbering footfalls of a massive bear.

Ethan tried to keep from shaking, concentrated on slowing his breath, on lying still so he wouldn't be detected. As the crunching steps grew closer, his feet jittered in his sleeping bag, and he was certain something would come tearing through the thin nylon walls of his shelter. He knew he deserved to die—probably deserved worse—but he couldn't keep his throat from tightening, his pulse from careening against his temples.

His fingers went to his quaking arm—to the scar—and his mind reeled back to a time when he'd raced his brother across the browning Petaluma hills—both on rusting thrift store bicycles—thinking that if he were the fastest brother, the wildest, he could pull himself free of his twin, like a star in a binary ripping from its orbit. Instead, he'd been clipped by a sedan after misjudging an intersection and toppled into a drainage ditch where he found two inches of jagged white ulna sticking out the back of his arm. His brother, only seconds behind him, had come skidding to a halt, and upright and unmarred had stared down into the ditch after him.

People always laughed and called him the bad twin, but Ethan didn't think he was bad. He was just unfocused, unlucky. He was always the one who was going to get hit by that car. And over the years it often felt as if they were still there at the side of that road. Two brothers, almost identical. One whole, one broken.

Ethan thought of the bodies back up the valley, mutilated by the wildlife his brother had loved. He'd papered the walls of their stuffy suburban room with maps of Glacier and Yellowstone. And now the wrong brother had hiked into those wilds—would die in it. Ethan held back a sob and waited for the flurry of violence to arrive.

The steps came to a stop at the flap of his tent before dissolving into a curious silence that seemed to bring the entire forest to a hush. He was waiting for the attack, for a gunshot, for a voice to speak his true name, for something, anything, to happen.

After half an hour he began to feel foolish. The steps must have been an animal, long gone by now, or more likely Wayne, up and looking for a place to take a piss, the trees echoing his steps back to them. No one looking for Ethan would ever make it this far into the wilderness. After an hour of perfect silence, the grating of his teeth slowly easing, Ethan began to doze, though as he was fading, he realized he never had heard the zipper of the other man's tent.

He dreamed that Wayne sat in the corner, watching him sleep with glinting animal eyes, hands reaching out to touch his face like a small child meeting someone new. Ethan raised his head to see a grizzly that walked on two legs crashing through the forest above them. But when he looked back, he realized there were claws gouging his face. Wayne was the bear in a crude human skin mask, and he was waiting for the perfect moment to take him in his teeth and shake.

⟡

On the trail the next day, Ethan paused to take a deep swallow of water from his Nalgene. He was wary of Wayne, but the man had greeted him with freshly filtered water from a nearby stream and did the bulk of the work breaking camp, an unfamiliar song whistling between his teeth. It sounded old, traditional, and Ethan couldn't place it. He could only scan the trees for any sign of his nocturnal visitor while chewing his morning protein bar. When he asked Wayne if he'd heard anything moving around in the dark, Wayne responded with a shrug and a smile. "The glaciers are melting, setting free what once was trapped." He turned his creased face up toward the mountain, the morning light dancing in his eyes. "These woods are full of strange and wondrous things," he said, adjusting the straps on his pack before stepping off, leading Ethan away down the nearly invisible path.

Ethan knew something was off, knew Wayne's story didn't add up, and his odd behavior the night before had him on guard, but there was little he could do before they found the research station. Wayne intended to continue his hike through the backcountry after they contacted the rangers, but Ethan had decided he was done. He'd fulfilled his purpose, documented his hikes well, and once they let the rangers know about the bodies, he'd ask for a ride out of the park. That was assuming the rangers had a way of getting a truck out this far. Ethan really didn't know.

He was still formulating his plot to escape the woods, to get away from Wayne and into a motel in Whitefish or Columbia Falls where he could plan his next step, when he noticed the trees begin to bow away from him as he moved near. The green of the needles was suddenly more striking than before, and the ground dipped when he tried to place a foot. Wayne was there to catch him when he stumbled.

"I don't know what's wrong with me," Ethan said, suddenly aware that a cold sweat was slicking his face. "Maybe that protein bar was off."

"Take your time," Wayne said, helping him get steady on his feet. "Here. Drink more water." He unscrewed his own bottle and handed it to Ethan who nodded and gulped the clean, fresh liquid. "Look," Wayne said, "the station is just around the next bend. That would be a better place to rest. Do you think you can make it?" His voice floated on the breeze, caressing Ethan's ears. The Montana accent was gone now, he thought, replaced with something more melodic. Something older and enticing.

Ethan nodded, already feeling better at the thought of a man-made structure. He took a few steps and found he could walk on his own if he focused on placing his feet, letting Wayne lead the way as usual.

The colors around him continued to brighten, but there was something else in the corner of his vision. He knew they couldn't be real, they disappeared almost as quickly as they emerged, darting out of sight when he tried to look at them head on, but he saw them all the same. There were people out in the woods. They were somehow all the same person, some in hiking clothes, some crouching naked in the brush, but each wore a different face. Sometimes Ethan even detected the jut of an antler or the curve of a snout, but as soon as his eyes focused there was nothing. He knew then that he was hallucinating, but the promise of the station pushed him forward.

By the time they turned the bend, Ethan was being dragged more than supported, and he mumbled wildly about the men in the woods and bears that walked on two legs. He broke free when he saw the wide clearing open before them, expecting to find a building, maybe even trucks or ATVs. Instead, he found the clearing empty. No, empty wasn't right because while there was no station, something else was there.

A crude but massive idol stood before them, hulking up out of the earth. At first, Ethan thought it must be a grotesque art piece created by the grad students, but then he was realizing there was no research station. There were no researchers, no ATVs, no radio. Only this enormous, obscene effigy. Mounds of rock and forest debris made up boulder-like shoulders and an upper torso while branches, twine, and assorted fragments of hiking equipment had been slicked together with mud and a darker substance to form two great arms supported by makeshift scaffolding that towered above them. It gave praise to something Ethan could not name. Atop the arms great talons had been fashioned out of sharpened sticks lashed with brightly colored paracord. Those arms appeared to sway as Ethan gaped at them in confusion and wonder, the structure a malformed, undulating abomination that tilted toward them as if about to strike.

A bear, Ethan thought, *it's meant to be a bear.* He dropped his pack in the dirt, moving forward to bask in its horrific splendor.

The thing's head should have been massive, full of barbarous teeth, but it was oddly small, a surprising mismatch for the heaping shape. The head had been impaled on what appeared to be sharpened pikes that protruded from the thick neck, human sized, no bigger than Ethan's or Wayne's, but painted in glistening slashes of white and red.

Ethan choked as it occurred to him that the head was human, probably the head that was missing from the body they'd found up the main trail. And the face wasn't painted but had instead been scraped clean down to the bone by what must have been a terrible set of claws. That realization cut straight through his shimmering world, and Ethan began to scream, howling in panic at the impossible, repulsive sight.

Stolen. The word repeated unbidden in his mind. *Stolen, stolen, stolen, stolen, sto—*

He was still screaming when he heard the *crunch* of something hard connecting with the back of the head, and he crumpled to his knees before the idol like a penitent, pain flashing a brilliant white behind his eyes before he finally collapsed forward into the dirt.

-‹o›-

He was back in San Francisco standing in the open door of the one-bedroom garden unit he'd been renting. They called it a "garden unit", but it was a basement. And now, his brother was dead on the floor of a mildewing basement, and it was his fault. His twin brother—the lucky brother, the successful, kind brother who must have stopped in before finally taking that trip up to Montana—was crumpled on the floor, bound at the wrists and ankles. Ethan knew he'd been shot in the back of the head because under the left eye his face was simply gone, a gaping hole of carnage in its place.

Ethan had been laying low for weeks, unsuccessfully scrambling to come up with money he owed men that no one should be indebted to. He'd been skipping his shifts at the bar, avoiding his apartment, sometimes sleeping on a friend's couch or even a bench if he had to. It wasn't until his mother started texting, asking if he'd heard from his brother, that it occurred to him he'd failed to warn his brother, tell him not to stop by. A pit opened in his chest that hadn't been filled since. They were identical. Easily mistaken for one another.

Standing there in the doorway, Ethan thought he would call an ambulance, call the police, call his mother. The guilt was already rising up, crashing over him and dragging him out to sea. Instead, he crouched over his brother and suddenly he was the brother staring down into that drainage ditch. The whole brother. The lucky brother. He took his brother's wallet from his pocket and swapped it for his own. The new fine leather was spattered with blood, but it was soft in his hand. His brother's car was on the street—clean and reliable. The tank was full. The backcountry permits were paid for. The rucksack was packed and ready.

If Ethan had plans to be in Montana, that's where Ethan would be.

◁◦▷

When he opened his eyes, he noticed the rocks around him were stained with a shade of rust that could only be old blood, like someone had been there before him, bleeding into the packed earth. Further out in the tree line there were piles of decaying packs and other equipment. A piece of neon green rain gear near the top of the heap flapped in the light breeze. It looked familiar, but Ethan couldn't remember why anymore. His sluggish mind stuttered with images of insects, and grass, and blood.

Then something more urgent was happening, a crushing pain in his lungs. Wayne was straddling his chest, legs pinning his arms. With animal-like fluidity, he grabbed Ethan by the head, fingers digging into the flesh of his scalp. The knit cap had been lost at some point or he'd removed it, and from this new angle Ethan could see Wayne's face was peeling at the edges, like it was ready to be free of him. Ethan was either still hallucinating, or some perverse magic had let this man wear another's face for days on end without detection. Ethan did not want to see what was underneath.

"Wayne—" Ethan coughed, not certain what he could say to save his own life.

"I am not Wayne," he said, the face slipping slightly off center, "I am Ethan. I have always been Ethan. Just as I have always been Howard, and Emmett, and Levi, and many others who have walked these woods." Ethan thought he heard Wayne's voice oscillating in tone and accent, as if searching for a match to his own.

The clearing was spinning, but a spark of rage lit in his chest when he heard his brother's name on the thing's tongue—he now suspected this was a thing and not a man at all—and with the last breath he could muster he roared up at it. "I'm Jacob, you asshole—" he spat a glob of blood in its ruined face "—Ethan was my brother."

With one terrific buck and twist of his hips, Jacob felt the Wayne-thing's balance waver and he rolled with all his might, sending it sprawling. Face down in the dirt, he began to crawl, the world still roiling around him. He had a sudden blazing idea that he would leap to his feet, cross the clearing on powerful legs, and dive into the forest where he would run and hide until he found the trail again. Eventually there *would* be a ranger's station. There would be survival. He would be Jacob again, no matter what that would mean, even if it meant another death in another place, or police, or facing his mother. But past the quivering idol, across the clearing, the treetops were shuddering, and he saw the jerky, unnatural movements of something massive skulking there between the trees, and he knew there would be no escape.

Laying there in the stained soil and the blood of countless others, he heard the voice behind him, shifting now in accent and pitch as if losing control.

"It visited you in the night, Ethan." The Wayne-thing's voice sang with an evangelical flow. "Yours is the face it wants for me. And the face it wants, I take as I have taken for years and years."

Jacob's terror gave way to exhaustion, and he tipped onto his back to find the Wayne-thing above him, a bloodstained rock in its hand, something loathsome and unknowable beneath the ripped skin it wore as a face. Tears filled Jacob's eyes, gratefully blurring his vision and the thing he had known as Wayne.

"You can't have my brother," he said. "Neither of us can."

The Wayne-thing shrieked like a wounded animal when Jacob's filthy hands tore into his own face, raking and clawing without hesitation, as fast and brutally as he could manage. Skin that happened to look like his brother's peeled away in blood-soaked sheets beneath his untended nails. Ethan was dead because he shared Jacob's face, but Jacob wasn't going to let Wayne—or whatever he was—take him out into the woods, to walk and talk and see again for some unknown and profane purpose.

The Wayne-thing let out a mournful, inhuman bellow, and Ethan could hear the great bear—the ancient creature that demanded stolen faces—lumber off through the trees, its crashing footsteps echoing across the valley. Jacob grimaced through the pain, a smile distorting his shredded face.

His eyes ruined, Jacob waited for the attack, for a rock to come crashing down against his skull, but it never came. It was as if a spell had been broken, and the Wayne-thing seemed to have lost the ability to speak. He could hear hissing and spitting as it retreated back into the woods. His head was pulsing with a blistering pain, but Jacob thought he could hear the gibbering of others like it out in the trees.

Jacob didn't know if the Wayne-thing was a man, or maybe had once been a man, but he figured he was no use to him now. He didn't expect he'd be allowed to leave the clearing, but it seemed beside the point. Blood was flowing steadily from the back of his head, from his face. The mud was slick beneath him.

Exhaustion threatened to pull him under, but before it did his brother's face swam up in his mind. They were the same in every way except for the crooked scar on Jacob's forearm where bone had ripped through skin. He had always felt as if their lives were inextricably twisted together, a frayed sense of duty and competition tainting their days. One twin forever gazing down into the ditch, one peering up from the bottom. Now, he wondered if he had been the one dead on the floor of a basement apartment, would Ethan have found himself in this clearing, bleeding his life away under the watchful eye of a looming idol? He hoped he wouldn't have.

Jacob closed his eyes, and he was back in Petaluma, his bike cresting a hill, brown-green fields stretching away to either side, heat bending the world as it poured off the blacktop, his brother like a reflection, racing by his side.

SHARDS

IAN ROGERS

Dawn came and they were still alive. All except for Marcie. Only at the end, they supposed she hadn't really been Marcie anymore.

She was the only one who didn't come to the cabin as part of a couple. Later on, the others—Chad and Annabelle, Mark and Donna—would all privately wonder if Marcie had been targeted the moment she walked through the door. If she'd been singled out for being single.

It seemed such an absurd notion, but after the night they spent at the cabin, their lives seemed to exist in a series of absurd notions, one following directly after another. The grief counsellors and psychiatrists told them this was a perfectly normal response to the trauma they had endured. That this was the way the human mind functioned when confronted with such terrifying and inexplicable events. The only way to move on was to accept the things that didn't make any sense.

Which, to Chad and Annabelle and Mark and Donna, seemed like the most absurd notion of all.

⟨◦⟩

They drove up on a Friday afternoon after classes ended. They went in Chad's new Expedition, an early graduation present from his parents. Annabelle sat next to him, playing navigator with Google Maps; Mark and Donna were in the back seat holding hands and staring at their smartphones; and Marcie was sprawled in the rear compartment with their luggage and groceries.

Chad glanced in the rear-view mirror and told her not to eat all their food before they reached the cabin, which earned him double fuck-you fingers from Marcie, who stood six one and weighed a solid two fifty, none of it fat. On the rugby field they called her the Steamroller.

The others ragged her about her size, but there was never any cruelty in their remarks. No more than the jibes they made about Chad's thinning hair or Donna's lazy eye. It was the way they'd always spoken to each other, ever since they were kids. The jokes and taunts that others used to hurt and humiliate, they turned into shields to protect themselves.

They'd learned early on that even though there was no perfection in the human body, there was plenty to be found in friendship. It was a strange friendship, to be sure. Their families and schoolmates didn't understand it; they didn't even understand it themselves. But they didn't need to. It worked—*they* worked—and that was all that mattered.

Looking back, it made a strange kind of sense—an *absurd* kind of sense, one could say—that they should be the ones who ended up killing Marcie. They would have died for her if the situation had been reversed.

If you looked at it like that, killing Marcie was really the least they could do.

⸗⸗

Still, there were some unanswered questions.

Like why did they dismember Marcie's body after they killed her?

None of them had an answer for that. A fact that—strangely, absurdly—provided even more support for their collective story.

The grief counsellors and psychiatrists would later say the survivors mutilated their friend's body because it was the only way they could externalize what they'd done to someone they'd known and loved since early childhood. Decapitating her and severing her limbs was their way of negating that relationship, of turning Marcie into a stranger, which, in a way, is what she had become to them during the course of the event.

The mutilation may have been vicious and violent, but it was also—strangely, absurdly—healthy.

-◦-

It was Marcie who found the trap door. She tripped over the ringbolt while they were bringing their stuff into the cabin.

"The fuck?" she shouted, stumbling forward a few steps and almost dropping the two bags of groceries she was carrying.

"What's the matter, Marce?" Annabelle said, dragging her suitcase through the doorway on its small plastic wheels.

"Damn thing almost killed me." Marcie went over and nudged the ringbolt with the toe of her shoe. "They should've covered it with a rug or something."

"They who?" Chad said, stepping around Annabelle with a large cooler. Mark and Donna came in behind him, still holding hands, still on their phones.

"Whoever you rented this piece-of-shit cabin from."

"Hey," Chad said. "It's got four walls and a roof. What else do we need?"

Marcie glared distrustfully at the trap door. "What the hell do you think is down there?"

Donna shrugged. "Probably the ghost of a demonic entity that will slaughter us all while we sleep."

She was wrong, but not entirely.

-◦-

After they unpacked their bags and put away the groceries, they made a fire in the stone-lined pit out back and roasted hot dogs and marshmallows. They washed them down with beer, then moved on to vodka. They finished the bottle—the *first* bottle—and Mark stuck it between his legs and chased the girls around the yard, thrusting his hips and crying out, *Hoo-ah! Hoo-ah!*

Marcie grabbed the bottle and looked at it skeptically. "We've all seen your dick, Mark, and this is way too generous. Maybe we could find you one of those little wee bottles you get on airplanes."

Mark dropped to his knees, head slumped. "Why you gotta wound me with the truth like that?"

Donna hugged him. "It's okay, babe. It's not the size that matters, it's what you do with it."

Mark perked up. "I gotta pee."

Donna backed away. "You can do that on your own."

Mark rose shakily to his feet. "I'm not sure I can."

The others watched him stumble off to the edge of the woods. Annabelle intoned in a narrator voice: "The police found his body the following morning. They thought his penis was missing, but it turned out they just had to look really, really hard to see it."

They all laughed while Mark peed against an oak tree. He let go of himself to flick double fuck-you fingers over his shoulders, then cursed and brought his hands back around.

"Don't get any on ya!" Chad called, and they all laughed again.

"Too late!" Mark called back. After he was finished he shuffled back to the circle, buttoning his jeans. "What's the matter, Chad, you couldn't spring for a place with an outhouse?"

"The cabin has a bathroom, numbnuts. You're the one who decided to piss in the woods."

"That's part of the cabin experience," Mark said solemnly.

"I'll be sure to tell that to the owners," Chad said.

"Who are the owners?" Marcie asked him.

"I don't know," Chad said. "I found it on Airbnb. Which reminds me . . ." He gave them his smooth lazy grin, the one that always preceded a bad joke. "After I graduate, I've already got an idea for my first entrepreneurial venture. It's similar to Airbnb, only mine will be aimed at the Spring Break crowd. You know: beach, booze, and babes. I'm gonna call it AirTnA."

The others groaned in unison. Annabelle threw a marshmallow at him. "Pig," she said, but she was smiling.

"Seriously," Marcie said. She gestured at the cabin with the hot dog skewered on her stick. "Who owns this dump?"

"How the hell should I know?" Chad said. "I checked the listings for a cabin in the woods, someplace within driving distance of the city, and this one looked good."

"And by 'good' you mean 'bad,'" Annabelle said.

"Didn't you talk to someone?" Marcie asked.

"No," Chad said. "I emailed. They quoted a price, I paid it, and here we are. What's the big deal?"

An awkward silence descended, threatening the pleasant mood of the evening. Since Marcie was the cause of this particular bring-down, she knew it was her responsibility to provide the requisite counterweight to bring it up again.

"Whatever they charged," she said, "it was too much. Just like your mom."

They all looked at her for a short beat, then burst out laughing.

Tragedy averted, Marcie thought.

And it was.

For the moment.

◄◦►

They went inside when the temperature began to drop.

Chad started another fire, this one in the big fieldstone hearth, while Annabelle made a round of drinks. Donna was checking her phone and marvelling at the excellent coverage they got way out here in the sticks. Mark was still outside, putting out the old fire and gathering up their trash.

Marcie was in the main room, staring at the trap door.

"If you're just going to stand there," Chad said, kneeling in front of the fire, "could you at least be useful and hand me some more kindling?" He pointed at the pile of cut wood next to the rack of fireplace tools.

Marcie picked up a piece and handed it to him without taking her eyes off the trap door.

She couldn't stop looking at it. When she was outside, sitting with the others around the fire, she hadn't been able to stop thinking about it. It was like when she tripped over the ringbolt something had dislodged in her brain, and now it was rattling around in there like the only penny in a piggy bank.

What was down there? she wondered. *Anything* was the answer. Including nothing.

But she didn't believe there was nothing. No, there was definitely something down there. She didn't know how she knew that, but she did. Something . . . or some*one*?

No. There was no one down there. She was sure of that, not because of any particular reason but rather a feeling that was telling her—insisting to her—that there was some*thing* down there. Something other than dust and dirt.

But what?

She didn't know, and while a part of her was okay with not knowing, a bigger part was not okay, because the not-knowing side was motivated by fear. She was *afraid* of opening the trap door and going into the cellar. She was *afraid* of what she might find. And she couldn't accept that.

She took a deep breath, then blew it out. She needed to keep herself together. Her coach said fear was the forerunner of failure. Pretty words, Marcie thought, but they didn't mean squat on the rugby field. She was the Steamroller, for god's sake. Was she really going to be stopped in her tracks by a trap door that didn't even look strong enough to take her full weight standing on top of it?

"Fuck no," she muttered.

"Fuck what?" Chad said, jabbing at the burning kindling with a brass poker.

When he didn't get a reply, he looked over his shoulder.

Marcie was gone and the trap door was open.

-‹o›-

Annabelle was handing out drinks. When she was done she had an extra one. "Where's Marce?" she asked.

Chad jerked his thumb at the trap door. "Down in the cellar."

Donna snickered. "We'll probably never see her again."

"You're one cold bitch," Chad said.

"The coldest," Donna said, her eyes glued to her phone.

Annabelle carried her drink (gin and tonic) and Marcie's (rum and coke) over to the opening in the floor and peered inside. She couldn't see anything beyond the first few steps of the wooden stairs descending into darkness below.

"Marcie!" she called down. "What are you doing?"

There was no reply.

Annabelle crouched, balancing the drinks on her knees, and tilted her head at a listening angle.

She couldn't hear a thing from the cellar, which seemed strange to her. If Marcie was down there, she should've been able to hear her moving around. Marcie was a lot of things, Annabelle thought, but light on her feet wasn't one of them.

"Come on, Marce." Her mouth had gone dry and she swallowed with an audible click. "If you're joking around, it isn't funny."

Mark came in the back door carrying a half-full garbage bag. "Shut the trap door and lock her in there," he said. "Now *that* would be funny."

Annabelle frowned at him, then turned back to the square-shaped hole in the floor. Locking Marcie in the cellar wouldn't be funny, but it would teach her a lesson. Teach her not to scare her friends like this.

Annabelle stood up and was actually extending her foot to push the door closed when she heard something from below.

It was a low scratching sound, almost like radio static, but gone so quickly she wasn't sure if she'd only imagined it.

She crouched back down and leaned forward, keeping the glasses in her hands upright so they wouldn't spill. She tilted her head to the side again, like a satellite dish trying to pick up a stray signal.

She reached the tipping point and was trembling on the balls of her feet when Marcie's face appeared out of the darkness and said, "Boo!"

Annabelle squealed and fell over backwards. The glasses flew out of her hands and spilled their contents across the plank floor. The others turned in unison, their startled faces turning to puzzlement as they watched Marcie climb out of the cellar.

She was carrying a record player.

⋅◦⋅

It was a very old device—a gramophone, according to Donna, the music major—with a hand-crank on the side and a big brass horn that looked like a metallic flower in full bloom. Instead of a needle at the end of the tone arm, there was a curved hook of smoky black glass.

Marcie put it on the coffee table and they all gathered around it.

"It was just sitting there on the dirt floor," she said.

"Sweet," Donna said. "We need some tunes."

Annabelle reached for the hook at the end of the tone arm.

"Careful," Marcie said. "It's sharp." She showed a cut on the pad of her index finger, still weeping a bit of blood.

There was a record on the turntable, a plain black disc with no label.

"What do you think it is?" Chad wondered.

"Nicki Minaj?" Donna said.

The others laughed, then a deep silence fell over the room as they examined the gramophone.

Donna ran her hands along its smooth wooden sides.

Chad tipped his head toward the brass horn.

Marcie put her finger on the record and rotated it slowly around.

Annabelle reached out for the hand-crank.

Something might have happened in that moment, but the silence was broken by the plastic rustling sound of Mark digging around in the garbage bag. Snapped out of their collective trance, the others turned to face him.

Mark was holding the empty vodka bottle. He grinned mischievously as he waggled it back and forth in his hand.

"Wanna play a game?"

◄◦►

They lost interest in the gramophone after that. All except for Marcie.

She was still kneeling on the floor in front of it, spinning the record around and around.

The others were on the far side of the room, sitting in a circle around the bottle.

Annabelle said she didn't want to play. Chad told her not to be a prude, and she accused him of only wanting to play so he could kiss Donna. Chad said his real plan was to see her and Donna kiss. Donna said she wanted to see Chad and Mark kiss. Annabelle shook her head and proclaimed them all childish. Donna said they'd be graduating soon and this would be their last chance to be childish, so they should enjoy it. Annabelle said fine, as long they didn't enjoy it *too much*, and shot a pointed look at Chad.

Mark put his hand on the bottle. "I'll start."

He gave it a spin.

Across the room, Marcie turned the hand-crank on the gramophone.

The record began to spin, too.

◄◦►

When the turntable was going at a good, steady speed, Marcie lifted the tone arm and placed the needle on the spinning record.

No, she thought. Not the needle. The Shard.

She wondered where that thought had come from, but only for a second, then she inclined her head toward the brass horn.

There was nothing at first except the hollow sound of dead air and the low, expectant scratch of the needle.

The Shard.

Marcie leaned closer, wondering if it no longer worked, if a record could die like an old battery.

She heard only faint scratching, and was about to pull her head back when she realized the scratching wasn't random: it had a pattern to it. It wasn't scratching at all. It was a voice, a very low voice, and it was speaking to her, whispering to her. Asking her a question.

Wanna play a game?

◂◌▸

A blast of sound exploded from the gramophone. A fusillade of horns so loud it knocked Marcie onto her back.

The squall rose to an ear-splitting level, then tripped back down the scale in a stuttering staccato that made everyone in the room feel as if icy fingers were tickling along their spines.

Their heads were all turned toward Marcie and the sounds coming from the gramophone—oblivious to the bottle in the center of their circle that continued to spin and spin.

As the horns trickled away, a tapping sound came in to take their place, a light pitter-patter as if of approaching footsteps. The tapping got progressively louder until it became the sharp rat-a-tat-tat of a snare drum, a percussive beat that sounded like gunfire.

The space between the drumbeats was soon filled by the razor-squeal of violins. A pained sound, as if the instruments were being tortured rather than played.

The auditory onslaught continued with a deep, pummelling bass that felt like a series of hammer blows against their eardrums.

Marcie suddenly jerked upright like a puppet whose master has pulled too hard on its strings. The music pounded out of the gramophone, causing the entire cabin to shake. The windows rattled in their frames. The floor was vibrating so much it looked like Marcie was hovering six inches above it.

Later on they would all agree she didn't turn to face them. She spun around. Like a record.

They knew right away something was wrong with her. Her eyes were glazed, her mouth hung slack, and her head was slumped at an unnatural angle. The autopsy would later determine her neck had been broken by that first burst of sound. She should've been dead, and yet she wasn't.

As the others watched, Marcie reached out with one marionette arm and snapped off the gramophone's tone arm. The record continued spinning on the turntable, and although there was no needle—no *Shard*—to play it, the sounds kept blasting out.

Sounds that became the soundtrack for everything that followed.

◄◦►

Donna was sitting on the front porch when the police arrived.

Who called them? she wondered.

Even though her arms were wrapped tightly around herself, she couldn't stop trembling. She thought that being outside to catch the first light of day would help to drive away the icy aura surrounding her. It didn't.

The first officers on the scene pointed their guns at her and told her to drop it. She didn't know what they were talking about, then realized she was still holding the fireplace poker. It was covered in blood. So was she.

She understood how it must have looked. Only some of the blood was hers. Most of it was Marcie's. There was a chunk of flesh stuck to the end of the poker. That was Marcie's, too. It had come from one of her massive shoulders. Hitting her with the poker had been like hitting the tough hide of some large animal. It hadn't stopped her, not at first. Not until the others joined in to help her. Killing Marcie had been a group effort.

Donna thought about letting the cops shoot her. She could stand up, raise the poker high over her head, and make like she was going to charge them.

She didn't do it. Not because she was unwilling but because she was so fucking cold she could barely move. Her hand felt like a frozen claw, and it took all her strength to open it and let the poker fall to the ground. The police told her to stand up and walk toward them with her hands raised. She ignored them. She was done. If they wanted to shoot her, they could shoot her.

They didn't. More cops showed up, and some of them stayed with her, watching her warily with their guns still drawn, while the others went into the cabin. Chad, Mark, and Annabelle were in there. And Marcie. Marcie was all over the cabin.

An ambulance arrived and a pair of EMTs tried to get Donna off the porch. She was hurt, they said, nodding at the slash wounds on her arms. She refused to move, wasn't even sure she could move. She was so cold it felt like her ass had frozen to the plank floor. One of the EMTs noticed she was shivering and put a blanket around her. It didn't help.

The EMT told her it was shock and would wear off eventually.

They were wrong on both counts.

⟨◦⟩

Detective Russo entered the cabin and almost stepped on a severed arm. It was a strong, muscular arm with a large hand lying palm-down on the floor. For a moment he thought the nails on the fingers had been painted with red polish. Then he realized it was blood.

There was more blood at the mangled joint where the arm was once attached to the shoulder. A few feet away was the shoulder, still attached to the torso. Over there was another arm. A leg. A head with blood-splattered hair pulled back in a ponytail. The room looked like a slaughterhouse. Russo's gaze drifted over to a pile of smashed wood and a dented brass horn, what looked like the remains of an old record player. What the hell happened here?

Two young men were seated on a ratty couch being treated by EMTs. The one on the left had a vertical gash running from his temple to the edge of his thinning hair. The other had what appeared to be a stab wound to his lower left side. A uniform was in the kitchen talking to a young woman sitting on a stool. She appeared uninjured.

Russo headed over that way, stepping carefully to avoid the puddles of congealing blood. As he was passing an open trap door, the head of another uniform popped up, giving Russo a minor heart attack. He froze in mid-step, clutching the mantel for support.

The uniform winced. "Sorry, Detective."

Russo closed his eyes. "What've you got?"

"Nothing down there." He looked around the cabin floor. "Looks like all the action happened up here."

The other uniform came over from the kitchen. Russo nodded at the open notebook in his hand.

"Tell me."

⟿

They told their story to the police, and from there it went to the media, and then out into the world.

Four friends had murdered a fifth after a night of partying at a cabin in the woods. The murder was committed in self-defence, after their friend experienced a psychotic episode and attacked them. Some reports insinuated that drugs may have been a factor, but this was never confirmed. There was no mention of the mutilation of the body.

Russo didn't like it. Not one bit.

When he questioned each of the survivors, they had spoken calmly and clearly, with no outward signs of lying or evasion. Their stories matched and their wounds were consistent with the makeshift knife they recovered from the scene. None of them had criminal records or a history of violence. All four were squeaky-clean college kids, due to graduate in a month. But there was something *wrong* about them.

"Wrong how?" asked the police chief.

Russo shook his head. "I can't explain it."

The chief spread his hands. "Try."

Russo paced back and forth across the office, running his hand through his hair. "The dead girl's body. Why did they chop it up?"

"You read the shrink's report. They claimed it was the only way to stop her. It's abnormal, but considering their state of mind at the time . . ."

"I know," Russo snapped. "Their story makes sense, I get it. But it's not the truth."

"What does that mean?"

"It means I don't like it."

"You don't have to like it," the chief said. "But you have to close it."

So that's what he did.

The coroner's inquest determined that none of the four survivors was criminally responsible for their friend's death and no charges would be brought.

The case was closed.

But not for Russo.

◂◦▸

Summer.

Donna couldn't get warm. One of the hottest summers on record and she was freezing. On the news, they talked about climate change and record-breaking temperatures. Donna was glad to hear it—if they were talking about the weather that meant they no longer cared about what happened at the cabin—but it didn't change the way she felt. She was still fucking cold.

All summer long she cranked the thermostat in the house, and her parents kept knocking it back down. They argued about it constantly. Donna's parents tried to be patient, figuring it was her way of dealing with the stress and the trauma. They told themselves it would pass.

One day in August, they returned from work to find the house so stifling it felt like they'd walked into an oven. In addition to turning up the thermostat as high as it would go, Donna had a roaring fire going in the hearth. They found her sitting on the floor in front of the dancing flames, clothed in three layers of sweaters and her winter coat.

Her parents yelled at her—Donna couldn't hear them at first with the earmuffs she was wearing—then sent her to her room, something they hadn't done in ten years.

Donna was holding the brass poker she'd used to get the fire going, and for a moment she considered using it on her parents. The way she'd used the poker at the cabin on Marcie. The way she'd used it on the empty vodka bottle.

When Marcie was dead and the music stopped, the bottle had still been spinning on the floor. It showed no sign of stopping, and to Donna this was the final indignity of the evening, so she smashed it with the poker. Smashed it and smashed it until it stopped spinning.

That was when she started feeling cold. It was like a chill wind wrapped itself around her, enveloping her, sinking deep into her skin. It ran through her veins like ice water, turned her bones into frozen sticks. It numbed her very soul and filled her with a hopeless dread that she would never be warm again.

Donna decided not to use the poker on her parents. She went upstairs like the good girl she'd been all her life. She thought about calling Mark—that's what she normally would've done—but she didn't. They hadn't spoken since the cabin. None of them had spoken to each other. It was strange. They'd always been so close; they'd always been there for each other. Now they were like strangers. She didn't feel sad about it, which was even stranger. She felt nothing about it whatsoever.

She climbed into her bed, pulling up the duvet and the heavy quilt she'd brought down from the attic. The heat from the fire and the furnace hadn't been enough. She was still cold. Her parents said it was all in her mind, but what difference did it make? Hot, cold—they were all signals sent from the body to the brain. How was this any different?

She decided her parents were the problem. She couldn't get warm with them constantly stopping her.

So she waited a couple weeks, until they went away on a weekend trip. They'd been spending a lot of time out of the house since Donna returned from the cabin.

After they were gone, Donna turned up the thermostat and made a fire. Like before, it did nothing to stave off the cold she felt deep in her bones and all through her body.

She stayed up late, shivering in her layers of sweaters as she fed one piece of wood after another into the hungry flames. It made no difference—she was still freezing, so she decided to make another fire, this one in the basement. She emptied a can of turpentine onto a stack of old wooden chairs her father had been meaning to take to the dump. Then she tossed a lit match onto the pile and went back upstairs to start another fire in the living room. And another in the den. She locked the front and back doors and went up to the second floor. She lit more fires in her parents' bedroom and the guest room.

She went back downstairs. Thick black smoke chugged out of the basement door. The living room and den were burning nicely; flaming particles whirled through the air like a swarm of fireflies.

Donna surveyed her handiwork and decided it would do. She retrieved the brass poker from the rack of fireplace tools and went upstairs. She climbed into bed and pulled up the covers, clutching the poker to her chest like a teddy bear.

She listened to the strident beeping of the smoke alarms and the rustle of flames as they grew louder and louder. A flickering light soon filled her doorway. She closed her eyes.

The fire slipped into her room, climbed up the door, and spread across the ceiling in a red-orange wave.

Even as the room was engulfed, even as the flames crawled across the carpet and leaped up the bedsheets, even as the fire surrounded her body and encased her in a burning cocoon, even as her hair burned and her skin melted, even as her eyes boiled and spilled down her cheeks, Donna trembled and shuddered and shivered.

Right up to the end, she was cold.

⟶

Fall.

Chad couldn't stand the silence. He could feel it nibbling at his mind, eroding his sanity. He couldn't believe how much of it there was in the world, with all the people, all the noise. But it was there, vast mountains of peace and small pockets of quiet, lying in wait, threatening to destroy him.

It didn't make sense. At the cabin all he wanted was silence. When the music had come blasting out of the gramophone, his first impulse was to shut it off, to stop those sounds from entering his head even if it meant driving iron spikes into his ears. The music was more than unpleasant; it was toxic, polluted, a raping of his auditory canals.

While Chad had taken no pleasure in what they'd done to Marcie, there had been a beatific smile on his face when they finally stopped the music. In the lull of silence immediately afterward, he'd felt a euphoric sense of calm and relief.

It didn't last.

He was fine when the police arrived. Better than fine, actually, because they bombarded him with questions—questions that began as thinly veiled accusations but quickly escalated into perplexed demands for the truth.

Chad didn't mind. He welcomed their inquiries, welcomed the sound of their raised voices, the louder the better. The others were sullen and barely coherent, but he was a regular chatterbox. He talked so much one of the officers suggested he might want to remain silent until his lawyer showed up. Chad couldn't do that; he was already growing suspicious of the silence. The only way to banish it was to fill it with sound.

So he talked to the police, to his parents, to the lawyer they got for him, to the press (even though the police and the lawyer advised him not to). He didn't care. He talked to anyone willing to listen, anyone willing to talk back to him, and it pushed away the silence. For a while.

Even though the cabin was big news that summer, interest waned over time and attentions eventually turned to the next tragedy. Soon Chad didn't have anyone to talk to—even his parents were tired of listening to him and responded only with single-word replies and grunts—and the silence returned.

It became a presence in his life, haunting him, infiltrating all the gaps of his existence that he couldn't fill with sound.

Nights were the worst. Lying in bed, trying to sleep with the house gone quiet around him. Leaving his television on helped him fall asleep, but in the depths of slumber the silence would return, telling him there was no escape even in the dreamworld. He'd wake up gasping, sometimes screaming, and although the sounds were caused by fear and anguish, they were sweet relief to his ears, reassuring him, telling him he was okay, when he knew he wasn't.

The people he could've talked to about this, the ones he *should* have talked to—his friends—he made no effort to contact. He couldn't say exactly why he didn't reach out to them, only that he knew on some level they wouldn't be able to help him. Just like he knew he couldn't help them.

He felt bad about not attending Donna's service, but the silence there would have been too great. There was no funeral, only a spreading of her ashes on the lakeshore, which Chad found ironic since ashes were supposedly all that had been left of her. The fire in which Donna had committed suicide ended up consuming almost every house on the street. The news said it was a miracle she was the only fatality.

Chad needed a miracle of his own, but he didn't think one was coming. No one wanted to talk to him anymore, and talking to himself only helped in a small, putting-off-the-inevitable sort of way. He figured it was only a matter of time before he ended up like Donna, taking his own life once the silence became too much to bear.

As the days grew shorter and the leaves changed colour, the silence took on a new aspect. Almost as if it were adapting itself to Chad's efforts to eliminate it.

Now when he entered a room, even if it was occupied, the silence was there. If he was at work, or a party, or a mall filled with people, he would experience a sensation like the volume of the world was being turned down to nothing. Then, at the moment he was about to start screaming, the volume would go back up again.

He went to the doctor even though he knew it was pointless. This wasn't a hearing impairment. It was a life impairment. A warning from the silence that it could get to him anywhere, at any time.

One day while he was out for a walk—and pondering the idea of buying a gun to blow his brains out—a car drove by with its stereo blaring. The windows were up so he couldn't make out what song was playing, but it didn't matter. The sound was what mattered. The *music*. It was like an oasis in a desert. A blast of sweet relief from all the crushing silence.

He wondered why he hadn't thought of it before. Talking to people, talking to himself, even leaving the television on while he slept. They were all stopgap solutions. The silence couldn't be sated by the mere babble of spoken words. It wanted something more mellifluous. It wanted the pitch and rhythm of music.

Chad ran home and went up to his room. He had a small stereo and a couple dozen CDs. He put on the loudest one he could find—Nirvana's *Nevermind*—and cranked the volume as high as it would go.

He nodded his head to the opening guitar riff of "Smells Like Teen Spirit," followed by the rumble of drums that ushered in the full blast of Kurt Cobain's power chords.

It was music, and it was loud, but he could tell right away it wasn't the solution to his problem. Even though it held back the silence, he could still sense it in the gaps between the music and the lyrics—lurking, waiting, biding its time, waiting for the song to end. It wasn't the miracle he needed.

The next day he went to a pawn shop and looked at a selection of record players. Many of them were old, although none were as ancient as the one Marcie had found in the cellar of the cabin. He bought one and brought it home. There were records at the pawn shop, but none that he wanted. Perry Como. Lesley Gore. The Beatles. No, no, and no.

He needed big sounds. Horns that could make your ears bleed. Drums that could pound your bones to dust. Music that could lift you off the ground and make your very soul tremble.

He thought of the record at the cabin, but it was gone, smashed to pieces.

He tried searching for it on the internet even though he had nothing to go on.

He searched and searched until he realized the answer couldn't be found on a computer.

The song was out there, somewhere, and he had to find it.

Before the silence took him.

◄◦►

Winter.

Mark couldn't sleep. He would drift, he would doze, but he could never enter the proper restful state that most people took for granted. It wasn't due to shock or stress or guilt or any of the other one-word diagnoses the doctors proposed to explain his condition. It wasn't that he didn't feel tired; he did, immensely so. He was simply incapable of shutting off his waking mind. It was like he'd forgotten how to sleep.

He tried drinking, he tried drugs, he tried drinking and drugs. He tried tricking his body by going through the ceremony of his sleeping routine: brushing his teeth, putting on his pyjamas, climbing into bed, putting his head on the pillow. All in the hope of drawing the attention of the Sandman.

To no avail.

His parents wanted to send him to a sleep clinic, but Mark refused to talk to any more doctors. They couldn't help the others—Donna dead, Chad missing, Annabelle crazy—and they wouldn't be able to help him.

Eventually he grew to accept his sleepless state—mostly because he didn't have a choice—and began to explore the new vista that had opened up before him.

Nighttime.

While everyone else was tucked into their beds, luxuriating in slumber, Mark walked the streets in his neighbourhood. He explored other people's houses, sneaking in through unlocked doors and windows. He never stole anything or damaged anyone's property. He simply strolled from room to room, checking things out, admiring the interior world of other people's lives. He told himself he was only killing time, of which he had plenty these days. It never entered his mind that he was practicing for his future career.

On one of his late-night wanderings he ended up at the police station. He'd been there many times over the summer, usually during the day and in the company of his lawyer. It felt strange to be there now, alone at night. And yet, in another way, it felt perfectly right. As if he'd been drawn to this place.

He took to watching the police station. It was never closed, but late at night there were usually only a couple people working in the building, sometimes only a single desk officer manning the front counter.

Sneaking around to the back of the building, Mark broke a basement window and slithered inside. He landed on the concrete floor of an exercise room, with various pieces of workout equipment and a stack of gym mats against one wall.

He exited into a darkened hallway and wandered around until he found what he was looking for.

The evidence room.

The door was locked, but on the wall next to it there was a key on a hook below a handmade sign that said: RETURN KEY WHEN YOU ARE DONE WITH IT. DO NOT TAKE IT HOME WITH YOU!

"Fair enough," Mark said.

He unlocked the door and went inside.

The evidence room was a long dark cave divided into narrow corridors by a series of free-standing metal shelves. Mark flicked a wall switch and fluorescent tubes sputtered to life overhead, filling the room with a cold, sterile light.

The shelves were lined with banker's boxes, each one with a different case number written on it. Mark didn't know their case number, so it took him a long time to find what he was looking for.

When he did, he sat on the floor with the box in front of him. It was like Christmas morning and he was about to open his present. Only he already knew what he was getting.

He opened the box and dug through a pile of evidence bags until he found the one with the gramophone's tone arm in it. He took it out—the cylindrical tube with the hook of black glass on the end—and held it on the palm of his hand. It felt like nothing. It felt like everything.

He remembered the night at the cabin when Marcie snapped it off the gramophone. He'd thought she was going to attack them with it. That she would let out a primal scream and come flying through the air, slashing and stabbing. That's what they told the police.

What really happened was that Marcie hovered in the air for a moment, clutching the tone arm in her fist, then she drew the obsidian hook across her own throat. As the skin parted and blood spilled out, the music grew louder and louder. It was unlike anything they'd ever heard before. It was the opening of something terrible, or something wonderful. They never found out which because they didn't let it finish.

Mark wondered now if that had been a mistake. If instead of killing Marcie and destroying the—

The door opened.

Mark leaped to his feet.

He expected to see the outline of the desk officer framed in the doorway, but it was a different shape. A familiar shape.

"Chad?"

"Hello, Mark."

Chad stepped into the room. His expression was calm, almost serene, as if he expected to find his friend here waiting for him. His gaze fell to the object Mark was clutching to his chest.

"I haven't been able to sleep," Mark blurted suddenly. "Not since the cabin. I thought if I found it . . ." He stared longingly at the tone arm. At the Shard.

"I have a song stuck in my head," Chad said. "*The* song. I thought that"—he nodded at the Shard—"would help me find it." He tilted his head to the side. "Maybe it's a lullaby."

Mark looked up hopefully. "It could help both of us?"

"Maybe," Chad said. "But I think we have to help it first."

"What do we need to do?"

"Things," Chad said. "Awful, horrible things."

Mark noticed his friend's hands. There was blood on them. He thought of the desk officer.

"They'll probably write books about us," Chad said.

"What about songs? Will they write songs?"

Chad smiled. He reached out and put his hand around Mark's, so they were holding the Shard together.

"I think they will."

And what beautiful music they would make.

◂◦▸

Spring.

Annabelle couldn't stop spinning. Her thoughts were awhirl as the one-year anniversary of the cabin approached. Her attention span was in tatters; sleep was virtually impossible. Her mind kept going back to that night—not to Marcie and the music, but to the game of Spin the Bottle they'd been playing before the horror began.

She should have been thinking about the violence of that night, the loss of her friend and the miracle of their own survival, but what kept popping into her head was the idea, the *conviction*, that Chad only wanted to play the game so he could kiss Donna. He had denied it at the time, but of course that's what she expected him to say.

In the weeks and months following the cabin, she became trapped in a circuit of denial and disbelief—thoughts of Chad and Donna kissing, touching, *fucking*, kept spinning around in her head like a torrid tornado—and there seemed to be nothing she could do to break herself out of it.

She stopped talking to them—which was easy to do, since the others stopped talking to her as well—but it didn't stop the whirling dervish of her thoughts.

The only thing that provided the slightest bit of relief was staying in motion. Walking, jogging, running, sprinting—it didn't matter as long as she wasn't standing still. When she stopped moving, that's when the thoughts returned, falling on her like a horde of vampire bats.

She went for long walks around town and in the woods behind her house. She went out at any hour, day or night, whenever the images in her head threatened to overwhelm her. Her parents grew more and more concerned, especially when a woman in town went missing. They tried to get Annabelle to limit her wanderings to the daylight hours, but she ignored them. She walked when she had to walk. This was the way it had to be. She knew there was no hope of clearing her mind; the best she could hope for was to quiet it.

And it worked.

For a while.

Over time the thoughts began to infiltrate her sleep, filling her dreams with images of Chad and Donna, their naked, sweaty bodies locked together, writhing on the gritty floor of the cabin, with the empty vodka bottle next to them, spinning, spinning, spinning.

On a cold morning in March, it all became too much to bear, and Annabelle was flung from her noxious nightmares like a circus performer shot from a cannon. She could actually feel her mind coming untethered, the guy wires of her sanity popping loose one by one.

She ran outside in only a T-shirt and a pair of pyjama bottoms, her bare feet punching holes in the fresh blanket of snow that had fallen the night before.

She ran and ran, but the images in her head remained. She couldn't outrun them, couldn't push them out of her head as she'd done before.

Crying out in fury and frustration, she picked up speed and ran headlong into a thick oak tree. She struck it hard, throwing her arms up at the last second to brace for the impact, and went stumbling into another tree. She bounced off it, her feet moving frantically to keep her from falling, and pinballed off a third.

She continued to twirl around, waiting for the inevitable moment when she'd hit something hard enough to knock her down. While this was happening, she became aware of something: those poisonous thoughts of Chad and Donna had vanished. They'd been knocked from her head just as her body had been knocked from one tree to another.

Finally she came to a stop, her breath pluming in misty gasps, her feet so cold they were numb. In the same instant, the relief she'd experienced began to evaporate and the thoughts slipped insidiously back into her mind.

She threw her hands at the gray sky and shouted, "*What do you want? What do you want?*"

She spun and screamed at the trees, her feet pounding the snow into the frozen ground . . . and the thoughts dissipated again. She slowed and felt them return.

It was the spinning, she realized. Not just moving but spinning! That's what kept the thoughts away.

She started twirling around and around with her arms stretched out to either side. The thoughts melted, like the snow beneath her feet, like the tears spilling down her cheeks.

She kept spinning until she made herself sick. Stumbling against one of the trees, she gripped the rough bark in one hand while she bent over at the waist and vomited onto the pristine snow.

She'd never felt better.

From that moment on, everywhere she went, Annabelle was spinning. She was like a human top, twirling and pirouetting as she walked around the house or strolled down the street. Step, step, spin, step, step, spin. She didn't have the grace of a ballerina, or the balance, and the dizziness that came with all the spinning contributed to a lot of falls and collisions. One time, on her way to the kitchen to make herself a sandwich, she walk-spun through the dining room and stumbled into the hutch containing her parents' wedding china. She was barely able to get out of the way before it toppled over and landed facedown on the floor, plates and cups exploding with a rattling, ear-splitting crash.

Her mom and dad were pretty upset about that one, but their anger turned quickly to concern for her mental state. They told Annabelle, as calmly as they could, that it wasn't normal for her to be spinning around everywhere she went.

Normal? Annabelle wanted to shout at them. *I left normal a long time ago. I left it at the cabin.*

That was when it first came to her, the thought of going back, although she supposed it had always been there, like the images of Chad and Donna that had taken root in her brain. Because the times she felt better—or as close to better as she got these days—were when she was outside, walking and spinning her way farther and farther from her house. At the time she'd thought it was only the relief of being away from her parents and their well-intentioned but mostly annoying concerns. Now she realized it wasn't just the spinning that drove the images away, it was the fact she was moving as she spun, spiralling outward from the nexus of her life to some unknown destination.

Only it wasn't unknown. She knew exactly where her spinning was trying to take her.

The cabin.

Going back was the last thing she wanted, but she knew there was no way she could keep spinning for the rest of her life. Unlike the empty vodka bottle, she would have to stop at some point, and when she did, all those horrible thoughts would be waiting for her. She wouldn't live like that. She couldn't.

So she went back.

She took her parents' car, telling them she was going shopping. They were relieved she was doing something so normal, something the old Annabelle would've done. They told her to enjoy herself. She said she would. They told her to take her time and enjoy the day. She said she would.

Even though she remembered how to get there, Annabelle took a circuitous route, driving away from her house and through her neighbourhood in wider and wider circles until she left the orbit of town and entered the woods.

When she finally arrived at the cabin, she was surprised to see it looked the same. She'd heard it had become a site of morbid notoriety for true-crime buffs, and that one particular kill club had even recorded a podcast here shortly after the police released the crime scene. She was especially surprised to find it empty today of all days. The one-year anniversary. Maybe the cabin was keeping them away.

Annabelle got out of the car and walked up onto the wide front porch. The door was open. She went inside and looked around and around, spinning as had become her practice these days. She expected to see skeins of old police tape on the floor, or empty beer bottles from the kids drawn to this place with tales of murder and mutilation. But there was nothing. It looked exactly as it did the day she and her friends had come here.

She was walking and twirling across the floor when her foot struck something and she went stumbling toward the fireplace. She managed to grab onto the mantel, then turned to see what she had tripped on.

It was the ringbolt in the trap door.

She went over to it, performing a quick spin without even thinking about it, and knelt. She remembered Marcie coming up from the cellar with the gramophone. She remembered the music that wasn't music, sounds that shouldn't have existed when Marcie tore off the tone arm, but continued to pound out of the brass horn. She remembered the way it felt when those sounds poured into her ears and entered her mind.

She remembered killing Marcie, their poor sweet friend, and destroying the gramophone and the record. Only that didn't put an end to the sounds. Because they weren't really coming from the brass horn. They were coming from Marcie. So they fell on her and dismembered her, chopped her body to pieces because that was the only way to make it stop.

And she remembered what happened afterward: the others taking the Shard and marking themselves with it. Donna slashing her arms. Chad drawing a jagged line across the side of his face. Mark stabbing himself in the side.

When it was Annabelle's turn, she stared at the Shard in her hand, the others watching her expectantly . . . and dropped it on the floor.

She couldn't do it. She wouldn't. She remembered the bottle, the one that wouldn't stop spinning until Donna smashed it with the poker. She remembered telling them she didn't want to play their game. She didn't then and she didn't now. She refused to mark herself.

Only it didn't matter. She was still marked, and the music was still alive, still playing in their heads over and over and over again.

That's what this was all about. That's what had brought her back to the cabin.

It was the song, and it wanted what every song wanted: to be heard.

She pressed her finger into the dust on top of the trap door and drew a spiral curving outward and outward. Then she made a fist and knocked on the old, dry wood.

She went over to the couch and sat down.

She didn't have to wait long.

Shortly after the sun went down, the trap door rose. Chad and Mark climbed out. They were filthy, their clothes smeared with dirt, their faces streaked with dried blood.

Annabelle was no more surprised to see them than they were to see her.

The dirt was from the cellar. The blood was from their victims. There had been seven, by her count—or at least that's how many people the news had reported missing in the past few months. The police were baffled. No bodies had been found. Annabelle could've told them where they were.

Chad and Mark crept stealthily across the room toward her, tiptoeing across the creaky wooden floor. Chad had something in his hand. Even though it was too dark for Annabelle to make it out, she knew what it was.

The Shard.

"You heard it, too?" Chad said.

Annabelle nodded.

"Can you make it stop?" Mark asked.

Annabelle said, "No," and Chad and Mark hung their heads.

Then she reached into her jacket pocket and took out the gun. It was her father's .38 revolver.

She looked up into their blood-streaked faces.

"Wanna play a game?"

⊰◦⊱

The police found the bodies a week later.

All three lay sprawled on the cabin floor, their heads surrounded by bloody halos.

Detective Russo crouched next to Annabelle's body. The revolver was still in her hand. Even though her finger was no longer capable of pulling the trigger, the cylinder continued to spin around and around.

Across the room, one of the uniforms hissed in pain and dropped something on the floor.

CHIT CHIT

STEVE TOASE

Diesel fumes leaked through the rusted floor into the back of the transit van and tainted every mouthful of air. I covered my face with my sleeve and tried to breathe as shallow as possible, not that it made much difference.

"Why couldn't you steal something decent?" I said, hardly able to hear my own voice over the engine noise. Vibrations from the worn suspension rattled me against the bodywork.

Karl half looked over his shoulder while trying to keep his attention on the road.

"I told you. There was nothing else available at such short notice, and a flash car was going to attract too much attention up here."

"You couldn't get a Land Rover? A Range Rover? Those wouldn't attract attention."

Chloe tapped me on the leg and shook her head. She sat opposite on the thin wooden seat, combat jacket collar folded up over her face.

She didn't need to remind me Karl was quick to temper. I'd seen the aftermath more than once. I looked back toward the driver's seat, and saw him gripping the steering wheel, knuckles almost popping out of the skin. Beside him Mick turned the radio on, his gold sovereign rings reflecting the moonlight, music struggling to be heard over the van trying to shake itself apart.

I still didn't understand why the job needed four of us for a simple recovery, but it wasn't really my place to understand the logistics. Apparently the client had insisted on it, and the client was always right.

We were far from any town, roads little more than grooves worn into the landscape. Each corner was a game of chicken with an unknown opponent.

I'd worked with Karl a few times over the years. I'd trust him to drive at speed down country roads far more than I would order me a beer in a pub. As long as he didn't have to talk to the public there was a chance someone wouldn't end up in hospital.

It was Chloe who'd brought us together. Had the link with the client. I saw her open Signal on her phone once more and update them on our progress. I'd worked with all three separately in the past, but never on a single job. At first I didn't know why they brought me in, but it sort of made sense.

After what happened to Pasha I'd retired to a small Romanian port on the Black Sea, far from my previous employer's influence, but money only lasts so long, and I had experiences a bank robber, a debt collector, and a con-woman didn't. Reaching into my pocket I brought out the creased map to check the route one more time.

The target was hidden in the corner of a small piece of moorland called Black Horse Acre. Over the years I'd searched for many different things in night-time fields. Unexcavated roman artefacts on archaeology sites. Sawn-off shotguns stuffed in mouldy holdalls. Caches of military grade explosives. Each one needed a specific search method. Horse skulls? They were harder to find. They needed intelligence, and intelligence needed an informer.

◄○►

I recognised the mark from several videos on YouTube, though he looked different wearing farm-stained tweeds instead of his ribbon fluttered mummer's costume. Grabbing myself a bourbon I sat down on the next table and watched him for a few minutes as I sipped the harsh, cheap, spirit. Several ash-smeared horse skulls stared down at me from the wall, bottle glass ground into the eye sockets.

I knew from Chloe's research that he never met anyone, every night just sitting by himself and drinking a single pint. A picture of rural isolation and misery. That research also told me he used to drink more, a lot more, and that whiskey loosened his tongue in a way that polite conversation couldn't.

Usually Chloe did the information gathering. Might be cliché, but people open up to a well-spoken young woman in expensive clothes, and when I say people I mean men. Not so much on the edge of the moors. In farming villages smart suits and posh accents mean authority, and authority meant someone poking around where they didn't belong.

Horse brasses glittered the light from the open fire. The taproom was too hot and I took off my jacket, tucking it on the windowsill.

"Can I join you?" I said, turning my chair around before the mark had chance to object. His beer was untouched. He shrugged and lifted the glass, coating his cracked lips in foam but barely drinking anything.

"What do you have there?" he said, as if noticing my glass for the first time.

"Bourbon, but it's pretty poor stuff. Got to make do I suppose."

"Scotch is better," he said, with the certainty of a man making a self-obvious proclamation.

"I'm sure you're right," I said, finishing the shot in one. He flinched at that. "But I know next to nothing about single malt. What would you recommend?"

He turned and looked at the bar.

"Start with a Highland Park," he said.

I came back and placed the second glass in front of him.

"As a thank-you," I said.

There was a flicker of doubt in his eyes as he stood at the top of a personal hill reaching for a treat he could no longer afford for himself. His scarred hand hesitated on the table. I lifted my glass and waited while his doubts left and he returned my cheers.

By the sixth drink we were best friends. By the seventh he was talking freely about the mummers, and by the tenth he'd marked on the Ordnance Survey map exactly where the horse skulls were buried in the field.

◄◦►

"We can't leave that there," Mick said, turning to stare at the van parked white and beacon-like beside the dry stone wall. The overheating engine crackled like burning leaves. "Someone will see it."

Karl looked around as if trying to find something lost.

"No garages. We'll just have to chance it. Unless you fancy driving it down to that village we passed and hiking back up while we shelter from the weather under a non-existent tree."

Mick said nothing, and walked to the back doors. He was a big guy, heavily tattooed with a taste for post pub fighting in car-parks. He was also very effective in problem solving, and the problem for now was keeping a lid on Karl's temper until we'd finished this part of the job. He passed me a shovel and closed the doors.

"Let's get going then."

◄○►

The plan was always for Karl to stop with the Transit. Just in case we needed to get started fast. While he waited, he doubled as look out, and interference if the police turned up. Though he would tear a nightclub to shreds over some imagined slight, in the presence of the Police he was always polite, forthcoming, and helpful. Hidden talents. We all had them.

Mick, Chloe, and I walked across the first field, threading our way through nettles and patches of stagnant water. The damp had got into my leg and stiffened my old knee injury, finding the metal and cooling it against the bone. Reminding me why I always got nervous going around country roads in the dark.

"He's the weak link, you know," Mick said, when he thought we were out of Karl's earshot. I said nothing, still unconvinced and unwilling to speak just in case.

"Someone always is," Chloe said. She turned her phone off, the stars and moon bright enough to navigate by. The heavy scent of peat washed down from the higher slopes on the breeze.

I led the way over the wall into the next field. I was the one with experience of stomping around the countryside at night finding lost artefacts. My workplace.

Chloe followed me, took the sketch map and looked around Black Horse Acre.

I didn't know if the client wanted the skulls for trophies or disruption, I didn't need to, but my money was on the latter. If it was a trophy we'd be revisiting the village pub after closing time. A full ritual skull was a far more impressive dinner party talking point than one freshly maggot skinned in the ground, still rot yellowed and dirt streaked.

"Over there," Chloe said, pointing to a far corner where the dry stone walls tapered to meet at a narrow point.

She tried to pretend she didn't belong, but I'd known her for many years and knew that she'd earned the right to be there as much as any of us. If Karl did lose his rag I'd let her deal with him. His fragile ego would be far more damaged by a beating from a hundred and twenty five pound woman. Baggy jumpers and designer jeans could hide a lot of battle scars and Chloe had been in a lot of battles.

◄○►

This was where I came in. I knew dirt. I knew topsoil and subsoil. I knew clay, silt, and bedrock. I knew when soil had been spade turned, and I was very, very good at finding things. I used to find changes in soil as a professional. Dig up old stuff hidden from sight for thousands of years. Qualifications and everything. Later in life? Let's say I was more work for hire than public service.

The ground was covered in thistles and patches of heather. Clumps of grass that even moorland sheep would pass on. I ran my hand over the ground. Felt the earth for any slight disturbance. The presence of something that should not be there.

Soil never goes back the same. Put a shovel in the earth and the land changes forever. Do it recently enough and someone like me will find it.

"Start there," I said, pointing to a clump of forget-me-nots growing amongst the choke of plants.

No-one questioned me. We all knew our jobs, and mine was to say where to look. The only thing I couldn't tell was how deep. How long we would be stood around in the corner of that field.

Mick started digging, hefting each shovelful of dirt to one side. Chloe just stood and watched. I noticed that her mobile had re-appeared, filming the job in progress so the client knew everything was going smoothly. Live-streaming. No escaping the signal, even on the moors.

I glanced toward the road. The van was still in place, and I thought I saw Karl moving around trying to keep himself warm. He never could keep still. Too much nervous energy.

"It's empty." Mick stood up and leant on the spade's handle, leaving room for myself and Chloe to kneel down. She turned her phone and switched on the torch.

There were no skulls but the hole was far from empty. Strands of horse hair stuck to the sides, tangled in the forget-me-knot roots. The rough trench reeked of abattoirs and tanning pits. I reached my hand back and Mick passed me the spade. Using the blade I scraped the bottom layer of soil away at the base. Hundreds of maggots came to life, until then hidden under a thin spread of silt. Shuffled and twitched like severed muscle. I flinched and stood up, pointed to Chloe's hand and she disconnected the video feed.

"Someone's beaten us to it," I said, stretching out my back. "They've already got the skulls. We can't do any more."

"Are you sure? These clients," she paused. "I don't want to go back to them empty-handed."

"Then I suggest you go to a stables and decapitate a couple of mares because there's fuck all under the ground here," Mick said. I watched him reach into his pocket for a packet of tobacco, slow and deliberate, resting the cigarette paper on his thumb and forefinger while he crumbled in his addiction.

"We need to check," Chloe said. "At least to say we've tried."

I nodded, took off my coat and hooked it on the limestone wall. Working fast I dug three more holes, cutting through the roots and stacking the dirt behind me. The quicker I finished the quicker I could get back out of the country. As soon as the metal blade hit bedrock I moved onto the next. Mick smoked and Chloe typed messages I couldn't see. I left them to what they needed to do. Dealing in their own ways with how things were panning out.

◄◦►

After the crash all those years ago all the memories faded, apart from the sound. The noise of bone on metal is very particular. One hardened substance giving way to another. Neither coming off unscathed. If Chloe and Mick hadn't turned toward the van, I would have thought it was another flashback. I'd not had one for a while. When I saw them looking in the same direction, well, it seemed a lot less likely.

Mick dropped his roll-up into the grass and stamped it cold.

"I'll go and have a look," he said, reaching to his belt for his knife.

"We'll all go," Chloe said. Something glinted across her knuckles, but in the darkness I couldn't tell if it was jewellery or a weapon. Maybe both.

I nodded, and followed them back across the field. We all walked in silence, making our own plans to deal with whatever was waiting for us. We were all capable and did not need to compare notes in situations like this.

Karl was no longer there, apart from a gouge of skin still attached to the ripped open metal of the driver's door. We moved around the vehicle falling into roles. I took the front, while Mick examined the wheels and Chloe checked out the rear compartment.

The bonnet had been torn open, inside the engine block shattered. Oil and water pooled underneath, collecting in the potholes of the lay-by, like the van had voided itself with fear.

Mick sat by the front wheel, running his finger over the buckled rim.

"Something's not right about this."

"You mean the van getting vandalised and Karl disappearing?" I knelt beside him, wincing as the surgical steel in my leg continued to remind me it was still there.

"The damage. Why not just slash the tires? This looks like something has gripped the rim and gnawed through the sidewall."

He was right. Wire sprung from underneath the rubber like splintered bone, the metal of the wheel buckled and torn.

"The back too," Chloe said. "Looks like it's been chewed free."

"And Karl?"

She shrugged, in a way that reminded me how hard it was for her to make a living in this business. How hard she had to be in return.

"We have to put him down to collateral. Get ourselves somewhere secure and regroup."

I nodded and stood, looked back to where we'd just been.

The figure was two fields away, dressed in white, its yellowed head streaked and stained to shadow. I watched for any movement but there was none. It did not approach or retreat, just stayed there watching us, limbless and empty eyed.

"I think we've got problems," I said. Chloe glanced up, and reached into her pocket for her phone. I watched her scroll a map to a destination, fingers zooming and scanning.

"There's a disused cottage about half a mile away. We get there and we wait."

I glanced toward the field once more. The figure had climbed the wall while our attention was elsewhere and was moving through the stagnant water and thistles toward us, each step marked by the chit chit of skinless jaws.

◄◦►

You can ignore chronic pain if you need to. You focus on the next thing because if you let the discomfort overwhelm you, that's your life worn away. I ignored my knee and ran, following Chloe and the glimmer of the mobile screen as she tried to keep track of the route. Behind us the figure was at the dry stone wall. Over the wall. Beside the van.

Mick was behind me, the tar in his lungs making each breath an effort.

There's an old joke with the punchline, 'I don't need to be faster than the bear. I just need to be faster than you.' I looked behind me at Mick, ignored the nerves in my leg that were trying to get me to slow down, and sped up after Chloe.

I don't know when Mick fell. I was too busy concentrating on following Chloe to the shelter of the cottage. She held the door open as I ran inside and collapsed on the floor, my knee finally giving way. While I recovered she locked us in and barricaded the way with mouldinfested chairs, and rotten sideboards.

"Are you OK?" she said, crouching beside me, and checking my pulse.

"As long as we don't have to run for a while, I'll be fine," I said. I tried to stand but all the pain I'd switched off came back in one single wave and I collapsed back to the floor.

"Did you see it?" I said, reaching into my pocket for a blister-pack of painkillers. They wouldn't work straight away but soon enough.

"I was too busy finding somewhere to run to," she said. She took off her coat and dropped it over the back of a dining chair. "Did you?"

I nodded.

"It had a horse's skull for a head."

She smiled as if trying to reassure a toddler.

"You're just seeing things. That knee injury distracting you, and the target playing on your mind."

"I know what I saw. Even at that distance."

"It's your first job in a while isn't it?" I nodded, because there was nothing to disagree with. "Adrenaline can do funny things."

The argument wasn't worth having, and we had more real world concerns than something I might or might not have seen.

"Get a fire lit," I said. "Then we can start planning how to get out of here."

She nodded and started to break up an old bed in the corner of the room, stamping the slats until they fitted on the hearth. Using handfuls of wallpaper as kindling. Soon flames blazed in the grate, smoke billowing into the room as if the chimney did not want to accept the offering.

I pulled myself up onto a chair and stretched out my knee, waiting for the drugs to kick in.

"What now?" I said, trying to get comfy.

"Now we wait until dawn," she said, placing her phone on the mantelpiece. "There's no cover, and I can't arrange an extraction until first thing. Someone is bound to report the van, so we don't want to be just wandering the moors waiting to be picked up."

The rattling interrupted her, coming from both sides of the building at once.

"Stay here," she said. I watched her climb the stairs to the first floor and listened as she moved from front to back of the building.

"And?"

"It's caught up with us. Trying to find a way in, but the building's secure for now."

"It? Can it be in two places at once? That noise came from the front and back at the same time."

"There's only one," she said. "You only saw one."

A white shape crossed in front of the window, then crossed back. I listened to the footsteps, first through the dirt of abandoned flower beds, then onto the stone path. I did not need to see it to know where it had gone.

The sound of banging on the door was incessant, splintering the old planks until cold air chased away any heat from the feeble fire. I looked around for Chloe. She was still upstairs.

"Chloe," I shouted, because we were far past concealing our names. "This barrier isn't going to hold forever."

Still no sound came down from the top floor.

It took me a moment to realise that the back door was also under attack, a moment longer to remember that it hadn't been reinforced.

Using the chair as a walking frame I limped across to the mantelpiece. To Chloe's phone. The screen glowed intermittently as message after message came in unanswered. I picked it up and pressed the display, left unlocked for speed. Read the message thread.

"Two targets secured. Third ready and unable to retreat to a safer location."

"Understood. Secure yourself out of the way and let them do what they need to. The transfer will be done when all three are created."

"When can you extract me?"

"As soon as all three targets have been transformed."

I slid her phone into my pocket and looked toward the back door. The creature ducked under the lintel and came into the cottage, horse's skull blackened with soot and ash, the white shroud almost glowing in the darkness. Where fabric and bone met I saw vertebrae exposed and strung with torn muscle. The cottage filled with the scent of charred fur, sweat, and urine soaked stables.

The creature stood staring for a moment, then walked forward, almost toppling with each step. The shroud lifted as it went to steady itself and an arm reached out. Gold sovereign rings glittered against tattooed hands. I ran toward the stairs as the front door finally gave way, hoping that the low arch would keep the creatures on the ground floor.

"I can't let you up," Chloe said, blocking the way. "I don't get paid unless all three of you are given and I really need to get paid." She held the knife low and, because of the difference in height, very close to my throat.

"Mick and Karl down there?"

She nodded. "And soon you. Three skulls. Three sacrifices. Three horses for the villages."

"How much are they paying you?" I asked, all the time watching where her gaze was.

"Paying me in kind. Money is not a problem. Sometimes you need a job doing in return. I'm sure you understand."

My intention was only ever to get beyond Chloe, into the safety of the second floor. As I launched myself forward she lunged with the knife. I grabbed her wrist and pulled, stepping past as I did. She lost her footing and fell down the flight of stairs. I couldn't keep my balance and slipped myself, catching the banister and wedging myself in the stairwell, just able to see the hobby horses moving onto the fallen Chloe.

They did not decapitate her. Instead the things that were once Mick and Karl gripped her head and slowly massaged her skull. The plates, solid since childhood, loosened along their seams and moved over each other, collapsing and shifting. They carried on manipulating, readying her for the next stage. Bone ground against bone. Her scalp snagged in the joins, tearing and cooking with friction. The cottage filled with the stench of burnt hair.

From under its shroud the creature with tattooed arms produced the third horse's skull, jaw already wired to chitter, and slid it over Chloe's now softened head.

Noises that might have been protests escaped from Chloe's shattered throat and just as the new adornment fitted into place the other two creatures reached out together and tore free her jaw, pulling away the skin and muscle from around her neck.

They were three now, united in their transformation. Creatures of the moor and the ritual. The Obby 'Oss and the Grey Mary. Mari Lwyd. The clatter against the door in the night that brings fear and nightmares to those inside.

With their triumvirate complete they turned away from me and walked out of the cottage into the darkness. In my pocket Chloe's phone rang. I pressed the green answer button and the speaker button.

"It was meant to be you, you know," the voice said.

I recognised it, though I'd only had one conversation with the owner, in a deserted taproom, overlooked by horse brasses and ash streaked skulls. He sounded different. In control. As if he was someone who never lost grip of a situation, even when he was on the outside of half a bottle of expensive single malt. "But that doesn't matter. We have our three horses now, ready for the winter plays. You can leave and make safe passage off the moors."

"And payment?" I said. I was used to keeping my voice steady in dangerous situations. At that moment I struggled.

"Your return flight is paid for. Consider yourself lucky you're leaving at all."

◄◦►

The knee injury happened a long time before the job with Chloe, Mick, and Karl on that deserted moor, but it's not the car crash I remember when cold gets into the surgical steel. It's the sight of a scalp being massaged and softened as a face collapses in on itself. Then I sit up all night with the lights on waiting for the memory of scorched hair and torn scalp to fade, but it never does.

POOR BUTCHER-BIRD

GEMMA FILES

Down here," he says, and I nod, like it's not obvious. Dip my head like I'm nervous, but a little shakily, too. Like I'm as excited as he is. You have to be careful about these things; he's dumb, sure, but nobody's *that* dumb.

You'd be surprised.

I had to work hard to hook up with this guy, who claims his "name" is Shrike93, just like his email. These Web-handles really crisp my arse-hairs, which I know makes me sound old—old enough to know what a Luddite actually was, any rate. The main good part about having once been a factory girl is, it keeps me small and weak-looking. Not a threat, supposedly, 'specially when stood next to some bro like the Shrike, all swole up with hormone-saturated meat and childhood vaccines. Nothing like. That, and I know not to sound how I think, either, when I speak out loud. Worked hard on that over the years. So much so, it holds pretty well, except when I get riled up; lucky how none of this posturing is quite enough to rile me, though. Not as yet.

He always picks two, and one of 'em doesn't tend to come back—that's the rumour. That's why I wasn't surprised I found another potential initiate waiting for him, when I got to our IRL meet-point; made sure to bristle a bit, then waited for the Shrike to step in once it got truly heated. Can't waste that precious red, now, can we? And he was quick enough to make his move, the minute this other wee pixie-haircut bitch pulled a flick-knife out. Which was just as well . . . for her.

She thinks she'll be the one gets picked, all right. But I *know* I will, and that's the difference.

Experience always wins, that's my motto.

So down we go, the three of us, the Shrike leading the way, with me and Pixie-Cut trailing after. It's almost always down, with these sorts. The house is an abandoned two-story box on a high-fenced lot somewhere in the Annex, thick inside with cobwebs and mouse shit and dust, except for the lane these slags have cleared between the kitchen's back entrance and the door to the basement. And at the bottom of those stairs there's another door—brand-new, very fancy, normal on the outside but heavier than it looks, with a neat little combination smart-lock built into its knob that has to be keyed from the Shrike's iPhone, using his thumbprint. He undoes it on one side, then does it back up on the other.

Note to self: Need to get hold of that thumb.

Inside, another stubby flight of stairs, going down half a story to some sort of sub-basement; might have been meant as a wine-cellar, maybe, or a bomb shelter. There's lit candles stuck in bottles everywhere, half-melted into wax stalagmites, and the air heavy with incense like it's 1969. Whole floor's paved with bare mattresses slicked in dark plastic on either side of a clear area, three feet wide by thirty long from the door on inwards, mosaic-tiled in red and gold—a ritual path to that joke of a shrine they've set up along the back wall. And there, at last, is that big red lacquer cabinet, inside which I can only assume they've got the thing—the person—I want.

The rest of the cult are all lined up on either side of it, too, not that they probably think of themselves as such: Twenty of 'em, all told, unless somebody else is hiding in the bog somewhere. Not that they seem to *have* a bog down here, that I can see.

They've all got names he insists on telling me, which I forget almost immediately, 'cause it makes it easier. Instead, I file 'em under characteristics: Blue Hair; (too much) Face-Metal; Green Highlights; Snatched Brows (with scarification); Needs More T. Not to mention Bare Midriff, Assless

Chaps and straight-up Topless (girl *and* boy), plus a variety of other mock-Goth costuming; leather, studs and vinyl, too-large hoodies paired with artfully ripped fishnets. There's even one in the back seems to be wearing a blood-stained fake fur-suit, bright pink, splotched all over like some naff bunny-leopard hybrid. Think I'll call him Anime Chimera, if and when it comes to it.

This is church night for them, I reckon. Get together with like-minded individuals, share something meaningful, go through the ritual celebration that gives their dull little weeks a goal—all dressed up with something to pray to, not to mention somebody to kill over it. And so blessed, blessed sure, in their black little hearts, how no one else ever does the same. Bloody children.

Still, kids can be tricky, 'specially when they're high, and armed. As I know from hard experience.

They're passing 'round bottles now, probably scarfed from parents' liquor cabinets: tequila, scotch, bourbon, vodka, red wine. I take a swallow or two, enough to make sure my breath smells like theirs, and mime the rest, while Pixie-Cut gleefully chugs whatever she's handed. By the time the Shrike stands up by the cabinet and loudly claps his hands, she's well and truly plastered.

"Brothers and sisters!" he shouts. "The moon's gone 'round again. It's that time!" Yells and cheers and hoots. "Time to renew ourselves, once more. Time to be *more*." More noise. I clench my jaw, holding my cardboard smile still. "Anyone have a story to share?"

A beat.

"I did it!" Green Highlights yells abruptly. "I found my boss. Told him I'd changed my mind, and when we were alone, I broke his nose and I knocked out his teeth—" this gets more cheers "—and then I carved PERV into his forehead, and I whammied him so hard he's never gonna know who did it! *Ever!*"

Howls of triumph fill the room; people hug Green Highlights, slap her back, hoist her hands into the air like she's won a boxing match. She's actually crying now I look close enough, poor cow. Still, I'm sure it feels good, while it lasts.

Up by the cabinet, Shrike's grinning like a preacher tallying up donations in his head. Calls for other stories, and gets them: All much the same, though none quite as righteously vindictive as Green Highlights'. Petty grudges, gleeful sadism, conquest-notches; the sort of selfish tat people dream about in bed or in front of a bathroom mirror, through clenched teeth, tears or panting, between the short strokes. The *I Deserve This* rag, I call it—high on their own drama, the sweet bile backwash. Pixie-Cut looks pretty much like she's already halfway to getting off herself at the spectacle, what with those big eyes and that flushed face, rapid-breathing through her nose; me, I make sure to keep on trembling just in case. Not that anybody's really looking.

Finally, Shrike calms the crowd down with a gesture and beckons me and Pixie-Cut closer, both of us shouldering past each other down the red-gold road to Paradise. Because tonight's the climax, right? The end of a months-long seduction waged over every form of social media available, led down a trail of whispers about transformation, transfiguration, apotheosis, *power*. Some new kind of kick, or—just maybe—a very, very old one, all dressed up in post-Millennial drag.

"Other people talk about confidence, or love, or tapping enneagrams," he tells us. "But we're not like that. Our shit isn't bullshit, it's *real*. Gotta be ready to handle it, though . . . to show how you're willing to pay the price. That you can *stand* knowing this sort of secret."

The crowd's stepped back by this point, clustered to hide exactly what's happening with the cabinet's slick red doors; behind them, I can hear a couple of flunkies wrestling with the gilded handles, grunting in effort as they heave it open and pull out *something*, heavy enough to scrape the floor beneath. The ones in front grin a bit to themselves, eyes studying our faces: Oh, they want a reaction, can't wait to see it, that first moment when—whatever it is we're gonna end up looking at—registers. Not that Pixie-Cut even seems to notice, her gaze still riveted to the Shrike's own, chest heaving pornographically.

"No rituals," Shrike goes on, smiling even wider. "All you need to do is see it. 'Cause when you do, I'll look at you, and I'll just *know*. That simple."

I nod, slightly; Pixie-Cut swallows, quick and dry enough I know she's going to ask, which means I don't have to. Blurting out, a second later: "Know *what*?"

"If you're one of us, of course."

He turns, smoothly—like he's rehearsed it. Steps aside to show what's standing there: a triangle of tarnished brass, three coiled legs topped with a wide, flat metal bowl big enough to wash in, and who knows, maybe that's what it was originally meant for. There's a half-mirror set above it, after all, fanned out like a glass ruff behind the thing that sits inside, haloing its awfulness in sullen, splintered light.

A gasp, from Pixie-Cut. While from everyone else—even the Shrike—comes a long, slow breath, drawn out rather than in. Half religious awe, half physical pleasure, admixed with just a hint of happy recognition: So *beautiful,* this artifact, this thing we serve and own. This thing that owns *us.*

It's really hard not to laugh, watching the other girl's face change. Watching her suddenly grasp that this isn't a joke or a piece of ego-boo, simple play-acting. That when they crow about violence wreaked on anyone who pisses them off, they actually *mean* it, and the only right move for any still-halfway sane and moral person who finds themselves in this particular situation is to scream and run forever.

Neither of which she has the brains to do, of course. Instead—

"That's a *head,*" she blurts out, yet again; can't stop herself from doing it, poor bint. Like she genuinely thinks maybe someone in here just hasn't noticed yet, and needs to know.

"It is," the Shrike agrees.

"A head . . . "

"Yes."

"You guys . . . *killed* somebody . . ."

The Shrike smiles, slightly. "Not exactly," he replies.

Which is when the head opens its eyes and blinks at us, blearily. Like we just woke it up. Like it's *pissed.*

Around us, the crowd whoops and claps. One of them gives this weird crooning laugh, a baby's crow of pure delight. The head opens its mouth, lips drawing back in a snarl, the corners slightly torn—think it'd be hissing, if it only still had a voice-box instead of that ragged bit of gristle and skin where the neck's been sliced through right underneath the jaw. The slightly uneven mixture of bone, tendon and sluggish black grue prevents it from standing straight up, like it's on a pedestal, so it has to sit cocked sidelong instead, off-kilter.

Pixie-Cut is shocked silent now, for which I don't blame her. The head in the bowl rolls bloodshot, ice-coloured eyes up at us, lids flickering spasmodically—I see its pupils narrow horizontally, u-shaped, cephalopodal. Its filthy mat of hair is snarled to the point I can't tell its original colour, let alone whether it's supposed to be curly or straight; the face, both gaunt and flat, has skin like black volcanic beach-sand, cheekbones like napped flint. The teeth are stained brown, serrated edges sharp enough to glint in the candlelight. Its jaws work up and down, trying to bite at empty air. Its nostrils flare, eyes snapping back and forth between me and Pixie-Cut, who's started to make a noise like a balloon deflating. I raise my eyebrows.

"Someone's not too good with surprises, is she?" I ask the Shrike, as his cult explodes in laughter around us. He doesn't reply, though; only sighs, like he's seen this before. Then he glances at me—I try to look thrilled, or not disgusted, at the very least—before nodding to the others.

They're on Pixie-Cut before she's even finished taking her first step backwards, one on each arm, one behind her; Green Highlights yanks her head back and cuts her throat with a big kitchen knife, while the other two shove her hard, backwards, into the cast-iron clawfoot bathtub they dragged up behind us during the Shrike's little speech. She trips over the edge, hands still trying to staunch her wound, quick enough her head slams into the tub's metal floor, ending her struggles instantly. And then there's only the sound of liquid, hot enough to steam a bit, glugging into the tub.

There's an odd little beat of silence, as if even the Shrike's startled how fast she went down. It sets me back a moment myself, truth told. Can't feel too much sympathy for Pixie-Cut; she wanted what these gobshites are selling, after all . . . just couldn't reckon the real price, not 'til it was too late. But it still hits hard sometimes, seeing life end like that: So sharp, so sudden, a blank face on a mound of cooling meat. Meat which used to be a person.

I'll probably go the same, one day—too fast to see it coming, let alone feel it happening.

The Shrike recovers himself, with a little shiver. He leans down and grabs Pixie-Cut's belt, hauling at the corpse 'til he folds her into one end of the tub, making room for her blood to pool at the other. Then he turns and reaches up, carefully, to lift the head from its dish. Hooks his fingers through knots of hair over its ears and makes sure to stay well shy of the teeth, slow and steady, same way a smith uses tongs to carry a casting cup full of molten metal. Gasps and whispers ripple through the crowd; they back away as he brings it within sight of the tub, which sets its jaws working even faster; the teeth grind against each other, making an eerie sort of *zizzz*, so much like flint striking I almost expect to see sparks fly from the mouth. But all that comes out is a slice of tongue, liver-coloured, torn where hunger's made it chew at itself.

"Who drinks first?" the Shrike asks, that same hyper, cultish, too-happy tone back in his voice. To which all the rest of 'em yell back, pretty much as one—

"*She* does!"

"That's right: Her first, then us. Blood in and blood out, blood come 'round and back again like every full moon, every time, forever." Turning to me, then, with a return of that oh-so-charming smile, of his: "And you drink too, of course, if you want to. Because . . . you *do* want to, don't you?"

And me, I don't even spare Pixie-Cut a blink, since that'd put me in the tub right along with her, most likely. Just hold his gaze instead, coolly, and reply, as I do—

"Wouldn't have come here in the first place if I didn't."

"Smart girl," he says, approvingly. And lowers the head into the blood.

The moment he withdraws his hand, they all surge forwards, gathering 'round with avid eyes and panting mouths. I let the crowd carry me, let *my* mouth hang open too, trying not to breathe too deep; can't let the scent get to me. Not just yet.

The change starts the instant the head sets down. Swollen threads of reddish-purple tissue crack their way through the sand-black skin, spiralling up jawline and cheekbones like time-lapse footage of vines growing, inflating out of nowhere. The eyes widen, their slotted pupils rippling, blooming circular; irises darken, sclera flushing abruptly clear—alert, aware, *human*. The lips plump out, tongue soft instead of shrivelled, blushing from purple back to pink the way jerky soaks up water. Beneath the black outer crust, smooth brown skin wells up, splitting it apart and shedding it in a rain of dark flakes; dust powders off the teeth, bleaching to old ivory, new ivory, salt-white. Even the hair thickens, darker and sleeker under its entangling slick of dirt.

All of a sudden, the thing in the tub is a living woman's head, face distorted with rage, eyes flashing around to glare at all of them, mouth shaping curses none of them would understand even if they could lip-read. The sight only makes them laugh, and applaud; Metal-Face actually leans down and mouths a version of her own words exaggeratedly back at her, like he's imitating a bad kung-fu movie dub. That just gets *more* laughs, making me sigh in disgust, if only on the inside: These bloody kids. No respect for anything, them. Not even themselves.

"Is that safe?" I distract Metal-Face by asking, when I can't stand to watch any more. "I mean . . . you're not supposed to look 'em in the eyes, right?"

He makes a raspberry noise, scoffing. "Nah, bitch can't tell you to do shit, not without lungs—just glowers at you, way she's doin' now. It's kind of a turn-on, actually." He grins at me, confidentially. I make myself grin back, choking down the spiky knot of fury in my gut. "'Sides which, sometimes if you get close enough, you can even kinda tell what she's thinking . . . you know, like all the stuff she wants to do to us for cuttin' her up in the first place, and yadda yadda. Like sharing somebody else's dream, and you're starrin' in it. Know what I mean?"

"I think so."

"You'll find out soon enough. It's trippy as hell."

The Shrike grabs the head by her hair again, lifting it high; the throat's ragged, severed edges have lengthened, strands of tissue twining down the way an avocado grows tendrils if you stick it in a glass of water, still soaking up red drops. I can see the white of bone amongst raw flesh—half a new vertebra straining to form itself, maybe—and the twin holes of trachea and esophagus. It's fascinating, if queasily so. The Shrike holds her above his face and shakes the drops into his open mouth, gulping them down, shuddering like it burns him good. Blood like scotch, like tequila, like mescal. Like Black Death vodka. Then he brings the head back down and smiles, right into her raging, champing face.

Next to him, Mr. Anime Chimera hands over yet another knife; no ripped-off cooking tool, this one, but a big, ugly thing with an ulna-length blade and a handle made from antler, fit to gut a wild boar with. The Shrike takes it, spins it like some hibachi grill chef at a teppanyaki restaurant. The head snarls at the sight.

"Open up, baby," he tells her—practically purrs it—before he jams the blade in between her jaws, stabbing through tongue and soft palate alike with a squelch, then slicing back and forth out through both cheeks with a flourish deft enough I know the son of a bitch must actually have *practiced*. Her mouth rips open in a soundless scream, tearing the wounds wider; I can see the helpless agony in her eyes before the Shrike drops the knife, forces the lower jaw shut and slams his mouth against her ruined lips, sucking up the spurting blood the way one of my old factory-floor mates might've slurped up the froth off the all-sorts keg's spigot when no one was looking—that hideous mixture of dregs sold for whatever pittance got offered at the local boozer's, right between the rat-fighting pit and the hanging meat. The bottom half of his face is a crimson mask by the time he's done, white eyes glaring through the spatters above it.

He raises the head high. His teeth are sharper. His nails have sprouted into claws. He howls, and his flunkies all howl back at him. For the first time, there's a note in their voices sends ice over my skin. They're stupid petty slags, these infants, but they're still monsters. Can't go forgetting that.

Shrike-boy turns the head so the mouth is facing away and holds it out, like an Aztec might show off a fresh-cut heart before throwing it into the flames. These blood-junkies all scramble up to it in a line, each one gulping down as much as they can before the rush knocks them crazy-eyed and reeling, stumbling away to make room for the next. Every few drinks there's a pause as the Shrike reopens the gaping wounds in her face, which keep trying to close. And then it's my turn, right at the last. Bastards actually start chanting, like it's a frat party, while Shrikey lifts the head towards my face.

I tip my head forward, touching foreheads with the thing like we're old friends. Through slitted eyes I see the head's nostrils flare; it can't breathe, but this close, my scent's got to be in its nose all the same. Any luck, that'll be enough.

I'm sorry, I think, trying to will the words inside her skull. *You've suffered so much, taken so much insult, such . . . indignity. But this is the last time, I promise.*

(We *promise.*)

I press my mouth to the hot, sodden, shredded lips and smear my own with the run-off, forcing dry-swallow after dry-swallow to make as if I'm drinking. Trying not to think about how, if the Shrike relaxes his grip an instant, she could take my nose and lips off with one bite; *probably* won't, if she's recognized whose spoor lies on me, and yet. At last I pull away, do my best job of screaming at the roof like the rest of them, and then suddenly they're all around me—hugging me, pounding my back, kissing my cheeks and forehead and red, dripping mouth. I grin back and let them kiss me, let the orgy take me, even though I want to puke.

-◦-

Metal-Face flops onto the mattress beside me, naked and grinning, blood-mask already drying to powder. "Rush, huh?" he sniggers, propping himself up on his elbows. "Like crack and meth and MDMA all together, an' it lasts for weeks. Barely need to sleep, and it never takes more'n five minutes to get it back up again . . . "

He rolls over and gestures proudly down at himself, like: see? (Schwing!) I drag my hand over my eyes, trying to look too shagged-out for him, stifling the urge to kick him there as hard as I can. If he senses it, it doesn't bother him.

"Don't worry," he laughs. "You're one of us now. We don't do anything we don't want. That's for them. Out there." He lies back and grins at the ceiling, letting out a long, slow, happy breath. "There are," he tells me, "so . . . many . . . little bitches out there never got told 'no' in their life, you know that? So many assholes think they own the world. That it owes them." He holds his hands up, drawing his lips back in a silent snarl, flexing the claws on his fingers so they slide in and out. "I live for that moment," he confides. "When I catch them, and they realize it's just me, and them. And everything they thought kept them safe, their money, their looks, their family, their guns, some of 'em . . . none of it means shit. I look in their eyes, and I know no matter how many pills they take, they're never gonna sleep again without screaming.

"That's why we try not to kill, you know?" he adds, suddenly earnest, in some weird mentoring-big-brother mode. "Like the Shrike says, anybody can kill. That's nothing. Leaving someone alive, and broken, and stuck that way, like a worm on a hook . . . " His gaze defocuses; the claws retract. "That's what it's really like."

"What what's really like?"

His eyes snap back to mine, looking almost startled.

"To be God," he says, simply.

Can't think of an answer to this that doesn't involve murder, so I just shut up. Not that I give two shits about God if he's even up there, and my own jury is still very much out on that.

Against the wall where the Shrike flung my jacket after pulling it off me, I can see the alert light flickering on my phone, fallen from pocket to floor. *Finally.*

I slip my panties on, quick and quiet. The rest can wait. I step over the Shrike, heading for the cabinet; he blinks after me, clearly taken aback by how fast and steady I'm suddenly moving, but too blood-drunk to quite realize what's going on. And then, before comprehension can hit, I'm back, his big fancy gutting knife in my hand. Down on my knees, free hand slamming his arm down, *whack.* It's a good knife, no denying that. Takes his hand clean off, quick as a guillotine.

Shrike's mouth opens ludicrously wide, his eyes bulging; he grabs his spurting wrist, so choked with shock he can't even get a scream out, only a kind of rattling gasp. The blood dulls pain, but I think it must really just be plain failure to understand what happened—he's gotten far too used to invulnerability. I don't give him time to recover. I grab up his iPhone from where he left it, on a cabinet shelf, then weave deftly through the rest of the junkies to the door. His thumb activates the phone, and the security code's pre-entered on the app.

I shake my head, amused. "Sloppy, sloppy," I murmur, triggering the app as I toss the Shrike's hand over my shoulder.

The door unlocks with an audible clunk. I pull it back.

The woman who stands there is—as ever—the most lovely thing I've ever seen: Angel-tall, her eyes and hair the same shiny black, skin the colour of rose-gold buffed with silk. When she smiles at me I feel dizzy, lit from within, ready once more to beg to be drained to death's point again and again, living forever in that moment just before my heart starts to stutter and my breath to catch, my blood mainly plasma, sucked transparent. I start to kneel, but she lifts me back up, effortlessly.

"Not tonight," she murmurs, and I know it must be true. She always knows best, after all.

"Milady," I agree, instead. And bow my head.

The Shrike's roar cuts through the air, shocking the ghoul-junkies to their feet, turning the post-orgy haze instantly into a cold blast of fear and fury; they're all on their feet, crouching with claws out, sharpened teeth glinting through snarls. He staggers towards us, and I can see that his wrist's already begun healing—give him a couple of weeks and he'll have his hand back, not that he'll ever get to see it. "Who's this bitch—?"

"She's my boss." I grin at him, this time, feeling like I'm washing away a week's worth of sweat. And then I point over their heads, at the cabinet behind them. At the head in the dish. They turn like they can't help themselves, and I finally let myself laugh as they see what I see. They gasp, swear, a couple even shriek.

The head is smiling. And its eyes are wide with joy, even as tears spill down its cheeks, trickling into the rotten grue around its throat.

"My boss," I repeat, "and *her* sister."

Milady smiles, close-mouthed, and shrugs off her cloak; it puddles to the floor, leaving her body nude and shining in the candlelight, like polished wood. Her eyes throw back the candlelight in a yellow-orange glitter. The ghoul-junkies instinctively shrink back, wide-eyed and slack-jawed, looking as much dismayed as terrified—like children about to cry, thinking only *Oh shit, someone caught us they caught us they* caught *us!* And then Milady lets her mouth spring open, and a forest of dripping fangs bursts forth. A long, purple tongue lashes out, whipping back and forth; drops of smoking spittle fly across the room. One hits Green Highlights' face. She screams in flabbergasted agony and staggers back, hand over her cheek; when she takes it away, her smooth pretty skin is a raw patch of oozing lesions, like leprosy gone mad. That *really* freaks the shit out of them.

Except the Shrike. I'll give him this, he must have been the only one with enough brains to think about this possibility. He moves fast enough even I can't follow, scooping up his knife with his remaining hand and flashing across the floor. In the next instant the knife's sliced almost spine deep through Milady's neck, in and out, while his wrist-stump smashes into her stomach and drives her backwards. She grabs her throat, genuinely surprised, as blood slicks her breasts in a crimson flood. I can't repress a gasp. The

Shrike pins her against the wall with his stump and poises the knife over her breast, point first.

"Head and heart, bitch," he rasps at her, panting. "Everything else in the stories, it's all bullshit—but the one thing they all agreed on? Head, and heart, and spilling your blood. How do you think I got hold of that thing in the first place?" A jerk of his head, back at the cabinet. Then turns his head, slowly, to glare at me, and asks exactly what I know he's gonna ask:

" . . . the hell are *you* laughing at?"

It takes a second to master myself. "Well—you, obviously," I finally force out, revelling in being able to use my real voice for the first time since this whole dance began. His eyes narrow. "Regular Van Helsing, you, eh? But I don't suppose it ever occurred to you that some vampires, they come from places *outside* Transylvania."

His flummoxed look only makes me laugh harder. Adding, as I do—

"Yeah, that's right. Like . . . *this*."

An unearthly noise rips through the air, between us: A sickening wet *crunch* like a hundred bones breaking at once, followed by a glutinous, bubbling, drawn-out squelch. Milady lifts her head, seeming to stand up taller—and taller, and taller yet, even taller still, as her blood-smeared body slips downward out of the Shrike's one-armed wrist pin and thuds to the floor. The torn skin of her sliced-open neck stretches wide, like a sphincter, shitting out a viscous tangle of pink and scarlet, purple and yellow; the acrid sour stink of acid billows into the room, so strong the Shrike stumbles backwards and half a dozen of the cultists double over, retching. Down against the wall like some cast-aside doll with her skull popped off, legs slid out in front of her beneath, an abandoned toy made from flesh. And then . . .

Then, Milady floats free, glorious as some bee-orchid floating on the tide, her beautiful head sat proud atop a hovering mass of slimy, shining viscera. Flowers of breast-fat cling to her fluttering lungs, her unshelled heart hammering fast enough to spurt blood with every beat, a thready red halo, jet upon jet upon jet. Her nude spine whipping like a wet glass-snake, a legless lizard, all scale and tail.

Penanggalan, *they named my kind, in my homeland long ago*, she told me, the night we met, laughing at my fumbling attempt to shape my

Southwark-flavoured lips 'round the word. Still can't really pronounce it, even now, but she never did make me try again, after that night.

Just the sight's enough to break some of them. Metal-Face is one, exploding into a frantic screaming sprint for the door, face stretched and blind with the terror the vicious little idiot thought a god never needed to feel again. He's not as fast as the Shrike, but he's still faster than a human—and it's not enough. Milady's tongue whiplashes through him like a razor, turning off his scream in a gurgle; he hits the floor in two pieces, body fountaining blood and his piercings clacking as his head rolls away. Howls, wails and screams drown the room once more; this time, though, there's no triumph, no joy. None but hers.

Milady floats forward as the blood-junkies cower away, sobbing, trying to push themselves back into the walls. I slam the door hard behind me, hearing it lock—should've kept the hand, shouldn't I? Ah, well, spilled milk; find it later, easy enough—and bend down to scoop Milady's abandoned body up by hooking my arms under hers, dragging it after her. The head is still grinning, still crying, as Milady draws up before it and lowers her eyes, her own tears welling up in sympathy.

"*Sister*," she says, voice gurgling like vinegar through old, slimy pipes. "*I am . . . so sorry we could not be here sooner.*" Gives a sigh like bagpipes tuning up, and cuts her wet eyes my way; I carry Milady's skin-suit to the cabinet and set it down, seated against the side, empty neck gaping upwards. Then I lift her sister's head—no need to be careful now—and set it onto the hole, positioning it carefully. Within an instant, I feel it jolt and twist in my hands; see the skin rippling as tissue weaves to tissue, sealing fast. The body jerks, hands thrown high, grabbing at the head to make sure it's on tight. A second of startlement, right before she knows she's truly free once more. Then she throws her head back, mouth wide in soundless laughter.

At that, Milady laughs too, a sound like a tar pit swallowing something helpless. Sister turns to me. *Can you still read lips, little one?* she mouths. I nod. Her grin turns savage. *Then tell them this.* She gives me the words, and as she stands, her fangs sliding out, I turn to the cowering crowd, and say:

"You owe this woman a *lot* of blood."

It's a different sort of orgy, after that. Milady lets her sister do most of it, though she joins in when the ghouls start fighting back at last, terror supercharging their strength and fury rather than sending them running; if they knew how to fight, or fight together, even Milady might have trouble with these numbers. But they don't. I go back to the door and stand guard, meanwhile, the Shrike's knife in my hand, making sure none of them escape. Which is why I get a great little surprise bonus when the boy himself comes at me, having managed to grab his iPhone again—I hear the door unlock behind me, as we struggle. Well, I've earned a little fun for myself, haven't I? So I step aside, let him by, watch him use that same blinding speed through the door and up the stairs—

Which is when I show him *my* speed. My strength. Catch him by the ankle just before he reaches the upper door, and with one hand I twist and whip him back down into the subcellar, hard enough to bounce him a yard high off the mattresses when he hits. Then I jump back down onto him and hamstring him in both legs, flourishing the knife the way he did when he carved up Sister's face—not that he'll appreciate that irony, but I do. I flip him over, then sit back down on his stomach, crushing the remaining breath out of him.

Most people when they know they're beat, they just crumple. Credit where credit's due, the Shrike isn't one of them. He glares up at me. "You *bitch*," he rasps, repeating himself. "Go ahead, kill me. I'll still die something you'll never be: *Free.* You work for monsters. I . . . made the monsters . . . work for *me*."

Believes it, too, even now; well, well. Some prats, they never learn.

So I cup his face in my hands and lean down, suddenly not angry any more. Just tired. "We're all monsters to somebody," I tell him, and twist, *hard*.

Still got enough of Sister's blood in him the broken neck won't kill him, right away. Nor will what I do next, which is to chop off every limb at elbow and knee; his boosted metabolism's sealed up the first amputation before I finish the last. He doesn't feel the pain, but I can see it in his eyes: Inside, he's screaming. And he'll scream until Milady and Sister finish him.

I take a deep breath, then, and let myself collapse sideways, finally resting, not moving as warm blood slowly pools 'round me like a comforting bath. Nobody left alive that's capable of running, not any more. And as always, my mind goes back to the past . . . my past, long past, a hundred years and more. When I made my choice, the choice *he* thought was such a joke, and why.

Milady wasn't the first monster I ever met, you see. But she was the one that changed me.

On the factory floor, we were all of us just meat to the owners, one mere mistake away from being maimed or killed, lit on fire or sliced apart by machinery gone wrong. I once knew a girl licked matches for a living, ha'penny a week, and called it good; she died with her face gone soft and her teeth rotted out, unable to eat for fear of choking on bits of her own phosphorus-poisoned jaw. Just like the hat-makers who went mad from mercurous nitrate fumes, or the dyers who puked themselves to death turning out yards of arsenic green just because it was that year's most fashionable shade, or the poor Radium Girls in their turn, glowing in the dark while their bones decayed from the inside-out.

But me, I was lucky; Milady took me away from all that. Fed me her blood, and fed on mine, though never enough to turn me. Only enough to bind us together and keep us bound so I could do her daytime work throughout the years, the centuries. 'Til I knew myself older by far than almost any other ghoul in North America, if not the whole world. I never had to give up the sun, or the taste of bread, or anything else most true humans think make their tiny, fragmentary, mirror-shard fragile mockery of a life worth living. I never had to give up nothing I didn't want to, did I? And I never, ever will.

The Shrike thought he'd got it made, breaking the chain like he did: All the perks and none of the labour, none of that hunger to love and serve and be mastered. Bloody child, like I said. But I'm no Renfield, nor is Milady any sort of Dracula. It's far more like being an apprentice than a mere employee. Far more like being someone's adopted child, loved for her dreams as well as her skills, her capacity to love and *be* loved. And no human gets in the way of that, ever.

But I'm something else now—a monster, a god. Servant to a god, sole priestess of She I worship. It's a better life than any I ever hoped to have, back when, or could ever hope to have, in future.

Milady comes—mother-lover, endless fount of knowledge, strength, power. *Eternity.*

Who raises me back up now from where I lie cocooned in these false ghouls' blood, her rescued sister at her side, and kisses my cheek, my forehead, my mouth.

Who licks the excess from me like a cat cleaning her kitten only to take my lower lip between hers and nip it lightly, tattooing it with the sacred symbol of her bite.

Who lifts me high in her cold embrace, her guts twining 'round me like tentacles, digestive acids burning at my skin, and cradles me against her doubly-naked bosom, pumping with stolen blood.

"My little London sparrow, my soot-grimed dockyards orphan," she calls me, knowing how I can't help but shiver with delight at her voice. "My lovely, faithful, poison-hearted little cannibal girl."

"Always, Milady."

Stroking my face, thumbing my eyelids closed, as the ecstasy comes on me—that deep, slackening, satisfied sleep which always comes after true slaughter. These fools thought they knew it, but they didn't know the half; couldn't, could they? No human ever will.

"My sweet, poor little butcher-bird."

I close my eyes and dream, glad yet once more how when death finally did come for me, it had nothing at all to do with industry. And in the dark behind my eyes, I see only red, the same endless hot salt sea that laps inside Milady's skull, the same thing that will surely drown me, eventually—take me down, drag me deep and ingest me, never letting me surface again until my flesh has changed to sharp-edged, quartz-toothed pearl, fit to stand at her side instead of kneeling before her. The same thing which will finally lick the last sad taste of my humanity from me forever and spit me back out, re-born into darkness.

TRAP

CARLY HOLMES

The first night there were over fifty photos of a fern growing from a crack in the barn wall, mostly captured between 11 p.m. and 3 a.m. The trail camera had shifted slightly on its makeshift perch of bricks, tipped forward just enough for its sensor to become blind to any movement in the wider space of the barn. Still, the images of the plant were interesting in their own way, the crimped fronds thrusting from a spindle of roots. There was an insect, a beetle maybe, on one or two of the pictures, a smudge of moth flickering across others. I went out to look at the fern properly in daylight, admired its tenacity and the deep gloss of its leaves. I looked the species up on the internet, wrote it down in my notebook. Hart's-tongue.

After that I used the strap that came with the camera, secured it to the frame of a rotting chair no one had sat on for many years. I got Jo and Stella to walk across the vast square of the barn entrance, leap or wave an arm from one side or the other, then move further away, out into the courtyard, and repeat. I checked the range, marvelled at the clarity of their marching figures, adjusted the angle.

"Just how bored are you, Mum?" Stella asked, as I picked my way through the heap of detritus at the far end of the barn, stooping to hold up desiccated lumps of god knows what between finger and thumb ("Look, is that an owl pellet do you think? I don't know, maybe just sheep shit . . . "). I told the girls to stay back as I slithered over upturned tables and cracked sinks slimed with decay, brittle binbags split and spilling naked plastic dolls and toy cars. Years of the things we throw away without actually bothering to take the ultimate step of throwing them away.

"I'm telling you, I saw it coming from beneath this pile of junk," I said, pausing to knock on the surface of a small side table and then heave it aside, ready to take indoors. "That'll do nicely for the living room. It was a stoat or a badger or something. It ran from there—" I pointed into the gloom of a corner, waited for them to lift their eyes from their phones and look at me, "—straight across the yard and under the hedge there by the door. I bet it's got a nest in here somewhere."

"It's my camera trap, I don't see why you get to take it over." Jo pouted at her phone screen, tapped and pouted, then tip-toed back across the yard and up the steep slate steps to the house. The fringed tip of the shawl she'd draped around her shoulders—my shawl—trailed behind her through the mud.

"Yes, the camera that I bought you for your birthday after you asked for it, and then left in its box for months," I called after her. "At least now we'll get some use out of it. And if you put the wellies on that I got you then you wouldn't need to mince around like that. You're ruining your slippers."

She raised an arm and jabbed her middle finger in the air, eyes still on her mobile. Stella giggled and looked at me expectantly. I sighed. "And that," I told her, "is an example of why my darling eldest isn't currently welcome at school."

I linked arms with her and walked back to the house. "I reckon I've got another year or so before you follow in her footsteps, and I'm going to make the most of every sweet second of you being my girl." I kissed the top of her head and held her for a second, before releasing her and following her indoors.

◄○►

I fetched the camera trap before breakfast the next morning, laid it on the table beside the coffee pot and cereal bowls. Its outer shell was misted with morning dew, gritty from the barn dust. I'd stayed in the yard for a while after I'd retrieved it, watching the encircling trees release their leaves, the starlings clattering from branch to branch. The knowledge that we'd have to leave this home of ours, our muddy, remote farmhouse, finally settled on me then as an inevitability and not just a passing anxiety I could twitch from my shoulders and ignore. The rent was too high, the girls too in thrall to the attractions of town. The long drive off the mountain just to get a loaf of bread or travel back and forth to school, the thick press of mist against the windows for days at a time. We'd loved it though, the four years we'd lived here. Maybe I'd loved it more than they had, but the space, the freedom to run and play outside, that kind of thing had to be good for their young souls.

I drank coffee and began to flick through the tiny images, glancing up when the girls shuffled in and pulled out chairs. "What did I tell you about screens at mealtimes?" I said.

Jo pointed with her mobile. "Hello? What's that then?"

"It's a different kind of screen. The kind that will hopefully prompt us to take a bit less interest in ourselves and a bit more interest in the world around us." I pushed the camera trap over to her. "Put your mobile down and take a look." I was a bit disappointed in the images I'd seen so far—just endless photos of the yard from what I could make out, no cavorting animals—but I didn't want to tell her that.

She shook a dozen cornflakes into her bowl and picked one up delicately, nipping at it. Beside her, Stella shovelled her spoon into her yawn like a clockwork toy, milk dribbling down her glazed morning face. Neither of them spoke.

"Okay, fine." I stood and plucked Jo's phone from where she'd propped it against the milk jug, the better to scroll through Twitter as she ate. "You get this back after you've actually written that essay you promised me you'd finished last week. I'm getting tired of defending you to the school."

My mood was precarious, the melancholy that had found me earlier threatening to overwhelm. I snapped at Stella to wipe her chin, tossed Jo's mobile into the fruit bowl as though it were some cheap piece of tat that hadn't cost me over three hundred pounds last Christmas. The water filling the sink bowl was flowing cool again; the pilot light on the boiler must have gone out in the night. Yet another reason to leave this place.

"Isn't that a foot?" Stella had pushed her empty bowl aside and was peering at the camera. She clicked through the images, forward and then back. "Yes, it is."

I wiped my hands on a tea towel and leaned over her. "Is it? It just looks like that piece of rock that sticks out from the bottom step, the one we catch our ankles on if we're not looking."

"No, it moves between shots, look." She pressed the tiny buttons on the side of the screen and pointed. "See, it's there, on the right, and then—" she pressed again "—it's there. Different place." She smirked across at Jo. "I know whose foot it looks like as well."

If I really concentrated on the grainy image I could almost see what she was seeing. Yes, it might be a foot. Wasn't that the pale jut of ankle bone, and the blur of a rabbit ear nodding at its tip? I bent to look under the table at Jo's slipper dangling from her naked toes, its ludicrous bunny face rendered grotesque by the loosened threads that secured its scratched glass eyes to the fluffy fabric. They hung from the hollows of their once-sockets, trembling with each slight bounce of her foot. I straightened up and checked the time of the photo: 3.18 a.m.

"What were you doing out of the house in the middle of the night?" I asked her. She stopped nibbling her eighth cornflake and looked at me. "What?"

"You were outside in the yard last night. In your slippers for god's sake." I spun the camera round and jabbed a finger at the screen. She leaned over it and stared, shrugged, sat back in her chair.

"That's the rock that sticks out of the bottom step. You can see the chunk of quartz on the end of it. Can I have my mobile back if I promise to finish the essay today?"

Something had woken me in the night, I remembered now. A car with a throaty exhaust, idling on the lane at the end of our long track. I hadn't checked the time, but I'd lay money it was around 3 a.m.

"You're fourteen years old, Jo, you can't just sneak out in the middle of the night. Have I got to start hiding the door key to keep you safely inside? Bolt you into your room at bedtime?"

She pushed her chair back and stood. "Do what you like, it wouldn't be hard to climb out of the window." She smiled. "Wouldn't be the first time either."

Stella was still looking through the photos, hunched over with her nose virtually pressed into the top of the camera. I wondered whether she needed her sight checked, it had been a while since the last test. "It disappears after two frames so it's definitely not the rock," she said triumphantly, "and you can see the ears." She pointed at Jo's slippers. Jo glared at her—"Stop being such a shit-stirring bitch!"—and marched out of the room.

I wasn't sure I shared Stella's certainty, even after staring at the images for long minutes. They were just too unfocussed to categorically be one thing or the other. I told her to get dressed, we'd be late for school, and while she was upstairs getting ready I went through the rest of the photos. There in the last half a dozen, just after dawn, was the animal I'd seen scuttling from the barn last week. It moved in a series of jerky stills, across the yard and round the side of the house. Face on, its eyes glowed like flash bulbs, its muzzle was pulled into a half-snarl. In the last photo something small was strung like a sacrifice from its jaw, some poor mouse or vole predated while going about its own night-time business.

Marvelling at the complexity and richness of the myriad lives playing out, and ending, yards from our own front door, I yelled at Stella to hurry up, grabbed the car keys, and went outside.

‹o›

I met with Jo's form teacher a few days later and promised, entreated, downright begged. As the adrenaline ebbed away afterwards, mission Back to School accomplished, and I was left with only relief and a lurking shame—was this more about my need to get her out of the house every day than concern for her education?—I vowed to be less complacent in the future, stricter with both of them. The free-range approach to parenting hadn't worked as well as planned and I didn't want Stella to go the same way as her sister.

The girls were arguing in the car when I got there. They'd been arguing when I left them half an hour ago, though the topic seemed to have progressed from stolen make-up to something more urgent. I tuned them out as I drove from the school carpark and pointed us towards home, switching the radio on and fumbling with a hand to check Jo was wearing her seatbelt. It was only when her voice hit that shrill note of near hysteria that used to precede a full-blown heel-drumming tantrum that I remembered my good intentions.

I held up a hand. "Okay, who's done what and why?" I smiled slyly and mimicked their old nursery teacher in singsong tones. "Use your words, girls."

They both began speaking at once, at me, craning into my face to be heard above the sound the other was making. I felt my foot pressing down on the accelerator in automatic response to the clamour, consciously eased off and forced myself to relax. "I can't hear either of you while you're both shrieking. Jo, you go first."

"She always wants to get me into trouble," Jo yelled. Stella thumped the back of her seat. "Why do you always get to go first? It's never me. Anyway, I wasn't actually going to tell her. God, you just can't take a joke."

"Tell me what? What have you done now?" I braced myself drearily for what I was about to hear, flicking through worst-case scenarios. But there was silence around me, the pair of them subsiding back into their seats. The radio murmured on and I slapped at the volume dial. "Well?" I shifted slightly to spot Stella's face in the rear-view mirror, try to catch her eye.

"Nothing. Just something I saw on the camera trap," she muttered sullenly, looking out of the window. Beside me, Jo hissed breath in and twisted her fingers into claws.

The narrow lane winding up and over the mountain was dense with fog. Once we left the main road and rolled over the first cattle grid I had to slow to a crawl and concentrate hard. Soon we'd be home, the fire would be lit and I'd be able to take something for the headache that had been throbbing all afternoon. Only a few more miles and then we'd all be free to scatter to our separate rooms, close doors and shut each other out. An average Friday night in our household.

"What did you see?" I asked, twitching the car away from the ditch that loomed suddenly on the left-hand side, largely guessing where the road should be. "I didn't realise you were even setting the camera up; I've been forgetting to."

"She didn't see anything. She's just making shit up to cause trouble. As usual." Jo's voice was flat and defeated. She didn't react when we slid onto the grassed verge as I steered us blindly around the tight final hairpin before our track, the car headlights giving me nothing but the fog reflected back, as though a white sheet had been thrown over the windscreen, obliterating everything. The tyres whined and spun; the car fishtailed briefly before straightening out. Stella yelped and twisted on the back seat, scrabbling to stay upright.

"I won't miss these lanes when we leave here," I told them cheerfully, palms slick and hot on the steering wheel. I'd mooted the prospect of a move nearer to town the day before and their enthusiasm, their glowing faces, had been the final nail in my rural-idyll coffin. They'd chattered through dinner, as much to each other as to me, ticking items off their list of absolute essentials for the new home. Watching them, seeing how they leaned into each other and nudged shoulders, I'd remembered how close they'd once been, how happy in each other's company.

We bumped down the track and parked in front of the house. I used my elbow to push the central-locking button down, imprisoning us all. "Before we go in and I see for myself, do you want to tell me what's on the camera?" I eyed them both.

Jo started tugging at her door handle and throwing her slight weight against the side window. The melodrama of it would have been more embarrassing if her distress weren't so palpable. If I couldn't hear her ripped, thin gasping for breath.

"Jo?" I stretched out a hand, but she flattened herself against the door as though my touch disgusted her, as though it might harm her in some way.

"She was outside again," Stella said from the darkness behind me. "Dancing around at 4 a.m. like some insane person. Barefoot this time. Full starkers for all I know. Now can I get out please? I've got homework."

I pulled the locking button back up and opened my door, at the same time reaching for my eldest. "Jo?"

She evaded my groping fingertips, arching away as she wrestled with the handle, her panic spitting her out onto the slippery cobbles of the yard—"I'm not going mad!"—her limbs flailing as though she were no more than a doll thrown from an open window. Landing hard and then fumbling to her feet and running inside.

◄○►

I spent that evening looking through the photos. I uploaded them to my laptop to get bigger images and scrolled back and forth, studying the frames until my eyeballs ached. There was definitely someone out there—wasn't there?—flickering and shimmering from shot to shot, murky calves crossed in one photograph and then legs scissored wide in another, pointed toes kicking out inches above the ground. And that did look like a chain looped around the joint of a hazy ankle. I could almost hear the tinkling of the tiny silver bells; the noise had driven me mad for the last few months. I wished I'd paid a bit extra last year for a better-quality camera, one with a video function and higher resolution, then I'd have more than a set of blurred images to judge.

Both girls were in their rooms, doors closed and music thumping. Neither had come down for dinner or responded to my calls. I filled plates and took them upstairs—"Room service!"—and left the trays out on the landing. Stella raised her head from her book and waved a hand when I peeked in on her, but Jo's door had been wedged shut and she didn't reply when I spoke. Pressing an ear to the thick wood, I was sure I could hear her sobbing, though it might just have been the wail of whatever singer she currently favoured.

Before I went to bed I deleted the photographs from the camera and my laptop. If Jo had been outside dancing it was a harmless enough thing surely, and certainly less concerning than her other activities over the last few months.

I reset the little machine and crept outside, placed it on the ground beneath the sheltered droop of the fuchsia bush and pointed it at the front of the house. Inside, I slid the top bolt across the door, securing us all, keeping us safe for the night.

◄○►

Jo didn't appear the next morning for breakfast. Stella, shuffling and stupefied by sleep, shrugged when I asked her to go back upstairs and fetch her sister. "She's probably sulking because she got caught acting like a psycho," she said, cascading cornflakes over a bowl already crammed with muesli. "I'd leave her be."

I watched her for a moment, saddened and repulsed by the lack of compassion or sympathy for her sister. No matter the wars my brother and I had waged on each other as kids we'd always banded together when one of us had got into trouble, sneaking food to each other if sent to bed without supper, lying to our parents if needed. The instinctive loyalty, the *us against them*, had been a given, something I'd never questioned or even appreciated. I'd just assumed all siblings did that, cleaved to one another and presented a united front when times were rough.

After I'd finished my second coffee I went upstairs to Jo's bedroom and knocked. The silence beyond the door rang with emptiness, as if she were gone, as if she'd maybe never even existed. In the second before I put my shoulder to the wood and pushed, the vision of what I would find was as clear as if I'd already seen it: a cold space containing nothing but boxes stacked against a wall, a curtainless window, the damp of unuse and vacancy filigreed in the corners.

Jo was an unmoving lump beneath the covers when I spilled into the room. So much smaller than I'd have thought she should be. I squeaked with relief and moved across the clothes-strewn carpet to lay a hand on the warm, curled bulge of her, pressing down to make sure she was real.

"Leave me alone," she mumbled, surely half-suffocating under the duvet. "I don't feel well."

"Do you want me to fetch you anything?" I asked gently, tugging the edge of the cover away so that I could stroke a strand of her hair between finger and thumb. "Do you want something to eat? What about some soup?"

She raised her head minutely from the pillow so that she could peer at me through one slitted, suspicious eye. The lid was puffy, as though she'd been crying all night. "Why are you being so nice? What did you do with my mother?" she asked. Then she burrowed back down and hunched a thin shoulder, the bones sharp beneath the milky flesh, so that her hair slipped free of my touch.

I kept the smile painted to my face. My lips felt as stiff and brittle as dried wax. "Well, just yell if you need anything."

Stella had finished her cereal when I returned to the kitchen, and she was poking blackened strips of burnt toast from the toaster with a butter knife. I leapt to her side and pulled the plug from its socket. "You could have electrocuted yourself," I told her, "and tripped all the fuses."

"That's a myth," she said. "And I'm still hungry, Mum, I need more food. Where's the camera? I wanted to look at last night's action, see if—" she rolled her eyes exaggeratedly at the ceiling "—there's anything interesting on it." She did a fussy little jig, flung her arms out—*Tah dah!*—grinned at me.

Ignoring the snide invitation to mock her sister, I carried the toaster to the sink and upended it, shaking the crumbs loose. "It ran out of batteries. I'll get some more next week." I looked pointedly at the clock on the wall. "Hadn't you better get ready if you want me to take you into town by midday?"

I watched her leave the room, waited until the thump of her feet resounded on the stairs, and then nipped outside and retrieved the camera, squatting quickly with one eye on the kitchen door, sweeping it blindly from its nest of fallen fuchsia blossoms and then tucking it beneath the pile of magazines on the kitchen chair.

◂◦▸

It felt like I was completely alone in the house after I'd dropped Stella off with her friends. There was that strange vibe of absence, of emptiness, again, as I walked through the front door. No sign that Jo had used my short trip to dash downstairs and grab some supplies before holing herself back up with her teenage angst and her music. The kettle was cool and the counter as clean as I'd left it. I called out, letting her know I was home. If she wanted to come down and talk, she knew where I was.

After a bout of half-hearted housework, I brewed a pot of tea and slid the camera out from beneath its glossy coverings. It whirred to life under the pressure of my fingertip, its screen lighting up. More photos of very little; the occasional leaf swirling up from the mat, a slug sliming its way purposefully towards the gap beneath the front door. I twisted and glared at the silvered trails spiralling across the tiled floor behind me, wondering where the slug was now.

When the camera's clock reached 2 a.m. I slowed my perusal of each image, examining closely every frame that inched the time towards 3 a.m., then 4 a.m. Still nothing of interest, nothing of concern. I hadn't really thought there would be.

At 4:22 a.m. there was a smear of activity in the bottom corner of an image. A scurrying mouse, or maybe that mustelid returning for another rodent snack? (I'd looked up the possibilities for our snarling night visitor and written the name of the species in my notebook, enjoying the achievement of discovering a new word.)

The next few frames were clear and empty; the creature must have passed through before the sensor had re-set. I sipped at my tea and glanced at my watch: still a couple of hours before I had to collect Stella. I should go and check on Jo, try and persuade her to emerge from her room and eat something. When had she become so thin, all pointed edges and scooped flesh?

At 4:27 a.m. there was something that looked like a branch carving the photograph in half. It sliced vertically through the image, so close to the camera I could make out the knots and knobs in its bark. It was there again in the next one, trailing a blur of movement behind it. I stared for a moment, then pulled up my sleeve and looked at my arm, flexing it slightly, pressing around the wrist. I looked back at the photograph and clicked forward to the next image, the one after.

Someone was crawling on hands and knees up to the front door. There were the forearms, first one and then both. At their base, palms were splayed across the slate slabs, fingers hooked and twisted as tree roots. Hair hung down between the arms, wisping like drifts of fog in the pre-dawn breeze.

In the second-to-last photograph the angle had changed slightly; the direction of movement, of focus, now aimed towards the watching camera. One of the hands was raised off the ground slightly, as if about to reach out.

The last photograph was of the drainpipe that ran down into the gutter beside the front door.

◄◦►

I couldn't remember whether the top bolt had been in place when I got up this morning. No matter how I tried to conjure an image of it, of me going through the actions required to open the door, there was just a blank. My before-coffee self, as the girls liked to say. *There's no point trying to get any sense out of before-coffee Mum.*

To tell them about this, or not? To accuse them—accuse one of them—of playing such a nasty prank? I looked through the images again, studying the earlier ones as intently as the later ones. The camera sensor was set to be triggered every five minutes, and then to take a sequence of five images in a row. If someone had emerged from the house they'd either have been captured doing so or they'd have known about the time lapse and worked around it.

The alternative, the thought that whoever had been crawling towards the house had never come from inside the house, wasn't one of us—that wasn't something my mind would let me settle on for more than a second at a time.

Movement from the other side of the room, a quick flicker of something, spun me around in my chair. Jo stood in the doorway, lost inside the dressing gown that used to fit her so snugly. She stumbled towards me with her arms out, "Mummy—", and then she saw the camera lying on the table. "Shit, no, no. Was I outside again?"

I tried to push it away at the same time as she grabbed for it. We tussled for a moment, but her desperation was greater than mine and I let her have it. "I'm not even sure what I'm looking at," I told her as she began to scroll through the photos. "The quality's so grainy it could be anything."

I watched as she reached the relevant images. Her body was completely still, her hair curtaining her expression as she stared down at the camera. It was only when she started heaving backwards and forwards, rocking in her chair, that I realised she was crying. I stood to hold her, to try and comfort her, but she rose too and held her hands up in front of her soaked face to ward me off.

"I think I'm going mad," she stuttered. "What am I doing, *crawling* around the garden like some wild animal?" The disgust, the loathing, distorted her features, adding grooves, so that it became unrecognisable, a caricature of a much older, deeply unhappy woman. She looked as crazed then as she'd said she must be.

"No, darling, we don't know it's you," I told her. "It's just an arm, it's probably not even that, it's probably just a branch blown off from one of the trees. It was pretty windy last night . . . " I trailed off and we both stood silently, until she gasped something through her sobs and jabbed a finger at me.

"Stella," she said. "It's Stella, screwing with my head. That little bitch." Her flailing hands caught her attention and she brought them up to her face, sniffing and examining the palms. She peeled off her dressing gown and bent to look at her legs. "See, clean," she said with vicious triumph. "And I haven't had a shower today. If I'd been outside on my hands and knees I'd be filthy, wouldn't I?"

"Stella?" I was still caught on my younger daughter's name, dazed with shock and a sudden sick suspicion I didn't want to confront. "No, she'd never do a thing like that, not to you. Jo, you're sisters for god's sake, why would she be so cruel?"

She turned away. "Why would she steal my favourite t-shirt and spill food all down it? Why would she call me fat? Why would she do any of the things she does? Because she's a spoilt little mummy's girl who gets away with everything. Look, she's clearly going to get away with *this*." Her voice was shrill and splintering.

"But she didn't even know I'd set the trap last night," I told her. "So how would she know to go out there and pretend to be you? You're wrong, Jo, I promise."

"Fine. Let me have it then, without telling her, let me set it up somewhere neither of you know about, and we'll see. Anyway, it's my camera, I can do what I like with it."

She left the room, conversation over. "What will we see?" I called after her. "I don't get how that will prove anything."

But I left the camera outside her bedroom before I went to collect Stella from town. If it calmed her down to be in control of the bloody thing that had to be good for her fragile mental health. I hoped she'd lose interest before nightfall, or be unable to work out how to use it. I wished I'd never bought it for her.

Stella was in a charming mood, glowing with the day she'd had. She chattered nonstop in the car, posting crisps into my mouth and joining me in the chorus for songs she'd usually dismiss as mum-music. I slid glances at her occasionally, trying to imagine this sweet girl planning an act as cruel as the one Jo had accused her of. She didn't mention her sister, didn't seem to be dwelling on yesterday's argument, and she seemed to have completely forgotten that there was any tension between them.

The evening was just the two of us, watching a dreadful film and eating junk food. Throwing peanuts at the TV when the drama got too clichéd to bear. It was lovely, though I didn't say that and felt queasy even thinking it. Still, it *was* lovely spending time with a child who smiled at me with open, simple pleasure, who wasn't judging everything I did, storing up every fault to flog me with later.

After I'd gone to bed I heard the top bolt on the front door grind loose. Jo leaving the house. I sat up in bed and waited until the door squealed closed again and I heard the bolt returning to its night-time harbour, footsteps on the stair, before switching out my lamp and settling to sleep.

◄◦►

Jo seemed to be stuck in the cherry tree outside the kitchen window the next morning. I tapped the glass and waved a mug at her.

She nodded tersely and swung down to the ground without grace, pushing the camera trap into the front of her dressing gown. I pretended not to see, motioned for her to come inside. Somewhere above me I could hear Stella dragging herself across the landing. She'd be starving, as usual, desperate for her breakfast.

I laid the table for three but Jo took her coffee and curled instead into the armchair by the unlit stove. She tucked her feet beneath her and sipped from her mug, glaring into the distance, transferring the venom to her sister when she entered the room, then returning to stare at the wall. Oblivious, Stella slumped into a chair and pulled a bowl towards herself.

We were silent as we ate and drank, the girls both seemingly unaware of anything beyond their own private worlds, and me watching them both, watching as Stella gobbled and slurped her way through her cereal and Jo nestled the camera on her lap and switched it on. I felt bruised with anxiety for her, tensed against a sudden screech and lunge across the room. If there were any evidence that might point an accusing finger at Stella, even obliquely, Jo would fasten onto it. I was torn between the hope that she might see something that would free her of her fear of madness, and the worry that she'd do just that. That she was right.

Stella finished her cereal and sighed with pleasure, burped quietly into her palm. She grinned at me. "I beg your pardon." I smiled back, loving her fiercely. From the corner of my eye I saw Jo jerk forward and clutch at the camera, bring it close to her face and then drop it with a yelp. She scrabbled it from its resting place on her thighs, kicking it towards me. I was up and between the girls before she'd managed to lever herself from the armchair, my arms out and rigid at my sides. "What is it?" I said sharply. She didn't answer, only pointed, her face blank and white.

I stooped to retrieve the little box, watching her warily, steeling myself for what I'd find. Please let it not be Stella. Please let her character not fall so far from my vision and hope for it.

The tiny screen was still lit up and showing the last image Jo had viewed. I looked at it with determined resolve, then bafflement. "What is it?" I asked again. Flicking backwards and forwards through the photos either side of the one that had upset Jo, I couldn't see anything of concern. I couldn't see anything at all really, other than a high, sharply-angled shot of the front door.

She moved to my side and clung to my arm, reaching for the camera. "There," she said, tapping the screen. "Right there."

I shifted my focus from the front door to the window in the top corner, and then I saw what she saw. A silhouetted figure, inside the house, gritty through the pane. It stood in the dark of the kitchen, almost exactly where we stood now. Jo pushed her face into my neck and laced her fingers around my wrist, tugging it down. "Don't look at any more of them," she whispered. "Just switch it off."

In the next photo the person was closer to the window and I could see the tumble of hair, falling beyond the shoulders almost to the waist, lifting hazily around its upper body. "Stella, didn't you get up for a glass of water last night?" I said. "I'm sure I heard you." But her hair was too short anyway, it was barely past her shoulders. And Jo's wasn't that much longer. Stella shook her head, barely listening, edging the cereal box back towards her.

She—she?—was only a little closer in the next photograph, still indistinct and shadowy. One of the arms was raised a little higher than the other, as if in the act of reaching towards the glass. But in the next, if I really squinted, I could see features floating in that bleached face. Deep eye sockets, cheekbones razed to ridges, a mouth open wide. There was a dull shine of moonlight reflected on saliva gathered in the corners of the lips. I could feel Jo trembling beside me, ducking her head. "Don't look," I told her. "Just don't look."

I clicked forward. The figure was right up against the window now, pressed against the glass. Torso flattened as it pushed against the pane, face distorted and stretched by the pressure exerted. Unrecognisable. Its face was all mouth, its mouth all teeth.

The next image, the second-to-last on the camera. 4:42 a.m. She—it?—had turned and was facing inwards. The back of the head, the sweep of that long hair flying out to the side, was purposeful and forceful. A person in the act of moving fast. Beyond the figure I could just make out the open doorway from the kitchen to the hallway and the stairs, to the upper floors where we lay sleeping. It gaped like a wound.

In the final image the kitchen was empty. My shawl, usually draped across the back of my chair, was on the floor. The door leading to the upstairs rooms had been pulled closed.

I'LL BE GONE BY THEN

ERIC LAROCCA

t doesn't creep into my mind the way it might for others who have known their mother all their life—a gentle realization of mortality when her hair begins to gray or when her hands start to prune with wrinkles.

It isn't delicately planted somewhere, like a beloved perennial to flower more amply each year until I realize the inevitable. No, instead it comes barreling into my thoughts like a home intruder; a masked assailant spraying the place with anthrax and laying carnage as I suddenly recognize the unavoidable: my mother is an affliction I wouldn't wish on anyone.

I make the horrible recognition as soon as one of the airport gate agents wheels her over to me while I wait at the baggage claim.

She's smaller than I remember from when I had seen her last. Although perhaps old age has robbed her of some of her stature, I can hardly recall such a loathsome scent shadowing her—a stench as vile as rotted flowers. I almost plug my nose, but I don't out of courtesy. Her skin is as transparent as parchment paper, her hair silky like cobweb. I notice her easily frowning mouth wrinkles slightly as she sees me, her lips puckering almost as if she recognizes me. I wonder if she does, but I'm answered immediately when her eyes begin to drift off and dim drowsily.

The gate agent flashes a hideous grin at me when she approaches, the imitation of joy etched into her face seeming to scream, "Please let this be over soon." She's dressed immaculately in a slim-fitted, powder blue pantsuit with a scarlet chiffon scarf draped around her neck like an open wound. As she approaches, grinning, I can't help but stifle a small laugh and wonder if her mouth hurts from smiling so unreservedly.

"Miss Vecoli?" the gate agent says, weaving through the crowd of passengers and finally arriving at me.

I slip my phone in my pocket and give her a halfhearted nod.

"Your mother was an absolute angel," she says, passing my mother's leather handbag to me. "Still a little sleepy from the flight. But we adored her."

"Is this it?" I ask, gesturing to the purse.

"Check Carousel Eight for any other bags," the gate agent says, already tiptoeing away from us. "Her flight from Rome was delayed a bit, but they should be delivering baggage there soon."

I search my mind, struggling to invent another question—anything to keep the young woman from leaving us. After all, once she leaves, the moment I've been dreading will finally arrive: my mother and I will be left alone.

"I was told she needed medication—?"

The gate agent is already backtracking and heading toward the escalator leading back to the main terminal. "Sorry. I wasn't told anything about meds."

Before I can utter another word, the gate agent climbs onto the escalator and disappears into the crowd.

It's finally here. The moment I've been quietly dreading for three months since my younger cousin in Vicenza phoned me at three in the morning, crying hysterically and apologizing that they could no longer care for my mother. It's an apology I certainly never deserved. After all, I'm the one who left Italy, abandoning my family in search of literary fame that never appeared even after nearly fifteen years of writing. Nearly two decades living in the States and I had a handful of literary magazine credits to my name, two maxed out credit cards, and an on-again, off-again liaison with a barista at one of my favorite local coffee shops.

I can't help but wonder if my mother still knew enough to resent me as she stirs slightly in her wheelchair. Whether her eyes avoid me out of spite or merely out of the disorientation that seems to cloud the elderly, I can't be certain.

Steeling my resolve, I kneel in front of her and place a hand on her lap.

"Hi, Mom," I whisper as if I were coaxing a fawn out of hiding. The word "mom" feels strange to say. "Did you have a good flight?"

My mother lifts her trembling head slightly to meet my gaze. I notice her eyes are dimmed and glassy like two small bowls of milk. Her lips quiver, as if trying to say something.

"A good flight?" I ask again, louder this time.

My mother lowers her head, eyes drifting as she stares off into the little crowd surrounding us.

"*Sono stanco oggi*," she says, her eyelids shrinking.

Even though I can understand what she says, it's something I don't care to encourage. I had left the language when I first abandoned my mother and father years ago. Even though the accent stalks me from time to time, I've done all I can to shrug off any indication of being a foreigner. I once read somewhere that people tend to not trust foreigners as eager as they trust their own kind.

I recall how an editor had once emailed me, telling me how he had adored the piece I had submitted, but that my surname was far too ethnic sounding to be included in his publication. That's why I've chosen to not only abandon the Italian language, but to also adopt a pen name. I had swiped at any opportunity to escape my past and yet here came a permanent reminder of everything I had tried to avoid, charging at me like a Gatling gun.

"Good flight?" I asked once more, as if hoping it might prompt her to respond in English.

She says nothing. Instead, she shrivels like a wreath of ivy abandoned in daylight.

I steer her toward Carousel 8 where we wait for the rest of her luggage. She dozes in and out of sleep like a drowsing toddler. I'll be damned if I'm going to wipe the saliva drooling from the corners of her lips. However, it's then I notice that people have begun to stare, children tugging on their mother's sleeves and pointing at the seemingly comatose woman. I fish in my handbag for a napkin and dab the threads of spittle trickling down my mother's chin.

After we collect her baggage from the carousel, I shepherd her from the terminal and into the nearby garage where I've parked my car. Once I've cleared the empty take-out cartons and empty coffee cups from the passenger seat, I unstrap her from the wheelchair. She fusses quietly but doesn't seem to object to my manhandling. Loading her into the car like a bag of groceries, it feels strange to hold her as if she were a child. She squirms as I lift her from the chair and buckle her into the passenger seat.

We amble out of the parking garage and are on the highway heading toward Henley's Edge in a matter of seconds. I'm so absentminded I nearly forget my turn signal when changing lanes, and a middle-aged man wearing glasses driving a Subaru Outback glides past, flipping me off. My mother doesn't seem to notice. She's drifting in and out of sleep, her head lowered as if deep in prayer. I can't help but wonder if she still wears the same rosary pendant around her neck she wore when I was little—a necklace I once treasured unlike anything else and then quickly despised when I began to think for myself.

I wonder what's to be done with her—all the arrangements I'll need to make for her to live comfortably in the States with me now. I'll have to schedule a preliminary doctor appointment to assess her properly since my cousin was less than enthused with the doctor from Venice she had taken her to. I'll have to schedule a dentist appointment considering the fact that she probably hasn't been to the dentist in almost ten years. After my father had perished unexpectedly during oral surgery in his late eighties, my mother had been adamant about not regularly attending a dental hygienist despite my cousin's pleading.

Something will certainly need to be done about her clothes as all she seems to wear is expensive-looking black. Then, of course, there's the issue of her citizenship if she's to stay with me. Thankfully, my cousin did most of the legwork when acquiring my mother's visa to live with me. But now that she's here, I can't help but wonder if she's even coherent enough to apply for citizenship if it came to it.

People with brothers and sisters don't have to worry about these things. It's a shared burden between siblings; a mutual hardship as they inherit their parents' legacy. What exactly am I to inherit? A few measly rosary pendants and a trunk filled with clothing as foul-smelling as embalming fluid. Not to mention, the slew of debts trailing my mother and her deceased husband from when they rented an apartment in Padua. I had always thought parents were to open doors for their children. Mine couldn't even be bothered to open a window.

"*Io ho fame adesso,*" my mother says, stirring from her sleep. Her voice is brittle-thin and damp-sounding as if fluid were collecting in her throat.

"In English, Mom," I remind her, gripping the steering wheel. My fingers flick the radio switch and music blares through the car speakers.

As we sail down the highway, the yellow arches for McDonald's drift into eyesight.

My mother points at them, her whole body straightening as if suddenly very much awake. "*Cibo,*" she says. "*Cibo.*"

I roll my eyes. I wonder if I should pretend I don't hear her—perhaps that might motivate her to speak English. After all, my cousin told me she was teaching my mother English words for when she was to eventually move here. Although she had only been quizzing her for three months, my mother had to have picked up on something.

I glance over in the passenger seat, and I notice my mother's attention glued to me, her eyes wet and shining. I certainly can't pretend I don't see her.

With a flick of my wrist, I nudge the turn signal and drift over into the exit lane. We drift down the rampway and meander into the McDonald's parking lot. I park near the trash cans and swing my arm over the seat to grab my purse.

"What would you like?" I ask her.

She doesn't answer. Her eyes are fixed on the teenagers skateboarding underneath the nearby streetlamp.

I nudge her again. "Mom. Food?"

She stirs slightly, her eyelids shrinking once more.

"I'll get you a burger and fries. A Coke to drink? OK?"

She doesn't respond, her mouth open and her breath gently whistling.

I fish my wallet out of my purse, haul myself out of my seat, and make my way into the restaurant. Even though it's mid-afternoon on a hot summer day, there's hardly anybody in the place. I'm about to go order my food when I realize I've left the windows of the car rolled up and the A/C off. The dreadful thought suddenly dangles itself like a jeweled fishing lure in my mind—my poor mother will overheat and die. I imagine paramedics prying open the locked car door, my mother's sun-wizened body sliding out and splaying on the sidewalk. I imagine the scrutiny from strangers— "How could you leave the poor woman locked in a car on one of the hottest days of the year?"

I'm about to turn and sprint back out to the car to turn on the AC when I realize I'll no longer have to take care of her. She'll be a thing of the past, a distant memory. Of course, I'll have to handle a fair amount of scrutiny from the local authorities for leaving her in the car in the first place, but isn't the reward far greater than the adversity? It won't pain her. She'll merely fall asleep while death's fingers squeeze the life from her. She won't suffer. More importantly, I won't suffer.

The cashier's face scrunches at me, bewildered. "Did you want to place an order?"

I'm brought back to reality at the sound of her voice, my shoes squeaking on the linoleum tiles, and the overhead lights whirring at me.

"Sorry," I say, my cheeks heating red. "Yeah, I'm ready."

"For here or to go?" the cashier asks, her fingers flicking across the register's screen.

My eyes once again drift to my car parked beside the trash cans, my mother's head barely visible above the passenger head rest.

I return to the cashier. "For here," I say.

After the cashier slides a tray filled with a cheeseburger, a small carton of fries, and a large drink across the counter toward me, I make the trek over to the window overlooking the parking lot. I have a perfect view of my mother residing in her little tomb. I catch her reflection in the rearview mirror, her head lowered, and eyes closed like an abandoned marionette doll. She resembles an encaustic portrait of a martyr in the act of supplication—so gentle and so exposed.

I unwrap the burger and take a bite, imagining how it might feel for her when it happens. I wonder if she'll struggle, clawing at the door handle or beating her fists against the glass. Or perhaps she'll been swaddled in a blanket of heat and gently rocked to sleep. I wonder how long I'll have to wait for it to be over. Maybe thirty, forty minutes at the most. I certainly don't want to return to the car too soon and be greeted with a task I'll have to finish myself if she's only half-dead.

My mind begins to wander as I snack on a handful of fries, and I think about the moments we had shared when I was growing up. Tender moments outside of Holy Mass were few and far between, unfortunately. Quite suddenly I'm reminded of slicing pomegranates in our apartment kitchen while my mother brings a pot on the stove to a boil.

"Grenadine never tastes as sweet when you have to cut the pomegranates yourself," she used to say in Italian.

I was never allowed to have a taste as her homemade grenadine was usually paired with a fine liqueur after dinner; however, over the years, I've come to reflect on what she said. Essentially, it translates to "taking care of others is a thankless burden." I can't help but wonder if that's why the bitch had me cut the pomegranates in the first place.

Just then, as my eyes drift out the window, I notice a middle-aged couple swerve into the parking spot beside my car. The wife seems to be pointing at my mother as she dozes in the passenger seat, her husband nodding as if in agreement that they have to do something. They crawl out of their idling car and approach mine.

That's it.

I've been caught.

I swipe my wallet from the counter, knocking the food tray onto the floor. Fries scatter everywhere. I can't be bothered with that right now. I sail out of the restaurant and sprint across the parking lot toward my car. The husband notices me immediately.

"Is this your car?" he asks me, lifting his sunglasses.

I'm out of breath, trembling. "Yes. Sorry. I ran in quickly. Forgot to leave the car running."

"Yeah, we were going to call the police," the wife says, circling the car and cornering me.

"No, it's alright," I assure them. I press the key fob, unlocking the car, and climb into the driver's seat. "She's OK. Right, Mom?"

My mother says nothing, her face flushed.

The man circles in front of my car, his eyes scanning the license plate. "Are you sure?" he asks me.

"Yes. Fine," I say. "I'm sorry. We're late for an appointment."

I shove the keys into the ignition and twist, the engine whirring alive. I'm backing out of the parking lot and veering onto the highway in a matter of seconds until the couple in the McDonald's parking lot are but a distant memory.

After the two-hour drive from the airport to Henley's Edge, we arrive at the small carriage house I've been renting on my landlord's property. As I lurch out of the driver's seat, I spy the remnants of the backyard swing set drowning in weeds behind my house—the place where my landlord's daughter used to play with her friends and remind me of the childhood I had robbed from me.

I haul my mother's wheelchair out of the trunk and prepare her throne. After I've finished loading her into her seat, I wheel her up the front pathway and steer her into the house. She doesn't seem to pay much attention to the papers scattered all over the floor or the half-eaten containers of Chinese food piled on top of one another. I notice her nostrils twitch, fingers plugging her nose at the stench waiting for us in the entryway. I had almost forgotten about the poor rodent that had met his untimely demise somewhere in the scaffolding behind the kitchenette.

"Sorry about the smell," I say to her. "Landlord's sending out pest control sometime next week to clean up the . . . remains."

There's a small, quiet part of me that hopes she won't be here next week.

Once I wheel her over to the window beside the couch, I clean the armchair of the bottles of soda and beer.

"If you'd like to sit," I say, gesturing to the empty seat.

My eyes suddenly dart to a pair of lavender-colored lace undergarments I had draped over the bathroom door. I snatch the underwear, tossing them into the nearby hamper.

I stare blankly at my mother, as if expecting some sort of penance for the ordeal in the McDonald's parking lot. She says nothing. In fact, she won't even look at me.

"I guess we'll order out for dinner," I say to her, shoving my hands in my pockets. "You still hungry?"

My mother's eyes close, as if distant and dreaming. She's probably lost somewhere in an insipid fantasy where she's accepting the Holy Eucharist from Christ, himself. I notice how her lips pout—her mouth like an untreated scar—as if she were being serenaded by a Requiem. There's no telling what's going on in her mind. After nearly fifteen years, it's like meeting her for the first time.

Part of me even wonders if she really is my mother, or rather if she's some monstrous creature wearing my mother's skin as a disguise. I think of pulling on her chin as if I were about to wrench away a mask of flesh and reveal a gruesome face pattered with blood beneath. I abandon the thought as quickly as it comes to me.

After we eat dinner in silence for what feels like hours, I show my mother to the sofa in the guest room where I explain she'll be sleeping until I can afford to buy a small bed. She looks at me with disappointment but doesn't say anything. Instead, my mother shuffles into the room and sits at the edge of the sofa, staring down at her patent leather shoes.

I watch her for a moment as if I were carefully studying an extinct animal. She'll never be happy here. I can't provide for her the way they're expecting me to. And why should I? It's not like she ever really took care of me.

I have to get rid of her. But how?

It's then I recall a news story I had seen printed in the local newspaper about a four-year-old who had been left by their mother at a laundromat a few towns over. The mother, probably unwed and young, was never heard from and couldn't be identified despite the authorities attempting to reunite mother and child. That's what I'll have to do. I'll have to leave her somewhere like a neglectful mother abandoning their child.

My mind races, imagining all the possible scenarios of somehow being reunited with her after I've left her. They can try to question her, but she can't speak English. Even if they brought in a specialist and he was able to communicate with her, she'd never be able to remember where I live. Then, I wonder if somehow they'll be able to trace her by her fingerprints. Yes, perhaps that's how they'll identify her. But what can I do? Burn each of her fingertips until they crisp black. No, I could never. I could barely stomach leaving her in a locked car in July heat. How could I possibly do physical harm to her?

They'll never be able to associate her with me. Even if they checked Italian dental records or fingerprints and finally identified her, they would never bring her back to me. I'll be long gone by then. Besides, I don't plan to waste away my life in Henley's Edge forever.

They'll send her away to some nursing home where she'll live out the remainder of her days feeding on mashed potatoes and Jeopardy reruns.

It's then I make the decision—tomorrow morning after we have our breakfast, I'll take her to one of the parks in Hartford and leave her there.

I can hardly sleep at night. I imagine what it might feel like wheeling her to a secluded spot in the park, inventing some excuse to step away for a moment, and then never looking back. I wonder how long she'll sit there before she realizes I'm not returning. Maybe some good Samaritan will intervene, struggle to communicate with her before he telephones the authorities. Whatever the scenario might be, it won't be my problem any longer. I'll be gone and she'll be my gift, my burden, for the world to receive.

The following morning, I prepare some eggs and bacon. She doesn't eat. As usual, we don't speak. I go through her trunk and locate her capsule of pills, shoving them in her pocket.

"You'll need these," I remind her.

I'm not a monster. I'd never leave her stranded without her heart medication.

After I explain to her that we'll be taking a short trip to run an errand in Hartford, I steer her toward the car and load her inside. The hour-long drive there feels almost unbearable. The radio hisses the latest Top 40 hits, but I'm lost somewhere in my mind, inventing scenarios of how it might transpire—how somebody might see me with her and then come looking for me. What if they describe me to the police? What if they somehow connect me to her?

As quickly as these thoughts arrive, I shoo them away and turn the radio dial up higher. Finally, we arrive at the small park hidden just beyond the highway. There aren't many cars in the parking lot today and I quietly thank God for little mercies such as that.

I pile my mother into her wheelchair and maneuver her through the portico leading into the park. We drift by the fountain arranged at the entrance—a statue of some obscure New England patriot, sword unsheathed, as he charges into battle. We pass by the small lily pond, a few swans gliding across the mirrorlike surface. Eventually, we come to a small apron of greenery curtained from the remainder of the park by a column of well-groomed hedges.

"Let's sit here, mom," I suggest.

I wheel her beside the bench and kick the wheels so that they lock properly. We sit for fifteen or twenty minutes. Each moment that passes, I wonder if I'll finally get up and leave. Finally, the moment arrives. I can't bear it any longer.

"Mom, I'm going to find the ladies room," I say to her. "Wait here."

She doesn't respond. When she's not looking, I swipe her leather handbag from the wheelchair's handle and begin my way down the path away from her. My pace quickens as I steer through the hedges and, finally, she's out of eyesight. It's done. I've finally done it. She's gone—a mere memory as she was once before.

I wonder if she'll tremble with fear, wondering when I'll return. Maybe she'll try to come looking for me. It won't matter. I'll be gone by then.

I'm back at my car in a few minutes, hurling myself into the driver's seat and tossing my mother's leather handbag into the passenger seat. Just then, the bag spills onto the floor and something heavy rolls out. I peer over the center console and see it—a small pomegranate. There's a piece of paper attached to it.

I swipe the pomegranate from the car floor and peel open the small note. Written in my mother's cursive handwriting are the words, "For my darling daughter" scrawled in Italian. I sense my mouth hanging open, tears webbing in the corners of my eyes. I don't even bother to wonder how she managed to sneak the piece of fruit through airport customs. Instead, I crumple the note, slamming my fists against the car horn.

"Fuck," I scream until I'm hoarse.

Without another moment of hesitation, I leap out of the vehicle and make my way back into the park. Weaving through parents with strollers and young children playing games in the grass, I hurry down the path and toward the hedges where I've left my mother. I skirt around the corner of the shrubbery, and I see the empty park bench. My mother nowhere in sight.

My head swivels in every direction as I scan the nearby area. I don't see her. I don't even see the little indentations of the wheels of her wheelchair in the gravel where I had left her. It's as if she was never even there.

I notice a young couple approaching, and I ask them if they've seen an elderly woman in a wheelchair nearby. They offer apologies and explain they haven't. Once they leave, I approach a pair of middle-aged gentlemen playing chess beside the fountain. I ask them if they've seen my mother. They both shake their heads, bewildered by my inquiry.

I wander the park for an hour or so before finally giving up and going to the police station. I file a report and fill out all the necessary paperwork. I give them her passport, her birth certificate, everything I have in her wallet. They tell me all I can do is wait for a response. So, I wait by the phone for their call.

But they never do.

It's been nearly three weeks since I first lost her, and I've found comfort in few distractions. The nights are hardest when I invent horrible scenarios of what might have happened to her—how some leering predator might have spirited her away and drained her body until it was limp and bloodless. Or perhaps some kind, gentle soul had discovered her and took her in as if she were their own.

I can't decide which thought hurts more to think about.

During my days off, I visit the park and wander the hedge-flanked paths like a specter. I carry the small pomegranate so that if, by some miracle, I find her she's able to recognize me. Sometimes I stay until after sundown—until the sky is a black velvet curtain scabbed with specks of tinfoil—calling out to her and waiting for the dark to answer.

JACK-IN-THE-BOX

ROBIN FURTH

Shall I show you the playroom now?"

I sat at the long mahogany dining table of Blackthorn House, located deep in that famous family's wooded estate. The wall opposite me was mirrored, and the wall behind was hung with heavy old family portraits in ornate gilt frames that stared grimly at their own reflections—and, I thought, at me. Tugging at my hand was little Jeremy Blackthorn. Jeremy was six years old and small for his age, but his large brown eyes were oddly hypnotic. As he spoke, he squeezed my hand. His fingers were cold with excitement and they trembled in mine. There was something almost unwholesome in his determination, something which struck me as far too old for one so young.

"Leave Miss Benjamin alone, Jeremy. She's not here to play with you. Now go and find your governess and return to the nursery." Jeremy's father, a broad-shouldered man of about thirty-five, spoke the words a little too sharply. Though he was handsome and pleasant enough, I'd taken an instant dislike to him. His flop of blond hair, tweed jacket, and lazy arrogance screamed Eton and Oxford. I was fresh from the States and still hadn't acclimatized to this aristocratic corner of England.

Jeremy's face darkened. "I wasn't speaking to you."

"No, you weren't," his father replied, carefully folding his napkin and pushing back his chair so that he stood to his full height. He was thin but tall and towered over the boy. I found myself suddenly glad that the table was between them. "But *I* was talking to *you*. Now go, or I shall carry you upstairs by the scruff of your neck."

"You're not allowed in the nursery!" Jeremy squared his shoulders defiantly. "Grandfather said so."

The pulse at Philip Branston-Smith's throat thudded visibly. "Your Grandfather is *dead*. Until you come of age, I am master of this house and I shall do as I please."

"That's not what—"

"GO!"

Jeremy's pale cheeks flushed with rage, but he hung his head and stomped across the wooden floor. At the door, he turned and glared angrily at his father. "You can only say such things because I'm little and you're big. When I'm big, you'll be sorry. Grandfather always said you were a cowardly custard!" Then Jeremy flung open the door and ran down the hall.

"Little monster." Philip Branston-Smith sighed under his breath as he sat down and swirled his single malt around in his glass.

Embarrassed, I dropped my gaze and stared at the table. Although lunch had been for two, almost a fortnight's supply of ham, cheese, and butter remained. I couldn't help but wonder whether the food would be thrown out and wished I had the courage or shamelessness to box it up and bring it back to my flat. I felt a throb of homesickness for New York, where I wouldn't need a ration book.

Branston-Smith appeared oblivious to the great waste on the table beside him. Though he'd barely touched his lunch, he knocked back the dregs of his Scotch and poured himself another two fingers. He held the decanter out to me, but I shook my head. It was only two p.m., and despite what was on offer I had eaten very little. Besides, a long train ride awaited me when this interview was over. Secretly, I couldn't help but wish that Mr. Branston-Smith had refrained from topping up his glass, since it made my job harder. As far as I could tell, he'd drunk a whole hand of whisky before I'd even arrived.

"Sorry you had to witness that little scene of filial disobedience, Miss Benjamin," he said.

"Mrs." I corrected.

"Ah." He smiled cynically. "A *New Woman*, working despite home and husband. I should have known. I do apologize. You look so young that I imagined you were still a *mademoiselle*. Your husband's a Brit, I take it?"

"He's English, yes," I replied.

"In the war?"

"Of course."

"Officer?" Men like Branston-Smith were always trying to discover where on the social hierarchy I belonged.

"Artist," I replied. That stumped him. I suppressed a smile.

"See any action?"

I nodded. "South East Asia Command. For a while, at least. But he spent most of the war camouflaging aerodromes."

Branston-Smith grinned. It was the first genuine emotion I'd seen on his face and it made him look ten years younger. "RAF man, was he? Jolly good! I piloted a Spitfire myself. Shot down my share of Jerries. Revenge for our lads, you know? Fighting the good fight. Good Lord. Those were the days."

His eyes drifted to the French doors and I saw his face fall into sterner lines, the recollected elation dissipating. "Do you have any children, Mrs. Benjamin?" Mr. Branston-Smith asked, breaking my reverie.

"No," I replied. I was only twenty-four and had been married less than a year. "But I do like them."

Branston-Smith gave a snort. "You obviously don't have any." He sipped his Scotch.

"It must have been hard for him," I said. "I heard . . ." My voice faltered, and I bit my lip.

Branston-Smith raised an eyebrow. "Yes?" he said. "I'm curious. What exactly have you heard about my son?"

I took a deep breath and absentmindedly smoothed my gloves, which rested in my lap. Upon accepting this assignment, I'd been warned that the Branston-Smiths were exceptionally sensitive to whiffs of scandal, but I couldn't really back out now. I'd always been a terrible liar.

"I heard that he found his grandfather's body," I said after a moment's pause. "That must have been very distressing."

Branston-Smith gave a quick and perfunctory nod. "Yes," he said. "Quite." Then he took another sip of Scotch and turned to stare out of the doors again. It was late May, and some swallows were nesting in the wisteria. I could see them fly past on their angled wings. The swift dips and turns of their flight made me think of children's kites, caught in a strong wind.

"Have you ever thought about the true meaning of the word *spoiled*, Mrs. Benjamin?" Branston-Smith did not turn to look at me, and the tatters of his boyish charm, which he'd been so eager to flaunt when I'd first arrived, had been carefully folded and put away. "*Spoiled*," he continued, "as it relates to infants and juveniles?"

I hesitated, uncomfortable with the direction this conversation was taking. It was not what I'd come about. "Not really," I said.

"No," he continued, still staring out of the French doors and swirling his glass absentmindedly. "I suppose you haven't. During the war, such thoughts were an extravagance, at least to those not forced to contemplate them." He raised his Scotch to his lips and paused. "One imagines a whining child, or a demanding brat whose wishes have been catered to so often that he believes all he need do is throw a tantrum to get what he desires. All *id* that has never been restrained." He knocked back his Scotch and topped it up again. "But a spoiled piece of fruit is rotten to the core. One bites into it and gags, discovering it is black at its heart."

"He's only a child," I said, then bit my lip again. The saying *Never contradict a Blackthorn* echoed in my mind once more. I could only suppose that this bit of advice applied to extended family as well.

"He's a child. Yes. Weren't we all, once? But this particular fruit has dropped from a rather nasty tree, as my poor wife can attest. I provided the seed but not the soil, so I don't believe I can be held completely responsible for how it sprouts."

I couldn't help but think that Philip Branston-Smith had already imbibed too much single malt and would regret it later that evening. He shook his head, as if to chase away some particularly horrid thought, and shuddered. Then he turned to me and smiled a winning smile, the kind I imagined they coached boys for in public schools. "But where were we before we were so rudely interrupted? And please, call me Philip."

"We were discussing Lord Blackthorn's study," I said, relieved to return to more stable topics of conversation. Philip's face darkened as Jeremy's had earlier, though he gave a humorless laugh.

"Ah yes. The splendid study of the famous Lord Blackthorn, orthopedic surgeon, researcher, and inventor extraordinaire." His face hardened. "Infamous would be a better word. The man was a blighter. Boy's just like him."

"Oh," I said, since I didn't know how else to respond.

"Even in his dotage, Lord Blackthorn couldn't resist a pretty figure or a pretty face, even those which—by the laws of common decency—were not his to take." Philip's lips were pressed together so tightly that they'd transformed into a thin white line. "It's a wonder his wife never divorced him. She had plenty of grounds. But then again, she was a scared rabbit and her stepson was an invalid. That's why my wife's nerves are so weak. Old man had them all under his thumb. Or perhaps a better description would be pressed under a glass slide."

Philip reached for the Scotch again, but then released the decanter with a sigh. His words were already beginning to slur. "By the way, I promised to pass on my wife's apologies for not meeting you herself. Her health is delicate, and sometimes the boy is too much for her. But where were we?"

"I'm writing a retrospective of Lord Blackthorn's . . . I mean Doctor Blackthorn's work, for *Country Life*. He was a great philanthropist, and because of his untimely death, our magazine wants to do justice to his memory."

"I would hardly call seventy-eight untimely," Philip snapped.

I took a deep breath. "But it was an accident, was it not?"

"Yes," Philip said, staring longingly at the sheen of Scotch still clinging to the cut crystal glass in his hand. "But old men and slippers and uncarpeted wooden staircases are a terrible combination." He put down his glass and slapped his thigh. "Well, I suppose we should get on with it. Shall I take you to the study?"

⟵◦⟶

I don't think I've ever walked through a house so large, either before or since. In later years I visited stately homes, but there were always sections reserved for the family—wings firmly closed by stout oak doors labeled PRIVATE, or corridors roped off with expensive braids of red velvet cord. Most of those aristocratic residences belonged to families that had hit hard times and needed to open up their abodes to the hoi polloi to gain tax credits, or something like it. But the Blackthorn family had no such troubles, in large part due to the accomplishments of the late Lord Blackthorn.

The hallway we were traversing was like the dining room—lined with mirrors on one side. They reflected the light, making the high molded ceilings look even higher, and the corridor itself both expansive and endless. The crimson runner beneath my feet—antique and probably Persian—was a little threadbare in places, and dust motes danced in the sunlight, occasionally flashing like little stars when they caught the light.

Between the many windows hung paintings. Not family portraits but expensive art. Though I was far from a connoisseur of such things, I recognized a Matisse and a Rembrandt as well as a sculpture by Henry Moore. And at the far end of the hallway, which we were fast approaching, was a grand oil by the occult artist Kenneth Osman.

It was one of Osman's Great War commissions, funded by the government. My husband had shown me an old article about the scandalous series not long before. This particular oil depicted a field hospital, probably just behind the front line. In the foreground, a young, wounded private was having his leg amputated by a surgeon in blood-spattered whites. Nurses scurried around the makeshift, unsanitary-looking operating theater as more wounded soldiers were carried in from the trenches, but it was the surgeon who commanded attention. He wielded a saw rather than a scalpel, and his expression was that of a hungry butcher rather than a doctor. It was unnerving, and I knew that the reaction wasn't just mine. Upon viewing the painting, the Imperial War Museum had banned it from public view.

"You have an amazing art collection," I said to break the moody silence.

"It's not mine, nor is it my wife's," said Philip. He had stopped before the final door and was searching his pockets for a key. In one of the mirrors I saw the reflection of his back. His head was bowed and his neck, just visible above his stiff white collar, was flushed. "The esteemed Lord Blackthorn willed everything to Jeremy. Even insisted that the boy take his name rather than mine since he is, by rights, the new Lord Blackthorn. Ah! Here it is!"

Philip Branston-Smith held up a small silver key. It shone in the late-afternoon sunlight. "We keep this room locked, since it wouldn't do to have the boy blundering in."

Deftly, he slipped the silver key into the lock, which clicked as he turned the knob. As the door swung wide, I glanced in and gasped.

"Yes," Philip said. "It is quite a sight, isn't it? A pathologist's dream, or so I've been told, though it gives my wife nightmares. My good lady insists that the maid clean the place the best she can each Thursday, but even she gets the shudders from it. She's a bull of a woman—you'd think the Devil wouldn't scare her—but she'll only enter here when the light streams in through the east-facing windows. Luckily for her, there's not much she can do. The old man left strict instructions that nothing should be moved or tampered with, not even a drawer opened other than the ones he specified, until the boy comes of age and does it himself."

I took a step into the room, which was, in truth, the size of a museum gallery.

"This is what's left of Blackthorn's private collection," Philip said. "If you'd visited fifteen years ago, it would have been much larger. I don't know whether you recall that bit of legal nastiness, when the ethics of certain medical men came under scrutiny and they were required to return all human remains to the deceased's heirs? Thanks to his connections, the old man kept his name out of the papers, but it was a scandal all the same. Fifteen hundred body parts returned, I believe. This collection used to fill the entire west wing."

"Oh," I said again. My father had been a surgeon, so I'd visited the Mütter Museum at the College of Physicians in Philadelphia, as well as La Specola in Florence and the Gordon Museum of Pathology in London, but I hadn't been prepared for, well, the *intimacy* of Dr. Blackthorn's collection. He had five of Clemente Susini's eighteenth-century wax anatomical Venuses, naked and erotically posed, though their thoraxes and abdomens had been removed so that their organs could be handled by medical students eager to learn their trade. Against the far wall was one of Ercole Lelli's flayed men—a real human skeleton partially clothed in wax representations of ligaments, muscles, and veins. There were framed human skins from Japan, carefully preserved because of their Yakuza tattoos. There were fetuses in bottles, one with two heads, one with a nose that looked like a proboscis. There were numerous wax torsos with the flesh and muscle clamped back, exposing their hearts, lungs, and intestines.

I paused by the flayed body of a man riding a bicycle. It looked as if he'd been partially dissected and then freeze-dried and coated in heavy varnish. "Is it real?" I asked.

"Oh yes, quite," said Philip. "This is one of Lord Blackthorn's own creations. He was very proud of his technique. Claimed that he'd rediscovered the process behind Honoré Fragonard's écorchés. Have you ever visited the Museé Fragonard in Maisons-Alfort?" I shook my head. "His Horseman of the Apocalypse is straight out of Dürer." Philip's mouth formed a rictus grin. "Blackthorn bought this fellow abroad. A convict, I believe. Though he may have been a political dissident. Not a very nice end for him."

"No," I said. I walked past the swollen gut of a man who had experienced a blockage and whose innards had swelled tight like a vellum balloon, then past a display of trepanned skulls. I paused again by a glass case of votive offerings that covered several square feet of wall space. The offerings were tin and silver charms, no bigger than my palm, depicting feet and arms and hearts.

"He bought those in Mexico," Philip said, standing a little closer to my back than I liked. I felt his breath on my neck and saw the ghost of his face, still flushed from alcohol, in the glass of the display case. "The old man had an interest in the occult, the blacker the better. He even belonged to an Order, if you believe in such tosh. But I doubt your editor at *Country Life* would be interested in such things." And then he laughed.

Displayed at the back of the room were more of Blackthorn's inventions. A repaired human pelvis—one of the earliest successful examples of that kind of operation—where the cradle of bone had been sutured back together and the ball of the hip joint replaced by a carefully formed sphere of metal. Nearby, under glass, was a human foot repaired with a tiny screw and bolt. Philip stood so close that I could feel the heat of his body.

"Blackthorn was a sly one," said Philip. "Even before there was a whiff of the coming legal scandal, he coerced many of his indigent patients—especially soldiers—into signing releases. If he agreed to repair their bodies, they'd will him their bones after they died. That was the secret clause in his medical philanthropy. Wanted to make sure that posterity would have samples to celebrate the glory of his work."

I stared at the bones of an ankle that had been crushed and then remade in metal and strange plastic polymers, and it struck me that the late Dr. Blackthorn had been a sculptor as well as a surgeon.

"Hip replacements, knee replacements, metal plates." Philip practically sang out the words. "Did you know that back in the day, orthopedic surgeons like Blackthorn would buy their screws and pins from hardware men? *A hinge for the door, Jack old man, and one for my wife's elbow.*" He gave another unpleasant laugh.

We'd reached a rear alcove, separated from the rest of the room by a curtained arch, though the heavy velvet curtain was elegantly tied back with a satin cord. The alcove contained a monumental teak desk behind which was a large arched window flanked on either side by towering bookshelves and tall filing cabinets. Wooden doors in each corner led, I presumed, to storage closets. Drumming his fingers on the desk, Philip paused.

"The old man saved every paper he ever wrote, every article about him, every credit that mentioned his name, no matter how minute. Wanted posterity to remember him, large as life. I suspect he believed he'd slip past death, but Death is a sneaky chap, don't you think? Gets us all in the end."

He pulled out Blackthorn's chair for me and I sat down at the desk. Chair and desk were so large, so rife with the departed man's presence, that I felt a breathless wave of vertigo.

"By all means have a nose through any of the unlocked drawers. The old man was fastidious about privacy. If he didn't want you to see something, he made sure that you couldn't."

Philip turned to go, then paused to ask, "How long do you think you'll need? Two hours?"

"More than enough," I responded, relieved that I would be alone for a while, even if it was in this creepy mausoleum.

Philip checked his watch. "Well then, I'll be back just after four. Feel free to call Jones if you'd like tea or anything stronger, and I'll make sure the boy doesn't bother you."

He must have seen the anxiety in my expression because he laughed. "Don't worry. I won't tie him up. I'll just make sure that the damn nanny finds some games for him to play. After all, that's what we pay her for. Cheerio, then. See you in time for a sherry."

The door closed behind him and I gave a sigh of relief, though I was secretly grateful not to hear the click of the key in the lock. Glancing around the office area, at the many overfull cabinets and bookshelves and drawers and filing cabinets, I felt momentarily overwhelmed.

On impulse, I stood and tried the knob of one of the closets. It was locked. So were the drawers of the first two cabinets I attempted to open. I felt a wave of disappointment, but when I tried the first desk drawer, it slid forward easily. At last!

As I began my search, I couldn't help but wonder what Lord Blackthorn had squirreled away in those locked closets and drawers, then thought it was probably best not to know. What my editor wanted was a cheerful two-dimensional human-interest story, nothing more. Though as far as I could tell, there wasn't much human about the Blackthorns. But these thoughts faded as I became engrossed in my research.

◄◦►

It turned out that Philip was right. Lord Blackthorn really had been determined to reserve a place for himself in the minds and hearts of posterity. It was almost as if the office had been left in careful order designed specifically for a researcher such as myself. All of his awards were systematically displayed and labeled, as were a series of articles chronicling the progression of his fifty-year career.

After about an hour, I came to a drawer that appeared to be stuck, but with a little diligent prodding and pulling finally opened for me. Afterwards I realized with dismay that it was probably supposed to be locked, but the mechanism had broken. Still, I was curious, and so pulled out the files. Each one contained copious notes, written in Blackthorn's own spidery hand. Most dated from forty years previously, the very beginning of his experimentation with alternatives to traditional arthroplasty and amputations.

At the back of the drawer was a metal box, about five inches long by seven inches wide and four inches deep. I removed the box and placed it on the desk, where the dull sheen of the metal shone in the late-afternoon sunlight. After a moment, I lifted the latch and opened it. The box contained black and white photographs which showed a boy of about twelve undergoing surgery. The photos were graphic, even for one who, like me, thought herself inured to the blood-and-guts of medical photography.

As in so many of the displays in Lord Blackthorn's collection, the boy's flesh and muscles were held apart by metal clamps, displaying the naked bone. But though some of the boy's bones had clean breaks, many appeared to be in pulverized fragments. How in the world could such extreme damage be repaired?

As I flicked through print after print, my concern transformed from confusion to wonder, and then finally to disquiet. Though the decimation of the boy's lower body looked complete, photograph by photograph, he was being rebuilt.

Taking a deep breath, I straightened the pile of photographs by tapping them on the desk. Then I searched through them again. Beginning with the first of the black and whites, I counted up the boy's injuries. Hairline fractures in the spinal column, partially crushed pelvis repaired with metal plates, two femoral heads and sockets replaced first with ivory, then with metal. Two metal knees, tiny screws and bolts in the lower left leg and in the heel, fusion in the tarsometatarsal joint, six pins in one arm, and a rebuilt wrist joint in the other. The boy was like a jigsaw puzzle, or Humpty-Dumpty, though it wasn't all the king's horses and all the king's men grappling with the fragments of a human life, but the famous Dr. Blackthorn.

Frowning, I turned one of the photos over and glanced at the date, written in Blackthorn's distinctive hand. *Blackthorn Hospital, 1920.* The earliest photos were twenty-eight years old, yet such repairs would have challenged the skills of a contemporary specialist. But there was Dr. Blackthorn in his surgeon's whites, younger than I'd imagined possible, gloved and gowned and masked, the flesh of the body before him peeled back, its skin and juvenile genitals pushed to one side, like unneeded clothing. Focused so completely on his surgery, Blackthorn looked every inch the heroic doctor, but something about his eyes unnerved me.

They were cold, like those of a wolf at slaughter.

There was a second pile of photographs documenting the post-op convalescence. From the boy's growth, I'd say he spent at least six months in bed, yet his limbs appeared to be lengthening as they should, nothing stunted.

Then there was a long phase in a wheelchair. Another year, at least. Then a makeshift walker, and, finally, an image of him as a fourteen- or fifteen-year-old, trying desperately to use crutches, his pain palpable.

There the documentation ended.

Carefully, I replaced the photos in the box. Either the lad had died, or, somewhere in a locked drawer, was another photographic catalogue. That more surgeries had followed seemed inevitable. But even as I latched the box, I couldn't help but wonder about the boy himself. The despair on his face was plain, as was the intensity of his agony. But lurking below the despair and pain had been another emotion, something just seeping to the surface, like molten lava forcing its way through every ground fault.

It was anger. I was sure of it.

I slid the box to the side of the desk. The boy in the photographs had reminded me of someone, but I couldn't place the face. Still sitting in Dr. Blackthorn's chair, I leaned my elbow on the wood and rested my forehead against my palm and closed my eyes. Suddenly it came to me. The boy's face was the ghost of Jeremy's.

From out in the hall a grandfather clock gonged four times. I jumped. The door opened and Philip entered. He was smiling and carried two small glasses of sherry. The faint strains of Lesley Douglass and his Orchestra drifted in behind him. Far away, in the kitchen, someone was playing the wireless.

"Let no one say that I am not a gentleman." He handed me a small etched glass. "*Cin cin!*"

We clinked glasses and I drank gratefully. He leaned his rear against the desk while I, still sitting in Lord Blackthorn's chair, crossed my legs. I wore flats, but my skirt had ridden up to my knees and he glanced down, admiringly.

"Find everything you needed for your little article?"

I nodded. "More than enough. But I was wondering." Unlatching the box again, I lifted out the black and white photos and handed them to Philip. "Can you tell me who this boy is?"

Philip took the photos casually enough, but as he leafed through them, he began to frown. "I've never seen *these* before. Where did you find them?"

"In one of the drawers," I responded.

He raised an eyebrow. "Picked a lock, did you?"

"Of course not!" I blurted, abashed. But Philip only laughed.

"I won't tell. No self-respecting journalist would want to work for *Country Life* after the age of twenty-five. You obviously have your sights set on greater things. An exposé, perhaps?"

"No, really—"

He pouted playfully. "Now, don't disappoint me. I'd be thrilled to have you *exposé* the old bastard. God knows there are more skeletons in this house's closets than in the old man's collection." He tossed the photographs down on the desk. "Those photos are of my wife Livvy's elder half-brother, Jack Blackthorn. He suffered a terrible fall when he was twelve, while the family was on a skiing holiday. Smashed his pelvis, his knees, and broke almost every bone in his body. His father put him back together again at great expense. Used up a good chunk of his inherited fortune doing so."

"That's amazing," I said, thinking of an angle for my story. "Lord Blackthorn must have been very devoted to his son."

Philip shrugged. "Depends on who you ask. According to Livvy, the old man pushed him."

My mouth fell open, and a moment passed before I could speak. "Did he walk again?"

"According to Livvy, yes. Youth can be remarkably resilient. Jack was never an athlete, as you can imagine. More of a bookish sort. He walked with a limp and used a cane in wet weather, more for the pain than anything else. Then, after he came of age, he decided to leave the country. Sick of being his father's guinea pig, I suppose. Livvy was a child at the time, but she remembers the arguments vividly. The old man swore till he was blue in the face. The boy was his masterpiece and he didn't want to let him go. Threatened to disinherit him, erase his name from the family records, the lot. But Jack walked out anyway. Or perhaps I should say limped out. Took the boat to America. Still there now, I suppose. Can only hope he did well for himself."

Philip glanced at the clock. "May I invite you for tea? I got a call from Livvy's doctor. Her nerves are better and they're letting her come home."

"No," I said. "No, thank you. I must be going." I slipped my notes into my purse and slid the strap over my shoulder. Grinning, Philip unsnapped my purse clasp and slipped the photographs in as well.

"Take these, just in case you run into old Jack when you return to America. See if he misses the family."

"My husband is English," I said. "We live in England now." But I didn't take the photos out of my bag. I was reluctant to touch them. In fact, part of me thought they were so awful that I'd burn them when I got home. History and posterity be damned.

⟪-◦-⟫

By the time I'd had a second sherry and then said my goodbyes, it was almost five o'clock. Walking down the gravel drive, I smiled with relief. The article would be easy to finish up. It would be complete pabulum, but pabulum was what I was paid for. I had just checked my watch when I saw Master Jeremy crouching behind a nearby hedge. He looked like he'd been crying, and his cheeks were smudged with black dust.

"Hullo," he said. "I'm glad I found you. They didn't want me to say goodbye, so I sneaked away and waited for you here. I knew you couldn't get home without walking down the drive."

"That was very clever of you," I said, my mood much improved now that the shadow of Blackthorn House was behind me. I hunkered down so that we were at eye level. "I'm glad you came to say goodbye."

"I had to," Jeremy replied. "Grandfather would have wanted me to. Don't you have a car? Mummy has a Bentley. It's yellow. Maybe we can give you a lift when she gets home."

"Maybe," I said. "But you'll have to ask your father first."

Jeremy wrinkled his nose. "Philip never agrees to anything fun." Then the boy's face brightened and he leaned conspiratorially close. "Did you find the box? The one with pictures of Uncle Jack? I tried to unlock the drawer, but it stuck. Then I heard you and Philip at the door and so I had to run away and hide."

Nonplussed, I blinked dumbly. "That was you, Jeremy?"

Jeremy nodded. "Philip treats me like a silly baby, but I'm not. I know all sorts of things that they don't. Like about the playroom. Shall I show you now?"

Thanks to the two sherries I felt dizzily indecisive. I hesitated.

"Please?" Jeremy said. "It's ever so important."

I glanced at my watch again. I'd already missed the five o'clock train, and the next wasn't due in until a quarter to seven. Bill knew I'd be late, and I'd left some cold meat for him in the larder. "Okay," I said. "But we'll have to be quick."

"Quick as lightning!" Jeremy bounced to his feet and took my hand. "We'll have to go through the maze and then take the secret way, so they won't catch us. Follow closely so you don't get lost."

◄◊►

In later years, I learned that the maze at Blackthorn House was roughly the same age as the one at Hampton Court. It was designed by the first Lord Blackthorn, who decided to plant not with hedge but with gorse. Evidently, he liked to stare out of the high house windows and watch his enemies, and more than one of his guests, as they desperately searched for a way out.

Standing before the entrance to the maze I felt daunted. The corridor leading in was narrow. The sculpted green gorse walls were twice as tall as me, and though they were still flowering with their small, yellow, coconut-scented blossoms, the thin thorns were the length of my thumb. Flanking each side of the green corridor were marble plinths topped with silver witch balls. I couldn't help but think of the entrance to Hell in Dante's *Inferno*: *Abandon all hope, ye who enter here.* But still, the journalist inside me was awake, wondering what Jeremy wanted so desperately to share. Up ahead, the little boy called my name.

"Come on, Miss Benjamin. Please! Come quick!"

I followed.

As Jeremy maneuvered the green twists and turns and forks, he chatted happily. "Grandfather taught me the maze," he said, "and I can do it blindfolded. It hurt my hands ever so much when I ran into the prickles, but Grandfather said that to master death, one must first master life, and life begins with one's home. Do you agree?"

I shook my head. "No one masters death, Jeremy."

"Grandfather could," Jeremy said with certainty. "Or at least he would have, if Philip hadn't been such a cowardly custard." Then he paused at a spot where the gorse corridor split in three different directions. He bit his

lip uncertainly for a moment, then, pointing at each path in turn, he began
a counting rhyme I'd never heard before:

Yan, tan, tethera, methera, pimp,
Break his knees and make him limp.
Sethera, hethera, hother, dother, dick,
Grab his wife and kiss her quick.

Grinning, Jeremy pointed to the left-hand path. "That way!"

A few moments later, we emerged in the maze's central square. It was a small
courtyard paved with white marble, but fragrant with flowering bushes and
hanging honeysuckle. Obviously, at least one gardener knew his way here.

At the heart of the courtyard stood a small folly shaped like a Greek
temple. Standing within, on a black marble plinth, was a golden statue of
Apollo holding a lyre. The instrument was strung and looked like it could
be played, so I wondered briefly whether it might be an Aeolian harp. But
what wind could find its way through such a dense maze to play it?

Climbing up the folly's gray-veined steps, Jeremy stood about a foot from
the base of the plinth. Folding his hands like a choirboy, he began to chant
in a sweet, high voice:

Apollo, quaeso te, ut des pacem propitious . . .

The Apollo was not a statue but an automaton. Raising its golden fingers,
it strummed the lyre's strings. A discordant note jarred the air, followed by
a great whirring of subterranean gears. To my surprise, the plinth lifted and
slid to one side, exposing a stairway.

"Follow me!" Master Jeremy cried and descended into the darkness.

◄◦►

The subterranean tunnel was twenty feet high and twenty feet wide, and
the arches and brickwork looked Roman. Side passages snaked off in either
direction, but we remained on the straight path, our way illuminated by tiny
lights embedded in the walls. They reminded me of fireflies.

Though his legs were small, Jeremy kept pace with me. His delicate
little-boy shadow wavered unsteadily in the dim light. Our footsteps echoed
hollowly, and I couldn't escape the sensation that this eerie tunnel was full of

the ghosts of many little boys, long ago sealed up in this underground maze and left to die. I was watching my own shadow scuttle, spiderlike, against the wall when I felt his hand slip into mine. I jumped.

"Do you have any friends?" he asked. His voice was followed by an unsettling choir of echoes.

"Yes," I said. "Some. But not as many here as I have back in America."

"I don't have any friends," Jeremy said glumly.

"Are there no children in the village?" I asked.

The little boy shrugged. "Grandfather forbade me from playing with them. He said they were peasants. He said that with old blood comes great responsibility, and our blood is even older than the house and all its secrets."

We were approaching the end of the tunnel. Up ahead was an archway that was probably Norman. "I thought only people had secrets," I said.

"No, silly!" Jeremy giggled. "Houses have *all sorts* of secrets. And they keep them better than people."

The heavy oak door filling the archway swung open into an old coal cellar, disturbing a great cloud of black dust. I started to cough, and Jeremy solicitously patted my back. After wiping my streaming eyes on my handkerchief, I reached into my purse and withdrew my lighter. I flicked it with my thumb and it flared into life, casting my wavering shadow against the floor. Removing the metal wick barrel so that I could use it as a candle, I held it aloft. The room was low and mean and shadowy. In one corner was an abandoned pile of coal. In another, a puddle of stagnant water. A thick layer of dirt and coal debris lay on the ground, disturbed only by the back and forth of little-boy footsteps. Nearby I could make out the faint traces of another type of footstep, one that belonged to a large man. Branston-Smith, perhaps? No. His feet were large but narrow and his strides were long. These marks appeared to indicate a shuffling, irregular gait, and perhaps even the use of a cane. Old Lord Blackthorn? Most likely.

Across from us was a spiral stone staircase that had probably once been for servants' use. At the base was an old coir doormat so discolored that it looked like it had absorbed a century of coal dust. Nevertheless, Jeremy wiped his feet on it assiduously, running the soles of his shoes back and forth over the coarse fibers before starting to climb. By the many sets of small, dirty footprints going up, I could see that Jeremy used this entrance frequently.

"If you stomp your feet the dust falls off quicker," he said, "so you needn't worry about treading it into the house." As if to show me what to do, Jeremy stomped up the steps. Once again glad I'd worn flats, I did my best to follow suit.

As we climbed the stone steps, each one worn to the shape of an old man's grin, I recalled the stories I'd been told about Blackthorn House. According to my editor, it had been built over the remains of an ancient monastery disgraced and shut down well before the Reformation. And the monastery? That had been built on the remains of an indigenous temple of some kind, the history of which lay sleeping in the building's foundations. Raising my metal candle higher, I couldn't help but wonder if houses had souls as well as secrets.

The staircase was as twisted as the inside of a conch shell, the stone steps worn to a slippery polish. I used my lighter again to illuminate my path as best I could, but the way was dark and treacherous. More than once I almost lost my footing, but Jeremy bounded from step to step almost as if he could see in the shadows.

"Grandfather and I were the same, you know," he said as he bounced up one step and then another. Faint light now trickled down the stairwell, leaving the little boy's shadow to stretch behind him, long and dark.

I blew out my lighter and slipped it back into my purse. "Oh yes," I said, glancing up. "When you grow up, you'll become the new Lord Blackthorn." I didn't intend it as a question.

"No, silly! Not just that!" Jeremy was holding on to the handrail and bending backward so that he could look at me upside down.

"Oh, please be careful!" I interjected. "The handrail might be unstable!" Jeremy giggled and made a face at me, but at least he straightened up.

"Do you play Jacks?" he asked.

"Not very well," I replied.

"I can do tensies!" he said proudly. "I can teach you if you like."

I smiled. "Okay. Maybe when we get to the playroom." Surreptitiously I glanced at my watch. It was a quarter to six. I had less than an hour.

Ahead of me, Jeremy stepped onto a narrow landing just below a high, narrow window composed of diamond-shaped panes. The leading looked very old. Although some of the panes were clear, others retained their original colors of red and vivid blue. Once, the window had contained an image, I was sure of it. Perhaps it had been smashed during the Civil War and then repaired? I could make out the tip of a wing and a fold of drapery. Had the window held an angel, once? Or had it been a devil?

I paused for a moment to catch my breath. We'd been climbing a long time. "Jeremy," I said, leaning my back against the wall and holding on to the iron railing. "What did you mean when you said that you and your grandfather were the same?"

Jeremy turned to look at me. The late-afternoon sunlight illuminated his light brown hair with an eerie, dust-laden halo. To his left was an old oak doorway, firmly closed. "The Lord Blackthorns have *always* been the same. I thought everyone knew that."

"The same in what way?"

"The same *person*. I'm Jeremy Blackthorn, and Grandfather was Jeremy Blackthorn, and *his* grandfather was Jeremy Blackthorn as well. See?"

"Just because you have the same name doesn't mean you're the same person," I corrected gently.

"The name comes first, then the sameness comes after," Jeremy replied. "Grandfather called it 'fusing.' He and I were meant to be together forever."

"No one lives forever," I said, still gazing up at the boy. "No one—no matter how much we love them."

"Grandfather could have!" Jeremy insisted. "He could do anything!"

Jeremy's face was still high above mine, and his expression was fierce. For a moment, I was taken aback. I had seen heartbreak and anger and even grief on children's faces before, but never this.

"Grandfather could talk to me without moving his mouth and nobody knew! Mummy could hear him sometimes—I saw it on her face. But it made her scared and she cried. But I *never* cried! I loved him! I loved him more than the whole world!" Then Jeremy's ferocious pride slackened, and he seemed to deflate. Once more he was a sad little boy.

"He was supposed to live inside my head after he died, so I'd never be lonely." Jeremy's brown eyes brimmed with tears. "I did everything Grandfather asked. Everything. When the blood made me retch and Grandfather said it was like eating rare beef at table but without the chewy bits, I drank it. But it didn't happen like we'd practiced. Mummy and Philip had an argument. Then Mummy took me to the seaside. Her eyes were all puffy. I was building a sandcastle when I heard Grandfather scream. Then I screamed and screamed until Mummy brought me home."

Solemnly, Jeremy descended a single step, then another and another. "He was lying at the bottom of the staircase when I found him. His neck was crooked. I tried to hold his hand, but he couldn't hold mine back. Afterwards my fingers smelled funny, like they did when I stroked my pet rabbit after it had been torn apart by dogs."

Standing on his tiptoes, Jeremy rested his small hands on my shoulders and leaned forward to whisper in my ear. "Sometimes I have nightmares that I'm standing at the top of the stair and Philip pushes me. I fall and fall, and then I wake up, screaming my name."

Abruptly, Jeremy let go of my shoulders. Turning, he rushed up the stairs and then flung open the landing door.

"Bad boys are always punished," he said, half of his face in shadow, "and that's what will happen to Philip." Then he ran into the nursery.

⟶⟨◦⟩⟵

What we entered was actually an old vestibule just to the side of the nursery. It had been converted into a closet, where toys and linens jostled each other on long white shelves. We exited the French doors and I found myself in a room full of the slanting light of a late-spring evening.

Like the rest of the house, the nursery was spectacular. There was a jungle gym and a painted rocking horse and model planes and stuffed bears and dogs. The ceiling was embellished with stars and planets, and the walls were the blue of a perfect summer sky, complete with fluffy floating clouds and treetops so real that an imaginative boy could almost climb them. Tracks for a perfectly modeled steam train looped around the perimeter. Remembering a much smaller version I'd seen as a child at a Christmas display, I leaned down and flicked a small switch located near the smokestack. *Toot-toot*, the engine cried as it began to chug its way around the room. Every toy a young boy could want was here, but Jeremy ignored them all.

"We have to go down again," Jeremy said.

I stared at him, perplexed. "But I thought you wanted to show me the playroom."

"This isn't the playroom, silly!" he said. "This is the *nursery*. The playroom was *Grandfather's*."

Hanging on the wall behind Jeremy was a life-sized painting of a clown. Jeremy reached behind it and I heard the click of a latch. The painting—now a door—swung open. From the main hallway came two voices and the sound of hurried footsteps. The first voice was pleading and belonged to a woman.

"But Monsieur, I don't know where he went. He *disappeared*."

"Six-year-old boys don't disappear, damn it! Not if you watch them!" The voice belonged to Philip. "Jeremy!" he cried. "JEREMY! *Where in the blazes are you hiding*? Your mother wants you! NOW!"

Jeremy took my hand again. "Come quick," he said. "They won't know how to follow us."

I don't know what frightened me more—the prospect of being caught with Jeremy when I was supposed to be on a train heading into the city, or the physical punishment that Jeremy would most certainly receive when his antics had been discovered. My heart was beating hard when I slipped through the clown door, ducking my head so as not to hit it on the lintel. Jeremy followed, latching the door behind us, then he slipped ahead and began to run down the secret spiral stair. I did my best to keep up, but the way was almost pitch black and I was in too much of a hurry to find my lighter. As Philip's voice faded to a murmur, Jeremy spoke without turning.

"He's not my real daddy, you know."

"Who?" I asked, suddenly confused.

"Philip."

I furrowed my brow. "Was your mother married before?"

"No, silly-socks!" Jeremy giggled. "Philip has always been Mummy's husband, but he's not my real daddy."

I took a deep breath. If Livvy Branston-Smith had embarked on an affair, it would go far in explaining her husband's hostility to her child. "Do you know who your real daddy is?" I asked.

Jeremy turned with a look of surprise. "Why of course! It was Grandfather!"

I felt like I'd been punched in the stomach. "No!" I blurted.

Jeremy stamped his foot. "It *is* true! Grandfather said so! Philip called me a liar, but I'm *not* a liar!" Tears of frustration and rage brimmed in Jeremy's eyes. He wiped them away angrily with one grubby fist.

"I asked Mummy, just to make sure, and she went all red and started to cry. Mummy is always crying. Then she went to the doctor's and stayed there for weeks. She only came home again because Philip made her, just like he made her take me to the seaside."

Jeremy was still crying, so I brushed the tears from his cheeks. My fingers, stained with coal dust, left long, dirty trails.

"It's not your fault," I said. "None of it. You're just a little boy."

Jeremy gave me the ghost of a smile. "Grandfather would have liked you. You're pretty, just like Mummy. Only I bet you don't cry half so much."

Bending down, Jeremy reached into his sock and pulled out a key. "This is how I opened the drawer for you!" he said. "They think I can't come in here, but they are such gooses!"

Jeremy slipped the key into the lock and turned it. The door swung open. We were standing in one of the closet doorways in Lord Blackthorn's study.

I followed Jeremy past the filing cabinets and desk and large windows to the locked closet on the opposite side of the room. Jeremy unlocked this door as well. As the door banged open, he flicked on the lights.

We were in a small, windowless, black-walled room. On the floor was painted a spider's web, and at the heart of the web, just the right size for a small boy to lie in, was a red inverted pentacle. Across the back wall were shelves of old manuscripts, and several clothes hooks from which hung two black cloaks. One was large enough for a grown man, one small enough for a child. At the side was an altar draped in black damask, upon which sat a heavy silver chalice flanked by large ebony candlesticks holding half-burned black candles. Mounted above it was the head of a stuffed goat. From the ceiling hung a censer. The whole room smelled faintly of incense.

Jeremy had donned the small black cape and hood and was already hauling a box the size of a sea trunk into the center of the web. He huffed and puffed, but finally managed to sit it at the heart of the five-pointed star. At the side of the trunk was a hand crank that looked like it had been taken from a Model T.

Crouching down, Jeremy began to crank the handle, singing along to the music.

Half a pound of tuppenny rice,
Half a pound of treacle.
That's the way the money goes,
Pop! goes the weasel.

Pop went the lid and out leapt a human skeleton, dancing a momentary jig. I screamed.

"Ha! Ha! Ha!" Jeremy laughed. "Ha! Ha! Ha! Grandfather's jack-in-the box scared you!"

Jeremy was right. Lord Blackthorn's jack-in-the-box *did* scare me. It scared me more than anything had in my entire life. You see, I recognized the metal plating in the skeleton's pelvis, just as I recognized the rebuilt femurs and sockets, the pins in the arm, and the fused tarsometatarsal joint in the foot.

Bad boys are punished.

Jack Blackthorn had certainly been punished.

Though the shock left me winded, I couldn't help but stare at the horrific parody of a child's toy that old Lord Blackthorn had made of his son. Like the other skeletons in the doctor's collection, this one had been carefully prepared. The long bones were perfect, the only mar being a faint mark where a fine blade, or perhaps a scalpel, had been used to slice away muscle. Like the rest of the remains, the skull was bleached a brilliant white, though in one yawning eye socket I glimpsed a fragment of black carapace—most likely the remains of a dermestid beetle.

Jeremy! Dang it all! Where are you? The angry voice of Philip Branston-Smith drifted toward us from the distant study window. It was followed by a second voice, which could only be that of his wife.

Jeremy? Jeremy, darling? It's mummy! You can come out of your hiding place now! I'm home! She sounded like an injured bird.

I turned to Jeremy. "Your parents are searching the grounds for you."

The little boy frowned. "I don't care."

"But your mother must be worried."

Sticking out his bottom lip, Jeremy scowled.

Standing, I brushed dust from my skirt. I didn't relish explaining why I had remained on the Blackthorn estate, but having participated in Jeremy's wild escapade, I knew I had to face the repercussions of my actions . . . and of my discoveries.

"It's time to go," I said as I held out my hand. "Come. We'll face them together."

"No."

"But—"

"I DON'T CARE!" Jeremy's voice rose to a shriek. "MUMMY IS NOTHING BUT A CRYBABY!"

Taking hold of his arms, I tried to lift him to his feet. At first, he would not straighten his legs, but even after he'd lowered his feet to the floor, he refused to move. I rested my hands on my hips.

"Come, Jeremy. You're a big boy now. You can't act like a baby anymore."

When Jeremy raised his face to mine, it was red and twisted with rage. Balling his fists, he screamed and charged at me.

Very occasionally, suffering through a childhood with three brawling younger brothers has its advantages, and this was one of those times. Stepping to one side so that his fists only grazed me, I grabbed Jeremy's wrist and caught him in a bear hug by turning him around and pressing his back against my chest. He fought me, but I was both bigger and stronger.

"Liar! Liar! Liar!' he bellowed as he kicked and stamped. "I'm not a baby!" I didn't respond, merely kept hold of him until he calmed. Within a few moments, his tantrum fizzled into tears and hiccups.

"I hate them!" he wailed. "I hate them, hate them, hate them!"

Philip's words about little boys and spoiled fruit came back to me then, but I dismissed them. After all, Jeremy was just a child, and in my experience, children were creatures of circumstance. I didn't believe in bad seeds, only poisonous soil.

"I promised we'd face your parents together and we will." Letting him go, I helped him remove his cape and then offered my hand. After rubbing his dirty fists against his eyes, Jeremy laced his fingers with mine. Together, we stepped into the study.

◄○►

Alone with the Branston-Smiths in a drawing room larger than the London flat I shared with my husband, I sat on the edge of a white satin chair. I clasped my hands in my lap; a demitasse of coffee, brought to me by one of the maids, rested on the side table, untouched. Jeremy was upstairs with his nanny, having a bath. Before being led away, he had been severely reprimanded by his parents. He'd listened to their complaints impassively, with a jaded expression on his face that appeared disconcertingly adult. When his nanny had placed her hand on his shoulder, he'd broken away from her grip and thrown his arms about my waist.

"I wish *you* were my mummy."

When Olivia Branston-Smith began to silently cry, Jeremy smiled.

Photograph by photograph, Lady Olivia now sorted through the record of her half-brother's surgery and convalescence. Elegant but frail in her yellow summer dress, she reminded me of a faded daffodil. When she'd finished perusing the images, she placed the stack of prints on the mahogany table.

Lifting her head, she scowled at me, and for a moment I wondered if she was about to have a tantrum worthy of Jeremy. That she didn't like me was obvious. Not only was I a commoner and a foreigner, but I was also a rival for her son's affections. Still, she treated me with cautious courtesy. After all, I was a reporter and for the moment her family's public reputation rested, albeit tenuously, in my hands.

"Such horrid things are better forgotten," she said with a frown. "Surely you don't mean to publish them."

Another maid entered the room, this time with a plate of delicacies in one hand. Thanks to the mad hunt for Jeremy, Lady Olivia Branston-Smith had not yet eaten.

"I'm sorry if they cause you distress, Lady Olivia, but it's important that I ascertain the truth." I paused before continuing. "Are you certain that the boy in these photographs is Lord John Blackthorn?"

"Of course it's Jack!" Livvy replied. "My husband told you that, didn't you, Philip?"

"That I did, my love." Much less hostile than his wife, he seemed curious as to where my questions were leading. "Although I suppose calling him *Lord* Blackthorn is a bit over the top. He forfeited his title when he left for America."

"I'm sorry, Philip. I am not doubting your word." My use of her husband's Christian name made Lady Olivia's eyes flash with petulant jealousy. I ignored her glare. "I just wanted to confirm Jack Blackthorn's identity with your wife, since you'd never met him in the flesh."

"What exactly is this about?" Lady Olivia snapped as she pressed her long, delicate fingers to her temple. "I've had a very trying day."

She did not yet know it, but her day was about to become much more trying. "Lady Olivia," I said calmly, "your brother never made it to America."

"Whatever do you mean?" Abruptly, Lady Olivia stood. I think she was about to call the butler to shoo me out of the house.

"His skeleton is in your father's study," I answered. "Jeremy showed it to me."

The cut-glass sherry decanter crashed from the maid's hand as Lady Olivia fainted.

◄◦►

I had to take the sleeper back to London. By the time my train pulled into Waterloo, the last tram of the night had departed, as had the final trolleybus. Rather than pay for a hansom, I decided to walk back to Brixton.

This part of South London had been heavily bombed, and the surviving wreckage bloomed with purple spears of buddleia flowers. I suppose it was a reminder that even after the worst devastation, land could heal, though I have never been certain whether the same could be said about people. I passed the shell of a church. The glassless shadow of its rose window reminded me of the blind eye of a skull, hiding fragments of a skin beetle carapace.

As I walked, I opened my purse and pulled out the three prints I'd secretly kept, detailing Jack Blackthorn's painful surgeries. The rest I'd handed over to the Hampshire County chief inspector in charge of homicides. The black-and-whites would probably be safe with him, but I wanted to make sure that such important evidence would not be conveniently lost. The Branston-Smiths had powerful friends, and Lady Olivia hated scandal.

That Philip Branston-Smith had murdered his father-in-law seemed obvious, though that particular crime would never make it to court. The nightmares of a six-year-old boy were hardly admissible evidence. Besides, given the fact that Blackthorn had purposefully crippled his son, his end had a certain poetic justice. As for Lady Olivia, I was fairly certain that Blackthorn had forced himself on her. Given Jeremy's age, the child had either been conceived while Philip was on leave, or while he was at the Front. I bet my money on the latter. What made me conclude it was rape was something that Lady Olivia had whispered to her husband after she saw her brother's remains: *Oh God*, she'd whimpered as she clung to his neck. *Jack didn't escape the old man, either.*

By the time I reached Stansfield Road, it was the small hours of the morning and our flat windows were dark. Bill was probably asleep. As quietly as I could, I opened the terrace's front gate, unlocked the front door, and tiptoed up the steps. Before slipping my key in the lock, I stretched and yawned. The sun would be up soon, but I could still catch a few hours' sleep before I returned to my typewriter. I had a story to write.

TIPTOE

LAIRD BARRON

I was a child of the 1960s. Three network stations or fresh air; take your pick. No pocket computers for entertainment in dark-age suburbia. We read our comic books ragged and played catch with Dad in the backyard. He created shadow puppets on the wall to amuse us before bed. Elephants, giraffes, and foxes. The classics. He also made some animals I didn't recognize. His hands twisted to form these mysterious entities, which he called Mimis. Dad frequently traveled abroad. Said he'd learned of the Mimis at a conference in Australia. His double-jointed performances wowed me and my older brother, Greg. Mom hadn't seemed as impressed.

Then I discovered photography. Mom and Dad gave me a camera. Partly because they were supportive of their children's aspirations; partly because I bugged them relentlessly. At six years old I already understood my life's purpose.

Landscapes bore me, although I enjoy celestial photography—high resolution photos of planets, hanging in partial silhouette; blazing white fingertips emerging from a black pool. People aren't interesting either, unless I catch them in candid moments to reveal a glimmer of their hidden selves. Wild animals became my favorite subjects. Of all the variety of animals, I love predators. Dad approved. He said, *Men revile predators because they shed blood. What an unfair prejudice. Suppose garden vegetables possessed feelings.*

Suppose a carrot squealed when bitten in two . . .Well, a groundhog would go right on chomping, wouldn't he?

If anybody knew the answer to such a question, it'd be my old man. His oddball personality might be why Mom took a shine to him. Or she appreciated his potential as a captain of industry. What I do know, is he was the kind of guy nobody ever saw coming.

◄○►

My name is Randall Xerxes Vance. Friends tease me about my signature—RX and a swooping, offset V. Dad used to say, *Ha-ha, son. You're a prescription for trouble!* As a pro wilderness photographer, I'm accustomed to lying or sitting motionless for hours at a stretch. Despite this, I'm a tad jumpy. You could say my fight or flight reflex is highly tuned. While on assignment for a popular magazine, a technician—infamous for his pranks—snuck up, tapped my shoulder, and yelled, *Boo!* I swung instinctively. Wild, flailing. Good enough to knock him on his ass into a ditch.

Colleagues were nonplussed at my overreaction. Me too. That incident proved the beginning of a rough, emotional ride: insomnia; nightmares when I *could* sleep; and panic attacks. It felt like a crack had opened in my psyche. Generalized anxiety gradually worked its claws under my armor and skinned me to raw nerves. I committed to a leave of absence, pledging to conduct an inventory of possible antecedents.

Soul searching pairs seductively with large quantities of liquor.

A soon-to-be ex-girlfriend offered to help. She opined that I suffered from deep-rooted childhood trauma. I insisted that my childhood was actually fine. My parents had provided for me and my brother, supported our endeavors, and paid for my education; the whole deal.

There's always something if you dig, she said. Subsequent to a bunch more poking and prodding, one possible link between my youth and current troubles came to mind. I told her about a game called Tiptoe Dad taught me. A variation of ambush tag wherein you crept behind your victim and tapped him or her on the shoulder or goosed them, or whatever. Pretty much the same as my work colleague had done. Belying its simple premise, there were rules, which Dad adhered to with solemnity. The victim must be awake and unimpaired. The sneaker was required to assume a certain posture—poised on the balls of his or her feet, arms raised and fingers pressed into a blade or spread in an exaggerated manner. The other details and prescriptions are hazy.

As far as odd family traditions go, this seemed fairly innocuous. Dad's attitude was what made it weird.

Tiptoe went back as far as I could recall, but my formal introduction occurred around first grade when I got bitten by the photography bug. Greg and I were watching a nature documentary. Dad wandered in late, still dressed from a shift at the office and wearing that coldly affable expression he put on along with his hat and coat. The documentary shifted to the hunting habits of predatory insects. Dad sat between us on the couch. He stared intently at the images of mantises, voracious Venezuelan centipedes, and wasps. During the segment on trapdoor spiders, he smiled and pinched my shoulder. Dad was fast for an awkward, middle-aged dude. I didn't even see his arm move. *People say sneaky as a snake, sly as a fox, but spiders are the best hunters. Patient and swift.* I didn't give it a second thought.

One day, soon after, he stepped out of a doorway, grabbed me and started tickling. Then he snatched me into the air and turned my small body in his very large hands. He pretended to bite my neck, arms, and belly. *Which part shall I devour first? Eeny, meeny, miny moe!* I screamed hysterical laughter. He explained that tickling and the reaction to tickling were rooted in primitive fight or flight responses to mortal danger.

Tiptoe became our frequent contest, and one he'd already inflicted on Greg and Mom. The results seldom amounted to more than the requisite tap, except for the time when Dad popped up from a leaf pile and pinched me so hard it left a welt. You bet I tried to return the favor—on countless occasions, in fact—and failed. I even wore camo paint and dressed in black down to my socks, creeping closer, ever closer, only for him to whip his head around at the last second and look me in the eye with a tinge of disappointment. *Heard you coming from the other end of the house, son. Are you thinking like a man or a spider? Like a fox or a mantis? Keep trying.*

Another time, I walked into a room and caught him playing the game with Mom as victim. Dad gave me a sidelong wink as he reached out, tiptoeing closer and closer. Their silhouettes flickered on the wall. The shadows of his arms kept elongating; his shadow fingers ended in shadow claws. The optical illusion made me dizzy and sick to my stomach. He kissed her neck. She startled and mildly cussed him. Then they laughed and once more, he was a ham-fisted doofus, innocently pushing his glasses up the bridge of his nose.

As with many aspects of childhood, Tiptoe fell to the wayside for reasons that escaped me until the job incident brought it crashing home again. Unburdening to my lady friend didn't help either of us as much as we hoped. She acknowledged that the whole backstory was definitely fucked up and soon found other places to be. Probably had a lot to do with my drinking, increasingly moody behavior, and the fact that I nearly flew out of my skin whenever she walked into the room.

◄◦►

The worst part? This apparent mental breakdown coincided with my mother's tribulations. A double whammy. After her stroke, Mom's physical health gradually went downhill. She'd sold the house and moved into a comfy suite at the retirement village where Grandma resided years before.

The role of a calm, dutiful son made for an awkward fit, yet there wasn't much choice considering I was the last close family who remained in touch. Steeling my resolve, I shaved, slapped on cologne to disguise any lingering reek of booze, and drove down from Albany twice a week to hit a diner in Port Ewing. Same one we'd visited since the '60s. For her, a cheeseburger and a cup of tea. I'd order a sandwich and black coffee and watch her pick at the burger. Our conversations were sparse affairs—long silences peppered with acerbic repartee.

She let me read to her at bedtime. Usually, a few snippets from Poe or his literary cousins. *I've gotten morbid,* she'd say. *Give me some of that Amontillado, hey?* Or, *a bit of M.R. James, if you please.* Her defining characteristics were intellectual curiosity and a prickly demeanor. She didn't suffer fools—not in her prime, nor in her twilight. Ever shrewd and guarded, ever close-mouthed regarding her interior universe. Her disposition discouraged "remember-when's" and utterly repelled more probing inquiries into secrets.

Nonetheless, one evening I stopped in the middle of James' "The Ash Tree" and shut the book. "Did Aunt Vikki really have the gift?"

Next to Mom and Dad, Aunt Vikki represented a major authority figure of my childhood. She might not have gone to college like my parents, but she wasn't without her particular abilities. She performed what skeptics (my mother) dismissed as parlor tricks. Stage magician staples like naming cards in someone's hand, or locating lost keys or wallets. Under rare circumstances, she performed hypnotic regression and "communed" with friendly spirits. Her specialty? Astral projection allowed her to occasionally divine the general circumstances of missing persons. Whether they were alive or dead and their immediate surroundings, albeit not their precise location. Notwithstanding Dad's benign agnosticism and Mom's blatant contempt, I assumed there was something to it—the police had allegedly enlisted Vikki's services on two or three occasions. Nobody ever explained where she acquired her abilities. Mom and Dad brushed aside such questions and I dared not ask Aunt Vikki directly given her impatience with children.

"I haven't thought of that in ages." Mom lay in the narrow bed, covers pulled to her neck. A reading lamp reflected against the pillow and illuminated the shadow of her skull. "Bolt from the blue, isn't it?"

"I got to thinking of her the other day. Her magic act. The last time we visited Lake Terror . . ."

"You're asking whether she was a fraud."

"Nothing so harsh," I said. "The opposite, in fact. Her affinity for predictions seemed uncanny."

"Of course, it seemed uncanny. You were a kid."

"Greg thought so too."

"Let's not bring your brother into this."

"Okay."

She eyed me with a glimmer of suspicion, faintly aware that my true interest lay elsewhere; that I was feinting. "To be fair, Vikki sincerely believed in her connection to another world. None of us took it seriously. God, we humored the hell out of that woman."

"She disliked Dad."

"Hated John utterly." Her flat, unhesitating answer surprised me.

"Was it jealousy? Loneliness can have an effect . . ."

"Jealousy? C'mon. She lost interest in men after Theo kicked." Theo had been Aunt Vikki's husband; he'd died on the job for Con Edison.

I decided not to mention the fact that she'd twice remarried since. Mom would just wave them aside as marriages of convenience. "And Dad's feelings toward her?"

"Doubtful he gave her a second thought whenever she wasn't right in front of his nose. An odd duck, your father. Warm and fuzzy outside, cold tapioca on the inside."

"Damn, Mom."

"Some girls like tapioca. What's with the Twenty Questions? You have something to say, spill it."

Should I confess my recent nightmares? Terrible visions of long-buried childhood experiences? Or that Dad, an odd duck indeed, starred in these recollections and his innocuous, albeit unnerving, Tiptoe game assumed a sinister prominence that led to my current emotional turmoil? I wished to share with Mom; we'd finally gotten closer as the rest of our family fell by the wayside. Still, I faltered, true motives unspoken. She'd likely scoff at my foolishness in that acerbic manner of hers and ruin our fragile bond.

She craned her neck. "You haven't seen *him* around?"

"Who?" Caught off guard again, I stupidly concluded, despite evidence to the contrary, that her thoughts were fogged with rapid onset dementia. Even more stupidly, I blurted, "Mom, uh, you know Dad's dead. Right?"

"Yeah, dummy," she said. "I meant Greg."

"The guy you don't want to talk about?" Neither of us had seen my brother in a while. Absence doesn't always make the heart grow fonder.

"Smart ass." But she smiled faintly.

◄○►

In the wee hours, alone in my studio apartment, I woke from a lucid nightmare. Blurry, forgotten childhood images coalesced with horrible clarity. Aunt Vikki suffering what we politely termed an episode; the still image of a missing woman on the six o'clock news; my father, polishing his glasses and smiling cryptically. Behind him, a sun dappled lake, a stand of thick trees, and a lost trail that wound into the Catskills . . .or Purgatory. There were other, more disturbing, recollections that clamored for attention, whirling in a black mass on the periphery. Gray, gangling hands; a gray, cadaverous face . . .

I poured a glass of whiskey and dug into a shoebox of loose photos; mainly snapshots documenting our happiest moments as a family. I searched those smiling faces for signs of trauma, a hint of anguish to corroborate my tainted memories. Trouble is, old, weathered pictures are ambiguous. You can't always tell what's hiding behind the patina. Nothing, or the worst thing imaginable.

⟨○⟩

Whatever the truth might be, this is what I recall about our last summer vacation to the deep Catskills:

During the late 1960s, Dad worked at an IBM plant in Kingston, New York. Mom wrote colorful, acerbic essays documenting life in the Mid-Hudson Valley; sold them to regional papers, mainly, and sometimes slick publications such as *The New Yorker* and *The Saturday Evening Post*. We had it made. House in the suburbs, two cars, and an enormous color TV. I cruised the neighborhood on a Schwinn ten-speed with the camera slung around my neck. My older brother, Greg, ran cross-country for our school. Dad let him borrow the second car, a Buick, to squire his girlfriend into town on date night.

The Vance clan's holy trinity: Christmas; IBM Family Day; and the annual summer getaway at a cabin on Lake Terron. For us kids, the IBM Family Day carnival was an afternoon of games, Ferris wheel rides, running and screaming at the top of our lungs, and loads of deep-fried goodies. The next morning, Dad would load us into his Plymouth Suburban and undertake the long drive through the mountains. Our lakeside getaway tradition kicked off when I was a tyke—in that golden era, city folks retreated to the Catskills to escape the heat. Many camped at resorts along the so-called Borscht Belt. Dad and his office buddies, Fred Mercer and Leo Schrader, decided to skip the whole resort scene. Instead, they went in together on the aforementioned piece of lakefront property and built a trio of vacation cabins. The investment cost the men a pretty penny. However, nearby Harpy Peak was a popular winter destination. Ski bums were eager to rent the cabins during the holidays and that helped Dad and his friends recoup their expenses.

But let's stick to summer. Dreadful hot, humid summer that sent us to Lake Terron and its relative coolness. Me, Greg, Mom, Dad, Aunt Vikki, and Odin, our dog; supplies in back, a canoe strapped up top. Exhausted from Family Day, Greg and I usually slept for most of the trip. Probably a feature of Dad's vacation-management strategy. Then he merely had to contend with

Mom's chain-smoking and Aunt Vikki bitching about it. Unlike Mom and Dad, she didn't do much of anything. After her husband was electrocuted while repairing a downed power line, she collected a tidy insurance settlement and moved from the city into our Esopus home. Supposedly a temporary arrangement on account of her nervous condition. Her nerves never did improve—nor did anyone else's, for that matter.

We made our final pilgrimage the year before Armstrong left bootprints on the Moon. Greg and I were seventeen and twelve, respectively. Our good boy Odin sat between us. He'd outgrown his puppy ways and somehow gotten long in the tooth. Dad turned onto the lonely dirt track that wound a mile through heavy forest and arrived at the lake near sunset. The Mercers and Schraders were already in residence: a whole mob of obstreperous children and gamely suffering adults collected on a sward that fronted the cabins. Adults had gotten a head start on boilermakers and martinis. Grill-smoke wafted toward the beach. Smooth and cool as a mirror, the lake reflected the reddening sky like a portal to a parallel universe.

Lake Terron, or Lake Terror as we affectionately called it, gleamed at the edge of bona fide wilderness. Why Lake Terror? Some joker had altered the N on the road sign into an R with spray-paint and it just stuck. Nights were pitch-black five paces beyond the porch. The dark was full of insect noises and the coughs of deer lurching around in the brush.

Our cabin had pretty rough accommodations—plank siding and long, shotgun shack floorplan with a washroom, master bedroom, and a loft. Electricity and basic plumbing, but no phone or television. We lugged in books, cards, and boardgames to fashion a semblance of civilized entertainment. On a forest ranger's advice, Dad always propped a twelve-gauge shotgun by the door. Black bears roamed the woods and were attracted to the scents of barbeque and trash. *And children!* Mom would say.

The barbeque set the underlying tone; friendly hijinks and raucous laughter always prevailed those first few hours. Revived from our torpor, kids gorged on hotdogs and cola while parents lounged, grateful for the cool air and peaceful surroundings—except for the mosquitos. *Everybody* complained about them. Men understood shop talk was taboo. Those who slipped up received a warning glare from his better half. Nor did anyone remark upon news trickling in via the radio, especially concerning the Vietnam war; a subject that caused mothers everywhere to clutch teenaged sons to their bosoms. "Camp Terror" brooked none of that doomy guff. For two weeks, the outside world would remain at arms-length.

◄○►

Mr. Schrader struck a bonfire as the moon beamed over Harpy Peak. Once the dried cedar burned to coals, on came the bags of marshmallows and a sharpened stick for each kid's grubby mitt. I recall snatches of conversation. The men discussed the Apollo Program, inevitably philosophizing on the state of civilization and how far we'd advanced since the Wright Brothers climbed onto the stage.

"We take it for granted," Mr. Mercer said.

"What's that?" Mr. Schrader waved a marshmallow flaming at the end of his stick.

"Comfort, safety. You flip a switch, there's light. Turn a key, a motor starts."

"Electricity affords us the illusion of self-sufficiency."

"Gunpowder and penicillin imbue us with a sense of invincibility. Perpetual light has banished our natural dread of the dark. We're apes carrying brands of fire."

"Okay, gents. Since we're on the subject of apes. We primates share a common ancestor. Which means we share a staggering amount of history. You start dwelling on eons, you have to consider the implications of certain facts."

Mr. Mercer shook his head as lit a cigarette. "I can only guess where this is going."

"Simulation of human features and mannerisms will lead the field into eerie precincts," Dad said.

"Uh, oh," Mr. Schrader said. "This sounds suspiciously close to op-shay alk-tay."

"Thank goodness we're perfecting mechanical arms to handle rivet guns, not androids. Doesn't get more mundane."

"Mark it in the book. Heck, the Japanese are already there."

"Whatever you say, John."

"Researchers built a robot prototype—a baby with a lifelike face. Focus groups recoiled in disgust. Researchers came back with artificial features.

Focus groups *oohed* and *ahhed*. Corporate bankrolled the project. We'll hear plenty in a year or two."

"Humans are genetically encoded to fear things that look almost like us, but aren't us."

"Ever ask yourself why?"

"No, can't say I've dedicated much thought to the subject," Mr. Mercer said. "So, why are we allegedly fearful of, er, imitations?"

"For the same reason a deer or a fowl will spook if it gets wind of a decoy. Even an animal comprehends that a lure means nothing good." Dad had mentioned this periodically. Tonight, he didn't seem to speak to either of his colleagues. He looked directly at me.

"Shop talk!" Mom said with the tone of a referee declaring a foul. Mrs. Schrader and Mrs. Mercer interrupted their own conversation to boo the men.

"Whoops, sorry!" Mr. Mercer gestured placatingly. "Anyway, how about those Jets?"

Later, somebody suggested we have a game. No takers for charades or trivia. Finally, Mrs. Mercer requested a demonstration of Aunt Vikki's fabled skills. Close magic, prestidigitation, clairvoyance, or whatever she called it. My aunt demurred. However, the boisterous assembly would brook no refusal and badgered her until she relented.

That mystical evening, performing for a rapt audience against a wilderness backdrop, she was on her game. Seated lotus on a blanket near the fire, she affected trancelike concentration. Speaking in a monotone, she specified the exact change in Mr. Schrader's pocket; the contents of Mrs. Mercer's clutch, and the fact that one of the Mercer kids had stolen his sister's diary. This proved to be the warmup routine.

Mr. Mercer said, "John says you've worked with the law to find missing persons."

"Found a couple." Her cheeks were flushed, her tone defiant. "Their bodies, at any rate."

"That plane that went down in the Adirondacks. Can you get a psychic bead on it?"

Aunt Vikki again coyly declined until a chorus of pleas "convinced" her to give it a shot. She swayed in place, hands clasped. "Dirt. Rocks. Running water. Scattered voices. Many miles apart."

"Guess that makes sense," Mr. Mercer said to Mr. Schrader. "Wreck is definitely spread across the hills."

Mrs. Schrader said under her breath to Dad, "Eh, what's the point? She could say anything she pleases. We've no way to prove her claim." He shooshed her with a familiar pat on the hip. Everybody was ostensibly devout in those days. Mrs. Schrader frequently volunteered at her church and I suspect Aunt Vikki's occult shenanigans, innocent as they might've been, troubled her. The boozing and flirtation less-so.

The eldest Mercer girl, Katie, asked if she could divine details of an IBM housewife named Denise Vinson who'd disappeared near Saugerties that spring. Nobody present knew her husband; he was among the faceless legions of electricians who kept the plant humming. He and his wife had probably attended a company buffet or some such. The case made the papers.

"Denise Vinson. Denise Vinson . . ." Aunt Vikki slipped into her "trance." Moments dragged on and an almost electric tension built; the hair-raising sensation of an approaching thunderstorm. The adults ceased bantering. Pine branches creaked; an owl hooted. A breeze freshened off the lake, causing water to lap against the dock. Greg and I felt it. His persistent smirk faded, replaced by an expression of dawning wonderment. Then Aunt Vikki went rigid and shrieked. Her cry echoed off the lake and caused birds to dislodge from their roosts in the surrounding trees. Her arms extended, fingers and thumbs together, wrists bent downward. She rocked violently, cupped hands stabbing the air in exaggerated thrusts. Her eyes filled with blood. My thoughts weren't exactly coherent, but her posture and mannerisms reminded me of a mantis lashing at its prey. Reminded me of something else, too.

Her tongue distended as she babbled like a Charismatic. She covered her face and doubled over. Nobody said anything until she straightened to regard us.

"Geez, Vikki!" Mr. Mercer nodded toward his pop-eyed children. "I mean, geez-Louise!"

"What's the fuss?" She glanced around, dazed.

Mom, in a display of rare concern, asked what she'd seen. Aunt Vikki shrugged and said she'd glimpsed the inside of her eyelids. Why was everybody carrying on? Dad lurked to one side of the barbeque pit. His glasses were brimmed with the soft glow of the coals. I couldn't decipher his expression.

Mood dampened, the families said their goodnights and drifted off to bed. Mom, tight on highballs, compared Aunt Vikki's alleged powers of clairvoyance to those of the famous Edgar Cayce. This clash occurred in the wee hours after the others retired to their cabins. Awakened by raised voices, I hid in shadows atop the stairs to the loft, eavesdropping like it was my job.

"Cayce was as full of shit as a Christmas goose." Aunt Vikki's simmering antipathy boiled over. "Con man. Charlatan. Huckster." Her eyes were bloodshot and stained from burst capillaries. Though she doggedly claimed not to recall the episode from earlier that evening, its lingering effects were evident.

"Vikki," Dad said in the placating tone he deployed against disgruntled subordinates. "Barbara didn't mean any harm. Right, honey?"

"Sure, I did . . .not." From my vantage I saw Mom perched near the cold hearth, glass in hand. The drunker she got, the cattier she got. She drank plenty at Lake Terror.

Aunt Vikki loomed in her beehive-do and platform shoes. "Don't ever speak of me and that . . .that fraud in the same breath. Cayce's dead and good riddance to him. *I'm* the real McCoy."

"Is that a fact? Then, let's skip the rest of this campout and head for Vegas." Mom tried to hide her sardonic smile with the glass.

"Ladies, it's late," Dad said. "I sure hope our conversation isn't keeping the small fry awake." Maybe he glanced my way while stretching.

His not-so-subtle cue to skedaddle back to my cot left me pondering who was the psychic—Aunt Vikki or Dad? *Maybe he can see in the dark,* was my last conscious thought. It made me giggle, albeit nervously.

◄◦►

Greg jumped me and Billy Mercer as we walked along the trail behind the cabins. Billy and I were closest in age. Alas, we had next to nothing in common and didn't prefer one another's company. Those were the breaks, as the youth used to say. The path forked at a spring before winding ever deeper into the woods. To our left, the path climbed a steep hill through a notch in a stand of shaggy black pine. Mom, the poet among us, referred to it as the Black Gap. Our parents forbade us to drink from the spring, citing mosquito larvae. Predictably, we disregarded their command and slurped double handfuls of cool water at the first opportunity. As I drank, Greg crept upon me like an Apache.

He clamped my neck in a grip born of neighborhood lawnmowing to earn extra bucks for gas and date-night burgers. "Boo!" He'd simultaneously smacked Billy on the back of his head. The boy yelped and tripped over his own feet trying to flee. Thus, round one of Tiptoe went to my insufferably smirking brother. Ever merciless in that oh-so special cruelty the eldest impose upon their weaker siblings, I nonetheless detected a sharper, savage inflection to his demeanor of late. I zipped a rock past his ear from a safe distance—not that one could ever be sure—and beat a hasty retreat into the woods. Greg flipped us the bird and kept going without a backward glance.

The reason this incident is notable? Billy Mercer complained to the adults. Dad pulled me aside for an account, which I grudgingly provided—nobody respects a tattletale. Dad's smirk was even nastier than Greg's. *Head on a swivel, if you want to keep it, kiddo.* He put his arm around my brother's shoulders and they shared a laugh. Three days in, and those two spent much of it together, hiking the forest and floating around the lake. The stab of jealousy hurt worse than Greg squeezing my neck.

Near bedtime, we set up tents in the backyard, a few feet past the badminton net and horseshoe pit. The plan was for the boys to sleep under the stars (and among the swarming mosquitos). Mrs. Schrader protested weakly that maybe this was risky, what with the bears. Mr. Schrader and Mr. Mercer promised to take watches on the porch. Odin stayed with me; that would be the best alarm in the world. No critter would get within a hundred yards without that dog raising holy hell. And thus it went; Odin, Billy Mercer, a Schrader boy, and me in one tent, and the rest of them in the other. We chatted for a bit. Chitchat waned; I tucked into my sleeping bag, poring over an issue of *Mad Magazine* by flashlight until I got sleepy.

I woke to utter darkness. Odin panted near my face, growling softly. I lay at the entrance. Groggy and unsure of whether the dog had scented a deer or a bear, I instinctively clicked on my trusty flashlight, opened the flap, and shined it into the trees—ready to yell if I spotted danger. Nothing to corroborate Odin's anxious grumbles. Scruffy grass, bushes, and the shapeless mass of the forest. He eventually settled. I slept and dreamed two vivid dreams. The first was of Aunt Vikki spotlighted against a void. Her eyes bulged as she rocked and gesticulated, muttering. Dream logic prevailing, I understood her garbled words: *Eeny! Meany! Miny! Moe!*

In the second, I floated; a disembodied spirit gazing down. Barely revealed by a glimmer of porchlight, Dad crawled from under a bush and lay on his side next to the tent. He reached through the flap. His arm moved, stroking.

These dreams were forgotten by breakfast. The incident only returned to me many years later; a nightmare within a nightmare.

◄◦►

Over blueberry pancakes, Dad casually asked whether I'd care to go fishing. At an age where a kid selfishly treasured an appointment on his father's calendar, I filled a canteen and slung my trusty Nikon F around my neck and hustled after him to the dock. Unlike the starter camera I'd long outgrown, the Nikon was expensive and I treated it with proper reverence. Film rolls were costly as well. Manual labor, supplemented by a generous allowance and a bit of wheedling, paid the freight. Mom, a stalwart supporter of the arts, chipped in extra. She encouraged me to submit my work to newspaper and magazine contests, in vain. Back then, the hobby was strictly personal. I wasn't inclined to share my vision with the world just yet, although I secretly dreamed big dreams—namely, riding the savannah with the crew of *Mutual of Omaha's Wild Kingdom.*

The sun hadn't cleared the trees as we pushed away from the dock. Dad paddled. I faced him, clicking shots of the receding cabins and birds rising and falling from the lake and into the sky. He set aside his paddle and the canoe kept on gliding across the dark water.

"This is where we're gonna fish?" I said.

"No fishing today." After a pause, he said, "I'm more a fisher of men."

"I don't get it."

"Time to begin reflecting on what kind of man *you* are."

"Dad, I'm *twelve.*" I inherited my smart-Alec lip from Mom.

"That's why I don't expect you to decide today. Merely think on it." He could see I wasn't comprehending him. "Ever since you showed an interest in photography, I had a hunch . . ." He cupped his hands and blew into the notch between his thumbs. Took him a couple of tries to perfect an eerie, fluting whistle that rebounded off the lake and nearby hills. He lowered his hands and looked at me. "I planned to wait until next year to have this conversation. Aunt Vikki's . . .outburst has me thinking sooner is better. Sorry if she frightened you."

"Why did she fly off the handle? Are her eyes okay?" I hoped to sound unflappable.

"Her eyes are fine. It's my fault. The Vinson woman was too close to home. Anyhow, your aunt is staying with us because she can't live alone. She's fragile. Emotionally."

"Vikki's crazy?"

"No. Well, maybe. She's different and she needs her family."

"She and Mom hate each other."

"They fight. That doesn't mean they hate each other. Do you hate your brother? Wait, don't answer that." He dipped his paddle into the water. "What's my job at the plant?"

"You build—"

"Design."

"You design robots."

"I'm a mechanical engineer specializing in robotic devices and systems. It's not quite as dramatic as it sounds. How do you suppose I landed that position?"

"Well, you went to school—"

"No, son. I majored in sociology. Any expertise I have in engineering I've learned on the fly or by studying at night."

"Oh." Confused by the turn in our conversation, I fiddled with my camera.

"Want to know the truth?"

"Okay." I feared with all the power of my child's imagination that he would reveal that his *real* name was Vladimir, a deep cover mole sent by the Russians. It's difficult to properly emphasize the underlying paranoia wrought by the Cold War on our collective national psyche. My brother and I spied on our neighbors, profiling them as possible Red agents. We'd frequently convinced ourselves that half the neighborhood was sending clandestine reports to a numbers station.

"I bullshitted the hiring committee," Dad said. He seldom cursed around Mom; moreso Greg. Now I'd entered his hallowed circle of confidence. "*That's* how I acquired my position. If you understand what makes people tick, you can always get what you want. Oops, here we are." Silt scraped the hull as he nosed the canoe onto the shore. We disembarked and walked through some bushes to a path that circled the entire lake. I knew this since our families made the entire circuit at least once per vacation.

Dad yawned, twisting his torso around with a contortionist's knack. He doubled his left hand against his forearm; then the right. His joints popped. This wasn't the same as my brother cracking his knuckles, which he often did to annoy me. No, it sounded more like a butcher snapping the bones of a chicken carcass. He sighed in evident relief. "Son, I can't tell you what a living bitch it is to maintain acceptable posture every damned minute of the day. Speaking of wanting things. You want great pictures of predators, right?" I agreed, sure, that was the idea. He hunched so our heads were closer. "Prey animals are easy to stalk. They're *prey*. They exist to be hunted and eaten. Predators are tougher. I can teach you. I've been working with your brother for years. Getting him ready for the jungle."

"The jungle?" I said, hearing and reacting to the latter part of his statement while ignoring the former. "You mean *Vietnam*?" There was a curse word. But he promised Mom—"

"Greg's going to volunteer for the Marines. Don't worry. He's a natural. He's like me." He stopped and laid his hand on my shoulder. Heavy and full of suppressed power. "I can count on your discretion not to tell your mother. Can't I?"

Sons and fathers have differences. Nonetheless, I'd always felt safe around mine. Sure, he was awkward and socially off-putting. Sure, he ran hot and cold. Sure, he made lame jokes and could be painfully distant. People joke that engineers are socially maladjusted; there's some truth to that cliché. Foibles notwithstanding, I didn't doubt his love or intentions. Yet, in that moment, I became hyperaware of the size of his hand—of him, in general—and the chirping birds, and that we were alone here in the trees on the opposite shore of the lake. Awareness of his physical grotesqueness hit me in a wave of revulsion. From my child's unvarnished perspective, his features transcended mere homeliness. Since he'd stretched, his stance and expression had altered. Spade-faced and gangling, toothy and hunched, yet tall and deceptively agile. A carnivore had slipped on Dad's sporting goods department ensemble and lured me into the woods. *Let's go to Grandma's house!*

Such a witless, childish fantasy. The spit dried in my mouth anyhow. Desperate to change the subject, perhaps to show deference the way a wolf pup does to an alpha, I said, "I didn't mean to call Aunt Vikki crazy."

Dad blinked behind those enormous, horn-rimmed glasses. "It would be a mistake to classify aberrant psychology as proof of disorder." He registered my blank expression. "Charles Addams said—"

"Who's that?"

"A cartoonist. He said, 'What is normal for the spider is chaos for the fly.' He was correct. The world is divided between spiders and flies." He studied me intently, searching for something, then shook himself and straightened. His hand dropped away from my shoulder. Such a large hand, such a long arm. "C'mon. Let's stroll a bit. If we're quiet, we might surprise a woodland critter."

◄◦►

We strolled.

Contrary to his stated intention of moving quietly to surprise our quarry, Dad initiated a nonstop monologue. He got onto the subject of physical comedy and acting. "Boris Karloff is a master," He said. "And Lon Chaney Jr. The werewolf guy?"

"Yeah, Dad." I'd recovered a bit after that moment of irrational panic. The world felt right again under my feet.

"Chaney's facility with physiognomic transformation? Truly remarkable. Unparalleled, considering his disadvantages. Faking—it's difficult." One aspect I learned to appreciate about my old man's character was the fact he didn't dumb down his language. Granted, he'd speak slower depending upon the audience. However, he used big words if big words were appropriate. My deskside dictionary and thesaurus were dogeared as all get-out.

While he blathered, I managed a few good shots including a Cooper's hawk perched on a high branch, observing our progress. The hawk leaped, disappearing over the canopy. When I lowered the camera, Dad was gone too. I did what you might expect—called for him and dithered, figuring he'd poke his head around a tree and laugh at my consternation. Instead, the sun climbed. Patches of cool shade thickened; the lake surface dimmed and brightened with opaline hardness. Yelling occasionally, I trudged back toward where we'd beached the canoe.

He caught me as I rounded a bend in the path. A hand and ropy arm extended so very far from the wall of brush. A hooked nail scraped my forehead. *Look, son! See?* Instead of pausing to peer into the undergrowth, I ran. Full tilt, camera strap whipping around my neck and a miracle I didn't lose that beloved camera before I crashed through the bushes onto the beach.

Dad sat on a driftwood log, serenely studying the lake. "Hey, kiddo. There you are." He explained his intention to play a harmless joke. "You perceive your surroundings in a different light if a guardian isn't present. Every boy should feel that small burst of adrenaline under controlled circumstances. Head on a swivel, right, son?"

I realized I'd merely bumped into a low-hanging branch and completely freaked. By the time we paddled home, my wild, unreasoning terror had dissipated. It's all or nothing with kids—dying of plague or fit as a fiddle; bounce back from a nasty fall, or busted legs; rub some dirt on it and walk it off, or a wheelchair. Similar deal with our emotions as well. Dad wasn't a monster, merely a weirdo. Aunt Vikki's crazed behavior had set my teeth on edge. The perfect storm. My thoughts shied from outré concerns to dwell upon on Dad's casual mention that Greg planned on going to war and how we'd best keep on the QT. Not the kind of secret I wanted to hide from Mom, but I wasn't a squealer.

He remained quiet until we were gliding alongside the dock. He said, "Randy, I was wrong to test you. I'm sorry. Won't happen again. Scout's honor."

It didn't.

◄◦►

Toward the end of our stay, the whole lot of us trooped forth to conduct our annual peregrination around the entire lake. We packed picnic baskets and assembled at the Black Gap. Except for Dad, who'd gone ahead to prepare the site where we'd camp for lunch. Another barbeque, in fact. Mr. Mercer brought along a fancy camera (a Canon!) to record the vacation action. He and I had a bonding moment as "serious" photographers. Mr. Schrader, Dad, and a couple of the kids toted flimsy cheapo tourist models. Such amateurs! Mr. Mercer arranged us with the pines for a backdrop. Everybody posed according to height. He yelled directions, got what he wanted, and joined the group while I snapped a few—first with his camera, then my own. I lagged behind as they scrambled uphill along the path. Odin stuck to my side, occasionally whining, but nothing dangerous appeared.

We trekked to the campsite. Hot, thirsty, and ready for our roasted chicken. Dad awaited us, although not by much. None of the other adults said anything. However, I recall Mom's vexation with the fact he hadn't even gotten a fire going in the pit. She pulled him aside and asked what happened. Why was he so mussed and unkempt? Why so damned sweaty?

He blinked, pushed his glasses up, and shrugged. "I tried a shortcut. Got lost."

"Lost, huh?" She combed pine needles out of his hair. "Likely story."

⟨○⟩

That winter, drunken ski bums accidentally burned down the Schrader cabin. Oh, the plan was to rebuild in the spring and carry on. Alas, one thing led to another—kids shipping off to college, the Mercers divorcing, etc.—and we never returned. The men sold off the property for a tidy profit. That was that for our Terror Lake era.

Greg skipped college and enlisted with the United States Marine Corps in '69. Mom locked herself in her study and cried for a week. That shook me—she wasn't a weeper by any means. My brother sent postcards every month or so over the course of his two tours. Well, except for a long, dark stretch near the end when he ceased all communication. The military wouldn't tell us anything. Judging by her peevishness and the fact she seldom slept, I suspect Mom walked the ragged edge.

One day, Greg called and said he'd be home soon. Could Dad pick him up at the airport? He departed an obstreperous child and returned a quieter, thoughtful man. The war injured the psyches of many soldiers. It definitely affected him. Greg kibitzed about shore leave and the antics of his rogue's gallery of comrades. Conversely, he deflected intimate questions that drilled too close to where his honest emotions lay buried. Dumb kids being dumb kids, I asked if he killed anyone. He smiled and drummed his fingers on the table, one then another. That smile harked to his teenaged cruelness, now carefully submerged. More artful, more refined, more mature. He said, *The neat thing about Tiptoe? It's humane. Curbs the ol' urges. Ordinarily, it's enough to catch and release. Ordinarily. You get me, kid?* We didn't speak often after he moved to the Midwest. He latched on with a trucking company. The next to the last time I saw him was at Dad's funeral in 1985. Dad's ticker had blown while raking leaves. Dead on his way to the ground, same as his own father and older brother. Greg lurked on the fringes at the reception. He slipped away before I could corner him. Nobody else noticed that he'd come and gone.

Aunt Vikki? She joined a weird church. Her erratic behavior deteriorated throughout the 1970s, leading to a stint in an institution. She made a comeback in the '80s, got on the ground floor of the whole psychic hotline craze. Made a killing telling people what they wanted to hear. Remarried to a disgraced avant-garde filmmaker. Bought a mansion in Florida where she currently runs a New Age commune of international repute. Every Christmas, she drops a couple grand on my photography to jazz up her compound. I can't imagine how poster photos of wolves disemboweling caribou go over with the rubes seeking enlightenment. Got to admit, watching those recruitment videos shot by her latest husband, my work looks damned slick.

◄◦►

And full circle at last. My coworker startled me; nightmares ensued; and creepy-crawly memories surfaced. Cue my formerly happy existence falling apart. 2 a.m. routinely found me wide awake, scrutinizing my sweaty reflection in the bathroom mirror. I tugged the bags beneath my eyes, exposing the veiny whites. Drew down until it hurt. Just more of the same. What did I expect? That my face was a mask and I peered through slits? That I was my father's son, through and through? If he were more or less than a man, what did that make me?

On my next visit, I decided to level with Mom as I tucked her into bed.

"We need to talk about Dad." I hesitated. Was it even ethical to tell her the truth, here at the end of her days? *Hey, Ma, I believe Pop was involved in the disappearances of several—god knows the number—people back in the '60s.* I forged ahead. "This will sound crazy. He wasn't . . .normal."

"Well, duh," she said. We sat that there for a while, on opposite sides of a gulf that widened by the second.

"Wait. Were you aware?"

"Of what?"

Hell of a question. "There was another side to Dad. Dark. Real dark, I'm afraid."

"Ah. What did you know, ma'am, and when did you know it?"

"Yeah, basically."

"Bank robbers don't always tell their wives they rob banks."

"The wives suspect."

"Damned straight. Suspicion isn't proof. That's the beauty of the arrange-ment. We lasted until he died. There's beauty in that too, these days." Mom's voice had weakened as she spoke. She beckoned me to lean in and I did. "We were on our honeymoon at a lodge. Around dawn, wrapped in a quilt on the deck. A fox light-footed into the yard. I whispered to your father about the awesomeness of mother nature, or wow, a fox! He smiled. Not his quirky smile, the cold one. He said, *an animal's expression won't change, even as it's eating prey alive.* May sound strange, but that's when I knew we fit perfectly."

"Jesus, Mom." I shivered. Dad and his pearls of wisdom, his icy little apothegms. *Respected, admired, revered. But replaceable.* A phrase he said in response to anyone who inquired after his job security at IBM. He'd also uttered a similar quote when admonishing Greg or me in connection to juvenile hijinks. *Loved, but replaceable, boys. Loved, but replaceable.*

"He never would've hurt you." She closed her eyes and snuggled deeper into her blankets. Her next words were muffled. I'm not sure I heard them right. "At least, not by choice."

◁o▷

Mom died. A handful of journalist colleagues and nurses showed to pay their respects. Greg waited until the rest had gone and I was in the midst of wiping my tears to step from behind a decrepit obelisk, grip my shoulder, and whisper, "Boo!" He didn't appear especially well. Gray and gaunt, raw around the nose and mouth. Strong, though, and seething with febrile energy. He resembled the hell out of Dad when Dad was around that age and not long prior to his coronary. Greg even wore a set of oversized glasses, although I got a funny feeling they were purely camouflage.

We relocated to a tavern. He paid for a pitcher, of which he guzzled the majority. Half a lifetime had passed since our last beer. I wondered what was on his mind. The funeral? Vietnam? That decade-old string of missing persons in Ohio near his last known town of residence?

"Don't fret, little brother." Predators have a talent for sniffing weakness. He'd sussed out that I'd gone through a few things recently, Mom's death being the latest addition to the calculus of woe. "Dad *told* you—you're not the same as us." He wiped his lips and tried on a peaceable smile. "They gave me the good genes. Although, I do surely wish I had your eye. Mom also had the eye." The second pitcher came and he waxed maudlin. "Look, apologies for being such a jerk to you when we were kids."

"Forgotten," I said.

"I've always controlled my worse impulses by inflicting petty discomfort. Like chewing a stick of gum when I want a cigarette so bad my teeth ache. I needle people. Associates, friends, loved ones. Whomever. Their unease feeds me well enough to keep the real craving at bay. Until it doesn't." He removed a photo from his wallet and pushed it across the table. Mom and Dad in our old yard. The sun was in Dad's glasses. Hard to know what to make of man's smile when you can't see his eyes. I pushed it back. He waved me off. "Hang onto that."

"It's yours."

"Nah, I don't need a memento. You're the archivist. The sentimental one."

"Fine. Thanks." I slipped the photo into my coat pocket.

He stared at a waitress as she cleared a booth across the aisle. From a distance his expression might've passed for friendly. "My motel isn't far," he said. "Give me a ride? Or if you're busy, I could ask her."

How could I refuse my own brother? Well, I would've loved to.

◄◦►

His motel occupied a lonely corner on a dark street near the freeway. He invited me into his cave-like room. I declined, said it had been great, etcetera. I almost escaped clean. He caught my wrist. Up close, he smelled of beer, coppery musk, and a hint of moldering earth.

"I think back to my friends in school and the military," Greg said. "The drug addicts, the cons, and divorcees. A shitload of kids who grew up and moved as far from home as humanly possible. Why? Because their families were the worst thing that ever happened to them. It hit me."

"What hit you?"

"On the whole, Mom and Dad were pretty great parents."

"Surprising to hear you put it that way, Greg. We haven't shared many family dinners since we were kids."

"Take my absence as an expression of love. Consider also, I might have been around more than you noticed." He squeezed. "

As I mentioned, despite his cadaverous appearance, he was strong. And by that, I mean bone crushing strong. My arm may as well have been clamped in the jaws of a grizzly. I wasn't going anywhere unless he permitted it. "They were good people," I said through my teeth.

"Adios, bud."

Surely was a relief when he slackened his grip and released me. I trudged down the stairs, across the lot, and had my car keys in hand when the flesh on my neck prickled. I spun, and there was Greg, twenty or so feet behind me, soundlessly tiptoeing along, knees to chest, elbows even with the top of his head, hands splayed wide. He closed most of the gap in a single, exaggerated stride. Then he froze and watched my face with the same intensity as he'd observed the waitress.

"Well done," he said. "Maybe you learned something, bumbling around in the woods." He turned and walked toward the lights of the motel. I waited until he'd climbed the stairs to jump into my car and floor it out of there.

A long trip home. You bet I glanced into my rearview the entire drive.

◄◦►

Later, in the desolate stretch that comes along after 3 a.m., short on sleep due to a brain that refused to switch off, I killed the last of the bourbon while obsessively sorting those photographs one more time. A mindless occupation that felt akin to picking at a scab or working on a jigsaw. No real mental agility involved other than mechanically rotating pieces until something locked into place. Among the many loose pictures I'd stashed for posterity were some shot on that last day at Lake Terror in '68. The sequence began with our three cheerfully waving families (minus Dad) assembled at the Black Gap; then a few more of everybody proceeding single-file away and up the trail.

I spread these photos on the coffee table and stared for a long, long while. I only spotted the slightly fuzzy, unfocused extra figure because of my keenly trained vision . . .and possibly a dreadful instinct honed by escalating paranoia. Once I saw him, there were no take backsies, as we used to say. Dad hung in the branches; a huge, distorted figure hidden in the background of tree trunks and heavy canopy. Bloated and lanky, his jaw unslung. Inhumanly proportioned, but unmistakably my father. Gaze fixed upon the camera as his left arm dangled and dangled, gray-black fingers plucking the hair of the kids as they hiked obliviously through the notch between the shaggy pines. His lips squirmed.

Eeny. Meeny. Miny. Moe.

HONORABLE MENTIONS

Ballingrud, Nathan "A Brief Tour of the Night," *Beyond the Veil*.

Baxter, Alan "Out On a Rim," *The Gulp*.

Bechko, Corinna "A Darkness a Little Too Bright," Corridor 1.

Birnie, Seán Padraic "Like a Zip," *I Would Haunt You If I Could*.

Brown, Gordon "It Looked Like Her," Nightscript VII.

Bulkin, Nadia "One Day Across the Valley," Corridor 1.

Campbell, Ramsey "First a Bird," *Uncertainties Volume V*.

Chapman, Clay McCleod "Stowaway," Southwest Review, Autumn.

Cisco, Michael "Milking," *Antisocieties*.

Coffman, Frank "The Decipherment," (poem) *Eclipse of the Moon*.

Cohen, Michael Harris "I Pay You," On Spec #118.

Cosby. M.R. "Dark Matter," *The Trains Don't Stop Here*.

DeLucci, Theresa "Only My Skin That Crawled Away," Weird Horror #3.

DeMeester, Kristi "A Good Boy," Corridor 1.

Duffy, Steve "The Other Four O'Clock," *Finding Yourself in the Dark*.

Enriquez, Mariana "Cart," *The Dangers of Smoking in Bed*.

Enriquez, Mariana "Meat," *The Dangers of Smoking in Bed*.

Evenson, Brian "The Barrow Men," Unsaid 8/*The Glassy Burning Floor of Hell*.

Fahey, Tracy "I'll Be Your Mirror," *I Spit Myself Out*.

Files, Gemma "Uncertainty," *Tales From Omnipark*.

Files, Gemma "Yellowback," *Beyond the Veil*.

Ford, Jeffrey "Inn of the Dreaming Dog," *Big Dark Hole*.

Fracassi, Philip "The Wheel," *Beneath a Pale Sky*.

Granville, Timothy "The Summer King's Day," Nightscript VII.

Hand, Elizabeth "For Sale By Owner," *When Things Get Dark*.

Hardy, Lucie McKnight "Dead Relatives," (novella) *Dead Relatives*.

Iqbal, Muhammed Zafar, "The Zoo," trans Arunava Sinha *The Gollancz Bk of S Asian SF*Vol2.

Jones, Stephen Graham "Ten Miles of Bad Road," *Attack From the 80s*.

Khaw, Cassandra *Nothing But Blackened Teeth* (novella). Tor.com.

Kiernan, *Caitlín R.* "Pygmalion As a Hammer," *Sirenia Digest 185.*

Langan, John "Uncle Bart's Map, Hymns of Abomination.

Langan, John "Washed in the Blood of the Sun," *Uncertainties Volume V.*

Link, Kelly "Skinder's Veil," *When Things Get Dark.*

MacLeod, Bracken "Weightless Before She Falls," *Fright Train.*

Madrigano, Clare "Little Doors," The Dark #70, March.

Malerman, Josh "Special Meal" *When Things Get Dark.*

Moore, Tegan "Tyger," Tor.com, February 24.

Oates, Joyce Carol "Río Piedra," Conjunctions 76.

Peréz, Lexi "Jamón Íberico," Underland Arcana 2.

Rowlan, Garrett "The Dentist," Horrorzine October.

Tbakhi, Fargo "Balfour in the Desert," Strange Horizons, May 17.

Tem, Steve Rasnic "Sleepover," *Thanatrauma.*

Warren, Kaaron "Warp and Weft," *Professor Charlatan Bardot's Travel Anthology . . .*

Whitley, Aliya "Envelope," *The Loosening Skin.*

Wilkinson, Charles "Where the Oxen Turned the Plough," Nightscript VII.

ABOUT THE AUTHORS

G. V. Anderson's short stories have won a World Fantasy Award, a British Fantasy Award, and been nominated for a Nebula Award. Her work can be found in *Strange Horizons* and *Tor.com*, as well as anthologies such as *The Year's Best Dark Fantasy & Horror*. She lives and works in Dorset, UK.

Laird Barron spent his early years in Alaska. He is the author of several books, including *The Beautiful Thing That Awaits Us All, Swift to Chase,* and *Blood Standard*. His work has also appeared in many magazines and anthologies. Barron currently resides in the Rondout Valley writing stories about the evil that men do.

Simon Bestwick lives on the Wirral in North-West England, and is still happily serving as husband and butler to long-suffering fellow author Cate Gardner. He is the author of seven novels, four full-length short story collections, and has been four times shortlisted for the British Fantasy Award. His latest books are the novella *Devils Of London*, from Hersham Horror, and the novel *Black Mountain*, from Independent Legions Publishing. His ambitions are to move to Wales, get a dog, and avoid honest work

Brian Evenson has published over a dozen books of fiction, most recently *The Glassy, Burning Floor of Hell*. His collection *Song for the Unraveling of the World* won the Shirley Jackson Award and the World Fantasy Award and was a finalist for the Ray Bradbury Prize. Other honors include the 2009 ALA-RUSA award for *Last Days* and the International Horror Guild Award for *The Wavering Knife*. He has received three O. Henry Prizes, an NEA fellowship, and a Guggenheim Award. He lives in Los Angeles and teaches at CalArts.

Gemma Files has been an award-winning horror author for almost thirty years. Probably best known for her novel *Experimental Film*, she has also published four other novels, five collections of short fiction, and three collections of speculative poetry. Her most recent collection, *In That Endlessness, Our End* (Grimscribe Press), was nominated for a 2021 Bram Stoker Award. She has two more collections upcoming, one from Trepidatio in 2022, one from Grimscribe in 2023, and a new poetry collection from Plutonian Press.

Robin Furth's fiction has appeared in *The Magazine of Fantasy & Science Fiction*, *The Year's Best Dark Fantasy and Horror*, and *The NoSleep Podcast*. She is the co-author of Marvel's bestselling *Dark Tower* graphic novels, and has been published by IDW, Vertigo, and Marvel. Her work has been nominated for Eisner and Harvey Awards, and has twice been chosen for YALSA's list of Great Graphic Novels for Teens. Her nonfiction book, *Stephen King's The Dark Tower: The Complete Concordance*, has been translated into five languages.

Christopher Golden is the *New York Times* bestselling author of *Ararat*, *Road of Bones*, *Snowblind*, and many other novels. With Mike Mignola, he is the co-creator of such comics series as *Baltimore*, *Lady Baltimore*, and *Joe Golem: Occult Detective*. Golden has edited and co-edited numerous anthologies, including *Seize the Night*, *The New Dead*, and Shirley Jackson Award winner *The Twisted Book of Shadows*. The author has been nominated ten times in eight different categories for the Bram Stoker Awards, and won twice. Golden is a screenwriter and producer, as well as a writer of audio dramas and video games. He lives in Massachusetts.

Glen Hirshberg's novels include *The Snowman's Children*, *Infinity Dreams*, *The Book of Bunk*, and the *Motherless Children* trilogy. He is also the author of four widely praised story collections: *The Two Sams*, *American Morons*, *The Janus Tree*, and *The Ones Who Are Waving*. Hirshberg is a three-time International Horror Guild Award Winner, five-time World Fantasy Award finalist, and he won the Shirley Jackson Award for the novelette "The Janus Tree." Check out his Substack at https://glenhirshberg.substack.com/. He lives with his family and cats in the Pacific Northwest.

Carly Holmes lives and writes in a small village on the banks of the river Teifi in west Wales, UK. Her debut novel *The Scrapbook* was shortlisted for the International Rubery Book Award, and her debut story collection,

Figurehead, was published in limited edition hardback by Tartarus Press. The paperback edition was published by Parthian Books in 2022. Her prize-winning short prose has appeared in journals and anthologies such as *Ambit, The Ghastling, Shadows & Tall Trees, Crooked Houses*, and *Black Static*.

Matthew Holness created and starred in *Garth Marenghi's Darkplace* for Channel 4 and his short films include *A Gun For George, The Snipist*, and *Smutch*. His stories have appeared in *Beyond the Veil, Black Static, At Ease With the Dead, Phobic, The New Uncanny*, and *Protest*. He wrote and directed the 2018 horror feature *Possum*, and his audio adaptation of M.R. James's *The Ash Tree* for Bafflegab Productions recently won Best Drama Special (Gold) at the 2020 New York Festivals Radio Awards.

Sarah Lamparelli is a librarian and a writer of dark fiction. Born and raised in Upstate New York, she now lives and works in the Chicago suburbs. Her short fiction has appeared in *Black Static*, and she is currently at work on her first novel. "Stolen Property" is her first published story.

Eric LaRocca is the Bram Stoker Award nominated author of several works of horror and dark fiction including the viral sensation *Things Have Gotten Worse Since We Last Spoke*. He is an active member of the Horror Writers Association and lives in Boston, MA with his partner. For more information, please visit ericlarocca.com.

Gerard McKeown was shortlisted for The Bridport Prize in 2017, and in 2018 he was longlisted for The Irish Book Awards' Short Story of the Year. His work has been featured in a number of journals and anthologies and broadcast on BBC Radio 4. More of his writing can be viewed at www. gerardmckeown.co.uk. He can also be found on twitter at @gerardmckeown.

Eóin Murphy is a writer from Northern Ireland where he lives with his wonderful wife and fantastic son. Eóin has been writing ever since he wasn't allowed to go see *The Monster Squad* so he wrote his own version. His previous work can be found, amongst other places, in *The Siren's Call* and *The Twisted Book of Shadows*. Eóin can be found lurking on Twitter at @Ragemonki.

Lee Murray is a multi-award-winning author-editor and poet from Aotearoa New Zealand. A *USA Today* bestselling author, Shirley Jackson and Bram Stoker Award®-winner, she is an NZSA Honorary Literary Fellow and a Grimshaw Sargeson Fellow for poetry. A Rhysling- and Pushcart-nominated poet, Lee's debut collection, *Tortured Willows: Bent. Bowed. Unbroken*, is a collaborative title with Christina Sng, Angela Yuriko Smith, and Geneve Flynn. Read more at leemurray.info.

Jonathan Raab is the author of *of The Haunting of Camp Winter Falcon, The Secret Goatman Spookshow and Other Psychological Warfare Operations, The Crypt of Blood: A Halloween TV Special, Camp Ghoul Mountain Part VI: The Official Novelization*, and more. He is the editor of several books from Muzzleland Press including *Behold the Undead of Dracula: Lurid Tales of Cinematic Gothic Horror* and *Terror in 16-bits*. He lives among the Gothic landscapes of Upstate New York with his wife, son, and a dog named Egon. You can find him on Twitter at @jonathanraab1.

Ian Rogers is the author of the award-winning collection, *Every House Is Haunted*. A novelette from the collection, "The House on Ashley Avenue," was a finalist for the Shirley Jackson Award, and is the basis for an upcoming Netflix film produced by Sam Raimi. Ian lives with his wife in Peterborough, Ontario. For more information, visit ianrogers.ca.

Michael Marshall Smith has published nearly a hundred stories and five novels, and is the only author to have won the British Fantasy Award for Short Fiction four times. 2020 saw a *Best Of* collection from Subterranean Press. As Michael Marshall he has written seven internationally-bestselling thrillers including *The Straw Men*; now additionally writing as Michael Rutger, he has published the thrillers *The Anomaly* and *The Possession*.

He works as Creative Director of Neil Gaiman's production company in Los Angeles, and lives in Santa Cruz, California, with his wife, son, and cats. www.michaelmarshallsmith.com.

Simon Strantzas is the author of five collections of short fiction, including *Nothing is Everything* (Undertow Publications), and editor of several anthologies. He has been a finalist for four Shirley Jackson Awards, two British Fantasy Awards, and the World Fantasy Award. His short stories have been reprinted in over a dozen best-of anthologies and appeared in venues such as *Nightmare*, *The Dark*, and *Cemetery Dance*. In 2014, the anthology he edited, *Aickman's Heirs*, won the Shirley Jackson Award. He lives with his wife in Toronto, Canada.

Steve Toase was born in England, and lives in Bavaria, Germany. His fiction has appeared in *Nightmare* Magazine, *Shadows & Tall Trees*, *Analog*, *Three-Lobed Burning Eye*, *Shimmer*, and *Lackington's*, amongst others. His nonfiction has been published in *Back Street Heroes Custom Motorbike Magazine*, *100% Biker*, and *Kerrang Magazine*. He writes regularly for *Fortean Times*. His debut collection *To Drown in Dark Water* is now out from Undertow Publications. He also likes old motorbikes and vintage cocktails. You can find him at stevetoase.co.uk.

Shirley Jackson award-winner **Kaaron Warren**'s most recent books include the re-release of her acclaimed novels *Slights* and *Mistification* (IFWG Australia), *Tool Tales*, a chapbook in collaboration with Ellen Datlow (also IFWG), which won the Australian Shadows Award, the novella *Into Bones Like Oil* (Meerkat Press), which was shortlisted for a Shirley Jackson Award and the Bram Stoker Award, winning the Aurealis Award, and *Capturing Ghosts*, a writing advice chapbook from Brain Jar Press.

A.C. Wise is the author of the novels *Wendy, Darling,* and *Hooked,* as well as a novella and three collections, the most recent of which, *The Ghost Sequences*, was a finalist for the Stoker Award. Her work has won the Sunburst Award for Excellence in Canadian Literature of the Fantastic, and has been a finalist for the Nebula, Sunburst, Aurora, Lambda, and Ignyte Awards. Find her online at www.acwise.net.

ACKNOWLEDGMENT OF COPYRIGHT

ABOUT THE EDITOR

Ellen Datlow has been editing sf/f/h short fiction for four decades. She currently acquires short stories and novellas for Tor.com and Nightfire. She has edited numerous anthologies for adults, young adults, and children, *When Things Get Dark: Stories inspired by Shirley Jackson* and *Body Shocks*. Her next original anthology is *Screams From the Dark: 19 Tales of Monsters and the Monstrous*. She's won multiple Locus, Hugo, Stoker, International Horror Guild, Shirley Jackson, and World Fantasy Awards, plus the 2012 Il Posto Nero Black Spot Award for Excellence as Best Foreign Editor. Datlow was named recipient of the 2007 Karl Edward Wagner Award, given at the British Fantasy Convention for "outstanding contribution to the genre" and was honored with the Life Achievement Award given by the Horror Writers Association, in acknowledgment of superior achievement over an entire career and honored with the World Fantasy Life Achievement Award at the 2014 World Fantasy Convention.

She runs the Fantastic Fiction at KGB reading series in the east village, NYC, with Matthew Kressel.

She can be found on the website Datlow.com, and on Twitter and Facebook (Google her).